DEKING THE PUCK

KATHY OBUSZEWSKI

"You can become overwhelmed, sink into despair, and allow yourself to live life as a victim, or you can rise above the pain and consciously take your life to a higher level."- Oni Vitandham

1

ALICE

Alice was dragging her oversized hockey bag and the two sticks into the ice arena. It's been a while since she last picked up her gear but with the new year, it was time to make some changes to her life. The resolutions that she had in mind were pretty simple: use the long-neglected hockey gear, read more and be as healthy as possible. So today was the day to tackle the goal of playing ice hockey again.

As she approached the older man who was manning the desk, she shifted the strap on the bulky bag hoping to redistribute some of the weight slightly so it wasn't so heavy. She didn't say anything at first and the man greeted her by asking, "Here for the open hockey time?"

"Yup."

"That will be ten dollars. Don't think there are any other girls here. Usually, it's all guys. Do you want to use a private locker room or just get changed with the guys?"

Alice thought about it for a moment. In the past, she

usually changed with the guys on her team except for the one time when it was offered to her at a roller rink. The girls locker room was nice since some of the guys' behavior could be rather gross especially when they took moldy equipment, rinsed it off and put it on. But the private locker room for girls could be a terrible shade of pink and super cramped. Yet this time, she didn't know anyone at the rink and it would be weird getting changed in front of complete strangers. So she said, "I'll like to use the private one, if that's okay."

The man looked down at the desk, almost as if he was looking at the schedule to verify which room he was going to send her to. Then he looked up and said, "Down the hall, last door on the right."

With that, Alice took her gear and started to head towards the locker room. She was trying to get her bearings at the rink since it was her first time there. So far it didn't seem too different from many rink complexes. There were two rinks on either side of the main hallway that seemed to house most of the locker rooms, there was a set of stairs to go to presumably a cafe space or office area. There appeared to be about four main locker rooms where the guys were entering and exiting either in street clothes or a full hockey kit. Alice also passed by a few closed doors that she guessed were various storage closets or a janitor's space. She was starting to wonder where her locker room was until she saw a door with a pull handle that attached to the hallway on the right-hand side and a glass door that appeared to be a side exit from the building.

After pulling open the door, she placed her sticks by the stick box that was close the door and started to turn her body so she could force the massive hockey bag through the door.

She really wasn't looking where she was going but did notice and was eternally grateful that the walls weren't Pepto-Bismol pink. It wasn't until she was through the door that she noticed a 6 foot 2, lean, red-haired man almost immediately in front of her. She very quickly realized that was Scott Wheiland of the Cleveland Sound, the captain of the local NHL team. She knew that she had gone into the wrong locker room since there was no way they would want people from the public using the team's private locker room when they were at the practice facility. Immediately Alice started to back out of the room, thankful she could just shove everything backwards to make a quick getaway. "Sorry, I thought this was the girls' locker room."

Alice was sure that she was blushing and was probably an insane shade of red from her embarrassment. But she was surprised when she heard him say, "No, no, you're good. I was just straggling."

"Are you sure?" Alice asked hesitantly and made her way back fully into the locker room. She was still tentative and didn't want to get anyone into any trouble.

"Yup. Ed knows that girls can use it if we don't have practice and gear isn't here. All the gear is being transported to the arena for tonight, so it's all good. I was just leaving."

Getting that reassurance that it was okay for her to be in the locker room and wasn't intruding on anyone, Alice just dropped the bag to the ground with an undignified thud. She was glad to let go of it since it was heavy enough and she was sick of lugging it around. She also started to look more closely at the captain. He was way better looking than she expected. His clothes were hugging his muscles just right where you could tell that he was solid muscle but also not overly built like a bodybuilder.

Scott broke the silence when he said, "So a Flyers fan, huh?"

Alice was a little surprised that he knew that since her bag was just a generic black CCM hockey bag. Then she realized that she was wearing a black Philadelphia Flyers t-shirt. In all honesty, when she left the house, she just grabbed one of her black tees from her workout/pj pile without even realizing what she put on since she knew it was just going to get disgusting while she played. It wasn't like she expected to run into someone that was so her type.

"Yup. What can I say, you can take the girl from the city but you can't stop me from bleeding black and orange. Won't lie, this has not been one of my favorite seasons especially with the high hopes at the beginning of the season but I love my team. Besides my dad would kill me if I abandoned them since he wasn't raising any bandwagon daughters."

Scott smiled some but Alice could tell that he was sizing her up. She didn't feel like she was being objectified. She was just being sussed out. "You clearly play hockey but are you actually any good?"

That question made Alice bust out laughing. She knew her own skills. She hadn't touched her stuff in years except to move it from Pittsburgh to Philly and then to Cleveland. Sometimes she swore the equipment carried more emotional baggage than padding. Between a bad breakup with a guy who played for her team and her own coping mechanisms of working so much that she couldn't think about the problems in her life, she was off the ice for close to 6 years. She was terrible since she was not comfortable carrying the puck on her stick. As good as she was playing floor hockey, the tempo of the game and the speed the puck moved on ice, it made it difficult for her to control so she would rather pass the puck up as quickly as possible so she wasn't a liability for her teammates. The other thing that made things slightly difficult was transitioning from figure skates to hockey skates since if she wasn't careful she would forget there wasn't a toepick up front.

"I'm going to be lucky to keep up and maybe make a friend or two so I can join a beer league. Honestly, I'm just hoping not to completely suck today" Alice shrugged her shoulders trying to keep things light but she had a feeling it was probably more awkward than she intended, but at least her voice was light and self-deprecating. She quietly cursed at letting herself get distracted by him.

"I should probably let you change. Sorry for surprising you."

"It's no problem. I'm the one who is apparently using your locker room. I don't want to rush you."

"It's all good. I was talking my with last-minute meetings and whatnot after getting the medical okay to play in tonight's game."

Alice couldn't contain herself and she let out the instinctual "Fuck" out of her mouth with a quiet voice. She knew that she was a biased Flyers fan who wanted to see The Sounds' best players off the ice, she just hoped her cursing was quiet enough that he didn't hear it. But since Scott's red eyebrow shot up and looked more than a tad cocky, Alice knew that he had heard her and she should explain herself. "Sorry. I'm glad to hear that you got cleared. I just wanted it to happen after tonight's game. It'll be a lot tougher for the Flyers to win tonight now that you're back."

He laughed at that and said, "Damn straight it will be. I've been dying to get back out there. Been too long since I played a proper game. Well, I should go and get some rest before the game."

With that, the delicious looking ginger walked out of the locker room leaving Alice a wee bit stunned and maybe a tad star struck. She was also heavily embarrassed that she swore at one of the hottest men she's ever seen for getting cleared to play against her favorite team later on in the night.

So much for the easy transition back into hockey, she thought to herself. *At least, there's no chance it could go anywhere or he would be interested in me. If he was, he would have tried to get my information or even a name. Instead, I just made a fool of myself.*

Alice knew that the thoughts were getting her into the wrong mindset and she needed to refocus. She shook her head and got back to what she needed to think about. She started with the task of putting on her pads. After getting all the pads on, she laced up her skates hoping that they would be tight enough. Although it seemed like the moment she started to do a couple of laps around the rink one of the skates wouldn't feel tight enough. Then it was time to put on the sweater, helmet, and gloves.

She headed towards the door and said to herself. "Let's try not to suck too much today. Just ease back into it."

Scott

Scott was in a nearly jubilant mood. He just got cleared to play after having to sit out for a little over a week with concussion symptoms from a cheap hit in a game. But in addition to being cleared to do the sport he loved, he got to meet a really cute girl in the locker room.

As he left the locker room, he kicked himself for not getting more information from the brunette beauty who clearly didn't need makeup to look good. He liked the mix of being self-conscious and yet there was an underlying fierceness that he could see especially when she talked about her team. He also liked how she clearly knew who he was but wasn't trying to get an autograph or be a puck bunny, instead she was at the rink to do her thing.

Now if I only could convert her to support my team instead of Philadelphia, he thought to himself.

He figured he would ask Eddie if he knew anything about the mystery girl. So instead of taking the side door that led out towards his car, he walked up to the front desk to visit with the old man who ran the rink and was an expert skate sharpener for anyone who didn't have access to the Sound's equipment guy. Hell, he's used Eddie's skills a couple of times when he needed his skates to be sharpened before the full team got to practice Scott couldn't help himself as he did a soft rap on the desk and said, "Hey, Ed."

"Oh, I didn't realize that anyone was still here. I thought you guys all left ages ago. I hoped there wouldn't be an issue with letting that girl use the locker room for the open ice hockey."

"It's just me, even the coaches are gone. I just lost track of time. But I did want to ask you about the girl."

"Timid little thing. Good chance she won't be back for a while."

Scott's face dropped some. That wasn't what he wanted to hear. Ed usually knew everyone at the rink and had a good instinct about the players' habits. He has been around the scene long enough to know.

"So she's not a regular then."

"Never seen her before today. Not sure if she's an out-of-towner practicing or someone new the area. She really didn't have much to say."

At least not to you. She was a little closed off but it wasn't like it was all one-word answers.

"Damn. I was hoping you might know her name and would have some contact information on her."

"No such luck Scotty. Don't tell me you are interested in her? " Scott blushed a little bit since he was completely busted and was striking out with Ed. But the rink manager just smiled and said, "Sorry, you are going to have to do it the old fashion way and actually talk to her."

"I did, but I forgot to get her name and other details like a dumbass."

"So what are you going to do about it?"

"I'll figure it out soon enough. How much longer does the open hockey go?"

"About an hour and a half."

Scott walked away from the front desk. He knew sooner or later an observant hockey player would try to come up to him for autographs or a picture, if not try to get him to play with them during the pick-up time. But he wanted to remain anonymous if he could since he was playing when he had a division game tonight. He knew that he should be getting something to eat and nap before the game. But the nap wasn't really an option at the moment since he had to know more about the petite brunette that he ran into. So he settled on getting some sushi to go, come back to the rink and spy on the open hockey so he could talk to the girl afterward. He didn't want to leave the rink just yet but the cafeteria area only ever had fried shit that would just make his stomach heavy.

After grabbing a sashimi platter, seaweed salad and some edamame to go from the place close to the rink, he headed back in. The meal should have enough protein to keep his muscles going while still being light enough not to weigh him down. Although he knew he should still make a protein shake and possibly take a nap before the evening's game. He also grabbed a Sound ballcap from the passenger seat and it affixed it low on his head trying to minimize his fiery red hair that always seemed to be his giveaway that he was the pro hockey player for the Cleveland Sound. Some of his hair flared out from hat. He just wanted to watch and interact with that beautiful girl from earlier.

As he hid out in the overlook area from the cafeteria, he casually ate his food but he was watching the play on the ice the entire time. It was pretty easy to spot the girl. She was smaller than most of the players by a good 5 inches and in most cases almost a foot short. She was on the leaner side with a small tuft of hair that was exposed in the back of her helmet. She definitely wasn't a star player and had no confidence but she could pass the puck cleanly and skate halfway decently. He couldn't help but laugh whenever he would catch her swearing to herself whenever she seemed to lose her balance, mishandled the puck or even on being given the puck. Her swearing wasn't audible at least not from his vantage point but he knew what she was saying since he's seen and heard enough players curse on the ice to know what she was saying. But she never did fall over and she was trying.

He guessed that she must have been a figure skater at one point since she seemed to have some good skate control at times but was more on the upright side and would sometimes put the weight near the toe expecting to have a toepick to help catch.

He couldn't help but think to himself, *she must miss that bloody awful toepick something fierce and needs to get used to a wider stance.*

Towards the end of the open hockey time, he noticed that even the guys on the ice were trying to have her keep the puck on her stick rather than just pass it up as quickly as possible which seemed to be her natural instinct. Although he was having fun watching what would normally be an uninteresting session of hockey, since the skill levels varied.

As soon as the players were starting to get off the ice, the rink staff started to open the doors to allow the Zamboni onto the ice so it could be cleaned. He knew it was time to make his move with the girl. But before heading downstairs he decided to give the Cleveland Sound a call to see if there was any way to get her a ticket for tonight's game. He had a feeling that there would be no way he could be denied a date if he offered her a chance to see her favorite team play. Fortunately, the front office could help him out but they needed to know the information that he didn't have just yet. But he was confident as he headed downstairs and was ready to make his move.

Alice

Alice was exhausted after playing hockey but she knew that today's tired legs would be far better than the muscle stiffness that would set in later. She knew she shouldn't get too comfortable on the locker room bench as she pried off the sweaty hockey gear.

Alice saw a shower area in the corner and decided to take a very quick shower before heading home even though she knew she only had a couple of microfiber towels that were more meant to absorb moisture off her skates rather than be for full body drying. She knew that the hot water would feel great on her skin and could help prevent some of the stiffness from setting in. Although she knew that was most likely wishful thinking. But instead of taking a long shower, she figured that she should get going since she really didn't feel all that comfortable being in that locker room. So after trying to dry herself off, she got dressed in her street clothes: black leggings and a purple dolman top. She also decided to apply some black eyeliner and mascara. As per usual, she skipped any foundation since she was never quite sure when she would get called into work to cover for one of her guards or if she would have a last minute swim lesson. Why bother to get dolled up if she was just going to get wet and have the makeup get wrecked. She then swung the wet hair into French braids, the easiest way to do her hair without a hairbrush since that seemed to be the one thing that wasn't in her massive hockey bag.

About 15 minutes after leaving the ice, she was ready to go home and rest until it was time to turn on the Flyers vs. Sound game. As soon as Alice started to push her way through the locker room door, she heard a vaguely familiar voice saying, "You are afraid of the puck."

Alice turned to see the gorgeous man from earlier leaning against the door frame to the locker room with his arms folded to show off his biceps. She was disappointed to see the baseball cap was covering his beautiful red hair and was kind of hiding his brown eyes.

"What's it to you? Why are you still here?" Then she realized what she was saying and immediately scrunched up her face in disgust with allowing her defensive side to just come out. She knew he was right but at the same time, she didn't want to speak it out loud. She then tried to calm herself some and said, "Sorry, I shouldn't have snapped. I just wasn't expecting to see you again and even less ready to get advice about hockey from someone like you."

Scott just smiled and seemed to be more amused by her outburst rather than offended. He took it all in stride and said, "You need to stop apologizing for just reacting. Be you. Besides I'm just trying to help."

Alice nodded. It was something she's heard before multiple times but she still did since she was also taught most of her life how she should be in control of her emotions. "I know I need to stop apologizing for everything, but old habits die hard. But do we have to make it real by saying what we both know to be true out loud?"

"Well if you can get over the fear of handling the puck, you wouldn't be half bad. You actually pass quite well. Do you ever play with the puck on your stick at home?"

Alice shook her head. "No. I know I should but with apartment living, I don't want to scratch up the floor too much or make weird echoey sounds for the neighbors." Alice was suddenly feeling increasingly shy as she was talking to him. It didn't help that in many ways he was the very embodiment of sex on the stick and he seemed to have genuinely taken an interest in her.

"If you want, I could maybe help you out with your puck handling."

"Really?" Alice said in genuine surprise. She literally couldn't believe it was something that was actually said to her. It was something that would be said in a romance novel but very unlikely to happen in real life.

"Sure. It would be a lot of fun." Scotty said as he was shrugging his shoulders, as if it was the most natural thing in the world. Why would it be weird for a hockey superstar to offer to help some nobody that he never met before? He then gave her a knee-melting smile, "Besides I want to get to know you better and that seems like a perfect way to start. But I should probably find out your name and get your phone number, so we can set up some time together."

Alice just blushed. She couldn't believe the attention that she was getting. Not only has it been a while since she was really been flirted with, she knew that he could easily have had his choice of girls. So she couldn't see what he saw in her.

"It's Alice. Alice Kercheck." Alice tried to say with some confidence before she let her uncertainty take over for a moment. "So you want to get to know me better?" But then she let her voice get a little playful. "What would you say if I told you that I would like to get to know you better as well?"

Scott's smile continued to grow and even revealed a dimple. He then leaned over and grabbed her heavy hockey bag from her. "Here, let me get that for you. It's practically the size of you."

His touch was warm and invigorating in a sensual way. Alice couldn't have imagined that it would be real but it was something she had often read about. Even if his touch wasn't amazing, it felt good to have the weight taken off her shoulders. "Thanks."

"No problem. Do you have plans tonight?"

Alice looked at him questioningly. She was thinking to herself: *Why is he asking me what I'm doing? He has a game tonight and I could have sworn that the game preview said that this was the first game of a back to back for the Sound. There is no way we can meet up or do anything after the game...*

"Just going to watch the Flyers game on TV."

"Wouldn't you rather go to the game?"

"Of course. But I couldn't afford tickets. Besides, do you really think that's a good idea? I'm sure no one would like to see that you got tickets for a Flyers fan."

Scott actually looked slightly hurt. But once he started to speak, it was clear he didn't have any hard feelings and was ready to tease her right back to her, "You mean you would still wear their stuff and root against me?"

Alice laughed some and found it so refreshing that he was teasing her in a similar way that her dad would tease her when their two football teams play against each other. "I wouldn't root against YOU but I can't say the same about your team. I told you earlier that I bleed black and orange. I could wear my Wheels sweater."

Wheels was a nickname for Chris Wheeler. The defensive man was selected by the Sound in the expansion draft from the Flyers. He was one of the young kids who looked to be part of the fresh look to the Flyers' defense, but they couldn't protect everyone and he was just beyond the age where he had to be protected in the expansion draft. She wasn't surprised to see how the gritty Canadian was continuing to blossom into an elite defenseman for the Sound.

"Wheels? Not even me?"

"Well, you never played for my guys. Why would I have a Flyers jersey with your name on my back? Besides I don't even own any Sound gear."

"I could fix that for you, you know."

Alice laughed. She was sure he could. But at the moment she didn't care. She didn't want to take advantage of his generosity; scoring a ticket would be more than enough. But in many ways, she just wanted to spend more time with him. But most importantly to her, she couldn't give up on her favorite team just because she met a player from the opposition.

"Thanks, I wouldn't wear it until after the game even if you fixed my lack of Sound apparel. My boys are my boys. Besides what would you get out of me going to the game?"

"Nothing other than getting a chance to see you smile. And I was hoping that you might join me for drinks before I have to fly to DC."

Alice smiled and nodded, "Yeah. That would be a lot of fun. Are you sure? I don't want to take advantage of you."

"Yup. But I will need to know your number so I can get everything fully confirmed. It shouldn't be an issue but I still have to ask." He dug out his phone, unlocked it and handed it over to her. She quickly inputted her contact information and saved it into his phone. When she handed the phone back to him, "I will text you to confirm everything tonight and keep you updated on everything."

"Okay. We should probably get going. I'm sure I'm keeping you from your normal pregame routine. Not that it would be a terrible thing that you are a little tired against my guys but that's probably not the best way to bounce back from an injury."

Scott nodded but didn't really give back anything to her teasing. So Alice was concerned that she might have gone too far with her comments. She was tempted to say she was sorry again but she decided not to say anything.

Scott pushed the glass door open. Alice immediately saw a large, shiny black SUV. Alice assumed that it had to be Scott's car. She realized that her car had to be on the side of the building and they were standing at the back but she wasn't a hundred percent if they should turn to the left or the right. Then she saw the sign to the building on the street and that allowed her to get her bearings again. So she turned to the left.

Alice broke the silence again and said. "Thanks for everything, Scott. Literally everything. I would have been happy not having to lug that thing back to my car. But then you offer to get me into the game...."

Alice's thoughts were disrupted when Scott grabbed her free hand as they walked together which sent warmth and heat through her body. With the way she reacted, you would have thought he kissed her. When they reached her beat up blue sedan, she was disappointed. It meant that they would have to separate and she was sure that he would come to his senses and completely forget about her. Plus she was slightly embarrassed he had to see her old car when she was sure he was driving the brand new SUV. She hit the button on her keychain to unlock the doors. She opened up the side door so they could put the bag on the back seat while she tossed her two hockey sticks onto the floor.

Scott said, "So I guess I will see you tonight." It seemed

like he was almost about ready to kiss her for the first time. He tilted his head but before he actually went in, he pulled back and seemed like he was second guessing the moment. Alice felt slightly cheated in that moment. She wanted that kiss. Not to mention, she wished that he wasn't wearing a baseball hat at the moment since she wanted to see all his hair, not just the stuff that stuck out every which way in the back.

"Yeah. I'm looking forward to that."

2

ALICE

Alice was still stunned from the events earlier in the day at the hockey rink. It was slightly insane to believe that not only did she meet, but she was going to meet up with a living, breathing vision of her dream man: gorgeous, muscular, and a professional hockey player. It just seemed unreal and something that belonged in a romantic-comedy rather than real life.

By the time that she drove home, she had a text from Scott saying that everything was all set at the arena for her. All she had to do was go to will call for the ticket. She knew that she had to be a grinning fool and was grateful that she had Fridays off and no one would see her looking like that. She also knew that she should keep everything fairly quiet. He was a public figure and deserved some privacy. Besides, she didn't even know if it would go anywhere at all since it was new and there is a chance he did that with all the girls. But she knew that she would explode if she didn't talk to someone.

So Alice decided to open up WhatsApp to start a chat

with her British friend, Jennifer. She trusted Jennifer immensely. Besides, Jennifer knew about Alice's love of hockey and gingers.

Alice: *I think that I might have a date tonight*

Jennifer: *Oh really?*

Alice: *Surprisingly enough with the captain of the Cleveland Sound after they play the Flyers. Hell, he even got me a ticket to the game.*

Jennifer: *Wait, What?*

Alice: *I practically ran into him when I went to play hockey. I feel like this couldn't really be happening.*

I feel like I'm a complete asshole, but I'm still going to the game to represent my Flyers. I don't care that the only reason I'm going to the game is because of freaking Scott Wheilan.

Jennifer: *Does he know about your Flyers obsession?*

Alice: *He does. He actually called me out for liking them since guess what shirt I was wearing.*

Then Alice got distracted by a phone notification saying that one of her guards was calling off for work for the evening shift. If she didn't find coverage, she would have to go into work like she normally did on her day off.

Alice: *FUCK! I have a call off to threaten tonight's plans*

Jennifer: *Don't you dare cancel your date!*

Alice: *I won't. Worst-case scenario, I go into work and leave early for the game. But FUCK! Why is it so hard to have a day off?*

Jennifer: *Grim. But don't do anything rash, this will be good for you. You need to get out more.*

Alice: *I know. But I won't. I just now have to look for some coverage.*

Jennifer: *Have fun tonight.*

Alice then started to turn her attention to work matters. She had roughly an hour to find coverage or start to head into work. She was hoping for a miracle so she could just enjoy the game and have extra prep time to make herself look presentable. Fortunately for her, she was able to find a replacement. So with that she had a couple of relaxing hours before she got into her gameday wear.

Scott

Pregame warm-ups were progressing well. It seemed like everyone was skating well and getting in some nice clean shots. Scott himself was distracted, hoping that Alice was at the game and the PR team was able to deliver the jersey like they promised they would. The stadium was awash in gold and wine that celebrated both The Sound and The Cavs who played at the arena. There was also a bunch of orange and black from an ample amount of Flyers fans that seemed to travel wherever they played. Besides getting her a jersey, he did ask for them to give her a seat in the crowd instead of having her sit in the family section. He knew he would get shit from the team if they found out that he invited a Flyers fan to the game. Hell, any girl would arouse a lot of suspicions and gossip since he hadn't dated anyone in a long time. He could only look blindly in the crowd hoping to see her face but that was proving to be absolutely useless.

All of a sudden he was covered in a snow shower, a spray of ice that came up from the surface of the ice if a player stopped too quickly all on the edge of the blade. He looked to see that Lager was the one to blame. With a dirty look, he said, "What the fuck was that for?" Snow showers were usually reserved for rookies and goalies.

Lager was short for Andreas Lagerfield. He was Scotty's

closest friend on the team. They have been line mates for years and have always seemed to click really well together. Scotty fought to keep Lager on his line earlier in the season when the coach was thinking about splitting them up. Lager could feed a pass better than anyone else on the team for him and if Scotty couldn't get it on the net, Pavel Dykstaman would.

"It's time to look alive," said a full barreled voice with a slight bit of a German accent. Lager was technically Austrian but he always sounded more German than most of the Austrians that Scotty ever knew. Then Lager dropped his voice so only the two of them would hear his whisper, "Quit worrying. She'll be here."

Lager was the only guy on the team who could tell there was that subtle crack in Scotty's cockiness and joy of returning to the game. Lager could sense the bit of anxiousness that was unusual for Scotty. Thinking that it was Scott trying to hide the fact that he still had concussion symptoms, Lager threatened to go to the trainers. Scott did that last year and got really messed up for weeks, so Lager was always on guard to make sure it didn't happen again. But it also meant that Scott had to tell him about liking a new girl and wanting to impress her tonight both in the game and after. Lager also knew how Scott was in a bit of a dry spell where he would have casual sex with girls but hadn't had any luck with a real relationship in a while, nor has Scotty's interest even piqued in the direction of a relationship. So Lager knew Scotty being was interested in a girl was a big deal.

Scott continued to casually feed pucks to the other forwards who were warming up on the ice. He gave Lager a death stare for even mentioning anything about Alice on the ice. She was supposed to be a secret until he was sure if it was anything at all.

Lager didn't seem to take a hint and said, "No one is going to be impressed with that stuff. Gotta step it up."

Then Lager sped off down the ice. He knew that if he didn't do that, Scott was likely to deck Lager or give him his own snow shower. But Scott wasn't going to let have Lager have the last word. Knowing that Lager was still watching him, he fanned on the puck, pivoted his hips and took a wicked hard shot on net that would give most goalies issues. Then Scott skated towards Lager, stole his puck and also shot that on net.

"Better?"

"Much. But this is only warm-ups. Don't show Philly all your tricks. They might try to catch on."

Scotty shook his head laughing. As he got close to Lager, he said, "There's no winning with you." It was time to get back to his own normal warm-up routine so he skated backward and started to get into the cycle.

"Never is." Lager said with a grin. It was actually a relief for Scott to just screw around some with Lager. Which was probably Lager's goal from the start.

By the end of warms up, Scott started to feel like it was going to be a good game and he was back to his old self. If he just played the way he knew how to play, he wouldn't have any issues. Plus he forgot about looking for Alice and instead started to focus on the game.

Once he was in the locker room again, he peeled off his warm-up sweater and tossed it in the laundry bin. He then quickly dug out his phone to see if he had any word from Alice. She seemed like a girl who would send a message of appreciation and not take advantage of him for his money. He was also hoping that she might have sent him a photo wearing the jersey. So he was excited to see the message:

Alice: ***Thanks for the jersey. But you shouldn't have.***

Scott: ***Glad you like it. But will you be wearing it tonight?***

Alice: ***No. At least, not until after the game.***

Scott was surprised how quickly she responded. In a way, he wasn't surprised by her answer. In a way, he liked the fact that she was so loyal to her team. He just wished she wasn't a fan of the enemy. He was about to text at least a frowny face when he saw:

Alice: ***Kick some butt tonight. Just not too much. I still want to see the baby get his first road win.***

He knew he had to put the phone away and couldn't really answer the message but he couldn't help but smile and feel completely at ease. They weren't supposed to have their phones out until the end of the game. But it was totally worth it to chat with her for a few moments. Just seeing her wish him luck was awesome and a mood booster. But seeing that even the Flyers fans called the rookie goaltender a baby was priceless. He could load up with all sorts of chirps for the game although Scotty knew the chirping would most likely come from Lager.

He sat back down on the bench to make the final adjustments to his pads. He wasn't too surprised when the camera crew did a pregame shot of him prior to changing to the game day sweater for the pregame show. If it wasn't his first game back after missing six games, it could have been anyone else in the locker room. Although since he was the captain, team leader in goals and points, and a fan favorite, they liked to focus on him most of the time anyway. He just ignored the camera like always but fortunately, they would just pop in and then leave nearly as quickly.

Everyone seemed to be in a good mood. It should be an easy win against the Flyers who were struggling especially on defense. The coaches didn't say much other than the reminders that you can't count them out, they are hungry for a road win, and to follow the system. It was based on trust and skill. While the Sound wasn't the best team in the league they had a solid footing in the Metro as the second best team in the division. Only the Capitals had a better record.

With that, it was time to head out of the locker room for the pregame ceremonies. On the way out of the locker room, Lager asked: "Better now?"

Scott nodded at first and said, "Yeah. She's here. Apparently, we are to kick some butt but not score on the baby too much."

"Seriously?!?! Does she fucking think you will listen to that and not try to score? She has to know we will be chirping at him something fierce knowing their fans think he's a baby too."

"Oh, I know. I have a feeling that this will be a very fun game. Let's see if we can shake the kid up."

Then from the hallway, they heard Coach Berman scream, "Quit dawdling, assholes. We have a game to play."

With that, the two rushed out to get into the proper area and get matched up with a kid. They skated out and stood for the national anthem. Then Scotty went to do the ceremonial drop puck for one of the most ginger drop pucks possible for the league. While Scott was the only redhead on the Sound, it seemed like the Flyers were filled with them including their captain.

Alice

For the first time ever at a hockey game, Alice was finding herself conflicted on who to root for. She figured that this game would be like when a favorite player got traded- she would root for the player while at the same time not mind if he got checked into the boards, hit, had a scoring opportunity nullified or took a blocked shot. For some reason, it was different when it was Scott on the ice.

Early in the first period, he took a crushing hit into the boards from Flyers defenseman. She was sure that if she was watching from home, it would have been the Great Check of the Game. But she found herself worried when Scott took his time getting off the boards and then was babying his hip as he got to the bench. She was watching him on the bench to try and gauge how serious an injury he had. It didn't seem like he went to the back of the tunnel to get some repairs. So that was good. She then realized that she was seeing a couple of streaks of orange and white streaking down the ice on a clear breakaway opportunity by Jake and JVR. They were practically on top of the goal mouth. She watched as JVR faked out the Sound goalie, Alex Crestor, into believing that was JVR was going to shoot onto net. Instead, he fired a laser at Jake, who fired the puck into an empty area of net since Crestor was still pulled down low on the non-glove side. She was elated to see her team get ahead. Then Alice looked towards the Sound bench, what she saw were some very frustrated faces and a missing Scott.

Don't tell me, that he's seriously hurt.

Then she realized that the top line with Scott, Lagerfield, and Dykstman were out to take the faceoff against the Flyer's ginger line. Giroux won the faceoff (which is pretty typical) but the Flyers immediately turned the puck over to Wheels who sent the puck forward to Dykstman while Scotty was skating forward to keep the pressure on the Flyer's defense. Alice was glad to see that Scott was skating well despite Philly trying to box him out. Dykstman passed to Lagerfield who was cycling forward. He took a shot on net only to hit iron and the rebound bounced to a Flyer stick. The direction shifted back down to the other side of the rink.

The game continued to be an up and down affair with neither team having any real dominance. They would take shots but they weren't going into either goal. By the end of the game, it was Flyers 1 and Sound 0. It wasn't for lack of trying by Scott. He hit iron at least four times during the game but not one of them broke his way. While there was a part of Alice that wanted Scott to get a goal, she was glad nothing ending up going into the net.

Scott

Scott was exhausted and frustrated by the game. He knew he should probably take an ice bath and a hot soak after the bone-crushing check from early in the game, especially since he would be super stiff for tomorrow's game if he didn't. But if he did that, he wouldn't be able to meet up with Alice before having to fly out. He already wasted enough time with his media requirements.

Eventually, he made his way up to the club level area that he asked Alice to wait until he was done. He saw the brunette looking at her phone rather contently. He decided that he wanted to take that opportunity to sneak up as quietly from behind and then he kissed her softly on her ear. While he backed away from kissing her earlier, he let his lust take over this time. Alice immediately snapped to attention and turned to Scott with one of the sweetest smiles and said, "Hey you! You had a pretty good game," as she started to return the hug. He tried to make sure that he didn't cringe when she was touching a fresh bruise on his arm.

"Pretty good?" he said as he raised an eyebrow. He was amused by how she wasn't playing to his ego. Most girls would try to stroke it. While he was cocky, he knew when they were lying.

Alice smiled and shrugged, "Well what can I say. You guys didn't win and you personally managed to hit the post, what four times? If you actually scored, then I might have said that was a good game."

"So you are going to bring that up? What are you going to say next, how the Flyers dominated the game?"

She smiled and started laughing. "No way. The breakaway goal was good. But between the missed power plays and the crap ton of turnovers, there was no dominance for either team. But the Flyers won so I'm not going to complain."

"But I am."

"About what?"

"You could have wanted me to win. Besides, I was hoping to at least see you wearing my jersey by now."

Alice smiled and said, "I always told you that I wouldn't wear it until the end of the game." Then she surprised Scott by pulling the vastly oversized Flyers jersey overhead. Since she was using a private locker room, he thought that she was shy with her body. Not that she needed to be shy with her body, everything he's seen in her in looked great. Then he realized that underneath the dress sized jersey was a black form-fitting tank top that showed off some of her curves. She wasn't actually getting adventurous and not really showing off her body in any way. She then grabbed the Sound one. Scott smiled to see how his logo actually cusped her boobs and the jersey started to hug her body rather than just hide it. She turned around and asked, "Better?"

"Mmhmm." Scott then picked her up and gave her a deep passionate kiss. His voice got lusty as he said, "I love that on you." He kissed her one more time before lowering her back to the ground. He knew their time would be limited and if they were going to get any sort of dinner together that they should leave. "We should probably get going. We really don't have enough time tonight."

"Well, whose fault is that?" While that comment could almost seem like a negative one, there was no malice in her voice. It was actually light and understanding and teasing. She grabbed her Flyers jersey, folded it and put in the same bag that she pulled the Sound one out of, "I'm ready."

Scott grabbed her hand and led her out of the arena to his favorite post-game haunt. He loved how well her hand seemed to fit into his. "I didn't make you wait too long, did I?"

"No. I figured that was going to take some time. You did just return to play. So of course the local media wants to talk to you post game. It's why I made sure my Kindle app had something good on it."

"Good. You might have to get used to that. I never get out super early like some of the guys."

"That's what's happens when you are one of the best. I get it. At least your time is getting eaten up by media purposes. Now it would be far worse if you needed to spend all the time in with the trainers."

"Yeah. But I'm not always a fan of the media. It was easier when I came into the league. I didn't have to worry about managing the accent or accidentally going into French." He then pulled her into the little bar's door with a slight pivot.

Alice surprised by saying, "Ici?"

Most of the girls he saw in the states didn't speak his native language. "Tu parles français?"

"Un peu. J'ai étudié français aux universités. But I'm not that good."

"You are better than most but you need to practice." He smiled and was actually really pleased with her speaking some French. It wasn't forced but rather sweet although the accent sounded off. "I can help you with that."

Alice started to smile so sweetly and started to laugh. "Why do I think this is becoming a theme?"

Scott led the way to a small little two top that was close to the bar. Almost immediately, Janet, his usual bartender came up to the table.

"Tough one tonight. So do you want your usual?" asked Janet.

That made Scott feel uncomfortable. He wished she would have not mentioned the loss or at least even acknowledged that Alice was there. But he said, "Yeah." Then he looked towards Alice for her order. She was taking a hard look at the beer list. Then her face lit up and he wasn't quite sure why.

"I'll have the bourbon barrel aged Black Star Dies."

Janet nodded and let them be.

Alice then said, "Why are you staring at me so intently? Did I grow an extra head or something?"

Scott laughed and said, "No, it's more I've never seen someone get so excited over a beer list before. Your face literally lit up when you saw that beer."

"I like my beer. What can I say? One of my favorite beer podcasts literally just highlighted that one and it sounded so good but I didn't think the brewery actually distributed here in Ohio. Even though I'm supposed to take a trip out to Philly next month, there is a good chance that it would be gone. So I'm excited that I can actually get to try it after all."

"So what makes it so special?"

"Besides the name? It's a bourbon barrel aged stout and the aging both mellows out the stout while strengthening the adjunct notes. The stout itself was a dark cherry oatmeal which was an amazing combo with a nice heavy mouthfeel. It's like a meal in your mouth. So I couldn't wait to see how it would taste with the aging process. BB loved it and I love the brewery in general."

She squinted her nose up as she realized that he wasn't fully following what she was saying. It actually made her look cuter. He was trying to keep up but it was almost like she was speaking a foreign language, but he knew she was passionate about what she was saying. Before Scott could say anything, Janet dropped off two pints of beer. His looked downright pale compared to hers.

She picked up her glass right away and she seemed to subtly smell the glass and said, "Skoal" as she stared at him. He lifted his glass and nodded.

Scott just loved watching her drink that first sip. It seemed like she was in heaven. He definitely never felt that way from his usual Yuengling. It was a solid beer and reliable. But he never thought about it being something that could create that level of joy.

"Do you want to try it?" as she started to pass the glass his way.

He figured why not. He was curious. He was immediately confronted with a lot of flavors at once. It was sweet but it was heavy in his mouth. He now started to understand what she initially meant by her explanation of the beer. He was actually really enjoying it.

"Wow. I wasn't expecting that. That's a lot of things going on. But I like it."

"Yeah, me too. It was exactly what I was hoping it would be." Alice leaned on the table so they could talk a little easier. "Do you ever experiment with craft beers?

"Not really. Some of the guys do but everything they drink is so bitter. Nothing like this." Scott took a second sip without even thinking about it at first. Then he felt guilty for stealing her drink. But she didn't seem to mind. She just seemed to smile.

"That's why I love to drink saisons, porters and stouts. They tend to be more mellow but can pack a lot of flavor into their base, especially the barrel aged stuff. You don't get hit in the face with hops. I enjoy the other beer styles too. But after something like this, I am full enough after a pint or two. Besides, I tend to like the heavy ABV so only two full size beers are needed."

Then Alice surprised him and said, "May I?" as she took a sip from his glass. She smiled and said, "That's pretty much what I thought that was."

"What?"

"A Lager. If I'm not mistaken a Yuengling. From one of America's oldest breweries. A drink that's synonymous with the term lager in Philly."

Scott rolled his eyes in mocked frustration with yet another Philly mention. She didn't mock his choice of beer for being boring like many of the guys on the team. Instead, she seemed to just embrace it. He was actually being charmed by her. "So what's with all the Philly love? Are you from there or something?"

"I am. You can't fully remove the Philly from a girl."

"So why Cleveland, then?"

"Got the job at one of the universities. Not all that different from why you came here. Okay, I wasn't drafted but I was offered the ideal job."

The conservation just seemed to flow as the evening went on. While they had different interests in some areas, they got along well. They had a second round of drinks. He actually let Alice choose for both of them. He trusted her to pick out something that he would like which he never did, but it seemed like she actually knew beer rather then pretended to, like the guys on the team. It was another stout for him and then she got something she called a saison for herself.

All of a sudden, Scott's phone started to blow up with a few dozen messages. He knew that wasn't a good sign. He started to dig out the phone from his pants pocket. Once he did, he realized he was late getting back to the arena for their flight. Alice even seemed to pick up on that and said, "I take it that you are late." Scott nodded in disappointment and started to fumble for his wallet. He was looking to see Janet who of course was nowhere to be seen. Alice said, "Go. I got this. Don't get in trouble over me."

She gave him a pointed look that came from a parent or a coach. So he put his suit jacket on and then his coat as she wanted. He did give her one more kiss for the road but it was only a quick one. As he pulled away, "I still feel bad. Besides, how are you getting home?"

"Either the red line or uber. Don't worry. It's not an issue. But you are going to miss your flight if you don't go."

Scott knew she was right. So he started to head towards the door and said, "Text me. When you get home."

Once he left the bar, he ran the two blocks back to the arena. He saw the charter bus in the parking lot. So he grabbed the wheely bag from his car and ran onto the bus. As he entered the bus, the coach screamed, "You're late, Scotty!"

"Sorry," as he ducked his head just so he wouldn't see how pissed the coach was. He quickly sat down in the open seat, and the bus was on its way to the airport for their charter flight.

By the time they got to the airport, Alice had texted him saying how she had fun and shared the link to her uber. He made sure to screenshot the address, that way he more or less knew where she lived. They exchanged a few texts before he took off.

While Scott felt guilty for leaving Alice and not paying for their drinks, he liked how she was completely understanding of the situation. He couldn't remember the last time a girl offered to pay for the drinks or even had such an easy conversation.

Scotty was ready for an easy quick flight to DC. He knew the coaches would be making them do a tough practice and be extra tough on him as a form of punishment. It would be a totally justified punishment. So he hoped for a peaceful flight to DC, unfortunately for him, Doctor Curren sat down next to him.

In a very pointed tone, Doc said, "If you think you can hide another concussion from me, you've got another thing coming. And pulling that crap being late isn't helping you."

"Whoa. I'm fine, honest. I met a girl and I lost track of time."

"A girl?"

"Yeah. We were having drinks at Mel's. Trust me, I learned from the last time. I'll take any test you want to prove that I'm totally fine."

"What about that hit in the game? Any after effects."

"My hip hurts but that was all that really rammed into the boards. Nothing more than a nasty stinger and a couple of bruises."

"You sure?"

"Yup." He was tempted to throw in that he would remember if he hit his head but he knew that probably wasn't a good idea.

"So what were you drinking with this girl?"

Scotty looked confused and couldn't tell if Doc was actually interested or testing him. Doc was looking at him intently just like he did when it was a physical. So it was indeed a test. "Well, we kind of shared a couple drinks. I ordered a Yuengling and she had the Black Star Goes Boom or something like that. It was a bourbon aged cherry stout. Then it was a Great Lakes Oatmeal Stout and some sort of saison."

"Wait, you actually drank something other than your usual? What made you change it up?"

"Alice" Scott smiled just thinking of her and the way she got so excited over a beer.

"So there really is a girl."

"Of course there is. Why would I make something like that up?"

"You should see some of the crazy things people do with a concussion."

"I have the text messages if that makes you feel better. Are we good? You aren't threatening to take my health clearance, are you?"

"You are good with me. But Berman could still bench you if you keep pissing him off."

Scott nodded. He was glad to hear that he could still play at least medically. But he knew he should start to get ready for the next game. So he pulled out his iPad and started to watch some of the videos of the Capitals. He wanted to get back into the win column. Plus studying up for the next game would keep his mind busy until he could touchdown and have another possible exchange with Alice. That's was if she wasn't asleep when they landed.

3

ALICE

Alice was amazed at how quickly her relationship with Scott seemed to develop over the next four days. Even though he had been on the road since their first date, they were constantly texting and doing the occasional Facetime calls in the evening. She was looking forward to the next day when he would be back home in town for a nice long home stand.

She was home watching the Flyers game when her phone went off. Right away she knew it was Scott since it was showing one of her favorite photos of him that she got from the internet. "Hey you, did you make it back okay?" The game took a turn that made her say, "Son of a Bitch" without letting Scotty get in a word in and she quickly added, "Sorry, I really need to have a warning label at times. Watching hockey, swearing can and will happen based on gameplay."

She just heard his throaty chuckle at first. She always loved to hear his laugh even if she wasn't sure if he was laughing because of the reaction to the game or finding out that a team in his division wasn't playing well.

"I take it you didn't like that last play then."

"No… Who likes going two men down thanks to ticky-tack sashing call?" Alice said not noticing how he didn't actually say how his flight went.

"The other team," Scott said in a deadpan voice, the perfect straight man for the situation. Then his voice switched to a much lighter note and was likely the reason for the call. "So, I think I'm close to your place. That is if the Uber map from the other night is correct. Do you have parking and what is the number to your place?"

"Wait, what?!?!?" Alice sputtered for a moment, not believing what she was hearing. He was coming over right then.

"I figured instead of waiting until tomorrow, I would stop by tonight. The flight got in early and I was hoping to see you. That is if that's okay," as he started to transition to a more doubting tone.

Alice was literally caught off guard and wasn't exactly ready for any visitors. She was in her favorite t-shirt which had a cut out in the back that celebrated one of her favorite former Flyer's foundations and an old pair of black leggings that she was planning on wearing to bed later on in the evening. While it was something she loved to wear, it wasn't something that she wanted to be seen in when trying to impress the new man in her life. She was glad that at least her hair was still in decent shape from the day since she never took down her work braids.

"Um, Alice are you still there? Did I do something wrong?"

"Yeah, sorry. I just got distracted for a moment by the

Flyers game." She even cursed at herself for the lame excuse especially since he might have heard the horn announcing the end of the first period a moment earlier. But she didn't want to admit that she was trying to figure out her embarrassment level for him to see her in that moment. She was hoping to see him and was really happy that he wanted to surprise her. "I'm at 2660 Bay St. But it's only street parking at night since my neighbors get cranky if you use their parking space."

"Okay." Alice heard the classic beeping sound to indicate that he was locking up the door. He wasn't kidding when he said he was close. So she grabbed her keys and went towards the security door. "I'll meet you at the door."

Alice walked out of her living room to see Scott was at the security door already. He was still pretty dressed up in suit pants and a dress shirt meaning that must have come straight towards her place. He seemed to have already ditched his tie and suit jacket. He looked so yummy like that but it made her realize just how truly dressed down she was. She opened up the security door and he immediately scooped her up and started to kiss her passionately with a lot of tongue. She moved her hands around his neck and through his shaggy long hair. He moved her into the apartment with a few quick steps. Once they were inside, she kicked the door shut with her foot. They continued to kiss up against the wall in the dark room.

"I've missed you and been waiting too long to do that," he said impishly. Then he seemed to notice that the TV that was sitting next to them was currently turned off. "I thought you said you were watching the Flyers game."

"I missed you too. But that's not the only TV in my place. I actually don't spend much time in this room despite the couch and easy chair."

She started to kiss him again and ran her hand against his chin and jaw where she could feel a little bit of stubble trying to creep through. At that moment, she was having fun and didn't care that the game was going to be returning to play in a few moments. Instead, she had easy access to kiss his lips and she wanted to take advantage of that since the moment he lowered her down, she would have had a lot more trouble since she was practically a foot shorter than him.

"Easy there. We have all night," he said in an almost amused fashion as he started to lower her to the ground before she could make a play to unfasten his belt. She did a mock pout but he was right. They shouldn't just have sex in the hallway and not have anything left in the tank for later.

He continued, "Besides, I was hoping to see what it's like to watch a hockey game with you."

Alice smiled and said, "Ok. But with two conditions. No cracks about my setup. I'm weird and I like watching it this way. I never have guests over to tell me how weird I am. And no rooting for the Flames."

Scotty laughed at that. He kissed her again but it was more of a nip than a lusty, passionate kiss. He then said, "But what if I want to see Johnny Hockey's team win and have them continue to help me in the standings."

Alice lifted an eyebrow and said, "You are seriously concerned about the Flyers chance to catch you in the standings?"

"Not really. I just wanted to rile you up some and see what you would say."

Alice playfully swatted at his arm as she said, "asshole".

Then she led the way into her main living area. She glanced at the score on the iPad and saw that the Flyers tied it up while they were in the other room and that they were kissing much longer than she thought they were. "Do you want anything to drink? I'm a little limited in my selection. But I got beer, water, and tea on hand."

"What are you drinking?" asked Scotty as he peered at her dark brown drink that was sitting on the desk.

"New Phone, Who Dis? A caramel macchiato porter by Evil Genius. Unfortunately, I don't have any more of that cold. I do have in the fridge a pineapple cider, a donut IPA, a vanilla snowdrift porter, a milkshake IPA and two holiday beers that have been aged in either maple or bourbon barrels."

"You gotta be pulling my leg. Half of what you listed can't be real ingredients in beer."

"They are and I think they are good. Besides I've tried some stuff at a brewery that is much weirder like a cucumber beer. I would never bring it home unless I liked it. Although at a brewery, I will have a taster of almost anything just out of curiosity."

"What would you recommend?" asked Scott still sounding a little skeptical. She knew that she was still pushing him out of his comfort zone with beers but she didn't have any lagers in stock. It was winter time and she tended to stock up on the darkest beers possible. She wanted to make a note to herself to get some Yuengling on hand for the next time he came over.

"Do you want something that's light or dark?"

"Um dark, I guess."

"Okay. I think I have one or two of those that you might

like. Just grab a chair. I can swap the view to the main computer. If you want to try my beer, feel free." As Alice walked into the kitchen area, she called out, "Do you want a t-shirt or a jersey to wear? I got stuff that would fit you that were given as promos. I just can't promise it won't be Flyers related."

"Nah, I'm good."

All of a sudden, she could hear the Flyers game commentators much clearer which meant that he must have pulled the game on her main computer. She peeked in from the kitchen once she heard that the Flyers were on a breakaway. She first started to say "Go, Go, Go," which was followed by an immediate "Damnit" as the puck got smothered by the goalie. Scott just laughed. She went back to get him a drink. She opened up the bottle which popped a little bit like champagne and poured the dark liquid into a glass. She capped the bottle and put it back into the fridge.

She walked back to the main room to see that Scott had opened up his dress shirt all the way. She could see his abdominal muscles pop through the undershirt that he was wearing. He had his legs stretched out on her little ottoman that she kept under the desk but it was pulled out further than she normally kept it so he could access it. She handed him the dark Belgian ale and sat down in her favorite chair beside him.

They quickly settled into the game. It was mainly her getting animated and cussing at the screen either in either happiness or frustration depending on what the Flyers were doing as Scott just laughed at her. He really didn't seem to have any stake in the game other than watching her. At times, she wasn't even sure he was watching the game at all. By the end of the game, the Flyers lost in OT and they both drank their beers.

At the end of the game, Scott said, "You really are a true Philly fan."

"What's supposed to mean?" She knew all too well that most people tended to have a negative opinion of Philly fans.

"You cursed out your guys as much as you root them on. Normal fans don't do that."

"Are you sure?"

"Yeah. I can hear the fans from the stands when I'm on the ice. The negative shit tends to come from the opposing fans. NOT the home crowd."

Alice knew that to be true. Not many other fandoms would get restless as quickly as Flyers fans or would forgive a bad play. She liked to think of it as just being expressive. They knew that they would have bad games, but she didn't have to like it. Especially when you knew how good they could be. But she knew that she was probing and pushing some when she said, "But do you really expect me to have a different style of rooting for you versus any other team that I watch?"

That's when Scotty reached over to pull her chair over to him so he could actually kiss her. "You aren't a normal fan. So no. But you are my type of fan."

Alice smiled and kissed him back, wishing that they were in more than desk chairs. This is when being on a couch would be perfect and far more comfortable. She knew if she tried to climb into his lap, she was sure bad things would happen.

"I can live with that." Then she noticed the empty beer glasses on the desk and said, "I never did ask, how you did like the beer?"

"Heavy but good. What was it?"

"Bourbon barrel aged Feats of Strength from Market Brewing. I figured it was appropriate to give you based on the fact you had a Gordie Howe Hat Trick this evening. It was a hell of a game and a hell of a good fight. What did he say to you to piss you off so much?"

"It doesn't matter, he was in the wrong and we settled it," Scott said a little coldly. She knew it must have been something personal and he didn't want to talk about it. She didn't want to push the issue. She knew enough about the hockey code. The score was settled for now and nothing needed to be said. Then his voice shifted to a much lighter and happy tone as he said, "So you watched the game?"

"Yeah. Of course, I did." Scott just started to grin and seemed almost surprised to hear that she was watching his game. So Alice continued and said, "Why wouldn't I be watching you play? Even if the Flyers are playing, I would run the duel devices so I can watch it all. I just can't decide who gets the big screen and who gets the little screen."

"Oh really? Why am I not instantly on the big screen?"

"Um have we not met before or did you forget what we were just watching? This isn't the only room with Flyers stuff on the walls. You should see my kitchen. I love the Flyers. I can't just bump them down to the little screen after meeting you only a week ago. Of course, if you give me the right reasons, I could be persuaded to maybe bump you up to the big screen status."

"Oh really? What might that be?" he asked with a devilish smile.

"I have a few ideas but you have to figure that one out yourself," said Alice as she flashed an equally devilish smile.

She was letting herself be way more forward then she normally would be. While she was drinking throughout the night, she would normally wall herself off and prevent herself from getting too close to anyone. In many ways, she probably wouldn't have even told him her address so quickly except there was something about Scott that was begging her to just let him in. It had nothing to do with his looks or profession although they were both awesome in her book, she genuinely loved his personality. She loved hanging out with him.

Scott

Scott was thoroughly enjoying himself. For as much as he loved to give her shit about her taste in teams or how she cheered on their team, it really wasn't all that different than what he would say on the ice as long as he wasn't mic'ed up. It was refreshing to be with a girl who knew the sport and enjoyed it as much as he did. Since he got into the league, he's been in cities like Cleveland that didn't always have the strongest hockey bases.

Scott loved that Alice was being flirty and inviting him to do more than just hang out. While he was quick to start making out and letting his affections to be known, he was slower to get someone into bed. Part of that was practical since he didn't want to worry about getting hit up for child support and part of it was just the general boredom of one night stands and easy girls. He knew that Alice wasn't going to be a one-night stand. Alice seemed way too guarded to really be one of those girls who were looking for a quick lay. He knew how stunned she was when he basically figured out her approximate address just to let anyone into her place.

Scott started to push back off the chair to stand up, "I bet you have a few ideas. But I may have a few of my own."

He then scooped up Alice for another long kiss and then pushed towards the kitchen area and what he hoped to be a bedroom area. He inhaled her scent: a mix of sweetness with lemon and a tiny hint of chlorine in the background. She was so easy to lift and maneuver with her petite frame. She wrapped her legs around his waist so that he could walk easily and he was surprised how her strong legs were even though he knew that she did a lot of activities that would help to create strong legs, but they also looked lithe like swimming and hockey.

When they got into the kitchen, he noticed right away that there were two doors open (one straight ahead and one off to the side). So Scott broke away from the kiss just long enough to ask, "Which way to the bed?"

Alice sounded lusty when she said, "Straight."

Soon enough they were in the bedroom. He could make out the outline to the bed and dropped Alice onto it.

She immediately started to unbuckle his belt but Scott wanted to reassert some control and give himself some time to adjust. So he reached towards her waist so he could get rid of both her leggings and pants in one good tug. He wanted to do so much to her body. Alice was already wet with desire but Scott wanted to make sure she enjoyed every minute of. He took it slow and started to lick her lower body. She started to moan and twist softly in pleasure. He loved seeing the look of elation on her face.

Once she reached a climax, she surprised him by doing the same thing back to him while he was still standing beside the bed. She removed his pants and boxers just enough so she could have easy access to his hardening member. She was kneeling on the bed. She started to massage his private parts with her tongue. Then she started to give him the best blowjob that he'd had with the right amount of pressure and moisture. He was too close to the brink.

He had to slow it down if they were going to do anything else. So he asked, "Wait. I'm too close." He then quickly pulled out his emergency condom from his wallet. He deftly ripped the foil and slid the condom on. Then he climbed onto the bed and straddled her. Before he tried to do more, he pulled her shirt off. He already knew that she wasn't wearing a bra since he could see her nipples through the thin T, but he used his left hand to massage, cup and pinch her nipple. He then used his hand to get her ready for penetration by using his fingers to get her nice and wet. She was tight but willing. It didn't take long for her to be completely ready. They were able to get into a nice rhythm. He was able to find her pleasure zones right away and Alice was practically purring as he continued to thrust and pull back. He knew he would be coming way too quickly for his tastes. It was too long since he had sex and the charge he felt with Alice as practically electric. He wished he could have lasted much, much longer.

After he came, he quickly excused himself to take care of the condom and then came to lay down beside Alice. Everything from the day just came to him at that moment. He was exhausted from the brutal hockey game, the flight, and even the sex. He wanted to do nothing more than cuddle with Alice and hold her all night long if not go for a few more rounds. But he knew he had to get home. He never planned to spend the night. He didn't pack enough clothes for it or even bring the suitcase out of his car. But more importantly, he knew that Chloe needed him to get home. He only asked the dog walker to come to the house for one walk and feeding. She would be going crazy and probably trying to eat anything she could get her hands on which meant either the couch or a shoe, neither of which his beloved pitbull should be eating. But at the same time, he just couldn't pull himself up from Alice's side and considered how long until he could go again.

Alice

Scott was looking at her with a bit of a dreamy look in his eyes. Alice wasn't sure if he was tired from the long day or if he was completely content after their recent sexcapades. She knew that she was fully sated but she wasn't sure if it was also good for him.

"So what are your plans for tonight? Do you want to spend the night?"

"I do but I need to get back to my place. Chloe is probably starting to go a little crazy."

"Chloe?" asked Alice. She knew that she was finding herself to be a little jealous at the feminine name. She propped herself up on her elbow so she could see him better. Scott just laughed as he must have realized that she was a little jealous.

"Yeah, my pitbull. I had to have mentioned her before," said Scott. That immediately made Alice feel at ease. She realized that he had mentioned his dog before but never the dog's name. Scott propped himself up as he grabbed his cell phone from the nightstand. He immediately pulled up a photo of him giving a large dark brown dog with a larger smile on her face a belly rub. Alice wasn't sure what she liked best, seeing such a happy dog or happy owner who was shirtless. "She's a good girl for the most part. But she doesn't like it when I'm away for too long. I have a dog walker who comes but she normally wants another walk and meal about now. And she's been bad when women have come over before."

"I take it that she was a rescue."

"How could you tell?"

"I've heard a few stories where friends got rescues who most likely were abused in their previous home and were afraid of a particular gender as a result. I hope that I get to meet her and that she likes me."

"Me too. Cause Chloe will always stay in my life. She's non-negotiable."

"Why wouldn't she be? Don't tell me you had someone ask you to choose them or your dog?" asked Alice incredulously. She knew that she just met Scott but she could never see herself making any sort of ultimatum like that with a partner.

"More than once," said a very quiet Scott.

"That's terrible. At most, if she didn't like me, I would ask to be in a separate area. Like for her to be outside or in a different room. But not to get rid of her. She's your dog. That's like asking to get rid a piece of your family."

"So you don't mind pitbulls?"

"Why would I? They can be the sweetest, most loyal dog out there. In many ways, they are a reflection of their owners. A good owner, a great dog. A neglectful or mean owner, a mean dog. But given everything that I know about you thus far, I'm sure she's a great dog."

Scott smiled and took a deep sigh. "I really should get going. She needs me." He started to get out of bed. But before he could fully leave the bed, Alice grabbed him and started to kiss him one last time for the night.

4

ALICE

Things were going well with Scott. They were able to spend so much time together thanks to the home stand. She knew that she was starting to fall for him which was something she hadn't done in years. In some ways, she was afraid of the emotions that were running through her since she didn't always open up her trust too quickly and she really didn't want to get hurt either.

She was watching the Sound play the Blue Jackets, when she got a call from her dad. So she automatically picked up the call.

"Hey Dad. What's up?"

"Not too much. How about with you, kid?"

Alice laughed. She knew that question was coming. "Just watching what's left of the Sound game."

"The Sound again? What's that, the third game this week that you are watching? What happened to the Flyers?"

"Fourth game this week for the Sound. Nothing happened to the Flyers. They aren't playing tonight. They will play again after the All-Star break."

"So you are seriously trying to tell me that you just got a sudden interest over the Sound for no reason?"

"No. There's a reason. The new guy in my life has created a vested interest with the Sound."

"Care to elaborate, kid?"

"Not particularly. It's new, dad and I don't know where it's going. But once I know where it's going, I promise to explain more."

"I want to meet him, the next time I'm in town."

Alice knew that was a reasonable request. But also she didn't want to say much about Scott just yet. It wasn't that she wasn't insanely proud of Scott, she was. It was just so new and while it felt so real and good, she knew it could all fall apart quickly.

"Maybe. He travels a lot for work. So it will depend on the timing of everything. But the more sure I am about things, the more I will tell you. I promise, Dad."

As she was saying that, she noticed that Scotty just broke the shutout and scored on Blue Jackets for the first time of the evening. They still had to get two more goals to even tie it.

"So are you guys going to be doing anything for your birthday?"

She started smiling. She was excited to have a date planned with Scotty for tomorrow night. It was the only thing she was doing for her birthday in town. The bulk of her birthday celebrations would be with her friends in Philly next month.

"Depending on the game tonight." Alice caught herself from saying how tired he would be afterwards or he wanted to hang out with the team since it was a big rivalry game and a bit of a tradition to hang out. "We might go out but I'm pretty tired. So it might just be tomorrow night which we are definitely going out."

"As long as you are happy, I am too. It sounds like you are very happy. Just be smart and safe."

"I will be, Dad."

"Good. I will let you get back to your game. I know you are missing some of it talking to me. Love you kid."

"Thanks dad. Love you too."

Right as she was hanging up the phone, she noticed that Scotty got his second goal of the game. She missed one of the goals by the Sound when she was distracted by her dad. That was making her happy to see the Sound climb its way out of the deficit to create a tie game.

Then the game got really knotted up with both teams playing whack-a-puck more than actual hockey. It was killing Alice since she could see the holes and the opportunities for the Sound to actually take a lead but they all got shut down. So she was cursing with way more frustration then she should have been.

There was 30 seconds left in the game, Scotty had the puck on his stick. He just rushed the net and worked his ass off to get towards it since he was drawing triple coverage. But they weren't able to stop him as he continued to control the puck and even did a nifty move to lift the stick of a defensive man so he could keep the control. But right at the last moment, he backhanded the puck to Lager who had the perfect shot on net creating the win.

Alice was happy for Scotty. To get a 3 point night was excellent and she knew how important it was for the Sound to beat their in-state rivals. Not too much later, she got a text from Scotty.

S: ***Hey babe, Don't hate me but I'm going out with the guys tonight.***

A: ***No big deal. Still on for tomorrow night?***

S: ***Of course. I'm picking you up at 8pm.***

While Alice knew she should be disappointed that Scotty was canceling on her tonight, she was relieved. As the snow was starting to fall, she wanted to pass out for the night. She was curious if Scotty had any clue it was her birthday. She hadn't mentioned it since she wanted to keep it low key and didn't really care about it. But she wouldn't put it past him since he did figure out where she lived without her really giving him the information.

As she went to bed, Cleveland was in the midst of the largest snowstorm of the winter thus far. Alice didn't have any problems getting to sleep. Before she knew it, she was sound asleep until she heard a slight thud and some rustling of papers that woke her up. She wasn't that concerned since she lived in an apartment complex and would be woken up with noises from her upstairs neighbor or cars in the parking lot. But there was something about the noises that made her concerned and thought they might be coming from within her apartment rather than from her upstairs neighbor. So she was on guard for a minute or two, but then the noises seemed to stop. Just as she was convincing herself that the noises were coming from upstairs and it was safe to go back to sleep, the bedroom door started to open.

Oh shit, this is real. I have to act.

She was in a mental fog and not really thinking straight despite knowing that she would have to act. So at first, she thought that it might be maintenance so she as she was jumping up out of bed, she said, "hello" trying to figure out what was going on. But as she was removing the eye mask that she normally slept with, she realized there was a lean figure about 6 ft tall in her doorway that was possibly holding a flashlight.

Fortunately for her, he immediately ran out of the doorway and headed out the kitchen door to escape. She heard the door slam shut with the keys rattling off the door. She rushed out into the main room while she was dialing 911 on her cell phone that she grabbed off of her nightstand. Even without the lights on, she could tell that her iPad was gone, that they went through the desk and she saw one of her decorative boxes was overturned in the main room. It wasn't a complete wreck but she could tell that things were opened up and moved around almost randomly.

In a haze, she relayed the information to the 911 operator as she ran her hand through her hair and she was trying to survey what was missing or moved. She was extremely careful not to touch a damn thing. She listened to thousands of hours of true crime podcasts and knew that she would have to wait for the police to arrive.

It seemed to take forever for the police to arrive at her place. But she knew that was most likely the adrenaline coursing through her and not actually a long time. She paced back and forth. At the same time, she played with her hair turning it from ponytail into a bun shape and then letting it go.

She fired off two texts, one to Jennifer and one to Scott: ***Worst night ever. Someone entered and broke into my place. Stole my iPad.*** She wanted to let Jennifer know since she might actually be awake and could help give her the practical support on what to expect. Scott was purely for support and hoping he was still awake from his night of drinking with the team.

Then finally the doorbell rang. Alice grabbed her glasses and the keys to let the officer into her place. There was only one officer at the door but he seemed friendly and very non-threatening. He entered the place and asked to turn on the lights so they could easily move around.

Immediately, she started to run through the events thus far and anything she noticed to be moved, opened or missing. This included the desk being opened up, the box in the front room being toppled over, a battery pack removed from one of her purses and left on the desk, a bag of Goldfish crackers that was moved into the kitchen, the silver nutcracker salt and pepper shakers that were taken out of the desk and moved onto another shelving unit, and the missing iPad.

The first thing the police officer asked her to do was to access her Apple Account so they could get the serial number of her iPad and get the tracking on it. She also had to describe her home screen and the iPad case. But she wasn't able to open up the account since it wanted dual-layer authentication but her only apple device was stolen. Then they tried to track her iPad on his phone. They were immediately able to get the location of her iPad on the phone. The officer immediately radioed the location to the other officers and apparently sent a screenshot of the map from the Find my Phone app to the officers in a group chat.

Then Alice had to write up the written statement about everything that was missing, moved, and whatnot. As she was starting to take a closer look at her desk area, she realized her Echo Dot was also gone. So the officer immediately radioed his officers to look for the missing virtual assistant as they were searching.

As Alice wrote her statement, the police officer was starting to process the evidence. There were some photos of everything. Then he collected touch DNA swabs throughout the apartment. This included the two different door knobs that the thief touched. Then it was Alice's turn to swab her cheeks so they could differentiate her DNA from the burglar's.

Then it was time to start fingerprinting the desk. Since Alice mentioned that she was rather interested in true crime podcasts, he took great care to explain what he was doing and even showed her some of what he was doing which helped to keep her calm and focused at the moment. It was neat to see how the feather-like brush would just expose any and all fingerprints on the white desk surface.

All of a sudden, a second police officer came in with a couple of brown bags that were in three different sizes. The second officer opened the conversation with, "So I have good news and I have bad news."

Alice wasn't sure what to expect. It seemed like it would be mostly good news by the look of everything. She didn't think they would be able to recover anything let alone so quickly. But she was still pretty stressed out and her voice wasn't being super cooperative- it was jagged and slightly panicky yet. So she just nodded instead of speaking.

The second officer set the bags on the one desk chair that was open. He then picked up one bag and said, "We think we found your Alexa. Do you happen to still have the box for it?"

Alice nodded and went over to the small shelving unit that was beside her desk that she kept a lot of her knitting projects. It was also littered with papers, notebooks, and the suede box for the silver nutcrackers. She had to shift a few things to get to where she left the box. She handed it to the officer. He was hoping to verify the serial numbers on the box and the Alexa itself. Unfortunately, you couldn't read anything on the Alexa's bottom. So they had to plug it in and see if it could connect with the Alexa app. That initially worked with the device going from an offline status to online status. Then there was the voice recognition with the app.

"So that's definitely yours," said the second officer as he walked over to the chair that he had previously set the various brown evidence bags on. He picked up the largest bag. "As for the bad news, this is what's left of the iPad that we recovered." He pulled out an iPad that was completely shattered, it was in 3 general pieces with wires and a miracle keeping the thing connected in one piece. There was no way to even think about getting it replaced. "Most likely once they realized that we were tracking, they just..." as he twisted his hands in opposite directions which would have rendered the device apart "and tossed it."

Alice honestly wasn't too surprised. She didn't think would recover anything, let alone something intact. Yet it still crushed her to see her tablet so completely destroyed, it was a constant companion and source of contentment and media.

She could tell from the occasional things on the police radio that they could follow the footprints in the snow and the two officers in her apartment were starting to call her place the primary site.

The first officer asked the second to see if he could help with trying to fingerprint the Alexa while he finished collecting prints from the desk. The Alexa was the trickiest to fingerprint since they had to use black powder on a black device. When they were trying to transfer the prints to the card, it was a crap shoot to see if they were actually transferring anything of value. After he did what he could do, he handed Alice the Alexa and said, "I did the best I could, so not to damage it," with that he started to pack up his evidence collection kit and left the apartment.

The first officer continued to finish up his work in the main room with the fingerprints. Then once he was done, he too packed up his kit. He gave Alice his card that had the case number, which was when she finally learned that his name was Officer LePrince. Then he left for the night.

By then it was an hour and a half later from when the burglar entered into her apartment. The gravity of it all started to settle in for Alice. She was becoming panicked and the anxiety just started to hit her, so she sat on her bed and was clutching the two teddy bears that she would sleep with whenever she wasn't sharing the bed with someone. She knew that she really needed to speak to someone. The first call that she made was practical and would be the calming influence if he picked up the phone: her dad. But since it was past 2:30 am, she wasn't surprised when she got his voicemail. The next call was to her sister. She figured that there was a good chance that Allison might pick up the phone since she was constantly up in the middle of the night taking care of her 4 year old. But that too was a voicemail. She also tried calling her mom, since her parents were divorced and you couldn't just call one parent anymore. That was the voicemail that she anticipated most.

At that point, Alice was starting to really lose her grasp on the emotions and her nerves felt like they were on fire. She decided to make the one call that she was hoping to avoid just because she hated how late she was calling knowing that he had a game coming up. But she knew that out of anyone in the area, he would be the one who would pick up the phone and would make sure that she wasn't alone. She decided to call Scott. It didn't matter that he didn't answer her text. She needed to talk to someone that she was close to.

Scott

Scott thought he heard his phone go off. He couldn't imagine who would be calling him at this hour. He was slow to react and missed the call completely but he continued to pull out his phone just to figure out who it was. His teammates would all be either asleep or getting laid- either way, unlikely to call him. He knew that Alice said she was planning on going to bed early after he changed up the plans on her. Then he saw the missed message and the call he just missed were both from Alice.

As he read the one text message, he just gave out the longest protracted "FUCKKKKKKKKK" of his life.

Scott was seeing red and wanted to hurt whoever broke into her place. He wasn't the biggest guy on the team and definitely not the best fighter but he always protected anyone he cared about and could usually hold his own in a fight. It was no different for those he loved off the ice. He was already getting out of bed to grab a pair of pants and a shirt as he started to call Alice back. He knew he had to keep his temper in check since Alice wasn't needing him to fight at that moment and instead would need support. He just hoped she wasn't in the hospital or something along those lines.

"Are you okay? What all happened? Do you need me to come and get you?" asked Scott in a rush. He knew he needed to slow down some but he wanted to get to her and he needed answers. He knew he couldn't get any answers if he didn't give Alice space to speak so he forced himself to stay silent for the moment.

"I'm more or less okay," said Alice in a fairly rough voice. He couldn't tell at first if she was crying or hurt. He heard Alice take a deep breath almost as if to steady herself before saying more but that pause was killing him. He needed to know more. Just knowing she was more or less okay wasn't enough, he wanted her to know what she wasn't saying. Finally, she continued, "I wasn't hurt physically. The guy fled the moment I jumped out of bed as he was entering my bedroom. But I'm really shaken up right now."

"Yeah, I get that." Scott was grabbing his keys off the nightstand and grabbed his wallet just in case he got pulled over. He hit the autostarter on his car so it could warm up as he got more details from Alice. He knew Alice didn't answer the question if she wanted him to come over, at this point he was going over regardless. "I'm coming over now. But it's going to take me a little bit to get there on the roads."

"Thanks. Just take your time getting here," Alice said. That kinda fired him up for the moment. It wasn't a dismissal because he could hear the relief in her voice when he said he was coming over. But to be told to wait for something he wanted to do was never a strong suit. It was that drive that helped to catapult him to the NHL as a young kid at 20.

"I won't take my time. I want to get there as soon as I can. I think the bigger question would be that after I get there, do you want me to stay the night or do you want to come back to my place?"

"Can I go to your place?" asked Alice really meekly. He was starting to realize that there were some tears and a lot of panic going on. So it was not easy for her to really talk or say much. He hated that. She was tough and yet here she sounded almost broken.

As he was getting into his car and waiting for the garage door to come to life, he said, "Of course you can. I wouldn't have offered if it wasn't okay. Can you tell me what happened?"

He was glad that the roads were plowed and the conditions weren't that bad. The snow had stopped but there was a lot of it on the ground. The roads were slick but he could get around without too many problems. He just continued to grip the steering wheel as tight as he could to keep his emotions in check. He knew that while he was angry at the break in, he needed to be there for her at that moment. She seemed so broken and not like herself and he wanted to fix it.

She was still taking her time answering his question. When she did, "Not really. How was going out with the guys?"

Scott hated that she wouldn't say what was going on in her mind and what happened. But he also realized that there was a good chance that she was trying to distract herself from reality for a moment and just needed to hear his voice. "It was okay. Nothing too crazy. Do you want me to talk for a bit?"

He could hear that she was still on the phone by the little

gasps and breathing but she didn't actually say anything. He chuckled as he asked, "Did you just answer me with a nod forgetting I can't see you?"

"Maybe...."

Scott took a deep breath. He knew he had to fill more of the conversational space then he usually had to. But he wasn't even sure what to talk about or what to say. He didn't want to upset her more or say something that sounded really dumb.

"I'm sorry kid that this happened to you. But I will be there soon. I promise." He then realized he could just fill the space with what they did that evening. "But my night was really pretty tame. We had a couple beers together as they had some of the west coast games on at the bar. Then people started to break off. A few of the younger guys went to a strip club. Not sure what happened to Misha and Toli. We think they went to find some girls but we are not sure. At least, Toli will look after Misha and make sure they are ready for tonight's game. Dkystman found a girl at the bar and left with her. When Lager wanted to head back and I figured it was a good as time as ever and left with him. I then crawled into bed. Not sure how I missed your initial message. Must have been right as I was crawling into bed."

He wasn't sure if Alice was still there. She wasn't making any noise like she did initially with a heavy breath that almost sounded like crying. If he wasn't driving in the snow, he would have looked down at the phone but he didn't want to take his eyes off the road. He was already driving faster then he probably should have been but after so many winters in Canada, the snow wasn't really that bad and he could take it faster than most locals.

"So Alice, I'm going to need you to talk a little. I know you are starting to settle down which is good but I don't know if you are still there."

"I'm here. I won't hang up. At least not until you tell me to."

"So did he get anything?"

"My iPad is gone. My Alexa was taken but returned by the police. He got into my desk but I don't notice anything being gone, but things got moved around. Oh he also got into my Goldfish."

"Goldfish? I didn't remember any pets at your place," asked Scott. He started to hear Alice giggling some in the background. He knew that was missing something or completely off the mark.

"Don't you remember Goldfish crackers? I know they are for kids but I still enjoy them from time to time. When I went home for Christmas, my niece wanted a bag of them with the cheddar and pretzel flavors all mixed up. Almost immediately, she decided that she didn't like them and I inherited the bag. But he ate my bag before I did."

That just sounded weird. Well to steal a pet goldfish is even weirder. Nothing about that part made much sense. "How could you tell?"

"Given that the bag magically moved between my snack table in the main room to the kitchen when I was asleep, it's a pretty good guess who did that."

"That it is. Still it's weird. Why would you have a snack in the middle of breaking into someone's place?"

"Don't know. I've been asking myself the same thing."

He was finally approaching her place. The next trick would be to find parking. He normally just parked in front of her place on the street, but that was covered in snow. They wouldn't be in her place for too long, so he figured why not use the parking lot at her place since there was almost no one on the roads due to the storm. So he found an open spot and locked up his car.

"I'm walking up now."

"Thank god."

Scott got to the door and saw Alice waiting there. She looked so out of sorts. Her eyes looked puffy and red from crying. Even worse, her eyes were both empty and fearful at the same time. All he could do was hug her as she opened up the security door. She just seemed to melt into him. Instead of lifting her up as he normally did, he just started to kiss her forehead. He also started to whisper, "Je t'aime. Je t'aime." He knew she would understand what he was saying and needed to hear some calming words. Normally he would never say such heavy words but seeing her in such a state, he knew he meant them and wanted to soothe her. So it seemed like the perfect time to tell her that he loved her. He was just glad that she understood French and knew what he was saying.

After a few moments, he switched back to English and said, "I'm so sorry that I wasn't there to protect you. I should have been there."

"This wasn't your fault. I'm just glad you're here now."

Scott knew that she was right but he still felt bad. There would be plenty of road trips where he couldn't be there to protect her. But he still wanted to keep her safe all the time.

While it felt good comforting Alice with one of his bear hugs, he knew that they should get going pretty soon. She had work and he had a game the next day. They both should attempt some sleep. Even if it wasn't already decided that they would go back to his place, he knew there would be no sleep happening in the apartment. He had no intention of leaving her place in an unprotected state. He was going to put as much security in place before leaving. There was no reason to have a second robbery take place.

"Hey, we should probably get going pretty soon. Before we do, lets get that door they used blocked. Which door was it?"

Alice was slow to say something and slower to move away from his embrace. Eventually she said, "Kitchen."

Scott nodded. This is when he could just take charge in the moment and do what needed to be done. He was anticipating to do it by himself but Alice followed him into the apartment and continued to hold onto his hand. It was like she was afraid to let go and just wanted to be touched.

Scott was surprised by what he saw. He could see that things were moved around and out of place. But much of the place also looked like it was untouched (at least from what he remembered from other night). He heard that a robbery looks different in real life and what that's what they meant on how it could look staged. He could still see where they were testing for fingerprints on the desk area since there was black smudges everywhere on what was a white desk. He knew that he could probably touch anything he wanted since she said that the police had already left but he didn't want to. He knew the main room wouldn't have anything appropriate to block the door. He didn't want to disrupt her normal routine too much and it had to be heavy enough to keep the door from being pushed on.

So he looked into the bedroom. That had both a small dresser and the A/C unit that he could easily move but would be large enough to cause issues getting into the bedroom.

Since he hadn't actually slept over at her place due to Chloe, he wasn't sure how much she would be using either. Since it was winter and the A/C unit was tucked between some other furniture, he assumed it wouldn't be in use but also it would be a pain to get it out of its winter spot. He asked, "Do you mind if we bring this dresser into the kitchen?"

Alice just nodded. He wasn't used to her being so quiet. She was timid until you got to know her but then she was open and could be quite talkative. It pained him to see her like that since he knew she was hurting. He hugged her before starting to move the dresser. He also said, "It'll be okay. I promise."

He lifted the dresser into the kitchen. He made sure she still had access to open the drawers since he really wasn't sure what she kept in there. It only took a minute to move it into the kitchen area. She just kept looking at him.

"You know, we could get another lock for your bedroom door, before you spend another night in here."

"You think?" almost as if that was a novel idea. Alice was wicked smart so he knew that if she had a chance to calm down, she would have thought of the same thing.

"Yeah. It might help. No sense in relying on the main door alone. It wouldn't be that hard to install. I can't promise that we can do it tomorrow but before I leave town."

Alice then kissed him as if he was a genius. He was so tempted to pull her into her bedroom and do what they normally do whenever he was at her place. But tonight wasn't a night for carnal lust, it was about giving her security and protection. So he hugged her and just kept everything pretty still except for the fact that he was getting hard.

"So are you all ready to go?"

"Yeah. I have everything in my work bag."

"Let's grab your hockey sticks too."

Alice looked at him as if he had lost his mind but she regardless started to head to the front closet where she presumably kept her hockey equipment. Scott felt that he should help carry something so he grabbed the backpack that she'd been carrying with her whenever she came anywhere after work. Most girls he knew carried purses but she always seemed to have a backpack instead. It seemed heavier than he expected. He knew it wouldn't have the weight of her iPad but at the same time, he knew she carried lots of other things that wouldn't have been taken like knitting and notebooks.

"Yeah unless you want to play some full pick-up again. I promised you that I would help you with your puck handling. Tonight is as good as night as any. It normally helps me to feel better."

"Swimming or skating does it for me. But it might be nice to work with the puck handling. Although it's more the speed of the puck on the ice that gets to me. I used to play floor hockey and I never had any sort of discomfort with the puck. If anything, I'm just lazy when it's off the ice."

"You aren't lazy. Grab your skates. We can try to get some ice time."

Scott was trying to think when and where they would have access to ice the easiest. He knew that Corey had some ice at his house but Scott wasn't sure if he wanted to go there. Sometimes Corey could be a bit of an asshole without meaning to be. Plus, everyone on the team would know about Alice since there was no way Corey would keep his mouth shut. He wasn't trying to hide Alice but she hadn't been able to make it to any of his games since her schedule made it impossible to catch the whole game (although she never had an issue meeting up with him after his games). The main reason he didn't want Corey to know was because he would be called pussy-whipped and they would all blame her if he didn't want to go out after games. He had time to figure out when they could to some ice since he didn't plan to let her sleep alone until he had to leave in three nights.

They left for his place. He took his time driving now that she was in his car. He could relax since he knew that she was actually physically okay although he could see it all over her face she was still majorly stressed. He knew that sleep would be an afterthought for him at this point. He just wanted to protect her. The car was getting a little too quiet for him. He knew there was still a good chance she would try deflecting his questions but he was hoping she would open up some.

"Did you think about calling off for tomorrow?"

"I have to go in. We are short staffed. It wasn't even a real thought to call off. Just not sure how well I will handle everything. I did let my boss know that I was likely to be pretty useless with the cleaning but I could be the adult in the room."

Scott looked at her in slight surprise and awe. He was glad to see that she was willing to go in and try. But he could see that she was still pretty much on the verge of another panic attack at any moment and she was not completely herself.

"Do you want me to come in with you?" He actually surprised himself by offering to go to work with her. At least she worked at a gym, so he could work out and do something useful for his game day prep as he stayed close by.

"Maybe. But you got your own stuff to do. Don't you have a morning skate and pregame stuff that you need to do? I already feel like a shithead for waking you up. The last thing I want to do is to screw up your game."

"You are not a shithead. I am glad you called." He took one of his hands off the steering wheel and started to rub her thigh since her hands were tucked away. He hoped that his touch was as soothing for her as it was magnetic for him. "I'm just so glad that you weren't physically hurt. If anyone has a right to feel like a shithead, it's me. I changed our plans tonight and I could have been there. Don't ever feel guilty for calling me when you need help. Not ever."

"Okay," said Alice too quietly and too tentatively. He didn't even need to look to know that she was second guessing herself.

"Honestly babe. It's okay to call me anytime. I will try to pick up. If I don't, I will hit you up when I see the missed call. I care about you sooo much that hockey and everything else in the world doesn't matter as much."

They then drifted into some more silence. He wasn't sure why he didn't actually put the music on the in car, most likely since he tended to favor heavy rock and hip hop and neither seemed right at that moment.

Scott pulled into his gated community. He was excited to bring Alice over to his place for the first time. It was much larger than Alice's apartment. They talked about going there a few times but just never got around to it. Part of it was his nerves about Chloe's reaction and if she would try to nip at Alice like she had at his previous girlfriends.

Alice smiled some. "I didn't realize you lived back here too. I used to do some computer help for one of my swim lessons clients here." Scott waited to see if she would say a name or elaborate but she didn't.

As he pulled into the driveway, he said, "Are you ready to meet the other girl in my life?" He was excited to show off his place and his dog. He knew it wasn't fancy and there was room for someone to make it nicer but it was his.

Alice was still being quiet when she said, "I guess so."

Scott reached back to grab her bag from the back seat as Alice slowly got out of the SUV. He left the hockey sticks in the car for now; figuring he could get them once she was a little bit more lively or tomorrow afternoon. He rounded the car to passionately kiss her. He did keep his temptation to just carry her up the steps and over the threshold at bay.

When he pushed opened the garage door, he was immediately greeted by Chloe. "Come on, Chloe you know you need to back up. We can't get into the room." His voice was firm but very playful. He knew he wasn't helping things since he was also scratching Chloe under the chin like he normally did. As the duo entered, Chloe surprised Scott in the best way possible. Chloe didn't act at all aggressive towards Alice. Instead, the pit bull sniffed Alice's legs and just started to brush up against her, most likely hoping to get a bit of an ear scratch which Alice obliged. After getting a bit of an ear scratch from Alice, Chloe stalked off towards the bedroom.

Odd, is she going back to bed already?

Alice's breath started to quicken again. He wasn't sure what was going on in her head at that moment but whatever it was, it wasn't a good sign. So he started to rub her back as he said, "Babe, what do you want? Do you want to sit in the living room or go to bed? Do you want something to drink?"

"Living room, I guess. Just hold me for a bit."

Scott scooped her up and carried her easily to his living room with a large TV and the oversized couches. He carefully sat her down on the couch and then he snuggled in beside her. Trying to do exactly what she wanted - to hold her and give her some comfort. He realized that he still had her backpack on his back, so he set it down by their feet in case she wanted to grab anything from it. Almost immediately, she grabbed out two small teddy bears that were at the top of her bag as he was running his fingers up and down her spine. Right away, he noticed that one of the two bears was wearing a Flyers hoodie.

"Hey, shouldn't that be a Sound hoodie by now?" he asked teasingly like he normally did. In all honesty, he thought it was fitting for her. The two bears both seemed well loved and he didn't think that she should have swapped the shirt out just to his team. He made the comment to give Alice any sense of normalcy he could. It seemed like she was settling down again as she sat there. He hated knowing that she was scared and fighting something fierce inside of herself that she wasn't sharing.

"No, Hextall will always be a Flyer. I don't care if he got fired as our GM. Hextall was the goalie when I was growing up and just fit all the ideas of what it meant to be a Flyer in my book: strong player, could score, protects his own and doesn't take shit from anyone. I would never switch out this guy's hoodie as long as he is named Hextall."

Scott was tempted to tease her about what would happen if Ron Hextall got hired by the Sound in some capacity. But figured it wasn't worth it tonight. Instead he wanted to know more about her.

"So if that's Hextall, who is the other guy?"

"China." She said it so simply like it was plain as day.

The bear had some sort of clothing on but it didn't look Chinese. Her other bear's name fit its clothing. So Scott felt like he was missing something. "Why China?"

"So it's actually China the Second. I have always wanted to go to China ever since I saw Big Bird Goes to China when I was super little. Someone told me you make names inspirational or a wish to the person. So the 3 year old me named my favorite bear China since I wanted to go there. Then I lost that one in London. It wasn't good and I brought home a bunch of bears trying to replicate the comfort China gave me. Of course, it was the bear given to me by doing a good deed on the flight back to the States. Literally from the moment I held him, it was like holding onto China again. So I gave him the same name."

Scott started to hear Chloe coming back towards them with slow deliberate footsteps. Once she came into the room, the pit bull climbed up onto the couch and buried her head into Alice's lap. That alone stunned Scott since Chloe was always a daddy's girl and seemed to be jealous of any woman he got serious with. After a few moments, Alice pulled a well chewed black hockey puck from her lap. Scott just chuckled as he realized what it was: Chloe's favorite toy. Alice just seemed confused.

"Chloe must really like you and wants to make you feel better. She almost never shares her hockey pucks with anyone except if I'm having a really bad day or if she wants to play."

"A puck? Is that even a good thing for her to chew on all the time?"

Scott just shrugged. He's thought about it a long time ago

but since she seemed like a normal healthy dog, he never even asked the vet about it. “No idea. But she would always steal pucks from me ever since she was a puppy. I just kinda gave up on the idea of taking them away. At most I will limit it to one or two pucks at a time. That way she has something to chew on. It keeps her happy but I don’t have too many pucks sacrificed to her.”

They kinda settled into the moment. In many ways, he wished he could take a photo of the moment. He had his two favorite girls with him on the couch and they were all cuddled up but he knew that moment wasn’t right even if it was Instagram worthy. He noticed the longer they sat there and the more relaxed Alice got, the sleepier she got too. He kissed her forehead again to help get her attention, “Hey, what time do you need to get up for work?”

“Um I guess 8am. I have to be there by 9:30am but I will need to take a shower in the morning and I’m sure I will have to talk to my family in the morning since I tried to talk to them before I called you but I left a few voicemails.”

Scott nodded and dug out his phone from his pocket so he could set the alarm. While he had a feeling he wasn’t going to fall back asleep anytime soon, he didn’t want to make her day any worse than it was by accidently oversleeping. He set the phone aside and held her for a while. As he was doing so, he noticed that Alice had fallen asleep. He waited a few moments to make sure she was fully asleep before he tried to pick her up. As soon as he started to pick up Alice, Chloe jumped down from the couch. She knew that they would be heading towards his bedroom for some real sleep.

5

ALICE

Alice felt so completely knackered when she heard an unfamiliar alarm go off. It felt like she had been run over by a truck and so much had happened to her that night, she hoped it was a weird dream caused by drinking too much even though she knew that she didn't drink the evening before. As she started to look around her, everything seemed unfamiliar. The walls were bare and the bed was a king size bed with grey sheets (not her normal double bed). She was also holding onto a puck in addition to having her two bears in the crook of her arm. She rolled over to see Scott looking at her. He looked too devilish good at that moment since he was half naked and propped up on his elbows.

"Hey there," he said with a sexy smile. Almost as if he had been waiting for her to finally wake up.

That's when everything rushed back to her and she realized the burglary wasn't a dream. It happened and he took her back to his place. The last thing she remembered was being cuddled up on the couch with him. He gave her so much comfort and made her feel so safe in his arms. There were a few moments where it seemed like he was the only one keeping her all together. Without him, she might have fallen completely apart. That being said, she found herself being just unsure of herself. "Hey."

His warm hands started to rub her arm, sending down nothing but warmth and heat through her body as he asked, "How are you doing this morning?"

Alice took a deep breath and was trying to assess herself. The more she thought about the evening, the more shaken she had become. But at the same time, waking up beside him was magical and for a few seconds she could forget the horrors. She wanted to wake every morning with him shirtless by her side.

"Okay given everything, won't lie, I'm still pretty shaken up." She knew she should probably tell him about how she felt in his arms but she didn't want to sound pitiful or needy.

He started to push himself up to seated position. His dog jumped off the bed and ran down the hall. Most likely in anticipation of food or a walk. Instead of moving from the bed, Scott passed over her cellphone and said, "Your phone has been going off all morning. You might want to check out what's going on."

Alice just flattened herself back into the bed. "Why didn't you silence it?" She opened up to see if there was anything she actually had to deal with. She saw it was silenced but the vibrate mode was on. "Ugh, I don't want to deal with birthday wishes today. Wasn't the burglary enough for one day?"

That's when Scott actually started to roll on top of her almost as if he wanted to start with some morning foreplay. She barely had time to tuck the phone into some pillows between them so it wouldn't get crushed under their weight. She already had to replace her iPad with a barely there budget, she couldn't afford a new phone on top of it. With her being pinned to the bed, she could see his scruff coming through which made him look even sexier. Although as soon as he spoke, she knew it wasn't for sexy time. He was looking at her seriously as he asked, "What do you mean birthday wishes?"

"It's my birthday today. I got to be one of the few people who had to deal with a break in and the police as the very first thing on their birthday."

Then Scott started to kiss her ear which just set off sparks throughout her entire body and he continued kissing her down the line of her neck. Once he reached the top of her white shirt, he asked, "Why didn't you say anything that it was your birthday? I could have gotten you something or done something to treat you."

"Because until this morning, the only thing I wanted to do on my birthday was to spend time with you especially since my Philly birthday trip won't happen until next month. We already had plans so why say anything. It just didn't seem like that big of a deal. Hell, you even had me all set up to go to your game tonight before our date. It was what I would have wanted. In some ways, I just want my birthday to go away so I don't have to think about this morning's events."

Scott then rolled them both over as he hugged her. So now she was on top of him but he continued to shower her with kisses as he pushed up the t-shirt that she was wearing and getting rather close to playing with her lower half as well. There was something that felt so sweet and perfect for her. He was keeping her anxiety at bay and she wasn't even sure he realized the kind of power that he held over her in that moment.

"Would you mind if I did get you something now that I know that it's your birthday, cause what kind of a boyfriend would I be if I got you nothing?"

"No. But more of this is perfectly fine with me too, you don't need to go overboard with anything," she said as she started to lustfully kiss him and fisted his hair.

Once they separated from the kiss, he said, "Would a new iPad be going overboard in your book?"

She had to think about that one for a second. In some ways, it absolutely was too much. She could never afford to spend the same amount of money on him for his birthday. But she was dreading having to purchase a new iPad on her budget since it would take a couple months before she could afford a new one and in the short time period that she had the iPad, it became an everyday tool for her. She would use it as her main media center: whether it was for podcasts, music or hockey games and she loved to use it at work when she needed to look up things quickly. She kept workouts on there and could answer emails.

She said, "Yeah, but nothing else except maybe a night where I can wake up next to you and we can do whatever we want."

All of a sudden she heard the familiar sounds of a dog nails walking on hardwood floor and an audible whine from Chloe. Alice started to roll off of Scott. Scott was looking guilty at that moment. "Sorry, she's not used to me being awake for so long and not getting up out of bed. She's hungry and bored. When you were asleep, it was easy for her to tell that it was still bedtime."

Alice realized the weight of those words and immediately felt guilty herself. She looked at him and said, "Please don't tell me that you stayed up all night long."

Scott didn't say anything at all. Alice could respect that he wasn't lying to her but she felt terribly guilty. She knew that he had a game. She just figured he would get some sleep too. He was the ultimate soothing balm for everything for her and she felt inadequate since she must not have had the same sway over him.

"Scotty. Why didn't you sleep when I was asleep? Hell, why bring me here if you weren't going to sleep yourself? I was fine cuddling up next to you on the couch, I wouldn't have noticed if you moved me or not." It didn't take a genius that he was the one responsible for her waking up in his bedroom.

"I couldn't sleep. I wanted to make sure you were comfortable all night long. It's okay, I swear. I moved you up here, so you could sleep comfortably." Then there was another more desperate whine from Chloe. "Go use the shower. It won't take me long to get her some food. I can then bring up your bag up afterwards. I forgot to grab that last night and I wasn't going to leave your side in case you woke up in a panic not knowing where you were."

Scott then kissed her forehead, almost as if he was saying it was okay and don't feel guilty. But it didn't make her feel any better. She hated imposing herself on others. But he just headed out the door.

Alice knew she should get into the shower as Scott said, but she was pretty sure that she saw she had a few missed calls on her phone before she got wonderfully distracted by Scotty. So she dug out the phone that got stashed among the pillows. Once she did so, she saw her phone littered with Facebook notifications which she was sure included a bunch of birthday messages. She had missed calls from everyone in her family and a missed message from her mom on Messenger. Subconsciously, she got out of bed and started to pace by one of his windows to see if he had a view of Lake Erie. So she started answering questions to her mom on messenger as she called back her dad.

"Hey kid, are you okay?"

"Yeah. More shaken than anything. But I was pretty lucky. As soon as I said anything, they ran out."

"So you did see someone. Did they get anything?"

"My iPad and initially my Echo Dot but the police recovered that."

"Are you still there now?"

"No. Scott picked me up last night after the police left. I'm still at his place but I have to get ready for work soon."

That piqued her dad's interest. His tone said that he knew what she was saying but at the same time, he needed her to confirm his suspicions. He even said, "You know, I have to ask you kid, who's Scott?"

"My boyfriend," Alice's voice immediately softened and you could hear the love that she had for him.

While she was she was close with her dad, she never liked to share any information about boyfriends until she knew they were serious and the last time she fully opened up to her dad about a boyfriend was her last serious partner over 5 years ago. Her dad seemed happy and laughed some. "So you are finally sharing his name. I was wondering when that would happen. What does he do?"

"He's the all-star center for the Cleveland Sound"

Alice was surprised as she was hugged from behind tightly. She felt the heat just raise up through her body. She heard Scott whisper in the ear that wasn't pressed up against the phone, "I love hearing you say that." She smiled.

In the other ear, she heard her dad laughing and going "Well that certainly explains why you are suddenly interested in the Sound. You weren't kidding when you said he was the reason you got all interested in the local team."

"Yeah. Sorry Dad, I got to go." knowing that she was starting to get way too distracted by Scott hugging her and kissing her ear. She could barely focus on what her dad was saying. She knew that she would need to get ready for work but she liked being in his arms way too much to think about work at that moment.

"Make sure you call your mom and sister. And I want to meet Scott the next time I'm in town."

"I will. I'll talk to you soon."

Scott turned her around so they were facing each other. She smiled and just felt so calm in his arms. She knew her emotions were still running wild and having to talk about the evening's events weren't helping her to stay collected. The shit eating grin that Scott was wearing was almost too sexy to handle.

"How much did you hear before you snuck up on me?"

"Enough. But don't you have a few more calls to make and/or a shower to get into?" He seemed to be placing emphasis on the shower. Probably hoping for an invite to join her in the shower.

"I'm getting there. I didn't ask before you went to take care of Chloe, are there specific towels that I should use?"

"Any are fine. They should all be clean. What do you want for breakfast?"

Alice wasn't used to so much attention in the morning. Then again, this was their first time they actually spent a morning together. While she wasn't much of a morning person and certainly didn't eat much in the morning, she was thinking she could get used to waking up with Scotty.

"Um, just a coffee with lots of cream and sugar."

"That's not a real meal," he said with a clear frown and was fully disapproving of her choice of breakfast. "I'm a pretty good cook. I can make you pretty much anything you could desire."

Alice went quickly into a defensive mode, "My stomach wakes up super cranky. I get sick if eat much of anything in the morning until I've been awake for a while. Normally I can tolerate coffee."

Scott still didn't seem to approve but conceded, "I'm still going to make breakfast while you get a shower. But I intend to stay with you a little bit longer and help you get through those calls."

"Oh you are incorrigible."

Scott laughed some before he started to kiss her ears. "Only slightly. If I was truly incorrigible, I wouldn't let you shower by yourself. But if you keep stalling, you are going to be late for work."

Alice just had to shake her head as she called her sister but it was incredibly distracting to do it with him holding her and kissing along her ears and neck line. Her sister picked up right away.

Allison immediately asked, "Hey are you okay?"

"Yeah. He ran off when I saw him."

"So that answered if you were there when it happened. That had to be so scary." Alice just nodded at that comment as Allison continued on to "Did they get anything?"

"My iPad is toast. Initially they got my Alexa too but they police gave that back to me."

"Oh no. Do you want me to get you a new one for your birthday?"

"No. That's okay. Scotty beat you to it and he wants to get me a new one. Besides you already got me too much stuff for my birthday." Then Scott started to toy with her hair.

Alice heard her niece, Noelle, starting to chatter in the background. Allison asked Noelle to say "Happy birthday" who immediately said it to Alice. Then the little one asked "Are you going to have a birthday party today?"

Allison stepped in, "Not today. She's having a really bad day."

Scott squeezed her a little tighter as he continued to snuggle up. It was like heaven in his arms and she could smell his wonderful musk. He was just keeping her safe and the panic in her body never fully rose to the surface. She didn't realize how hard she was fighting back her feelings.

"Yeah. But at least the police were helpful and Scott's been great. I don't know what I would have done without him."

"Okay, time to share some details. Not that you are just seeing a guy. You don't call a guy who means nothing to you. After a burglary, you call someone who can make you feel safe. He means way more to you than just a casual fling."

Scott then started to nibble on her ear. It was making her feel way too distracted. But she knew that her sister wouldn't let her slide for much longer.

“He’s my new boyfriend. We met when I played hockey a couple weeks ago. He plays for the Sound. Well not just plays for but he really carries the team. You’re right, I don't think of him as a fling but it’s new. He came over last night and barricaded everything before we went back to his place. I’m still there now.”

He seemed to be enjoying her comments about him. Alice was enjoying the moment but she could tell her sister was getting into a bit of a mama bear mode. Alice couldn’t tell if Allison approved or not. Not that she had ever approved Alice’s prior boyfriends, so there was a part of Alice thinking that Allison might not. Then Allison surprised Alice by asking to speak to Scott directly. Alice was shocked since Allison never asked about that before. Scotty looked equally surprised. But she knew it wasn’t worth the fight so she just passed the phone off to him. Scotty moved away from her as he said, “Hello.”

Alice hated how he wasn’t holding anymore and she couldn’t hear what was being said. She knew that she had to keep her hands busy. First, she got her work clothes out of her bag that Scott placed on the bed. Then she grabbed the bears, thinking she should pack them up when she heard Scott say, “I promise, I would never hurt her. I want to provide her with everything she ever wants. Neither of us were looking for a casual fling. She’s special to me.”

Scott went silent for a second. He was looking a little grim at the moment. Which only set Alice’s anxiety up even more. Holding her bears wouldn’t be enough. So she walked over to Scott and started to hug him.

“I don’t know what would happen if I got traded. We never talked about that in part because I have a non-movement clause and I just got signed to a five year deal with the Sound before the start of season. So I doubt that would happen."

All Alice could think was *Shit this is a far more serious conversation than I thought it would be. And they wonder why I don't want to introduce a guy when I start seeing someone.*

Alice couldn't hear what Allison was saying. All she knew was the conversation was not what she was expecting. Scott spoke up again and said, "If she moves, then we will make it work. I can fly her to me on the weekends and stay with her in the off season. I wouldn't want to hold her back. I know how important work is to her, it's why I didn't try to talk her out of going in today like normal. In fact, I think it shows how strong she really is."

Alice started to lean into Scott's clavicle and kiss it. She could feel his body's tension ease off some but then again it might have easily been her mind playing tricks on her. Then she heard how light and happy his voice sounded when he said, "Yeah, I do talk a little funny, don't I? It's because the first language I learned to speak was French when I was your age and then I learned English later."

Alice knew that Noelle must have piped in. She smiled at how sweet he sounded to her niece. Then even her own anxiety started to dissipate. He leaned down and kissed her nose lightly as he asked, "Do you like hockey?"

Because of how close they were, Alice could hear Noelle say, "Yeah but are you one of the good guys or the bad guys? Do you know Gritty?"

Scott arched his eyebrow at Alice. She feigned innocence. But she knew he was going to poke fun at how Alice introduced Noelle to the Flyer's mascot. But Alice loved Gritty and loved how much Noelle would giggle anytime she saw Gritty. So every time Alice saw her niece, she would show Noelle Gritty videos.

"Yeah. I'm definitely of the good guys. I play for a different team. We have a different mascot so Gritty won't be there. I can bring you to one of my games."

"When?"

"We will have to figure it out with your mom. Most likely it will be the next time that you come to visit your Aunt Alice."

That sounded like the perfect trip to do when her sister came to town. She knew that he would treat the whole family well when the time came. But it was something she would never ask him to do.

Her sister continued speaking and said, "Be sure you look after her. She tries to be strong but I've seen her break down before and each time it happens, she puts up more walls. It sounds like she's about to break again."

"I promise. I don't want to hurt her in any way. It killed me that I wasn't there for her last night until she called. I wish I could have done more than to give her a safe place to sleep and some comfort," he said earnestly. Much like when he went to take care of Chloe, he kissed her forehead again to seal that invisible promise. He then leaned down and took a super quick but chaste kiss to her lips. Then he handed the phone back to Alice and shooed her towards the bathroom.

"He seems nice so far. But I still need to meet him before I can really tell my feelings about him."

"Okay. Just pick a date when the Sound are at home and we will do something together. I really should get ready for work."

"If you need to talk, just call. I know how vulnerable you feel after something like this and I never saw the guy who stole my laptop in college. I can't imagine what it's like knowing you were there. I'm glad you are okay and you were with someone the rest of the night."

"Thanks."

"Love you." she heard both Allison and Noelle say together and Alice said, "I love you too". Alice didn't always say 'I love you'. It was something she saved for people who deserved it and wouldn't ever give an empty 'I love you.'

Then Alice hung up the phone and realized the time. No wonder Scott was starting to shoo her into the bathroom, it was getting late. She texted her mom a few more times as she waited on the water to get nice and warm. She realized that Scott had different shower stuff then she used. But she didn't think to grab her own stuff last night so it would have to do. She reminded herself, she would be getting another shower after her swim lessons in the afternoon.

In about ten minutes, she was dressed and her hair was pulled back into two braids like normal with a ponytail hanging loose at the nape of her neck. She grabbed her work bag and started to walk towards the kitchen. She could smell sausage and eggs which smelled delicious but made her stomach angry. When Scott saw her, he waggled his eyebrows trying to entice her into eating. She just politely shook her head no. She wasn't hungry at all even if her stomach wanted to cooperate with the idea of breakfast.

"I'm good." She said as she sat down at the island on one the wooden barstools. She watched as Scott filled up his plate. He did hand her a travel mug full of coffee. She quietly accepted the drink. It was much stronger than she anticipated. It was much more like one of her lattes with extra shots that she would order as a free treat reward from Starbucks.

"I'm sorry about my sister. I didn't have any idea that she wanted to give you the 3rd degree today but I should have known when she asked to speak to you."

"It's all good. She worries about you and that's how family should be. She didn't scare me away. I'm still here for you like I said. Just give me a moment to eat some of this while it's hot and then I can take you to work. Did you want me to come with you until I have to go to the morning skate?" asked Scotty as he was eating his breakfast. "Also how did you want to handle when you are done with work?"

Alice watched him eat as she sipped her coffee, "I think I can handle work on my own. Sundays tend to be pretty quiet and I have about half my day in the pool. If need anything, I will let you know." Although she was thinking to herself that she was most likely going to turn to someone else so he could get some rest. "I can take the RTA to the game or I might run home to get my car."

Scott seemed surprised and said, "Are you sure?"

Alice just nodded, "Honestly, I feel so guilty that you stayed up all night, especially since you let me sleep so soundly. I want you to get some sleep. Besides, I normally take the RTA to games anyway. It won't be a problem."

Alice continued to sip on her coffee. She was amazed at how much it fit the bill of what she wanted that morning. This cup was literally perfect. It was strong and sweet, almost like her favorite drink at Starbucks, and she had to ask, "How did you know I wanted something this strong and this flavorful."

"I had a feeling. Do you have enough for work?"

Alice shook her head in the positive. As much as she loved her coffee, she always nursed it. Especially her first cup of coffee of the day. Scott set his empty plate in the dishwasher and grabbed his own coffee mug that he had tucked beside him. Then it was time to go to work.

6

SCOTT

The morning skate was not going well for Scott. Being tired and not being able to focus on the game in front of him was bad enough; but he still had Alice's sisters words going through his head about trying to make sure that Alice doesn't completely break down from all the stress despite appearing to be strong in the moment. He was making terrible plays left, right and center. If he wasn't overshooting the puck, he was having it stripped from him.

"Okay. What's the deal, man?" asked Lager when they were in line for a shooting drill.

"Rough night," Scotty said dryly.

"No shit! You better get yourself fucking sorted out. I'm not losing to the Habs because you can't get your shit together."

Scotty felt bad. They have been talking about this game for a while. The two of them always pulled out their A game when they were matched up against their old teams that let them get exposed in the expansion draft. He knew that Lager needed him to be the setup man tonight and really make the Habs regret their decision. It didn't matter that the expansion was over four years ago at this point. Lager would do the same anytime they played the Predators for Scotty.

"I will." Scotty said with absolute certainty. "I just need to get some sleep. I'll be ready."

When it was their turn, Lager sped through the middle and Scotty went right to draw the defender away from the net while he brought the puck through the middle. Everything was all ready for the pass to Lager so he could have an easy shot on goal but Scotty shanked it again.

Berman blew his whistle to end practice. The guys all started to clean up the pucks and the nets as the doors opened up for the zamboni to clean the ice surface for the next skating session. As Scotty was coming off the ice, Berman said, "Wheiland, my office in 10."

FUCK!!!!! That's never good. I was sucking hard today but I can't get scratched tonight.

He knew that he was going to get reamed for his lack of focus. As captain, he was supposed to be the leading example for the team. He wasn't supposed to have off days and he always lived up to his commitment as captain until today. While it was his job to be the star player, he couldn't keep Alice off his mind. It sucked to see how even though she was more herself in the morning, the light in her eyes was clearly missing and some of that spark was missing too.

Scott stripped out of his gear and went into the showers much quicker than normal. He knew that he had to get into Berman's office before the ten minutes if he had any hope in playing tonight's game. Normally he liked to take much longer than ten minutes. He got changed. He didn't bother to look at his phone to see if there was word from Alice. Right now, the only thing he had on his mind was trying to make sure he didn't get into any more trouble than he was already in.

The coach's door was open when he came up to the office. Instead of walking straight in and risk pissing off Berman even more, he knocked on the door frame before entering.

"Get the fuck in here and shut the door."

Scott did as he was told and sat down in the chair across from Berman's desk. Berman's office was a standard collection of piles of current team research papers, playbooks, old memorabilia on the wall and an iPad docking area.

"Care to explain where you mind was at today?" asked Berman. While it was left unsaid, Scott knew that there was a huge undertone of it better be a fucking good reason.

Scotty was tempted to say he was sorry. But he knew that would be him living up to the Canadian stereotype and it wouldn't do him the least bit of good in this situation. He just had to tell it straight, like he would do with the players when he saw issues.

"I didn't sleep much and I was worried about my girlfriend. I was thinking about her most of practice." Berman's face was inscrutable at the moment. He wasn't raging with anger but he wasn't giving any indication of what he was thinking. Quite frankly, that was just as scary. When he was pissed, you at least knew where you stood. But right now he wasn't so sure, so Scotty just kept talking, "She was broken into last night while she was sleeping. She saw the guy before he ran off with some of her stuff and she needed help. She was in rough shape as you can imagine with an on-going panic attack for a bit. Even though I took her back to my place, it was either stay up and protect her while she slept or going out to do something super stupid like trying to kill the guy. I decided not to do something stupid but I'm paying for it now. You have every right to be pissed off at me and I should have slept more. But I will fix it before tonight."

Berman started to roll his mouth around as if he was trying to chew on each and every word he was going to say. He was staring down Scott which wasn't helping Scott's confidence levels or giving any indication on what the coach was thinking. After what felt like a lifetime, Berman finally said, "That wasn't what I was expecting to hear. But I should have known that you would have a damn good reason for your focus to be off. At least it's not another injury. I take it she was okay by the end of the night?"

"Yeah. She was unharmed in the burglary but she was shaken up something fierce. She already seemed much better this morning."

"That's to be expected. How pissed off are you at the situation?"

With absolutely no hesitation, he said, "Very!"

"Can you focus that anger to be placed against the Habs and be at least halfway decent again before game time?"

"Yeah."

"Okay. Well then, you will play tonight as long as you don't look like shit in the warm ups. If you do, I will scratch you."

Scott nodded and he knew it was time to get going before

Berman had a chance to change his mind. As Scott was starting to stand up to leave, Berman started to talk again and said, "Don't blindside me again. You were utterly useless today and I expect better from you."

Scott nodded and quickly made his escape. Instead of hanging out with the guys in the locker room like he normally did, he headed out the door.

Scott wasn't expecting to see Lager waiting for him and leaning up against his SUV door. While they used to sometimes drive together since they only lived a few houses apart, that stopped a while ago. Lager and Brigitta let Petey live with them until Petey found a place locally. If Lager would carpool with anyone, it would be with Petey. Scott wasn't looking for ass chewing number two from Lager. He just survived the reaming from Berman and all he wanted to do was get home and pass out. It's why he headed out the side door without hanging out in the locker room. At least he had already picked up the replacement tablet for Alice before he practiced.

Lager reached out for the keys and said, "You are NOT driving home today."

While Scotty wanted to just say WTF, he decided to stay calm and collected with Lager. He asked, "What about your car?"

"Petey drove us in today. Now hand over your keys before I have to forcibly take them from you."

Scott just glared. He knew that his friend meant well but that didn't mean he had to like it or he was just going to hand over his keys. He was exhausted and about to put up a fight when Lager said, "Dude, you missed your one-timer at least ten times today. You weren't even close to the goal mouth. Normally, you have complete control over that and make Crestor or Clay sweat it out. You didn't even test them at all today. I can't remember the last time that happened. Do you think I really trust you to drive your car home safely? Don't make me fight you for your keys, you dumbass."

"Fine" said Scott in resignation. He knew that he couldn't really say anything to contradict or make a better argument. So he tossed his keys over and started to round the car to sit in the passenger seat as Lager climbed into the driver's seat. Scott had to move the tablet out of the way so he wouldn't crush it when he climbed into the car.

Lager continued to lead the conversation as Scotty just attempted to stay in silence, "Okay what happened last night? Don't tell me you and Alice had a fight and broke up already."

"It wasn't anything like that."

"Well I know it wasn't from too much sex. I've known you long enough that if you are getting laid, your game improves. It doesn't go to hell in a handbasket. So tell me what happened?"

When did he learn that phrase? I don't even use hell in a handbasket and I've heard of it before. Lager would occasionally go into spurts of learning English idioms and then use them way too much. But it always seemed so forced. Although at that time, it actually sounded like proper use.

"Alice was broken into last night while she was sleeping and I had to go pick her up after she was done dealing with that shit."

"Fuck man. Is she okay?"

"Yeah for the most part."

Fortunately Lager knew enough not to pry about the last

part. Although the Austrian did continue to ask questions. "Did they get anything?"

"Her iPad is apparently destroyed although the police were able to locate it along with her missing Alexa device. But she really didn't say too much about the night she was just in the midst of a massive panic attack. This morning, she would just give the broad ideas of what happened or didn't want to talk about it at all. The panic attack freaked me out almost as much as the news of the break in the first place. I've never had to lead the conversations with her. It was always easy talking to her but this time she was so shut down. If that wasn't bad enough, I'm also a shitty boyfriend."

That made Lager's right eyebrow go straight up to question Scotty wordlessly as he drove. Scott knew that if he didn't say anything, Lager would ask why. So he just beat him to the punch. "Would you believe today is her birthday and I had no clue? Even Chloe knew enough to give Alice something this morning. I would still have felt like a shitty boyfriend since I wasn't there to protect her but this was something that could have been avoided."

"Okay man, two things. What the fuck did your dog give your girlfriend? And were you supposed to know?"

Scotty suddenly felt like he wasn't getting interrogated anymore. Instead it was just two guys talking. Lager always seemed to know when to change the tone to a more lighthearted conversation and make Scott feel at ease when he was stressed out much like he was doing today.

"Chloe gave up her hockey puck. You know how Chloe never gives up that thing. Sure, she was doing it as a consoling measure. Which was awesome since I really thought she might hate Alice." Then Scott took a deep breath as he switched to the other question that Lager asked, "No to knowing about the birthday. She gave me no clue until this morning. I only found out because she was..." Scotty took the time to find the right word. She wasn't disappointed or really pissed. "She just didn't want to deal with any birthday wishes she was getting on her phone. It's almost as if she connected the two things together as being the same thing and she wanted to forget it as quickly as it happened."

Lager shook his head in disbelief. "So what's the problem? It sounds like one of the few girls who don't expect anything on their birthday."

"I don't want her to hate her birthday or think of how the day started off. I want to help turn it around. I'm just not sure how."

"You said that she will be able to come to tonight's game and actually hang out with the other wives and girlfriends, right?"

"Yeah. We finally have our schedules synced up so she could come up. She was excited to come out before this all happened since the last game she actually made it to was against the Flyers. We both knew it would have been a mini-disaster in the making if we introduced her to everyone at that game especially since I met her earlier that day. She's been working so much in the evenings that it was just easier to watch at work or at home. She was still on board this morning but it seemed to be an afterthought for her. Then again, so was most everything else today."

Lager switched gears and said, "Any luck on convincing her about the errors of her ways for supporting the Flyers?"

Scott laughed some as he said, "Nope. I doubt I ever will. Besides it's actually wicked to cute to see how worked up she gets when watches them. She does root for the Sound though. I have a feeling she's just as vocal with the Sound playing but I haven't been able to prove that idea. She just roots for both team so that's not too bad."

"Well I guess I can live with that. If you want me to see if Bridge can get something put together inside the box, I can."

By then Lager was starting to turn into Scott's driveway. Lager turned off the ignition and handed the keys back to Scott. Lager was quiet for a moment waiting for Scotty's response. He just nodded and said, "That would be great. But nothing too crazy. She was hesitant about the birthday already. I did get her a replacement tablet that I was going to wrap up. We need to make sure that gets up there with whatever Brigitta can get put together..."

Then a wave of fatigue worked its way through Scotty. He let out an epic yawn, making Lager go, "Get your ass to bed. I can't have you playing like shit tonight. I need you set me up for a hatty."

"A hat trick? Really? Just that? Like those grow on trees. Do you think that Price or Neimi are just going to give one up so easily?"

"I never said it had to be a natural hat trick. I would be just as happy with a Gordie Howe hat trick. But I would prefer a natural."

"I will see what I can do," said Scotty with a laugh knowing full well that was a big ask but he would do what he could. If they were able to get Lager his hatty, the Sound would be in good shape for a win. That's what Scotty wanted in every game.

"Sleep. I will do what I can do you make your girl's birthday a bit less shitty".

"'Kay."

Then Scott went into his house and climbed up to bed. Before setting his head on the pillow, he made damn sure the alarms were set so he could do his pregame stuff and get to the rink on time. Chloe followed him upstairs as if she was just as worn out from the evening events as Scotty.

7

ALICE

As the day went on, Alice's sense of vulnerability and panic set back into her again. It was amazing how much comfort Scott provided her just by being there for her. While she was at his place, she felt so safe and secure especially when he was holding her. She was never someone who looked for protection in someone else's arms, she always relied on herself. So to find comfort in someone else's arms was shocking. She figured that it had to be a mixture of two things: the true connection that she had with Scott and the absolute terror of the evening. She barely comprehended how Scotty told her that he loved her that evening during everything but it sunk in during the morning as things replayed in her head.

Alice knew that her work was almost nonexistent since she was spending most of the time trying to keep her emotions in check. There was multiple times she wanted to text Scott and ask him to come to the gym. She already hated herself for even calling him last night but she couldn't have done it solo. But she couldn't bring herself to do it, instead she just clutched onto her two teddy bears that she took to work with her. She knew that the boys (as she typically referred to her bears) couldn't provide the same sort of help as Scott gave her the night before but he needed rest after staying up all night watching over her. Plus deep down, she just didn't want to appear weak despite the fact that holding onto bears while she was in the office was just that.

The only time she found herself feeling halfway normal was when she was teaching a couple swim lessons. She had to put on a happy facade and pretend that things were okay. She knew that she was more distracted than she should have been. But she was just grateful that when she was working with her clients that she didn't think about the break in as much as she did most of the time.

As she was rinsing off the chlorine, she realized that she forgot to pack anything for the Sound game. They have been talking about the game for days now since it would be the first time that she would be sitting with the other players' significant others. Hell, they even talked about the game in the morning. She wouldn't miss the game for the world since the All-Star Break started up after tonight and there would be no games for a week. Scott will be playing in the All-Star game. The Flyers were already on the break, the Sound got to play a few extra games before the break but they would have a couple games off afterwards. She knew that she would have to run back to the apartment before the game started.

The All-Star Game would also mean that she wouldn't get to see Scott for a few days since he was selected to play on the Metropolitan division team with the usual suspects like G (Claude Giroux), Sidney Crosby, and Henrik Lundqvist. Alice was so excited that Scotty got selected even if she dreaded knowing that he would be out of town for the week.

Knowing that she had to go home before the game just so she could be properly dressed, she decided to be both a bit bold and chicken all at the same time. She said, ***Hey, I have to run home before the game. Should I grab clothes for the next few nights?***

Before he could respond, she got a call from the police. They had a few more questions for her. Most of the questions were straightforward. Did she have any enemies or past boyfriends who could hold a grudge? She did have to admit that she was currently dating Scotty but that was it was very new and she didn't think anyone even knew they were dating. Then she had some questions related to her relationship with the landlords but she couldn't understand why they would ask someone else to commit a burglary. Then the police said they had to come back to her apartment for the bag of goldfish to add that to the evidence since it wasn't collected the evening before. Since she was only doing a quick pit stop at her place, they decided they would have to come back after the Sound game and they would send out the same shift that helped her the previous evening.

She heard a few notifications beep while she was on the phone with the police, so she hoped that she would be seeing a message from Scott giving the okay for her to stay at his place until he had to leave for the All-Star game but knew they were likely birthday messages. Low and behold it was more birthday wishes that she didn't really want to look at. The only good thing from the radio silence from Scott was it meant he was finally getting some rest, and she knew there was a good indication that he might be waking up soon. But she knew he would need to know about the latest kink in their plans.

A: *Hey, the police have to come by after the game. Sorry to throw yet another wrench into the plans.*

S: *It's okay. I'll come with you and we can do something after.*

A: *Thanks. You are the best.*

S: *I was hoping you would stay until I had to leave for the All-Star stuff. Get what you need then.*

A: *Thanks!*

S: *How's it been today?*

A: *It's been up and down. Still feeling afraid and off.*

S: *That's to be expected.*

A: *I know. But I don't have to like it. I want to feel normal again.*

S: *It will get better.*

A: *Did you get some sleep?*

S: *Yeah. If I didn't Lager will kill me.*

A: *Why?*

S: *He's still pissed that the Habs didn't protect him in the draft. So he always wants our A game when we play them.*

A: *Now I feel like a real shit head to mess up your evening.*

S: *Don't! I would have been pissed if you didn't call after something like that.*

S: *I have to get going soon. But I can't wait to see you! Ping me if you need to vent.*

A: *Kick some ass for me tonight.*

S: *Will do. Je t'aime.*

A: *Je t'aime.*

Alice was definitely feeling better after that exchange. She couldn't believe she told him that she loved him and he said the same thing to her. There was a part of her that knew he was saying that last night as she was so completely freaked out that she really didn't comprehend those words especially since he said them in French, not English. Her brain wasn't ready to make much of anything by the time he picked her up. But now that she was a bit more coherent as time elapsed from her trauma, she could let the words start to sink in. That carried her through the last thirty minutes of her work day without too much in the way of anxiety (at least in comparison to the last 24 hours).

Alice immediately ran home to get into her Sound jersey. While she was at home, she tried to make herself up as much as she could. Fortunately, she hadn't cried much today so she didn't have to try and cover up any puffy eyes. But she did have the purple rings underneath her eyes from lack of sleep and her eyes seemed to be so lifeless that her makeup skills just couldn't completely fix it. She did her hair with a fancy ponytail with some curls coming from it. She felt good about being in her jersey, jeggings and studded booties.

But she took longer than she would have liked, so she decided to drive to the arena to save some time. She parked her car in one of the lots that surrounded the arena and went inside. She was a little nervous about meeting the other players' wives, girlfriends and possible kids. Even on the best of days, she wasn't always super comfortable in social settings where the majority of people were new. But given her stress levels, all she wanted to do was hide in a corner with a beer and swear the stress out as she watched Scotty play.

The box was about half filled by the time she got there. She was glad to see there was a full bar and some light snacks. She got herself a Platform beer (a local craft beer that she was surprised the arena had). She saw that there were a few seats up front of the box that were open so she headed to get into the seat but got distracted as she started to watch her man on the ice. He was so easy to spot with his red hair being unhelmeted. It seemed like he was having fun and seemed relaxed during the warm ups. He was chatting with his teammates and handling the puck well. Nobody watching the game would ever suspect that he stayed up all night.

As Alice was watching down ice, a tall blonde woman who appeared to be about her age said, "Wie gehts?"

Alice was a little surprised to hear her talk to her in German and clearly addressing her. She knew enough German to answer but back but that was practically the extent of her German skills. Plus she wasn't sure how the woman would even know that Alice could respond back.

"So-so. Und du?"

"Gut." Then the woman laughed for a moment and said, "Sorry. Been home all day with the little one and I sometimes forget how to speak English since we are trying to always use German at home so he can be bilingual. So please don't be afraid to remind me to speak in English, but I'm impressed that you actually could answer back."

That made Alice smile, "Trust me, I would have said something soon since that's about the extent of my German right now. German has always been my weakest language."

"So are you Scott's new mysterious girlfriend?"

"I would hardly say I'm mysterious but yeah, I'm his new girlfriend. My name is Alice."

Alice was a little surprised that they seemed to know right away who she was and which player she would have been connected with. Alice noticed how the woman made a signal with the tilt of the head to someone who had to be standing behind Alice since it felt a little off. Then she said, "I'm Brigitta. I'm Ander's wife."

Alice knew that she had to have confusion on her face. She was still trying to pick up on all the Sounds' nicknames for the major players and even some of the 3rd and 4th line player names. It wasn't like the Flyers who she had been following for years and only had to learn a few names and faces each year. She was learning a full team all at once.

"You probably know him as Lager." Alice nodded and took a sip of her beer. As soon as she heard that, she knew exactly who Brigitta was married to. That was one of the people she was looking forward to meeting and wanted to make a good impression on. She knew that Lager was Scotty's best friend and things could go south quickly if they didn't end up getting along. "It's nice to finally meet you"

"Same. Sorry I haven't been around more this homestand. My work schedule was not cooperative and it didn't make sense to come in for the last period."

"Trust me, I get it. I know Klaus and I don't always make it out all the time. Why don't you meet everyone?" As she started to direct them towards the back of the box.

Alice was surprised that the room had changed from when she walked in. There were now more people and one of the cocktail tables was covered with several gift bags. She was hoping that they were for someone else but she had a nasty feeling that they were for her. The phone buzzed in her pocket, so she pulled it out to see a message from Scotty.

S: ***Don't be mad. I asked for a little help to transform your bday into something better.***

Alice shook her head. She fired off a quick text back. He

knew that she wanted to downplay the occasion but she couldn't blame him for trying to give her a reason to celebrate.

A: ***You're lucky that you are cute and I love you. Kick some ass tonight.***

S: ***I will just for you.***

S: ***Je t'aime. Don't forget that!***

Her heart soared in that exchange. It was like it was before the break in for a minute. She didn't have any moments of sadness or anxiety during that moment. She was amazed at how easy it was to hear him say that he loved her. She knew that she had to have a cheesy grin on her face. It was nice to have someone who could just make her happy even if it wasn't always what she expected. He also had stellar timing on and off the ice in that moment. Trying not to be too rude, she stuffed the phone back in her pocket and gave her attention back to Brigitta who was smiling.

"I take it that was a quick word from your man."

"That obvious?" Alice was ashamed to have it be that clear for someone else to see it.

"A little. Everything about you got more relaxed in that moment. Besides this is the only time the guys can send out a message for the next few hours." Then Brigitta stopped a boy who looked to be about three with blonde hair and a face fairly similar to Brigitta's who was running around the box. Brigitta turned the boy around and said, "Klaus, this is Alice, she's friends with Uncle Scotty."

Alice knelt down and shook hands with the little tyke. She was touched to hear that Scott was known as Uncle Scotty. It showed Alice some of Scott's giving nature and close friendship with the whole family. "It's nice to meet you Klaus."

While the boy had no problem in shaking her hand, he remained on the silent side. Neither Alice nor Brigitta forced him to talk. Instead Brigitta let the boy go and he immediately went back to chasing the slightly older boys who looked to be about five or six.

Brigitta immediately said, "Those two are Dima's kids. Klaus wants to be just like them and do whatever they do. Fortunately they are good kids, so I don't mind if they run about some. He always sleeps better after hanging out with them."

Alice nodded. She followed Brigitta up to the gift covered table. She had no clue what to expect. She hadn't met any met anyone before so it just felt awkward. Part of her wanted to be mad at the situation but she knew that everyone was just trying to be kind.

"So I figured we could do the introductions by gift. That way you can get a feel for who is who a little bit easier. We'll start with the one from my family," as Brigitta handed over a red bag.

"Okay." Alice said as she started to open the bag. She smiled when she saw a Sound Henley T-shirt with Scott's number on it. It was something cute and she would wear it a lot. Then underneath the shirt that she pulled out, she saw a few other things: pepper spray and some door stop alarms. Alice was both grateful and alarmed all at once since the burglary was back to being front and center in her mind. Brigitta stopped her from pulling out those items and said in a very quiet voice, "Anders told me what happened. We, well more him, thought those would be useful but you don't need to share that if you don't want to. I didn't tell anyone and from what I could tell, Scotty only told Anders."

Brigitta quickly passed over another bag and another beautiful woman stepped up to the table and introduced herself. Alice was just glad to know that the break-in was a secret and she didn't have to talk about if she didn't want to. They went quickly through the rest of the gifts. It was a blur of faces and names. She mostly got Sound apparel and gift cards. Stuff that anyone would like but you didn't have to know them personally too much. At least, the majority of the Sound stuff all had Scott's name or number associated with it and surprising enough all seemed to be more or less in her size.

There were a few names that stuck out in her mind. Becca (Wheels' longtime girlfriend) and Callie (Dkystman's current fling according to Brigitta). There was also Diane who headed the charitable causes and was Donnie's wife who wanted Alice to get super active with some of the causes since "everyone just loves Scotty and they will love you too especially if you can bring him out to the events."

There was one last bag on the table. Alice was pretty sure that she met everyone there. As she peered into the bag, she knew right away who the gift was from. Only one person knew that she would be in the market for a new iPad. Plus he was the one person who couldn't be there. The card had a romantic saying on the front but the inside had a hastily written message which absolutely made Alice swoon:

I love you so much. I just want to make you smile each day and get a chance to wake up beside you as many days as I can. Je t'aime.

Toujours,

Scotty

Alice heard the goal horn sounds. She knew that meeting everyone and opening up the gifts would likely mean missing out a little bit of the game. At first, she thought it was the horn to announce the start of the game but they had already paused with introductions to stand for the national anthems. That's when she realized that she had missed the first goal. Naturally, she cheered even if she didn't know what happened so tried to peer back to one of the mounted TVs showing the game. Fortunately, the TV was showing the replay where it was a quick breakaway play where Scott won the faceoff and got the puck to Dykstman. Dykstman flew with the puck as Lager was crashing the net and Scott was flying up on the left side. Dykstman passed the puck behind to Petey instead of shooting on net. Petey did take the shot on the goalie who let off a wicked rebound off his pad which sent the puck straight back to Scotty who took a clean shot on net with his wrister. That gave her so much pride in that moment. She also couldn't believe his timing, that while she was melting over the card he wrote, he was getting shit done on the ice surface. While she knew that he wouldn't see it until after the game, she fired off of a text to say: ***Only you could melt my heart with timing the opening of your card at the same moment you score a goal.***

From then on out, Alice was paying much more attention to the game. Both Brigitta and Diane were talking to her almost non-stop. Brigitta would talk hockey or was trying to catch Alice up on the dynamics of the box.

Diane had a one track mind though. She wanted to get Alice involved in the various wives' charity events as quickly as possible. Brigitta said she helps out some but it gets complicated with a little one and wasn't nearly as involved as Diane was. Sometime in the third period, Alice went from helping with the player's favorite things basket that was basically obligatory for submission, to helping with set up and on the committee. Part of Alice was sure she would regret taking on such a big role, especially since she worked so much. But it would be something that she would enjoy in the long term.

She was just glad to be enjoying the game. Scotty and Lager were on fire that evening against the Habs with 4 points apiece (2 goals and 2 assists each). With a little over ten minutes left in the game, she was hoping to see a hattrick by the end of the night. But she started to notice that there was something weird going on with the top line. Scott was trying to feed it to Lager, Lager was doing whatever he pleased and Dykstman kept trying to get it to Scott. Hell, even the defense were just as guilty for trying to set up Scott instead of Lager. In the meanwhile, they were all blowing the scoring chances and just eating up the clock while they played pass the puck.

Scott

The game was starting to breakdown and it was pissing him off. It was such a good game until the last seven minutes. Him and Lager were on the same page for most of the night but the game was starting to weigh on them. It didn't help that the Habs were trying to make a comeback after spending most of the game down three goals.

As Scott was climbing the boards with Lager, he said, "I got him. Just pressure down the line. We will feed it to you."

Scotty was thinking they could get a one-timer once Lager was in position. Although the next thing he knew, the puck was on his stick. He wasn't the one who wanted a fucking hatty tonight, that was Lager and he was trying to get it done.

He didn't even have a good opening at that moment. So he tried to deke it so he could get an opening since he was going to babysit the puck to waste the time off the clock. It didn't seem like he was going to get past the defensive pairing that was starting to swarm him but fortunately he knew he could be quicker than them. So he changed his weight so he could get onto his inside edge and push past the defensive pair. Lager was open and Scott knew he just had to keep his feet moving and finally he could get the puck over to Lager. Or least he hoped he did, since he never got a chance to see if the puck made it to Lager. He was blindsided from the late hit and was fully seeing stars from the impact of the blow.

"What the fuck?!?!?" Scott was pissed. He got to his feet. He was glad that there was a bit of a scrum going on behind him with both Dykstman and Lager squaring off between the two Canadien players. Scotty was just trying to shake off the hit and was glad his team had his back in the moment where he didn't have to exact retribution on his own. Plus he saw Petey chattering away and getting into another player's face. It seemed like Dykstman and the Hab player were more than willing to confront each other but neither were going to do a shove. But Lager was in full on fight mode and Scotty knew that would get Lager ejected before they could get him the hatty. The cursing was getting quite elaborate in several different languages.

Scotty knew that he should try to get some calm in that situation but he was still trying to get his legs going again so he could be useful in the power play that should be coming up. Plus he wanted to make sure he wasn't due for a trip for the quiet room but it didn't feel like he got another concussion. After a few moments, the fights were ending and everyone was finally getting separated. A linesman came up to check for blood on Scotty.

As expected, both Lager and Deslauries were ejected for fighting. Thankfully, there was no instigator call on Lager, so the Sound could maintain the power play. It was the last two minutes of the game, so he knew that Montreal would be trying to pull their goalie to see if they could do something but that would be next to impossible now. Losing Lager on the power play would hurt but it wouldn't be the first time where their top line of the power play unit would have to get switched up this season or the last. Besides, they wanted to keep it with a two man defensive pairing on the power play instead of switching down to one since Berman was expecting the Habs to pull try some last minute heroics and go for a shortie or two.

In the faceoff circle, Scotty got low and wide so he could get the puck. Faceoff wins was the only element of the game that didn't improve with sleeping that afternoon. So he wanted to try and get at least one more win before the night to not screw up his faceoff statistics. Up until tonight, he was one of the best in the league and he knew he would be leaving the fourth place in the league but he wasn't sure how much of a hit that would be. Unfortunately, he was trying to react a little too quickly and he got tossed.

Dykstman had to take the faceoff for him. The puck flew towards Scotty but it wasn't at the right angle for him to get his stick on the puck, so he had to go retrieve it from the boards. It started to be a bit of a pissing match to dig the puck out with one of the Canadiens. Finally, he was able to kick it out. It went to Dykstman and Scotty made his way to his favorite post. The Habs didn't get a chance to pull Niemi from net since the Sound was pressuring it so much. He was able to break free for a moment and get to his back office, the high point, so he could fire off his quick wrister with just enough lift to clear the leg but it was a deceptive little shot since goalies could seldom get their gloves down in time. As expected, the horn sounded to signal a good goal and the hats just rained down on the ice. He couldn't help himself in the moment the kid in him came out and he pulled a Jagr salute before he realized what he was doing. He knew that wouldn't go over very well on social media but too late to take it back.

Being up by four, they could get comfortable for the last minute and a half. The whole bench was excited and Scotty was trying to play it cool from that point on. He grabbed a towel to wipe his visor. Berman actually said excitedly, "Now that's a way to bounce back from a terrible skate. Just don't think you can get away with it again." Scott just nodded. It was still cool to see how many hats came down onto the ice, he just felt bad for the guys who helped to take care of the ice since it was always a lot of work to collect the hats.

The rest of the game finished up without anything of note. As soon as they got into the locker room Lager launched a towel at Scotty's face and said, "Nice hattrick."

Scotty was tempted to throw the towel back at Lager but just tossed it in the basket instead. He did say, "That could have been yours if you didn't get yourself ejected."

Lager shrugged as he nonchalantly said, "True, but it was worth it."

"Thanks for always having my back."

"Of course, that was a cheap ass hit. Nobody should get away with that shit. Besides, I never liked Deslauriers."

Scott laughed. He was just glad that Lager was in a good mood about the whole thing. As soon as everyone was in the room, the coaches did their usual talk of the good points and the missed opportunities as they got off their gear. Scott was given the puck that netted him his hattrick. The whole room was jubilant. There was just enough time to get a quick shower and change before he had to start talking to the reporters. He looked for Berman to make sure he was in the loop, especially after he was so pissed about the morning skate. Berman surprised him and was even willing to suspend all the interviews for Scotty today if he needed to but that seemed like it would be overkill and a way to invite journalists to dig for a story that didn't need to be told. He knew that it would be a while before he could sneak off to see Alice. Knowing that she was watching him tonight was awesome and he couldn't wait to get her game feedback. Then he felt a bit guilty as he remembered that they were supposed to go to her place to meet the police, now he was going to make them even later than usual. He was about ready to shoot off a text when he saw one from early on in the game. He had to laugh but he was curious which goal she was talking about to melt her heart while he was on the ice. Instead of asking, he just sent off: ***Probably going to be a while. Do you need to head off without me?***

He really didn't want her to go alone since he wanted to make sure she was okay. While she was trying to put on a brave front, he could see it in her eyes that she was having a tough go of it in the morning and he didn't expect it to be much different in the evening. He wanted to protect her much like how his team protected him tonight. But he didn't want her to get into trouble for being late, especially when it would have been his fault that they were late.

A: ***It should be okay. If it's getting late, I'll drive back but I will give you the heads up. Besides Diane wants to go over some charity stuff.***

Scotty had to laugh. Donnie's wife had been relentless in trying to get everyone involved with the wives' charity events. Well almost everyone. Dykstman never seemed to keep the same woman for more than a week so Diane stopped trying to recruit his current girlfriend to help. He knew how much Alice liked to work and wondered if that would be too much with everything else going on or just provide a good distraction when he was out of town.

After they were done with the media requirements, a few of the guys were hoping that Scott would come out after the game for a few drinks to celebrate his natural hatty and Lager's Gordie Howe hat trick. But since it was Alice's birthday, he had the perfect excuse to say how he had plans this evening without mentioning the fact that there was a less than happy note about some of the plans.

Eventually he was good to go upstairs to gather up Alice. She was engrossed in conversation with Brigitta and he had his favorite opening with Alice. He came up from behind and hugged her tightly as he nuzzled her neck. He also whispered in her ear, "Hey there, beautiful."

She looked back and said, "You're not too bad yourself. Good game tonight." She was smiling, that seemed true enough, but he could see how dull and brown her eyes were. He loved how when she was really happy they had flecks of gold and were mostly green instead of going to a dark brown.

It wasn't hard to notice how ever since the burglary, they were dark and slightly lifeless compared to what he's seen.

"Hey there, Scott," said Brigitta in a quiet voice. That's when he noticed that Lager's kid was passed out in her arms. He was glad that he didn't make Alice squeal when he started to hug her. But that's where she was awesome, she would be somewhat surprised but always quiet and would instantly melt into his body.

"Hey Bridge. Thanks for taking care of Alice tonight."

"No problem. It was my pleasure." Brigitta started to stand up with the ease only a parent could have when holding on to a child. He secretly hoped that one day he and Alice could have some of their own. Brigitta turned to Alice and said, "Good luck with everything tonight." As she was passing, Bridge mouthed "I like her. You better keep her." Scott nodded and thought the same thing.

Scott continued to nuzzle Alice's neck and kissed along it. He loved holding her and it seemed like she was enjoying it just as much. She just melted into him rather than even try to turn and face him. It was just the two of them in the box looking onto the ice. He was so tempted to do more but that's when Alice said, "We should probably get going." Then she said almost in the same breath, "Oh shit. I wasn't thinking and I brought my car."

Scott smiled as he ran his hands up and down her forearms. There was a part of him that was disappointed by the news. He liked dropping her off at work this morning but he knew it was more practical for her to have her car in the long run. "No worries. We can both drive to your place or we can try to see if either Petey or Lager could drive my car over to my place."

"Okay," as Alice leaned up and started to kiss him. It was a tame kiss for the two of them but it was appropriate for being in public and it still lasted a while. Eventually she broke away from the kiss and they both picked up a few gift bags that were by her feet. They were slow moving and it was easy to see they were one of the last ones in the arena. Scott was tempted to ask about the presents as they were walking out but she surprised him by asking him, "So towards the end of the game, what the hell was going on with your line? Why weren't you guys on the same page? I saw you trying to give them plays and direct things but it was clearly not working. It didn't even see like a lack of communication. You never stopped talking."

Scott chuckled at that. He was wondering some of the same thing but at the same time, he knew how quickly things on the ice happen and didn't dwell on it. Especially since his line was so solid most of the time. "Things happen. I would bet that one, Lager never told anyone but me, but he was hoping to get a hattrick tonight. Two, the guys just trust my ability to see a shot. I would bet that the guys forgot that me and Lager had pretty much the same stats: 2 goals and 2 assists tonight. So they were trying to get me the hatty when it was Lager who really wanted it."

He found it so refreshing to be with someone who understood hockey and really enjoyed it and wasn't using it as a way to get laid or find a sugar daddy. He loved how Alice would pick up on the little nuances that he didn't see from the game. He sometimes wondered if she could do something more with her knowledge. He kissed her on the nose and asked, "Any other burning question from tonight's game?"

Alice smirked for a moment as she was thinking up a

good question. Then she came out with a doozy. "When will your other lines contribute to the scoring? It's been what something like 10 games since anything but the top line scored? You guys are so top heavy on the front line. Hell, I've been waiting to see when Berman would split up your line for at least a few games to jump start the secondary scoring. I know the other lines are solid defensively and you don't get stripped in the neutral zone like my other team but still..."

The only reason Alice stopped with her train of thought was because he interrupted it by kissing her passionately. He didn't like the direction the conversation was going. He knew that the local analysts were probably asking the same thing. But that didn't mean he wanted it to happen. He had the best line that he's ever been on. They just click together on the ice. Sure off the ice, he didn't really hang out with Dykstman because of the language barrier and they just had different priorities. But him and Lager were thick as thieves basically from since they met. It was cute how well Alice knew hockey. Alice was clearly breathless from the kiss and Scott said in a hushed voice, "Have I ever told you how cute you are when you talk hockey? But shhh. I like my line just the way it is. We have enough offense for the team."

Alice shrugged her shoulders and let the conversation drop at the moment. Scott was just happy to see Alice talking more and not dwelling on the previous night's events. He just hoped he could get her eyes to light up again like he could before. Scott then steered the conversation back towards her. He was curious if she was really upset with him or if they were cool.

"So did you get anything good for your birthday?"

"Yup. Got to see my special guy get his 3rd career hat trick along with some other good stuff for him. He even said that loved me for the first time. I'm starting to think he's too good for me."

She surprisingly made him blush. He always felt a wee bit self-conscious whenever he blushed since guys weren't supposed to blush. Not only was she okay with what he did for her birthday, she was happy for him and his career successes. The only thing that he didn't like was how she was putting herself down, so he nipped at her lip before saying, "Could be that you are just as special to him and if anything you might be too good for him?"

Alice smiled and said, "Nah. I might be just as special but he's definitely too good for me."

Scotty just shook his head. He knew that Alice was stubborn on some things. But he would make her one day see his point of view.

Alice

Alice was actually surprised about how much fun she had at Scott's game. Everyone was so nice and welcoming. Only a handful of people knew about the break in and that was so comforting not to have to talk about it. She wasn't sure if she could have handled it if she had to. Then after the game, Scotty was so flirty and that kept her in such good spirits. It was actually kinda weird not to just get into the car without Scott as they headed back to her place. But by the time they were ready to leave, it was too late to have anyone to drive Scott's car home since they were one of the last ones there.

As she was getting closer to her apartment, her anxiety started to creep up again. Every ounce of fear just started to come back to her. She didn't want to be there but she knew that she would have to reclaim her place eventually. Scott was waiting for her to pull in by his SUV. He seemed to read her better than anyone else and he came up and scooped her up in a hug the moment she stepped out of her car. He whispered in her ear, "It'll be okay."

Once they were inside, she just looked around. Not sure what she wanted to do first. There was a part of her that was a little hesitant about the fact that the police weren't already there waiting. But part of her knew that it would be a good thing to be in her place without the police and take the time to be there again. At least she had Scotty with her in that moment. She started to look around (still really careful not to touch too much) in case she was missing things. Her Danish experience started to kick in while she was looking at stuff from her desk as she found her container of kroner. The Danes were all about hygge, a homey, comfortable space that you want to be in and part of that meant lighting some candles. She knew that she need to re-establish the hygge around her. But at that moment, all she wanted to do was wrap herself in Scott's arms. It was almost insane how much she wanted to be held after the burglary. While she always loved PDA when she was in a relationship, that feeling seemed to be intensified since the burglary. It was hard to put that feeling into words.

Scott's leadership qualities kicked in first. "Let me pour both of us a drink. Any preference? I know you are trying to see if you missed anything, is there anything that I could help with after getting us drinks?"

Alice looked back at him and nodded although in all honesty, she didn't care if she had a drink or not, "Sounds good. Just pour anything that looks good."

Alice started to look closer at her drawers that were still

left open. She thought maybe the boxes she kept some of her foreign change in might be missing but at the same time, the Danish Kroner was still there. As she was trying to remember if the money was even in the drawer, she said quietly, "Maybe I didn't put it back after Paris. I know I spent all the bills."

Scotty came up and handed her a dark amber drink while he was holding a bottle of Yuengling that she picked up for him. She wasn't surprised that he kept to the safety of his favorite drink but that's why she bought it for him. As he was starting to pull her close with his free hand, he asked, "What did you say?"

Alice took a sip and realized that he poured her some of the maple aged Christmas beer. Then again she kicked herself for having to taste in order to figure out what it was since that was the only amber drink in her fridge. She really shouldn't have needed to taste the drink in order to know it was the Festivus. But she knew that she should respond to Scott rather than kicking herself for not immediately knowing what beer she was drinking. She tried to force a smile as she said, "Just talking to myself. Trying to remember if I put my spare pounds and Euro coins away after I went to Paris or if I spent it all. I just can't remember."

Scott smiled and asked with simple curiosity, "You went to Paris? When and with who?" The last part could have come off as if he was jealous but that didn't seem like it. He was just interested in learning more about the trip.

"Yeah, in October for like ten days. It was wonderful. I went by myself."

"Really?" That seemed to impress Scott. Then again before the break in, she was strong and so independent. She didn't think twice about going to a different country on her own other than to give her family and best friends an itinerary of her trip. That's when she knew things broke her some in the past 24 hours when she was scared and wanted to be held. While she knew it was expected it still didn't sit well with her.

"Yeah. I needed to take time off and one of my swim lessons offered to pay for my flight so I could practice my French. Besides the best way to insure that you wouldn't get called into work is making sure you are out of state or better yet, out of the country. It was a lovely trip and I did so many things that I adored."

"You will need to tell me more about it. I don't think I've ever really traveled solo unless it's for hockey or to see my parents. But once I'm there, I know people. I don't think I would have thought to take a trip to another country and not know anyone."

Alice shrugged her shoulders. The more she talked about the trip, the more she knew that it was a little weird to put together the trip in less than six weeks and to do it by herself. But as she thought about the trip, it made her want to travel again. Maybe go abroad with Scotty.

"Hey can you do me a favor and light the candles in each room for me?" Scott smiled at the request and immediately acquiesced as she continued to look about things. At least he didn't ask why she wanted the candles lit or thought it would make the apartment all smelly.

She looked in her purse for the JCPenney gift card that she won on Black Friday with her sister. Over the holidays, Alice was thinking about giving her sister the gift card since Allison liked shopping there more but couldn't remember if they followed through with the idea. Her sister confirmed that didn't happen. Sure enough, that was missing too but at least Alice wasn't too worried about that since it was only $5 and she didn't really care about spending the money at JCPenney.

It didn't take long for Scott to return and say, "I think I got all of them but I didn't see one in the kitchen" as he put the matches back on her desk. She appreciated how he put them back in nearly the same spot that she pulled them from. That's where he was so observant and made things easy.

"Yeah. Sorry there wasn't one in that room. Can you remind me to ask about the iPad charger?"

"Sure" Then Scott pulled her close again and held her by her waist. He just nuzzled up against her and it was the perfect emotional grounder. He stayed quiet for the most part, while she realized that the travel journal box that she had was up was opened up and she knew she didn't pick up on that one last night. She leaned her head into Scott's strong body as she slowly sipped her beer. She was doing the best she could to try and be calm but it wasn't always easy. He picked up on when she needed it by saying steadfastly, "It'll be okay."

"I know that it just takes time. But that doesn't always make it any easier right now. But thanks for just being here and letting me stay with you."

Scott started to kiss her forehead as he said, "Anytime."

Finally the doorbell rang. Scott offered to get the door but Alice said she will get it. She was immediately put at ease when she saw Officer LePrince again. When she was told that one of the second shift police would pick up the bag of goldfish for evidence, she never expected it would be the officer that took care of her the entire time that she had police in her home.

He was pretty straight to the point when he said as he was coming into the front room, "So I think the officer who talked to you earlier said that the detective wants to get that bag of Goldfish into evidence. Is there anything else you noticed that was missing?"

Alice shook her head and took a deep breath. She saw that Scotty was coming into her peripheral vision. Just seeing him was reassuring. She was wondering if the police from earlier told them everything or if she would have to explain Scott's presence. LePrince immediately greeted Scott by saying, "Good game man."

Scott had his hands in pockets and said "Thanks." Almost as if he got hat tricks every day. Scott then stood close to Alice and helped to make her feel at ease again. So she gathered up her voice and said, "Um, I noticed that my travel journal box was opened up and a JCPenney gift card was missing in my purse. Also I know I noticed this last night but I don't think I put it in the statement, but my iPad charger was also taken from the plug and it was attached to the iPad that was stolen."

Alice didn't mention how she wasn't sure about the money. She was already silly about bringing up a missing $5 gift card. She also felt like some of her costume jewelry that she kept by her desk might be missing but she couldn't put her finger on anything specific that was gone. It just felt off.

"Okay. I will need to take some pictures before gathering up the evidence. I will need you to fill out another statement. Just like from last night. Include the iPad charger since you didn't mention it before. Make sure you include that we are collecting the Goldfish as well."

Alice nodded her head. Alice sat down on her couch and Scott sat down beside her. He just let her snuggle up and he was running his hands up and down her body. It was giving her warmth and steadiness. She started to fill out the statement as was requested. When she was almost done, Officer LePrince said, “Do you mind if we also collect the journal as well? I'm not sure the best way to do the evidence on it.”

Alice said, “Sure. That’s okay. I don’t need that just yet.”

So she added that to the statement as well. As she started to stand up, the officer asked, “Where was the goldfish prior to last night?

Alice pointed to a busy area on the snack table. He snapped the photo of the snack table. She had the goldfish tucked away between a couple different snacks somewhere but Alice wasn’t paying enough attention to really know where she was storing them.

“So that should be everything. We are questioning some witnesses and the detective actually assigned to the case should call you either tomorrow or the next day. Do you have any questions for me?”

“I don’t think so.”

“Okay that should be it then.” Both Alice and Scott got up to help escort the officer to the door. As he left, he said, “Happy birthday again. I hope it got better.” Between the written statements, and her moment of rambling when he first entered the night before that she didn’t want to deal with her birthday wishes, the officer knew that it was her birthday. At least that was up until Scott tried to make things better. Alice nodded and Scotty was starting to lock up for her after the Officer left.

Alice took a deep breath. She looked up to Scotty and said, "Thanks for being here. It was a huge help."

"No problem. Now that's done. What do you want to do for the rest of your birthday?"

Alice smiled and thought for a moment, "Could doing nothing or the other extreme of copious amounts of sex be a viable answer?"

Scott laughed at her response. "Yup. Both are good options. But what would you prefer?"

"I'm not sure. Sorry. I know I sound so lame but I think I just want to be held. Maybe later, I can take advantage of the other option."

Scott nodded and smiled wickedly. He seemed to be okay with her request. "So let's get you packed up. Let's grab your hockey gear too."

"Really? We didn't use what we grabbed this morning. What makes you think that the next couple of days would be much different?"

Scott smiled, "Cause I know we have a few more days together. You are calmed down and we can do some things more than just cuddle on the couch, unless you want to do that. Besides I already talked to Corey about using the rink in his basement tomorrow night. It should only be just the three of us."

"Seriously?!?!" Alice looked at him incredulously as he nodded in assent. She couldn't believe that Scott would set that up for them to do. Knowing that it would be private was also good since that would mean Alice could swear to her little heart's content when she was messing things up. Although knowing she would play with two professionals, she was sure she would be more self-conscious then normal even if she enjoyed hanging out with Scott. She leaned up to him to kiss him and said, "You are the best. Also thank you for setting it up with him and having it be private. I definitely prefer to limit how many people see how badly I suck."

"You don't suck that much. You just need some work on the skills. Besides you usually work in the water, not on ice." Scott then started to kiss her softly and allowed the passion to rise up. He lifted her up as he tended to do so she didn't have to balance quite so much to reach his lips. He also immediately started to carry her to the bedroom.

Alice didn't realize how unprepared she was to be back in her bedroom. Since the moment they went to bed, she was seized up by moments of panic where her mind replayed the previous night's event and she was worried that someone would walk in on them. She stopped kissing Scott and just started to breathe heavier as she was trying to make sure she suppressed the urge to start crying. She wanted to bury herself into his muscles and hide the fact that she felt so vulnerable in her own bedroom.

"Crap, I'm sorry Alice. I wasn't thinking. Are you okay?" Scott first started to hug her tight as he realized what had happened.

Alice nodded. She was slowly asserting control over her emotions as Scott just started to rub her back. "Sorry. I just really haven't been back in here since it happened and I wasn't expecting the rush of everything so quickly. I shouldn't feel so vulnerable in my own bedroom."

"It's to be expected. I just wasn't thinking. It's just where we do everything when we are here. Do you want to head out or do you want to stay here?"

Alice thought about the options for a moment. She knew

it would probably be better in the long term if she just tried to stay there, especially if they were there together doing their usual stuff. But she wasn't really ready to stay there any longer then needed. "Let's go ahead and leave. I still need to finish up packing my bag with a couple things. I'm almost done. I'm sorry."

Scotty looked at her like she was crazy at that moment. He didn't want her to be hurting but the apology was a step too much. Alice just threw some stuff into a bag, not paying attention to what she was grabbing. She wanted to get back to Scotty's place and go back to what they were doing without having her brain playing tricks on her.

8

SCOTT

Normally leaving for the All-Star break would be easy and a fun trip. The whole event was a media day, a skills challenge and a couple games to try and win $1 million dollars. It is always nice to play with some of the best in the league but in a very laid back fashion. But leaving Alice was tougher than he thought it would be. The last few days were pretty awesome as they settled into a routine and he could wake up next to her each day. He knew that their schedules would be changing once he was off the bye and back from the All-Star break but he liked having Alice at his place. He liked how Alice wasn't a ball of anxiety most of the time anymore and becoming more like her old self. While he saw more of the internal strength she had even when she was being hard on herself for feeling vulnerable, she loved the time hanging out together. But nights are always when she struggled the most, it was rough at times getting her to relax enough to fall asleep and she would jump at the slightest unexpected touch. He could see the dark circles and the purple tinge around her eyes just grow daily, he knew that she wasn't sleeping.

The flight to the All-Star game was uneventful. He traveled with a few people from the Sound PR team so they could promote the event but they were all working together and seldom said much to him. So he started to play on his Nintendo Switch to keep himself busy on the cross country flight.

Once he got to the hotel, he decided to do a quick video call with Alice but she didn't pick up which was disappointing. He knew she was most likely busy at work. So he got ready for his media day: a shower, took care of his hair and shaved. The shaving was probably the most important thing for him to do since he realized that his scruff was almost a beard but not quite one either. He stopped shaving when Alice started to stay at his place. He was too busy fussing over her and got lazy. He got mixed reviews from the guys in the locker room, not that it really mattered. But the person who mattered most never said if she liked it or not. He was hoping to ask her on the video chat but since that wasn't to be, he played it safe if only for the PR guys. While his hair could get a little crazy, he's pretty much always been clean shaven except for the playoffs.

Arriving at the arena, the atmosphere was that everyone was in the 'let's have fun' mode. All the players were in a great mood and a few of the guys even brought their kids around. There was a lot of chatter as people were catching up and getting to know the new guys. Scott hadn't been selected for the All-Star game for a couple years. So it was fun and he was enjoying the current format of the game: a 3 on 3 knock-out tournament based on divisional placement. He was curious how the Metropolitan would fair. He thought they were pretty deep despite not having some of the studs that the other teams had.

The media day was pretty uneventful. There were a few silly games that he had to do like the wiggle where he had to get 15 ping pong balls out a tissue box without using his hands and the 40 cup stacking game only using one hand. He had no idea what they were going to use the videos for with those games but the NHL wanted him to do it. So he did. He was just glad that all the players had to look pretty silly doing it. There were lots of interviews in between too.

He had to laugh when he saw that he was placed next to Claude Giroux in both the locker room and in the media booths. He knew that Alice had a thing for the Flyers captain prior to meeting him. There were times he actually wondered if he was a poor-man's substitute for Giroux in her eyes. But as he got to know her, he wasn't a substitute for anything in her book. She craved Scotty more in ways that counted most.

The best part of the day was when they finally got to play some hockey. All the equipment was brand new and had some sort of special sensors in it that allowed for more tracking. Scott was just glad to start breaking the equipment in and get a chance to feel if the sensors changed the feel of the gear. Fortunately for him, it didn't seem any different from the regular stuff he would wear. Plus it was nice to just get a feel of what it was like to play with the other guys. While they all played against each other about four times a year, that's different than being on the same line with a guy. Scott wasn't surprised by the fact the two Penguins players were on a line together and how they fed off of each other. He was surprised that he actually played really easily with Claude Giroux and they were forming their own ginger line for the All-Star Game. He hoped it was a lethal combination.

By the end of the day, he was exhausted. He just wanted to talk to Alice and then crash out. Fortunately, the hotel was close to the arena. He used Facetime to call Alice. This time, she picked up right away. He was a tad disappointed to see that she returned to her apartment rather than stay as his home. But he knew it would be good for her to go back there some. She'd been avoiding it like the plague.

"Oh hey you!" she said with a smile. She looked exhausted and a bit anxious. "You shaved."

"Yeah. I hope you don't mind. How was your day?"

Scott was a bit surprised that Alice didn't really give any indication if she liked the shaved or the unshaven look. Instead she just said, "It was uneventful." Then Alice went quiet for a moment. You could practically see her think and downplaying something in her mind. Scott wished he knew how to get her to open up. Although this time, she surprised him with how quickly she could switch a conversation. "How was your day? Did you have to do the weird thing where you had to wiggle out ping pong balls from your back?"

Scott laughed hard. He couldn't believe that she knew about that. Once he got done laughing he finally could ask, "How in the world did you know about that?"

"The Flyer's posted G's attempt to Instagram and my best friend sent it over to me. I figured you had to do that too. How did you do?" Alice too was laughing and smiling with the most pure joy he'd seen since the burglary that didn't involve sex. "Did you do any downward facing dog, too?"

"Nope to the downward facing dog. Just mainly hopped around and used some of my mad dancing skills." Alice raised her eyebrow as if she questioned his ability. "Seriously. Do you need me to take you dancing to prove it?"

"As long as it's not a club, why not." That was surprising to Scott. He never had a girl turn him down in a halfway fashion. Hell in juniors, going to the club and dancing was one of the easiest ways he had to pick up girls. Alice followed up by "Strobes give me migraines."

"Definitely no clubs then." He liked the idea of taking Alice dancing although that would limit some of his moves if he was going to be avoiding bright lights. He knew he was smiling. "But my day was good. I wished I could have played a little more hockey today if only to get used to the new gear. But I think you will like the lines if things stay the way they are."

"As long as you aren't with the asshole, I'm sure I will."

Scott chuckled. Her Philly was showing through and he knew it. He wanted to rib her just to see the reaction. So he teased, "Do you mean that guy from the Flyers?"

"Oh hell no! You know damn well that I would never call him an asshole. I'm pretty sure you know that it would probably be a Penguin. I will call Crybaby Crosby an asshole any day of the week but I am starting to suspect that you are one as well," said an extremely animated reaction. It was pretty much what he expected from her. But it was cute to see her get all riled up. He loved seeing how worked up she got. It was so funny and he was laughing again. Plus he hadn't heard the Crybaby nickname in forever. He forgot that nickname was still in use by Flyers fans.

With the sternest face he could muster, although he knew it was more a smile "You know you kinda have to like him for a couple games."

"Nope! Not going to happen. It took me like 35 games to stop cursing out every time Jagr touched the puck when he played for the Flyers. I only disliked Jagr. There is something about Crosby that I absolutely can't stand. There isn't enough time to get me to somewhat like that asshole. He's talented and I rather you play with him then against him but I **hate** him. If it helps, I won't curse out any other of the guys playing for the metro if that makes the difference. I do want you to win."

Scott nodded. He wasn't actually surprised by Alice's comments. He knew she was a typical Flyers fan and there is some pure hatred between the Penguins and Flyers on all levels. He wanted to watch a Flyers vs. Penguins game to just watch her reactions during a game and see how visceral it went. He was sure that some of her hatred had to go deeper than just a cross-state rivalry. He wasn't sure what was at the root of it. He hoped that he could learn about what was really at the root of her Crosby anger. He then noticed the time. It was approaching 10pm and he was 3 hours behind of Alice. So he knew his question was going to sound a little dumb, "Still having any issues getting to sleep?"

"Yeah. But I'm trying and I've taken some extra precautions like using the new lock and barricading my bedroom door. I'm trying to help ease myself into being here again. So I was just reading until you called."

Scott hated hearing that. He wished he knew how to help her but it was tricky and they both knew it. At least when she was at his place, he knew she got some sleep even if it was fitful. He wasn't sure she would be able to sleep at her place. She shot him down flat when he suggested just staying at his place without him. This was despite the fact that she was going there a couple times a day to help take care of Chloe.

"Can I help in anyway?"

"Just be you." She gave a forced smile which let him know that he was stirring up the demons within her. She then changed the angle of the discussion again- probably to avoid the thoughts going on in head at the moment. "Do you know the assignments for the skills challenge?"

Scott shook his head. "Not yet. There was a couple debates on a couple of the assignments."

"What are you hoping for?"

Scott took a deep breath. He really hadn't thought about it too much other then doing a few run throughs of each drill earlier in the day. It was just a showcase piece for the weekend. In many ways, it was something the fans cared about a bit more than most of the players. He didn't want to come in last place. "Um, I guess the accuracy shooting or the puck control. I know, I definitely, I don't want to do the fastest skater."

Alice laughed. Scott had to marvel how hockey might be even more therapeutic for Alice then it was him. She was mostly just a fan who watched the game and only played occasionally. He never thought hockey could make anyone else happier and more relaxed than him. But it was doing her good and he was happy to see that. As she became more relaxed in their conversation, he hoped that she would go to sleep soon. She teased some when she asked, "Don't think you can beat McDavid?"

"That little fucker is quick. There's no way I can touch him in a foot race."

Alice nodded, "That he is. Still not quite sure how

Manning ever kept up. Then again it helped that those two have/had some serious bad blood." Alice was definitely questioning herself over with her word choice. Then again, Scott couldn't blame her for questioning her word choice given the fact those two were on the same team. Scott barely knew about the bad blood until the unnoteworthy trade became the talk of the league since apparently the front office asked McDavid for his approval for the trade.

Scott turned the question back onto Alice, "What would you like to see me do?"

"Probably the puck control," she said with a yawn. Her exhaustion seemed to be catching up with her. "That's all you and G for that in my mind."

He nodded. He knew he should encourage her to go to sleep but he had a feeling that she would try to push off the idea so he decided on a different tact. "Hey baby, would you mind if I head off to bed?"

"Yeah. No problem." While she said it was totally okay, she didn't move to try and end the call. This is when he got to be the protector in the relationship and he could look after both of them.

Scott forced out the yawn to help make his act seem even more convincing, "You know that does mean of one of us has to hang up first." Alice nodded. "Alright. Sleep well. If you need to talk to someone in the middle of the night, just call. Je t'aime."

"Okay. Sleep well. Kick ass tomorrow. I love you too."

Alice

Alice had a really rough time with sleep. Even after talking with Scott, she wasn't any closer to falling asleep than before he called. She wasn't sure if it was because she was back in her place for the first time since the break in and missing Scott holding her if not both. She definitely relaxed when Scott called. Hearing his voice was soothing and she could focus on the noises that she was hearing as she laid in bed and realized they were natural creaks of an old apartment. But the wind kept picking up and she couldn't actually settle down.

The one thing she couldn't stop thinking about was the fact he shaved again for the first time in a week. She didn't realize how much of her actually liked the scruff that had developed that was starting to look like a solid beard since she started staying at his place. But she also wondered if he stopped shaving because she was too much of a distraction to have around. She was tempted to ask him about that but didn't know how. Besides it was up to Scott what he wanted to do with his facial hair.

After finishing up another book and mulling over ideas, she let her tired mind take the wheel for a moment. Even though she was sure that he would be asleep, she decided to text him.

Alice: ***Missing you something fierce.***

Scott: ***Me too.***

Alice: ***Wait, you are up?***

Scott: ***Yeah. The fire alarm went off and we are waiting to get the all clear. Why are you still up?***

Alice: ***That blows. I just can't get myself settled down. My mind keeps want to freak out.***

Scott: ***I wish I could help.***

Alice: ***You do help. You holding me or even talking to me has been huge. I know part of it is because I'm back.***

Scott: *I would hold you right now if I could. Why not stay at my place if your place is freaking you out?*

Alice: *Cause I miss my bed even if I'm failing at actually sleeping in it.*

Scott: *Don't feel like my place isn't a home for you. Besides Chloe would love the company.*

Alice: *I know and I'm grateful that you would let me stay there even if you aren't there. But it won't be better there. Over half the issue is the wind is freaking me out. It will be just as windy if not more so at your place.*

Scott: *I just got the all clear to go inside. Do you want me to call you once I'm back in the room?*

Alice wanted to say yes with every fiber in her being; but she knew it would rob him of sleep too. It was bad enough that she wasn't sleeping that night. She shouldn't make it impossible for him as well since she knew he would stay up to talk to her. So she ruled it out.

Alice: *Nah. I think I'm going to try to sleep again. Sleep well and Je t'aime.*

Scott: *Je t'aime.*

Alice placed the phone back on the nightstand. She was so glad that she could talk to him even in text form since every text was read in his voice and it was almost as good as a real call from him. She was definitely feeling more settled down so she rolled over one last time to get at least a couple hours of sleep.

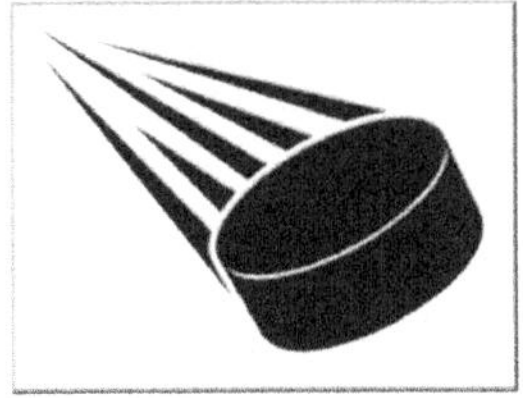

Alice was waiting for Scott at the airport. She was surprised that he wanted her to meet him at the airport since their original plan was for him to take an uber back and they would meet up the next day since it was going to be a super late flight. It didn't help that she barely slept the entire time he was away.

Finally, she saw Scott coming into view. She was surprised that he had a bag on his shoulder that she didn't remember him having before. He was grinning like mad when he saw her and practically trotted over to her. His pace was dampened by the fact he was trying to keep the shoulder bag from moving too much. Once he reached her, he scooped her up into a hug and said, "I've missed you."

"I've missed you too."

Before anything else could happen, there was a high pitched little arf that penetrated the air. It was so tiny sounded that she knew it had to be a super young puppy. Scott set her down on the ground again and with a Cheshire smile he started to pull something out of the bag by his side.

"So I was a wee bit impulsive while I was away and I got you something. So close your eyes and hold out your hands."

Alice did as she was told and was really unsure what was going on. All of sudden there was something moving between her hands and she tried to get a good grip as she opened up her eyes. She immediately saw a tiny puppy that reminded her of Chloe in general shape but she knew there was some differences like the paws and ears.

"What? A puppy?" asked a very shocked Alice.

"Yup." Scott looked pleased with himself as Alice tried to process everything. She couldn't have pets at her place. Where would the little guy live? Could they even care for such a tiny little puppy? How did they even let him board a plane with a puppy that young? Surely it was too young to be away from its mom.

Scott continued in a steady calm voice. "I figured you needed to have some back up with you when you are by yourself at night. He's going to get much bigger than what he is now. But isn't he adorable?" He scratched behind the dog's ears causing him to start to lick Alice's hands. "I know it seems crazy. But I talked to the breeder and they think Chloe should be able to nurse him. If that doesn't work, we can bottle feed him but he's eating food and water some too."

Alice was slowly falling in love with the little guy with each and every lick he gave her and with Scott's excitement, she knew deep down it was utterly absurd and crazy. She couldn't hold the laughter in anymore and said, "You're insane. I love the little guy but we can't take him to my place. My landlord will kill me."

That's when Scott started to kiss her almost as if to silence and calm her down from rejecting everything right out of hand. "I thought about that too since I had a feeling your place didn't allow pets. I know this is a big ask and you will probably think it's crazy but hear me out. Move in with me. You won't have to do anything. I have plenty of space where you can have your own separate rooms for stuff. But before you can think of every reason you can't, just think about how we were together every day before I left. It can be the same thing as before except you don't have to run to your apartment to get something and there won't be so many reminders every night. Plus don't you want to wake up next to me and this little guy every day?"

Alice wasn't sure she could have been more speechless. If she thought the puppy was a crazy thing to bring home over a weekend, being asked to move in seemed even crazier. It was a tempting offer since he was right, it would be a nice thing to do. But she couldn't just leap into moving into his place. "Would you hate me if I asked for more time to think about it?"

"I wouldn't expect anything less from you. As long as you and the little guy come home with me right now and you promise me that you will at least think about it."

"That could be arranged," Alice said with a sexy smile. She had been waiting for him to return. Despite chatting daily while he was gone, she missed him fiercely and wanted to sleep with him so badly. Not even sexually, she just wanted to sleep with him.

The puppy kept squirming in her hand and she had a feeling all he wanted to do was explore but Alice knew that she had to keep a grip on him or else he would run away since he didn't have a leash on. Scott was right: the gray and white puppy was adorable. As Alice continued to struggle to hold onto him, Scott scooped him up and put him back into the bag that he had and zipped it up.

He kissed her ear as they left the airport and sent shivers down her spine. He then lost some of his smile and had a little uneasiness about him as he asked, "Are you mad?"

"I'm not mad. I'm in disbelief for sure. You bought a

puppy without saying a word. And you want me to move in. It's kinda crazy since it's been what like a month since we met and you want me to move in. It just seems so insane."

"But I'm crazy for you and the timing seems perfect. You've said it the past several days, you can't sleep at your place. Don't lie and say that you did. It's all over your face that you haven't. You know you get some sleep at my place, especially when I'm around. When I'm not, you can be with Chloe and Backup who will protect you."

Alice nodded. Scott's idea made sense and she knew it deep down. But she couldn't just jump in at that moment. She needed to think about how quickly everything was moving. She was learning towards saying yes since Scotty was right about everything. Maybe it was the anxiety that was holding her back. But at the same time, if the burglary never happened, she wouldn't even entertain the idea since it was far too soon.

As they got into the car, Alice let out what she was thinking, "You really are perfect. What in the world did I do to deserve to have you in my life?"

Scott just accepted it and threw the line back at her, "I've been asking the same thing about you. Apparently we were meant for each other."

Alice felt anything but perfect lately and she knew it. Although, she did agree that they did seem well suited for each other. "I know that I've been like a scared puppy lately. Even I know that I'm not the same bubbly person I was before the break in no matter how I hard I try. I just feel bad that I'm not the same and that even in my own book, I'm feeling more or less broken."

Scott grabbed her hand and started to rub it with his

thumb. "You aren't broken and what you feel is normal. As much as it sucks, I honestly would be afraid if you didn't feel this way after the break in. I'm not trying to rush things. It will be better soon enough. Until then, I just want to make you happy and safe."

"I do feel that way when I'm with you."

"Good. So you will consider moving in, right?"

Their conversation was briefly interrupted when the little puppy started to yawn but it sounded more like a mew then it did like a noise a puppy would make. It was as if the puppy was making his voice heard and wanted to know.

"Yes, I will consider it. Hell, I'm leaning towards saying yes."

"Really?" asked a surprised Scott. Then again her own words surprised herself. But things were so good with him and it seemed like a good idea.

"Yeah. But would you want me to give up my lease?"

"Not if you don't want to. I was more thinking of bringing your stuff over to my place. You know I have a few rooms that are practically unfinished. You can have your office/library area that I know you love to watch hockey games if you don't want to watch while lounging downstairs and your bed would make a perfect guest room bed. Hell your couch/chair could play with the stuff in my living room too. It can be our home together. Where we can be happy together."

Alice liked the idea of that. It seemed so perfect and so ideal. He really seemed to think of everything. As impulsive as he was, it was well thought out and he clearly thought about the potential consequences. It was much like his style of play on the ice. He could be creative and make a risky rushes but he always seemed to know what he was doing.

"I like the sound of that. It feels like it's too soon. I know my whole family will just flip out and I'm not sure I want to deal with that with everything else in life. But at the same time a home together sounds so awesome. So I need time to think."

They were at a lone stoplight that forced them to stop at the red light. So Scott took the time to kiss her delicately almost as if pacing himself until they got home. Alice enjoyed that a lot even if it was too brief. The light turned green way too quickly and they drove on. He said, "Take all the time you need, babe. I'm not trying to rush you too much. I just think it would be good for both of us."

It seemed so damn impulsive but Scott had the answers to her questions thus far. So she had to ask the obvious question before they got back to the house. "How do you want to introduce the little guy.... Wait, did you say his name was Backup? Isn't that a Veronica Mars reference?" Scott shrugged his shoulders about the reference question. She knew that there was a really good chance that Veronica Mars didn't make it to Canada and even if it did, he was probably too focused on hockey to really know the show. She knew that she got sidetracked without finishing her question so she revisited it. "Sorry. But how do we make sure that Chloe doesn't get jealous or think he's a snack?"

Scott smiled knowingly. All his cockiness was back. "Chloe typically loves puppies. So I was thinking we will enter the house together. I will hold Backup in the bag while you help to get Chloe settled down. We will leave him in the bag until she can sniff him out. Then we will slowly unzip it and they'll start to play. It'll be fine."

When they got home, everything went as smoothly as

Scott thought it would. Chloe was interested in the puppy and the puppy just started to follow her around (at least as much as he could). But when Chloe needed a little break, she jumped onto one of the sectionals and Backup had to just look up to her. Alice knew that soon enough Backup could do that on his own but for now he would need help to get onto the sectionals and Scott's bed. Initially, Scott was playing with the two dogs as Alice sat on the couch since she was just overwhelmed. He then settled in beside her and she snuggled into his side. He first nibbled at her ear before asking, "You're awful quiet again. Everything okay?"

"Yeah. Just a lot on my mind."

"I'm guessing adding Backup to our lives and offering to have you move in didn't help you as much as I would have hoped."

"Not yet. I know you are doing it all from love. It just feels like everything is changing and I wonder if it's going to be fair to you. I know I won't be able to make as much or contribute to the household as much as I would like. This month is nuts. I won't be there to help train Backup like I should."

"Oh?"

"I have a conference for work and a belated birthday trip to Philly to see the Stadium Series game. Not to mention god knows how much time that will be needed to help with a charity event with Diane."

"That sounds like all good stuff though." Alice nodded her head and Scott continued on, "If it's too much with Diane, I can speak with Donnie to get you out of it. You aren't my wife so you aren't obligated to help out with that stuff. Besides, it's not like I won't be out of town a fair bit myself. I still have the dog walker booked for Chloe. He can also help to train and take care of both of them when we are gone."

"Sounds good." Alice said rather quietly as she was stifling a yawn.

"We should probably get to bed."

Alice nodded as she started to move off from the couch. Backup was right by her feet so she scooped him up into her hands. Scott kept his hand on her low back and he guided them to his bedroom. Chloe just followed them wordlessly. It wasn't the sexiest trip up to his bedroom, instead it was a family that had a long day. She knew if she did move in, they would be happy and most mornings would be like this.

They all climbed into bed. Almost immediately, they all fell asleep. Alice was in Scott's arms. Backup curled up on the pillow by Alice's head while Chloe took up the space at the bottom of the bed.

9

ALICE

Alice didn't stay asleep for long or at least it didn't feel like long. She didn't look over at her phone to see what time it was. Initially Alice just marveled at Scott's body. He looked so comfortable spread out on the bed. His arm muscles and abs were on display. Alice remained unmoving for a little bit loving the new family but she convinced herself to close her eyes again in search of some more elusive sleep.

After a little bit, it seemed like everyone was stirring. Backup started to move around and then eventually stepped on her head. She tried not to move since she didn't want to wake up Scott or freak out the little pup. She was about ready to move her hand by her eyes to keep Backup from stepping there; when she heard Scott say in a sleepy voice, "Hey, don't step on your mom like that. She needs her sleep. Let's go get some food," as he was picking up the little puppy from her head. There was no anger and he just took care of the situation as quietly as he could.

Alice was left alone in bed since Chloe immediately

followed Scott to get some food. She was tempted to follow and help him with the two dogs but she was comfortable. She figured she would wait ten minutes or so to see if she either fell back asleep or if Scott would return to the bed.

Soon enough, Alice felt the bed move some as Scott climbed back down into the bed with her. She opened her eyes and smiled. He was smiling and had lust in his eyes.

Alice said quietly, "Hey you."

"Hey. You weren't really asleep were you?"

"Nope."

Alice was tempted to say more but Scott said "Then it's a good thing I came back then" as he started to kiss her passionately. He pulled her t-shirt off as she started to pull at his pants. She noticed that he was already hard so she only softly caressed his member. That was about the time he got rid of her pants. She fell back into the bed as they started to swap positions. Alice wrapped her legs around his waist as he started to suck on her breasts and even nipped at her. She was ready to have him inside of her but he pulled away to a tabletop position which Alice was sure that it was so he could grab a condom. The tearing of the foil only confirmed that suspicion. The two of them made love together. He fell back on the bed and Alice breathed out in pure pleasure as he pulled her closer into a warm cuddle.

Being incorrigible, he said "Isn't this the best way to spend the morning before work?" The only thing he didn't say was that we could do this every morning if you move in.

"Yeah. Although, next time Backup can step on your head when he wakes up."

"That sounds fair. Want any breakfast?"

Alice shook her head in the no as per usual. She knew

that Scotty would be giving her a disapproving look so she didn't immediately turn over to look at him. But when she did turn to look over at his gorgeous face that had a couple scars by his nose and his blue gray eyes, she said "How about instead of breakfast, you join me in the shower?"

Scotty lifted her up and carried her to the bathroom while smothering her in kisses. He only paused long enough to throw the spent condom into the trash and to start the shower. He was kissing and caressing Alice the whole time. They had a fun round two under the water and there was a part of Alice that knew it had to be a bit risky but they didn't care. At least they had a good shower since he scrubbed her body clean after they had their fun.

As they finished up in the shower, Alice swore that Scotty was going to ask about moving in again and she didn't want to deny him anymore although part of her didn't want to rush. He had a sneaky grin on his face like he was up to something when he came up from behind and pulled her close. Instead of asking the question that she feared, he asked, "Up for some hockey after work?"

"Sure, but with who?" Alice was always a bit self conscious about the way she played. Especially since she knew she was a beginner at best and him and his friends completely outclassed and outplayed her. She hated making a fool out of herself.

"Some of the guys from the team. It'll be fun, I promise."

"For you, sure. But I'm just going to suck and hold you guys back. Are you sure you want me around for that?"

Scott squeezed her tight and said, "Don't be so hard on yourself. You will be fine, I promise. You know I won't set you up to fail. It will be a night for the guys to get their legs under them after a few days off. No one is looking to do more than a light skate. You'll be fine."

"Okay." and Alice then decided to switch the conversation to "What's your plan for today?"

"Just the usual. Workout and spend some time with the pups. Then get ready for tonight."

"Sounds like an easy day."

"Yeah. But the break will be ending soon enough. Then it's back into full tilt and I'll be away again. It's half the reason I'll be going heavy with the weights today and wanted some ice time. "

"Roadtrip?" asked Alice with some disappointment.

"One home game, two away that will be the start of a home and home series and then a few more games away after."

"Damn. Which means the guys in orange and black are mostly home." Alice continued to get ready. "The problem of trying to keep two team schedules in my head. I was thinking it was the reverse."

Scott gave her a forced smile. They both knew that he wanted to be home and Alice didn't want to make him feel bad about having to travel. Alice did her hair up in her usual braids with a low ponytail as Scott asked, "Are you sure you don't want anything real for breakfast besides coffee?"

"Yeah. I won't be able to eat anything just yet. Although I might grab something to eat later. I know that I should. Also let's just go ahead and do it. I'll move in."

Alice was a wee bit surprised with herself on the last part of that statement. It was unprompted but she was thinking about how perfect it would be to move in. To have someone who wanted to make meals for her, even if it's the ones she didn't want to eat, was perfect. She knew it was something she shouldn't balk at. Mornings at Scott's place were too perfect. So why not just make it official and make it more permanent. Plus it would end that awkward situation in her head where she knew that she would be dreading when he would ask her again.

Scott swung her around and said, "Really?" as he started to kiss her ears and neck. He was so elated by her decision that it caught her off guard. He kept hugging her and twirling her.

"Yeah. But you are going to make me dizzy if you keep spinning me around like that." Scott put her down and just looked at her so intensely for a moment. Probably looking for some doubt in her eyes. Alice smiled and said, "It seems right. But there's a lot of details that we will need to go through later. I can't do it now since I'm already cutting it close to making it to work on time."

"Alright. As long as you want to move in, that's all I care about. We can sort out the details later." Scott then started to kiss her neck some and said, "You know how to make me so damn happy. What were you thinking about for food for later? I can get it ready for you."

"Some fruit and yogurt."

"Okay. That's easy enough. I'm excited that you are going to move in." He snuck one last kiss before leaving the master suite bathroom. Alice smiled and continued to look at herself in the mirror in order to assess if her braids looked halfway decent and to apply some eye makeup. Although what Alice was really looking at in the mirror was looking at how her eyes are increasingly starting to express life again and contemplating the enormity of the decision to move in. She couldn't see a life without Scott but officially moving in with him also meant that they were a real couple. That was the part that seemed to be the scariest thing of all since Alice rarely let anyone get close to her. She rarely went on dates with guys in the last several years and then she fell into her very serious relationship out of nowhere. Now she was actually making the massive leap and moving in with someone. What would be next, actually getting married?

Scott

Scott was so happy. The morning was perfect for him. Alice never ceased in her ability to surprise him. He never thought she would agree to move in so easily and let alone this morning especially how she just shut down after he suggested it last night. He hated how she would get super quiet when she was stressed. He never knew what was going through her head in those moments. When she woke up that morning so damn playful, he really wanted to have that every morning and every night. He figured he would let her think about moving in for a while and wait until after coming back from his next two road trips before mentioning it again. He never imagined that she would just agree to move in unprompted and so soon.

If Alice wasn't over, he might have slept in a little bit longer although he wasn't sure if Backup would have let him. He liked his routines if only to give him some stability despite all the travel. Chloe was so good and well behaved and made it easy to keep his routines. He would always start the day with making some breakfast and coffee. He hated how Alice never seemed to eat anything other than coffee. His usual breakfast was light on the stomach with plenty of protein.

By the time he was done cutting up the fruit for Alice,

scrambling up egg whites and veggies into a frittata, Alice walked into the kitchen. "Hey beautiful." He noticed how she only smiled at the compliment. She never did say much whenever he called her beautiful. It was as if she didn't believe him. Instead of trying to get her to believe him, he would let it slide.

Their two dogs didn't really pay attention to him at this point. So they walked over to Alice hoping for either a walk or some more food. It didn't surprise him at all as she immediately rubbed both the dogs' ears and under their muzzles.

"The coffee should be ready. I haven't checked on it yet. Want anything else before you go? I got the fruit over here and you know where the yogurt is."

"No thanks. You are amazing for getting this ready. You didn't need to do that. Thank you," Alice said before kissing him in appreciation.

"No problem."

Almost as quickly as Alice came into the room, she left for work. That didn't actually surprise Scott. They fooled around a lot in the morning and it seemed like that Alice never gave herself a ton of time to get ready in the morning. Just enough to do the trick and she was out of the house. So he had the house to himself and the dogs for the rest of the day. He loved having lazy mornings at home with Chloe, now it would be with two dogs.

After a little bit, Chloe signaled that she wanted to go outside. He figured that it would be a good time to take both dogs. Chloe was always a breeze to walk and Backup being a little puppy, even Alice could easily walk both of them at the same time. Scott knew that he and Alice would have to train Backup to be as good as Chloe on walks so Alice would always be able to walk both dogs once he got older, especially since he will be bigger since he's part Great Dane. Scott pulled out both Chloe's and Backup's leashes.

Chloe came right up to Scott and he leaned over to ask, "Do you want to go fast?" Chloe jumped in excitement and he knew that she was on board with him skating as they went on her walk. He just hoped that Backup could keep up. He knew if worse came to worse, he would have to skate with the pup in his arms.

It didn't take long for Scott to get his inline skates on and start walking the two dogs. They didn't get to start going fast since almost immediately as they passed Lager's house, Scott heard Lager say "Yo, Scotty" as he was chasing his son in the yard. So Scotty pulled slightly on Chloe's leash to let her know that they were going to be stopping and he hoped that Backup would catch on without an active cue.

They stopped right in front of Lager's house and Lager came towards them. Scotty asked, "Hey. How's the bye treating you? You guys went to the Bahamas, eh? How was it?"

"Warm and sunny. It was pretty lazy when we aren't chasing this guy around," replied Lager as pointed towards his son who was making a beeline for the two dogs. "How was the All-Star Game?"

"Good. Couldn't complain about that. Getting a share of a million dollars is never a terrible thing."

"True. So what's with the little dog?"

"It's our new dog, Backup," said Scott rather casually.

"Wait. Ours? Does that mean what I think it means?" asked Lager rather confused.

"If you think that it has to do with Alice planning on

moving in and I got another dog to help protect her when I'm not around. Then yes, it's exactly what you think it means."

Lager let out a slow, low whistle before saying anything. "You aren't messing around are you? I know you aren't going to like what I am going to say next but hear me out 'cause I have to ask as a friend. Are you sure that Alice isn't like... What's her name, your ex?"

That hit like the lead balloon that Lager thought it would be and he was pissed off. Alice was nothing like his ex. Lager only knew about Denise since he was still a bit of a wreck when he first came to Cleveland over the breakup of that relationship. The year before the expansion draft, Scotty found out that Denise was sleeping with one of his teammates and only using him for the money. He was both livid and hurt by the whole situation. It also didn't help that his roommate, Matty, was the one to break the news to him after he walked in on Denise doing it. Literally the only good thing that Scotty found comfort in was the fact that he never married Denise. His game was off that entire season leading to the draft (and was the main reason he got exposed by the Predators) and even the first few months with The Sound. Most of the league writers assumed it was growing pains and assumed that Scotty just wasn't going to live up to the early career potential. Only Lager knew the real truth after a very drunken confession following a loss to the Preds. After that, Lager helped him to get over Denise and helped him realize that it wasn't his fault that she was a manipulative gold digger. He also asked Lager to caution him if he moved in too quick on the next relationship. For the first time in the past four years, Lager was calling him out.

Scotty's mood was definitely darkened by Lager's accusation. It wasn't a situation where it would damage their friendship. But Scotty responded the only way he could, "Really?"

Lager just shook his head and said, "Did you think this through? Do you really know Alice?"

"Of course, I thought it through. What do you take me for?"

"I'm not trying to be an ass, Scotty. You are the one who said that you jump into relationships hard and fast. After the last time, you wanted me to temper that habit, remember?" Lager took a deep breath, making sure his voice stayed measured. "From what I know, she's good for you. But you guys have only been dating for what, like a month, and you are already asking her to move in. You didn't even tell me that you guys were serious before the bye or even mention that you were considering this. So yeah, I have to question if you thought this through."

Scott just nodded. He didn't really want to admit that Lager had a point. Then he looked down at his two dogs to make sure they were doing okay from all the attention from the three year old as he was trying to keep a check on his temper and made sure he was careful with his word choice since the Lagerfields had a strict no swearing policy around Klaus. Fortunately for the dogs, Chloe was just patiently sitting while Klaus chased Backup in a tiny circle.

Finally he was able to trust himself to say in a low voice that was controlled from any anger but showed the subtle amount of doubt that Lager started to plant. "I thought it made sense. I was missing her so much and she was too scared to sleep at her place whenever I talked to her so I had to do something. I figured that since we were together constantly and practically living together before I went to the

All-Star game, why not ask her to move in? I know it's all of a sudden but I did think through things. And I can promise you that she's different from Denise. She wanted to keep her own lease for a bit yet and already was talking about what it all meant."

"Are you willfully ignoring any warning signs?" asked Lager carefully.

That Scott could answer quickly and strongly, "None. She's never asked for money or anything like that."

"But you got her an iPad for her birthday. That's not nothing."

"Only because hers was stolen and if I didn't offer to replace first, she would have let her sister replace it for her birthday. I got the feeling that if it wasn't for the fact that it wasn't her birthday, she wouldn't have let either of us replace it. She never asked for a new iPad, I offered to replace it first and same thing with her sister."

"So what has she asked for?"

"Time. Mostly. Especially after the break-in."

"Alright. But what is she like around other guys? I remember you said that one of the things you missed right away was the fact that Denise was a shameless flirt with all the guys on the team and it should have been obvious that she was probably hooking up with someone else."

"I haven't seen Alice flirt with anyone. But I'm bringing her out tonight. You can see for yourself. Alice is clever with her word choice to allow for double meanings but it's not flirting in the traditional way."

Lager nodded his head. He said, "Alright man. I don't want to police your relationship. Just trying to look out for you liked I promised. I trust you, dude. As I said before, I think Alice is good for you. If you're happy, I'm happy. So, are we good?"

"Yeah. We're good," as Scott gave Lager a bro hug. Although he was still a little pissed off at Lager for questioning his relationship with Alice, he knew that Lager wasn't trying to be an asshole and was doing what any good friend would do. "Well I should probably get out of your hair and get back to walking these guys before they get too restless."

"Wait, I'll go with you. I just need to grab my skates and get Klaus inside," said Lager as he scooped up his son and ran into the house.

Scotty knew that as annoying as their conversation was, it would be fun to race against Lager on his skates. While he knew that he actually played while they were on the break, Lager most likely didn't. So the more they can fool around, the better. Plus he knew that Chloe would love to get a chance to really run. He could tell that Chloe was ready to get going again as she stood back up. "Wait girl, I promise it will be worth the wait."

Just then, there was his linemate with a set of inline skates on coming down the driveway. "Alright. Let me take one of the dogs off your hands."

"You want to take Backup? But I will warn you, since he's so young, he might need to be carried if he can't keep up."

"Yeah. That's not a problem. Also that's a weird name for a puppy. Just saying." as he reached for Backup's leash from Scotty's hand. Lager then turned to the puppy and said, "You can run super-fast, can't you Little Guy?" Lager turned towards to Scotty and said, "Race you to the gate."

"Oh. Chloe and I will own you. On your mark: ready, set, go."

With that both guys went off using their quick powerful strides. Chloe was running at full tilt and had her tongue hanging out like she normally did when she ran. Scott and Chloe took an easy lead. Lager couldn't keep Backup running quick enough to really race. About midway down the street, Lager actually gave up and scooped up the pup. Lager had no chance to challenge since Scotty and Chloe were already nearly at the fence.

Once Lager got to the fence, he complained, "No fair. Chloe is a ringer and you knew it."

"You are the one who wanted to race. It's not my fault that Chloe is my fast running girl. You even knew that she's one of my favorite training partners before we started." Scott leaned down and rubbed his pitbull's sides as she basked in the attention and from the run itself. "You seriously can't cry foul."

"Watch me," said an indignant Lager.

"Which path do you want me to take?" asked Scotty. They could go to the right and have a longer trip around the gated community. If they went to the left, it would be a short trip.

"Let's go right. Do you want to switch dogs?"

"Okay." Scott lifted the little pup from Lager's hand. He then passed off Chloe's leash with Lager. "Hey little guy. How was your first skate? Did you like it?"

Unfortunately for Scott, Backup threw up onto the ground, catching a little bit of Scott's shirt. Scott pretended that it was nothing and said, "Awww. We must have gone a little too fast for you. I'm sorry." Scott set Backup onto the ground. He looked towards Lager with a lot of humor in his voice, "You knew he was getting motion sick didn't you? Looks like we have to take it slow for a bit and let him walk it off. But when we get back to the fence, we can do one more race. I'll take care of Backup."

They had a casual skate, Lager immediately said, "Sorry about your shirt. I didn't realize he was getting sick. Although I probably would have still given him back to you, if I realized."

"No worries." Scott just said, "Chloe was the same way when she was at that age. He'll outgrow it but I just need to be careful at first. I should have thought about it more. It's been a while since I had a pup this young."

By the end of the skate, he was in a better mood again. He was considering what Lager said earlier about rushing into things a little with Alice. While he didn't doubt that's what they should do, he realized how some people might question their decision and think it's a bad idea. People weren't going to just be excited for them or see how much they loved each other.

"So want to join me for weight lifting or are you needed on for babysitting duty until tonight?"

"Babysitting duty for now. Bridge has a class this afternoon but I'll see you tonight."

10

ALICE

Alice finished up with work after a long day where she found out some discomforting news about the break in from the local newspaper that was she was trying to ignore and headed to the rink as she promised Scott, but she had severe reservations about joining them. She didn't see any cars in the front of the rink like last time so she had a feeling it was going to be just the Sound guys. She knew she had limited skills and was on the slow side even on a good day and that was before playing with actual skilled players who had the speed to play on the NHL level. She didn't stand a chance and she knew it. Yet she decided to walk into the rink with her gear.

"Good to see you again. Can't have you use the same locker room as last time," said the elderly rink manager. If the Sound was playing even in an official capacity, there was no way he was going to let her use their locker room. Nor would she really want to use it when it was filled with her boyfriend's teammates.

"Kinda figured. Is there a specific locker room that I should use?" asked Alice.

"Any of the general locker rooms would do."

"Okay."

At that moment, Alice was even more sure that she was going to be the only one not playing in the NHL tonight. If it was a true family night, she would have thought that there would be an assigned locker room for family members to use. She got dressed and started to head to the ice. The closer she got, the more she knew it was going to be a bad idea. Alice was about ready to turn back and hide when Scott skated up to the boards with a huge smile. He said, "You're here. Come on, Alice and meet everyone."

Alice swore hard and long under her breath as she continued onto the ice. She walked towards Scott as she heard one of the guys say, "Who's the nerd?"

Scott whispered into Alice's ear before letting her get away from the bench. "Ditch the helmet, you won't need it for now."

Alice took off the helmet and tossed it towards the benches. She shot Scott a dirty look as she came onto the ice. She was actually pissed off at him for deceiving her. This was going to be a longer night than she was ready to deal with. Scott put his arm around her back which typically was a soothing move for her by him but in that moment, it wasn't helping things. He said, "You have nothing to worry about. I promise."

Alice knew he promised that in the morning too. But he also knew how she didn't want to make a fool of herself and was self conscious about her hockey ability. She wanted to trust him but everything she was seeing was just feeding her doubt rather than helping her expel them. She also knew that Scott had never done anything to break her trust and he had a plan. He's been her real life knight in shining armor so she was trying.

"Guys. This is my girlfriend Alice. She's going to join for some shooting drills. But then she's going to help coach/ref us for some 4-on-4. While she's a newbie playing, she knows hockey. So I expect you to listen to her when it's time. Alice, we have Crestie on net. Then you know Lager and Corey. You also got PK, Wheels, Karlson, Andy, Dykstman, Hunter, Donnie, Sammy, and Hartsy."

As soon as Scott mentioned that he wanted to her coach while the guys could scrimmage against each other, her mind went into overdrive trying to come up with a plan. Alice recognized a few of the faces right away but she was glad that Scott introduced her to everyone. That way she could start to put the team nicknames to faces and knew what to call them as they were playing. They had three defensemen and seven forwards. She knew that she was going to piss off Scott with one of her moves but she thought it was going to be for the best. Plus it was a little subtle payback for putting her on the spot and making her sweat about her lack of hockey skills in front of his friends.

The shooting drills weren't that bad. She was starting to develop a wrister which actually surprised her. None of her shots even tested Crestor in the slightest. But she was just glad that she was doing the drills and it wasn't that terrible. She continued to feel much more comfortable passing the puck but if she seemed to be doubting herself, Scott would shoot her a reassuring look or give her confidence boost with a comment or two.

Then it was time for the 4-on-4 for the last thirty minutes. The guys initially self-selected their teams and it didn't really surprise her with the initial set up. On one team it was Corey, Lager, Dykstman, Scotty, Sammy and Wheels and on the other side it was the younger guys together who were normally on the same lines: PK, Karlson, Andy, Hunter, Hartsy and Donnie.

As Scott's normal line started to line up, Alice said, "Wait. I want to try something. Dykst, head off for a second. Corey go to the right and Lager head to the left wing." That raised a ton of eyebrows as Lager had been pretty much used as a right wing his whole career with little changes. So she explained herself calmly and dropped a little hockey knowledge to get their attention. "Lager, you played left in the AHL the year you guys won the Calder Cup, right? I know it's been a while but just do it. I think this combo could work out really well but you got to swap sides to make it work for the full impact."

Lager nodded his head and the guys did as she asked by going to the assigned places. Then Alice turned towards Hunter and said, "Don't forget the hip check. You will slow down guys like Scotty better than always going to the poke check throughout the game rather than just on that play."

"Shit, man. I think she might be gunning for you," said Anderson (Andy) said as he matched up against Scott.

"You actually have to win the faceoff for that to happen," said Alice. She knew Scott could defend himself and had one of the best faceoff records in the league. Hunter on the other hand was terrible at them. As she said that, she was feeling the boldest she had in a while and let her bolder side out onto the ice. "You know what, let's make this really interesting. Dykstman switch with Andy."

Alice couldn't help but notice that everyone turned towards Scott for approval. She understood why people were trying to defer to him but she didn't want to have to beg for respect. But Scott said dryly, "Just do it. She's right Andy, you couldn't win a faceoff against me if you tried. Dykstman could." So the guys did as they were told which was a relief but she hoped that she wouldn't need to rely on Scott for everything tonight.

Alice dropped the puck and then immediately things got under way. Scotty grabbed the puck and sent it to Corey. Almost right away, they were off to the races trying to get onto the net. They were looking like they were going to score and Hunter came at Lager with a hip check that landed him solidly on the boards and popped the puck loose. "There we go! Good Hit!" called out Alice as Dykstman took the puck out towards the line. Then he passed towards PK who was in a great position to take the one-timer on Crestor that he had a clean read on and caught with his glove hand.

Alice heard Scotty tell Corey, "If you lose, go out." To which he just said, "okay."

Once everyone was set, Alice dropped the puck again and Scott won it. This time it was a tic-tac-toe style play going from Scotty to Lager who had to swing behind the net. Corey was waiting for the puck to be passed off from Lager along the side wall and he was able to catch Crestor off guard as Corey was able to get the puck slammed into the net. Crestor didn't see the shot since he was being screened by both Hunter and PK.

As Alice was grabbing the puck from Crestie, she said,

"Watch the lines. Both of you screened Alex and he had no chance."

Alice was surprised how much fun she was having as a coach. It was like when she coached swimming but so much faster and the guys knew to make the changes after just saying the word. She was also having fun using ideas that she had from watching games and talking with Scott but never had the opportunity to use. For the most part, they were working out. Dykstman wasn't the ideal center but he improved the play of both PK and Karlson. Dykstman won more faceoffs then Andy would have since Anderson probably had the worst capability of winning faceoffs in the league.

The time flew by. Eventually Ed came out with a whistle and said, "Alright guys. Time to head out. Next group is due up and we got to clean up the ice."

Everyone grabbed their stuff, the pucks and the net. It didn't take long at all for everything to be ready for the zamboni. Alice started to head off when she was grabbed from behind by Scotty. He was smiling and pulled her close as he said, "See that wasn't so bad."

"It was fun. But you are insane."

"So you keep telling me but I don't see you running away yet."

Alice shook her head and said, "True and I don't plan to run anytime soon."

"Good. Are you mad at me?"

"A little. It's just been a really long day and I wasn't expecting that. I don't know what I was expecting, probably more of a family or open skate thing. But it wasn't awful."

"Good. See you on the other side," Scotty said he had to

go the opposite direction for his locker room as Alice. But before he left, he kissed Alice. She melted slightly in his hands and it was hard to stay mad at him.

Scott

Scott was tired but happy after practice. He was surprised how easily they settled into the line formations that Alice asked for. They were definitely different formations then he would have come up with but they were oddly functional and allowed for some good plays. His line with Corey and Lager was scoring a ton. It seemed so crazy when she suggested it but he wasn't going to invite her to play and undermine her role there. Although, he might have fought her if she tried to split up him and Lager but that was not an issue.

Heading into the locker room, Scott was unsure what to expect from the guys. He knew he might take some shit for inviting her in the first place but she surpassed all his expectations with her ability to coach. Her personality was definitely much more mild mannered then Berman. He seldom heard her get so sassy and was unafraid to call bullshit when she wasn't watching Flyers hockey. She rocked in his opinion and it was a good warm up before going back to a real practice in the morning.

Scotty wasn't even surprised when heard Lager go, "Dude, what was that?"

"What do you mean?" Scott was curious about what Lager actually meant by the comments. Was he upset about having Alice there or impressed?

"You are dating someone can actually coach and understand hockey. Shit. I mean seriously, she's a freaking novice in her own skills and a girl but she has good ideas on how to actually create offense. Would not have expected that level of hockey knowledge."

Scotty smiled and said, "Oh that. I take it you liked today then."

"Yeah. Dude, we need to do that freak line of you, me and Corey in a game. It would give teams fits. Plus it was fun to be on that side again for a few shifts. I can't believe that she even knew I was on the opposite side when the Bears won, that was like seven years ago and it was only that year I wasn't on my natural side."

"Yeah. I had no idea that she knew that and it worked out a lot better than I would have even thought. I'll talk to Berman about trying it out in a game. Maybe on the power play since that's been so problematic lately. I think our current line is pretty damn strong for 5 on 5. We don't want too many people knowing that you can play both left and right wing."

"Plus she actually got Hunt to do more than the damn poke check" chimed in Andy "Although I still can't decide if that was a good thing or a bad thing. That was a little rougher than I expected it to be."

"Oh did I hurt you?" asked Hunter incredulously.

"You wish," snapped back Andy.

"So where did you find her?" asked either Karlson or PK. He was leaning that it was probably Karlson due to the subtle hint of an accent. But the two always sounded so similar that it was only on the ice, he could the two apart.

Scotty had no qualms about saying how they met, "Ironically enough right here. She came in for pick-up hockey and I was being a rink rat. We just ran into each other and there was something about her and I wanted to know more."

"Damn!" said Dykstman which surprised Scotty. He was never really close to Dykstman off the ice. Scotty had mixed feelings about having his approval of girlfriends since he knew how Dykstman seldom stayed with a girl for long and it stirred up some feelings of jealousy. Yet at the same time he liked that she was liked by the guys.

"Yeah. I'm just glad that you guys didn't hate having her tonight."

"Nah, man. It was inspired in the end. Although next time just bring her to coach. You work on her game later," said Lager speaking for the team.

"Kay. I know her game needs work. Hell, she even knows it too. I'm pretty sure she would have walked out if I didn't intercept her at the beginning. But I knew she would be a good coach and just not in the field of aquatics"

"Aquatics?" asked Lager.

"She runs a pool or pools, I'm not quite sure, over at one of the universities in town. She coaches swimming and teaches people how to swim but mainly she will keep the pools up and running with lifeguards even if she has to do it herself. I don't fully understand some things about her job. I just know that despite being a Flyers fan first, she gets hockey in addition to being a coach."

Wheels always had an opinion on the Flyers, the whole team knew that he would love to be back with them if they would pay him the same amount of money as the Sound. He said, "Dude, Flyer fans are no joke. Rough at times but that's because they know their team."

Then Donnie asked a question as he was starting to finish up getting dressed, "I've been meaning to ask, if only to get Diane off my case about charity stuff. Although after tonight,

I'm curious about it myself. Is this a keeper or a semi-serious fling?"

Scotty didn't even have to think about it. He knew what he wanted even with having to watch Alice work through her emotions and deal with the break in stuff, he wanted her in his life. "Keeper."

Lager decided to add in his two cents and tell the team everything. "So much so that the asshole asked her to move in over the break."

"Hey." Scotty said, "What can I say, it seemed like a good move to me."

But the announcement that Scotty was asking anyone to move in was big news. It was definitely met with mixed reviews by the guys. Some of the guys were shaking their heads in approval but everyone was just shocked. Scotty just smiled and didn't care since he was happier than ever. Earlier in the day, he was wondering if they were moving too fast after the conversation with Lager. After spending time with her on the ice, he knew that she was right for him. That was his forever girl. He just needed her to fully buy in.

They all finished getting changed and showered. Scotty was one of the last ones to leave as per usual. He hoped that Alice would still be there waiting and didn't just drive home without saying anything. He didn't see any messages from her on his phone, so he figured that she was likely waiting for him. So he headed out to the lobby and saw her talking with Lager and nursing a bottle of coke.

"Hasn't anyone told you that's a terrible recovery drink?" asked Scotty with a smile as he came up to them.

"I know but I like it. So," said Alice with a smile. He half expected Alice to stick her tongue out at the end of the statement but she didn't. Instead she just took a defiant swig of her soda.

Scotty was tempted to pick her and just snuggle with her but with her hockey bag hanging off her shoulder and Lager around, he realized it would be better to just stand close to Alice. He was behind her side and she started to lean her head back onto his shoulder and he asked, "What were you two talking about?"

"Oh nothing important. Just about maybe getting some swim lessons for the little man," said Lager.

Scotty nodded. He was surprised that Lager's wife wasn't going to teach him swimming, but it wasn't his place to question. Alice looked up towards Scott's face with a bit of a wistful look in her eyes and asked, "Ready to go home and/or get something to eat?"

"Mmhmmm."

Alice turned her gaze back towards Lager and said, "We can touch base about the lessons later. Just email or text me. Brigitta has my contact information."

"Sounds good. I will let you lovebirds be. You better talk to Berman or I will about the freak line." Lager said.

"I will. Have you known me to not bring something up to him like that?" replied Scotty as Lager headed back towards the Sound's locker room so he would have easy access to his car. Scotty took pride in his captain's role and wanted to do what's best for the team. That meant making sure he talked with the coaches about the lines and if needed doing his own meetings. Hell, it was why he wanted to bring in a coach for the OTA practice even if it was her girlfriend.

Alice looked up towards Scotty and asked, "The freak line?"

"That's what Lager is calling the line that you came up with with Corey, him and me. He's seeing it as a great way to increase scoring and I agree."

"Ah, that makes sense. I should have thought of all the lines that would be the one most appropriate to be called The Freak Line since it's such a weird concept on paper."

"Won't lie, I wasn't so sure that line combination would work when you tossed out Dkyst. Although I'm not surprised that you split up the three of us up but why Corey? Also how did you know about Lager being able to do both sides?"

"For Corey, that's obvious. He has great breakout capability that's not typical in most third liners. That and the three of you are friends off the ice and that always helps with the communication. I've noticed that half the time you consider Dykstman as an afterthought except when you are the ice together. So I was trying to figure out how to make that work. It wasn't until I remembered there was a few games that Lager did on the left wing in the Calder Cup playoffs that I knew it actually would work. Him succeeding in that role helped to kill the Phantoms hopes to get the Cup that year."

"The Phantoms?" Scotty knew the team but he was trying to figure out which era of Phantoms she was talking about since they moved around a bit recently. He could see her liking them since they were the Flyers farm team and she was a fan who would enjoy watching the prospects develop.

"The Philadelphia Phantoms use to have cheap tickets for college students. Jenna and I would go to games all the time in undergrad."

"Don't tell me you were a puck bunny back in college?" asked Scotty incredulously. He honestly couldn't see it but he knew a few girls from school that were pretty wild in college and really tamed down as they got older.

"Have we met?" asked Alice as she squinted her eyes. "I am not a person to throw myself at every hockey player they see. I strictly went to the games to watch hockey. I never had the confidence to believe that I stood a chance with a professional athlete even if they were in the AHL. I was a geeky, quiet girl back them who knew her sports. I **really** didn't believe anyone who said I was pretty back then. So there was no throwing myself at anyone let alone a hockey player."

"Seems like you have gotten over some of that. Cause when I see you, I see a mostly confident, geeky girl who loves sports and is gorgeous to boot" said Scott as he kissed her on the nose. She didn't flinch or blush. She just tilted her chin upwards to kiss him on the lips. When their lips separated, he said, "I'm pretty lucky to have you all to myself. You really rocked it out there today."

"Thanks for trusting me to try out some of my crazy ideas and letting me coach at all. I seriously had no idea that this was what you were planning when you invited me to come out tonight. But you could have told me."

"No problem. But I knew if I told you what I had in mind, you would have bailed." he smiled as he kissed her one more time. "Hell, I know that you only came onto the ice at all because I stopped you from running. You have to get over you fear of sucking and show the world the talents that you have."

"I'm trying."

"I know and that's all I ask." Scott started to look into her eyes, trying to get a read of what was going on in her mind. When he first came out, he thought she saw the spark of pure happiness in them. But now they were starting to get a little less of that spark of joy in them as they talked about her insecurities. He wasn't sure what was causing that dullness, was it just talking about her past or something else entirely. So he continued, "Besides, I think you are awesome and did a great job today. Let's go get some dinner before we head home. How about we get some sushi?"

Alice shook her head and said, "That sounds positively devine."

Alice

Alice followed Scott to the sushi place that he suggested. It didn't take long for them to arrive since it was close to the rink. Scott was waiting for her outside of his SUV. He was smiling with his red hair kind of flowing to the side as he had his head tilted with a goofy smile on his face. He looked absolutely gorgeous in that moment. Although she thought she saw that he had a hat or a beanie tucked in his pocket most likely to help hide his hair and his identity.

She was exhausted after hockey and work but she knew that the night was far from over. At least they could talk about their future together as they ate one of her favorite meals. She was so happy when he suggested getting sushi for dinner.

"Hey babe," he said as she exited her car.

She said a stupid little "Hey" back at him as he grabbed her hand. He lead her into the small restaurant. Upon entering the place, Alice knew that Scott had to be a regular there since all the staff knew him. That and when they were seated, he didn't even look at the menu at all.

Scott opened the conversation with "So do you want to talk here or wait until we get home?"

"You are making this sound way more dramatic than it

should be. I'm not going to back out of moving in. I just want to make sure we are on the same page for stuff."

"Really?"

Alice laughed to try and soften the tension some by saying, "Yeah. I'm moving in. It's kind of a big deal. All I want is a plan. I don't want to freeload but my salary is tiny, especially in comparison to yours. So I don't know how I can honestly contribute in a fair way. Nor do I want you to take on my debt. That's my shit to pay."

Scott grabbed her hand and started to run his thumbs over the hand trying to relax her. He didn't say anything right away since the waitress stopped by their table for the orders and almost immediately set down their drinks in front of them. But the entire time, Scott was looking and marveling her. She nearly asked him what was so strange.

"It's cool babe. Are you really that afraid that you can't pay any bills? "

"Yeah. Basically."

Scott looked at her with a mock serious look on his face as he said, "What if I told you that I don't want your money?"

Alice shook her head as she drank some of the tea that she ordered. She smiled and said, "But that's not fair to you. I should help out with some of the bills."

"Do you have anything in mind?"

"Maybe the food shopping, cable and another utility. I would want to see where things are at after I pay my other bills first."

"Sure, babe, whatever you want to pay. I don't really care. But you know I can eat a lot. Not everyone skips breakfast like every day of the week."

"I know but at least I can be contributing."

"Okay."

Even though Scott was being super agreeable and easy going about the situation, it was making Alice feel more and more ill at ease. She wasn't sure if it was the anxiety from the burglary stress and letting everything get to her. "You are really being so agreeable with this. It's like you don't care."

"In some ways, I don't. I'm just happy that you want to move in. I don't care if you help out with the bills. It's just money."

"Must be nice not to have to worry about money or think it's not a big deal." That's when Alice knew she was letting things get to her and she was lashing out in a way that she wasn't happy with. It was something she hated about herself. "Sorry. I am being an asshole and letting stress get to me. I shouldn't have said that."

"It's cool. I remember having to have multiple jobs to help pay for hockey before I got drafted and getting worried about money."

The server returned with their orders so they momentarily paused their conversation. Alice was still beating herself up for not having a better control over her emotions and snapping at Scott. But she was intrigued about hearing about Scott's past. She didn't know much. "So you had multiple jobs too?"

"Yeah. But I hated them. Construction in the day and bar backing at night. Neither were fun but they allowed me to play juniors. Knowing how much work it was, kept me focused on making it in hockey. You at least like your jobs. So I understand and just contribute any way you can."

"Okay. The other issue will be telling our families. We haven't met each other's family. I don't know about your family, but mine will freak out, especially since they haven't met you. They will think that we are rushing things."

"Take a deep breath. I'm going to meet your family soon. We can do a trip to visit my family once the season is over. They will love you."

"They aren't coming to anymore of your games this season?"

"No. Not unless we go deep into the playoffs. Then maman would insist upon coming to the games. It's hard for them to come to a lot of games. I grew up in a fairly rural part of Quebec. It's not easy to arrange trips. Plus like you, my parents don't want me paying for everything. They would rather do it on their own so they don't get to visit often. But we can Facetime with them tonight if you like. They know about you. Hell, they have known your name for a while now."

Alice shot him a look. She knew he was teasing her about how vague she was with dating life to her family and didn't mean any harm with his comment. That's where they were just different people in some ways: Scott didn't care who knew about them and she was just more reserved. "Sure that will be okay. I just hope that it goes well."

"It will. It's amazing how not even an hour ago you were working with a bunch of NHL players with hockey and you completely impressed them and yet you are doubting that you can impress my parents. There's no doubt you will impress my parents if that makes any difference," said teasing Scott

"One those are two very different skills. Just because I can give direction to people who live and breathe hockey, it doesn't mean your parents will like me. Besides, have we met?

I can be rather good at self-doubt. It's your parents, I want to be able to impress. Some self-doubt is normal, just like I want your friends to like me as well."

"Which is why I keep telling you that it's absurd to even worry. You are amazing."

"You act like I have no confidence. I do. I just more.... Well I'm not cocky. I'm a bit of a planner. If I think about the worst case scenario ahead of time, it's not a big deal in the moment and it almost never happens. I know what I'm doing."

"Yeah I know and I know you have confidence too. You traveled to Paris on your own. That's not something anyone will do. But you should be cocky on some things."

"That might never happen," Alice said with a bit of a laugh. Scotty was smiling at her.

"Should we head back to the pups?"

"Oh yes."

Scott paid for the dinner and they headed back to their cars. As she was about to unlock her car, he turned her around and kissed her passionately. She returned the favor as she started to massage his tongue with hers. Alice pulled away. "I'm sorry again for being a bit off tonight. I know you just want to make everything easy. I've just had a lot on my mind. While I was at work, I found a news article about my case. Let's just say a lot more happened that night than I thought and not in a good way. I found out that there may have been multiple people who broke into my place and I got off really lucky since one of the people arrested was arrested with a bullet. Then you threw the hockey at me which I really enjoyed but it didn't help with the stress levels. So all in all it's been a long day and I don't mean to get persnickety."

Scott chuckled in disbelief, "Persnickety? Who uses that word in real life? Let alone to talk about themselves?"

"Apparently me."

"That's one of the reasons that I love you. You keep me on my toes. But I think you could relax a little and let people help you. Or at least, let me. I don't care if you piss off other people by second guessing everything or not letting them help." Scott then leaned in for another kiss. This one was shorter and sweeter.

"Yeah. I know and I'm trying. You do mean everything to me."

"It's okay. But let's get home. That way you can make it up to me there in the privacy of **our** home."

Alice shook her head and said, "You are absolutely incorrigible sometimes."

"But you know that you love it."

The thing was Scott was absolutely right. Alice loved when he was being forward with her and wanted to do it all the time. Just like she didn't care if he told the whole world that they were dating. For the first time in forever, she was in love and absolutely believed that he wanted to protect her while at the same time let him grow. She knew that she didn't need to be so independent all the time.

"True. But maybe I just love all of you."

11

SCOTT

They got back to his place. It was a fairly short drive. He was ready to kick back with his family at home. He just hoped that dinner would be the end to Alice of worrying so much about moving in. With the burglary, he understood that Alice needed to work through stuff and would get stressed out and he knew that his place was the best place for that.

As he entered the house, his phone went off. He knew it had to be his parents since Alice was behind him and those were the only people who would typically call at this hour. He picked up the phone as he greeted the dogs that were waiting by the door. Since he was distracted by his mom, he didn't shut the door quickly enough and Backup ran out the door. Fortunately, Alice caught Backup as he was leaping down the steps. "Whoa there. We can't be running out there with no leash or parent. You know that, Backup," Alice said softly as she grabbed the little guy. Scott was glad she was there to back him up in that moment especially since his mom was complaining about how he didn't call right after the All-Star game or when he got back to Cleveland.

Before he had a chance to apologize saying how he was busy was, "I bet it's in part due to your new girlfriend," his mom said in jest. Although Scott felt guilty, he remembered how Denise didn't like to spend time with his family since she couldn't speak French and didn't like being left out of the conversation. So he didn't talk to his family a whole lot when they were dating and he still felt guilty about withdrawing from his family and how much pain he caused everyone.

"I flew back late last night and I've been busy today with trying to get the training schedule back to normal. I lost track of time. I'm sorry maman. But I would like to introduce you to Alice and we have some news. Can I call you on FaceTime?"

"Sure."

Scott hung up the phone and looked towards Alice. He was surprised to see her playing with the two dogs by passing the puck side to side with his one of his sticks as the dogs tried to catch it. He knew it was his stick since it was way too large for her. It was so adorable that he decided to film it. He mostly filmed the two dogs trying to snag the puck away and all that could be seen of Alice was her feet. Once he got a few seconds, he threw it up as an Instagram story tagging Alice as he did with the phrase "So this what happens I'm not looking."

After that was done, he kissed Alice's nose and asked, "Ready to talk to my parents?"

Alice leaned his stick against the wall and said, "As ready as I'm going to be."

Scotty knew that she was nervous and he hugged her and

said with a reassuring smile, "You'll be fine. Just remember my mom speaks only French. It doesn't have to be perfect. Just trying will be enough and I can help to translate if needed."

They both moved over to the sofa and she snuggled into his side. He had a feeling that she was trying to hide some but he didn't really give much room to do so. He dialed his mom's phone using FaceTime. Almost instantaneously, his mom said, "What took so long?" Clearly directed at him and then she looked towards Alice and smiled and said, "Is this is Alice?"

"Yes, madam," said Alice in a super formal tone, but it was in French. Scotty just pulled her in close and started to rub her arm after he did so.

His mom beat him to saying, "Don't be so formal. So you speak some French?"

"A little. I can typically it understand it when I hear it but I get shy speaking in French and I forget the words."

"I'm the same way, it's why I have the boys translate for me."

Scotty nearly dropped the phone in surprise. He never knew his mom understood a word of English. Him and his dad would always translate for his mom. He tried to hide his shock but he knew his mom would know right away. He knew he wasn't doing a good job at hiding his shock since his mom immediately said, "Don't act so surprised, Scotty. I watch all your games and I live in Canada. It's hard not to know some English." His mom paused a moment before saying with a wink, "Besides, it's sometimes useful when people don't think you understand what they are saying. You get to see their true selves."

"True. I've seen that a few times myself." added in Alice. She didn't elaborate but he knew there had to be a story or two in her. He just hoped he could get them out of her.

"It's nice to actually be able to converse with you. His last girlfriend wouldn't even try to speak to me if Scotty or his dad wasn't around."

Scott winced at that comment. He still harbored guilt over how Denise was awful to his mom. He hoped that it would be better with Alice and that seemed to be the case thus far. His mom was all smiles and joking around. Plus he still couldn't believe how his mom actually confided that she could understand English. That was unreal.

"I'll always..." Alice paused and whispered in Scott's ear looking for the word to try. He gave it to her. He almost gave her the slight grammar correction but she caught herself as she restarted and said, "I'll always try."

Scott was proud of his girlfriend.

"Which is all that you need to do. So Scott, you said you had some news that you wanted to share," said his mom.

"Where's dad? I want to make sure he's here too," asked Scott.

"He's here" as his mom held the phone so they could see that his dad was sitting next to his mom, much as he and Alice were sitting. His mom was clearly just keeping the phone super close to her initially. "So what's the news?"

"As you know, Alice has been staying with me before the All-Star game due to the burglary. Well, I liked having her here. I asked her to move in permanently and I got her a puppy."

"So what did she say?" asked his dad, always a bit impatient. He knew that his dad wouldn't care about a dog.

"I said yes this morning," said Alice.

"That's wonderful!" said his mom. "We'll have to meet your family, and what do they think?"

Scotty didn't want Alice to get grilled by his mom. He said quickly, "It was decided today. They don't know yet. We can arrange something where everyone meets up. But it's been a long day."

"Okay fine. We will leave you be. I know you just want to get off the phone so you can be together. It's fine since we know what it's like to be young and in love. Congratulations. We love you. Both of you."

"Love you too. Night mom and dad," replied Scott.

"Good night, Mr. and Mrs. Wheiland," said Alice.

"Alice, don't be so formal with us. Good night." said his mom as she was hanging up the phone. Scott set his phone down onto the sofa. He then laid his head on top of Alice's and kissed her forehead.

"So that wasn't so bad, was it?" whispered Scott?

"It really wasn't. Your family seemed really nice."

Scott felt like keeping the mood light. "You know that's the most I heard you speak in French and you know what, it's not half bad except for one thing. What's up with your accent?"

"What do you mean?" asked Alice in an obvious innocence ploy. Scott was tempted to tickle her sides to let her know that he was onto her but instead he just kissed her forehead.

"Your accent. It's really jacked up."

Alice looked at him with mock seriousness. "What do you expect an American to sound like when they were taught a

Parisian accent in school but had to turn to friends from Quebec to pass their oral exams to sound like?"

Scotty smiled, "Touché, but we will need to fix it. Get something that doesn't sound so jacked up."

"You can try. " Alice said with a small laugh. Then she went slightly more pensive. "You really think things were okay with your parents?"

Scott was smiling, "Yeah I do." Scott reached for his phone. He knew that his mom wouldn't hold back on her opinion. While she was too polite to say anything on the phone if Alice was in earshot, she would always text her opinions to him. He realized it might not have been the best idea to post on Insta before calling his parents: his phone had so many notifications. He ignored those and then went to look for the text messages. He saw the message from his mom just like he thought he would see. He kissed Alice and said, "Would you like to see proof?"

Alice nodded and he showed his phone to her. She read the message that his mom said thought Alice seemed liked a keeper but don't rush into it too much. Alice smiled deeply and melted into Scott as she fully relaxed.

"That seemed too easy. You know my family won't be that way. There will be 20 questions at least. Do you still want to do it with all the road games? I could reschedule if you like," as Alice started to ramble. Scott kissed her lips to get her to quiet her worry.

"It'll be fine. Don't reschedule, if you do it will cause more issues. I wouldn't have agreed to it if I thought it was going to be a problem." Then Scott pulled her on top of his lap and had her look into his eyes at that moment. "Besides, who suggested the date your family comes over?"

Alice closed her eyes and it looked like her uneasiness about her family coming over was starting to subside. Scott just didn't get what the big deal was. He knew the family visit would go okay, why wouldn't her family like him or see how happy she was with him. Alice spoke and said, "You. And I know you're right. I shouldn't be freaking out and I need to relax. It just seems like since the break in, my emotions have been all over the place."

"I know babe. I would do anything to see you feeling okay again all the time. But until then, we will go through it together. It will be okay. Also, there might be some hope for you after all. You are finally playing around with a puck. It was so utterly adorable to see you use **my** stick to entertain our dogs. Do you do that often when I'm not looking?"

Unsurprisingly, Alice rolled her eyes at Scott and said, "How many times do I have to tell you I'm not afraid of the puck when it's floor hockey. The ice makes the puck move so much faster and I lose control. I suck and I don't like sucking. And yes, I do it sometimes with Chloe."

"You don't suck. Okay, you kinda do, but that's because you need to practice. You can't just pass it up or not play around with a puck. And you know what, if you improve the stick handling, I'm sure you could get yourself a hockey coaching job. You were pretty awesome and could do it with a moment's notice."

Alice smiled and said, "No thanks to you. But what if I don't want to be a hockey coach and stick with my current stuff?"

Scott kissed her on the nose and said, "If you are happy, that's all I care about."

12

SCOTT

Scott was dead tired after the last game. It was a hard fought win against the Blues. They were being stingy with allowing goals in the net. Fortunately, Crestie was just as stingy as rookie netminder which meant it went into a shootout. It was a long night and getting back to the hotel was a godsend.

Collapsing on the bed, he pulled out his iPad so he could check in on Alice and see her thoughts on the game and how her day was going. Even though they had a couple days together. If he was being honest with himself, he missed sleeping and lying beside her at night.

As soon as Scott saw Alice's face, he knew that all was not well and most likely it was more than just him being gone. So while he was trying to stifle a yawn, he said, "Hey babe, what's up?"

"Long day." Alice said. At first, he wasn't sure if he would actually hear what was on her mind. But after taking a deep breath, it was clear that she was steeling herself up some before continuing on. "I got a letter from the prosecutor today. They charged a kid in my burglary. I need to write a victim impact statement."

Scott was surprised that she didn't seem particularly happy at the news then he realized it brought up all the emotions that she was trying to hard to bury and avoid. But she was talking, that was an improvement than a lot of days. At least, in her lap were both of the dogs and she was just rubbing them casually. He knew that he should put a positive spin on the situation although the whole time all he wanted to do was hug her. So he took comfort that she wasn't alone and both of the dogs would help to keep her spirits up.

"Well at least they caught someone," supplied Scott.

"Yeah that's what I'm telling myself. But it's in juvenile court so I know regardless of what happens they will only be sentenced for a short time. It just sucks. It brings everything up again. I'm just not ready to write the victim impact statement."

Scott couldn't blame her. It seemed like it was a lot on her and he hated that he wasn't there to help. The only thing could do was see if there was a chance he could be there to hug her as she filled it out so he asked, "When do you need to send back the victim impact statement?"

"A week."

"That's not so bad. I will be back before the week is up so I can be there to help you through as you write it. Maybe writing the statement might help you heal."

Scotty pulled up his travel calendar. He knew that the Sound would be in playing in Philly soon but he couldn't remember how that trip lined up compared to Alice's travel schedule. He was hoping he could surprise her with a trip to the game. He saw it exactly as he thought.

"That's what they say. I'm just not quite ready for it. I might wait until you get back."

"That's fine. I know it's both welcome and unwelcome news."

Alice shifted the subject quickly by saying "So tough game tonight."

"Yeah. That wasn't the win I was hoping for."

"They seemed tougher than I thought they would be. I should have known Berube would expect excellence but that didn't seem like an awful team. But seems like Crestor had things under control."

"Yeah. I still hate the shoot out."

"I do too. But you got the win."

"We did. I just hope they don't get a hefty upgrade at the trade deadline."

"Cleveland might get an upgrade too. It's an interesting market if the rumors are true. While I would hate for Petey to be sent down to make room for a trade there are some interesting names being bandied about and it's not just potential free agents."

Scott didn't like the direction that the conversation was taking since it meant changing up the team dynamic and he wasn't sure if that would be a good thing. Besides he needed him to talk about something else entirely so looking at the schedule would be pointless if he didn't switch topics, so he said, "Maybe. But I'd rather not think about too many trades before anything happens. I can't control it. Hey quick question do you have anything planned on February 12th?"

"I don't think so. Just working that day. Why?"

"No reason. Just curious if you were home between conferences."

"Yeah. Do you want me to keep the date open for something?"

"I think so but I'm not sure if everything will work out."

"Okay. Just let me know one way or another."

Scott was grateful that she was distracted by her emotions. He knew that normally she would be asking so many questions and trying to figure out what he had up his sleeve. Instead she was being open to the idea of doing something with him without prying or even questioning why he was trying to plan something when they were away. He was going to take it.

"Will do babe." Scott actually couldn't stop his yawning any more. "So I think some sleep is called for."

"Yeah. I know I should sleep but it's not the same when you are gone."

"Trust me, I feel the same way. But it will help make the time go faster and I will soon see you."

"I can't wait."

That's when Scott kissed his fingers on to the screen and said, "Night babe. Je t'aime."

Alice returned the gesture and she said, "Night Scotty. I love you too."

"Night, I'm going to hang up now" Scott said teasingly but he knew that he wasn't ready to hang up despite the fact that he was just yawning and staring at his girlfriend. He wasn't actually fully ready to hang up on the call.

"Alright."

They both weren't eager to shut off the phone. It was something where they smiled and just looked at each other for far longer than they probably should have. Eventually Scott said, "Try to get some sleep" and he hung up the phone.

While he was glad that the police caught someone, he hated seeing the toll all the stress was doing on his beautiful girl. He wanted to make her smile and he had an idea on a way to make her smile especially since she knew that there shouldn't be a massive shoehorn thrown into the mix. Instead of turning off his iPad, he decided to do a quick search. He looked at airline and hockey ticket prices in Philly. He realized that while the tickets weren't cheap, they weren't that expensive that he would feel guilty about it. It would be easy to treat Alice to a game in her favorite city and maybe get to hang out with some of her friends. The only thing that she might hate was for her favorite team to lose but he wasn't going to play dead again just to make her smile.

Alice

It was still dark, so Alice knew it had to be rather early in the morning. It was clear from everyone's reactions that Scott was home. If she didn't know that he was coming back in the early morning, she probably would have let her panic taken over. Hell, she panicked momentarily until reminding herself that it was just him. Instead, she just opened up the bedroom door. Immediately, Chloe ran towards the hall in an extremely excited state while Alice walked out much more cautiously. She left Backup on the bed.

As she was coming down the stairs, she heard Scott say in a hushed voice, "Shh, Chloey girl. You're going to wake up the whole house." Alice knew that he was rubbing behind her ears even before she spotted him. But the moment she saw him, she laid her head against the wall with a lazy smile on her face. He just seemed too perfect: had the chiseled good looks, so caring and adorable with his dogs.

Alice decided to speak up, "Too late on waking up the whole house." Alice didn't mention of course she was awake if Chloe came down the stairs that quickly.

Scott looked up with an evil grin on his face as he said, "Hey, who said you could wear that?"

Alice looked down to see the Sound t-shirt that she was wearing. She knew she stole one of Scotty's t-shirts before going to bed after realizing she was out of her clean pj tops and was too lazy to do laundry at night. But she just smiled since she knew it was his, it was comfy, smelt like him and showed off her legs.

"You weren't here to ask. So I let myself. I hope that's not a problem."

Scotty set everything down and come right towards her. He immediately pressed her to the wall and started to kiss her passionately. On instinct, she wrapped her legs around him and fisted his hair. After a few moments of passionately kissing, he pulled back slowly to say, "No, no problem. But I will have to take that back eventually."

"Were you planning on doing that tonight?" asked Alice more hopeful that they weren't going to sleep.

Scotty started to kiss down her neck before saying, "Between the game and your family coming over, sleep is definitely called for. But I haven't gotten to touch you for so long. So I just might."

Alice could see the lust in his eyes and she personally loved it as she gave into the pleasure centers that Scott was igniting with each and every kiss along her neck as she said, "But you want to stay awake doing this, don't you?"

"Oh yes."

Then Chloe climbed up the stairs and headed straight for the bedroom. It was clear that she was ready for bed again. Alice and Scott knew that love making while the two dogs were in the room was always problematic. So they would likely just try to look for a different location. Hell, Alice was even comfortable doing it right there on the wall but it seemed like Scott was having some second thoughts.

Alice said, "Wait, I thought we were going to delay sleep a little longer."

Scott looked up at her and said, "But Chloe just took back the bed. I know that even though I haven't seen the little guy just yet I'm assuming he's still on the bed. I know the guest room isn't set up with a bed yet since the movers aren't coming until next week."

Alice was being just as lustful in the moment and didn't want to just go to bed. She was so glad her boyfriend was home. Sure they had the new relationship energy going on but it was fun and she missed Scott while he was on his road trip. Knowing that he was only in town for a couple days made her want to use all the time they had together. So she said, "Who said we needed to go do it in bed? We could do it right here. Beds can be a tad overrated..."

"Oh you minx" Scott said as he started to go full force with the unbridled passion. He pushed the t-shirt up and massaged her breasts as she started to remove his belt, pants and boxers. It didn't take long for him to slip into her. It was hard, powerful and sexy. Alice clawed at his back. She could feel his release into her just as she reached her own point of ecstasy. As quickly as it happened, they were done but they were both happy.

They walked back to the bedroom. Chloe was already asleep in her usual spot after greeting Scott and then deciding it was time to go to bed. Backup on the other hand was wide awake and was seeking as much attention as he could from his dad. Alice couldn't help but smile blissfully as she started to climb into her side of the bed. She loved seeing Scott with the dogs and was looking forward to seeing how he was with her niece in the morning.

As Scott was rubbing Backup some, Alice asked, "How was the trip back from Columbus?" She knew enough not to ask about the game itself. It was a tough loss where the guys just looked like they were dead on their feet the whole time.

"Long and tedious. Just glad to be back."

"I am glad you're back too. Missing you is only one of the reasons why I borrowed one of your shirts."

Scott moved Backup to the side so he could lie down on the bed next to Alice. He grabbed Alice tightly and started to snuggle in. "You know, it's pretty sexy seeing you in it. I'm half tempted to ask you wear that every time I'm coming home."

As Scott snuggled into her neck and tickled her some with his scruff, she felt at home and could drift to sleep easily for the first time in days.

Alice heard Scott's alarm go off earlier then she wanted. She turned over in dismay. She always planned to get up early when his alarm went off since he always got up with her when she got up for work and to help get ready for the day, but in the moment she wasn't a fan of the decision. She felt Scott let go of her and he silenced the alarm. He was trying to be quiet and let her sleep for the most part even though he kissed her ear which sent everything tingling.

"Ugh, it's too early," complained Alice.

"Sorry. I have morning practice. I'll be back soon. You don't have to get up."

"No I want to get up with you today. What do you want for breakfast?" asked Alice as she started to push herself up to a sitting position.

Scott smiled in surprise as he said, "Hey, isn't that my line?"

"Well normally, I'm the one who has to get out the door early. I figured that since it's you getting up early today, I could return the favor and make some food for you."

"Please tell me that means you will eat breakfast with me too."

Alice shook her head and said, "Yeah, not with these nerves. My stomach is crankier than usual. I will be lucky to stomach a coffee today." Scott was giving Alice a look and was clearly disapproving. "Just because I have a cranky stomach, doesn't mean I can't make you anything. Do you want your usual or would like something else?"

"The usual is fine." said Scotty who was clearly disappointed in Alice.

"What?"

"You should eat."

"I will. Just not anytime soon. It'll be fine. I'd rather have my stomach settle down so I'm not immediately following the meal with meds." Alice reached towards him and kissed him lightly. She said, "Go shower, I'll make an egg white omelet and a side of Canadian bacon."

"You know we just call it bacon," said Scotty with a kiss clearly teasing her. "But sounds good."

Alice started to get up and that cued the dogs that it was time to go downstairs for food. Chloe immediately hopped off the bed as usual. Surprising everyone, Backup decided to try and leap off the bed as well. Scotty actually caught Backup before the little pup crashed to the ground from such a tall distance for a little puppy. Alice immediately asked "Is he okay? I knew it was going to happen sooner or later since he decided yesterday that he could handle the stairs in both directions. But I figured he would realize that this bed is much larger than the stairs for a couple more days."

"He's good. But we might want to get some landing pads for him set up around the bed" Scotty said as he set down the confused pup. He leaned down and said to the puppy, "You gotta watch where you are landing. I know you are growing up so quickly and soon you will be able to leap down without getting hurt but you need to grow a bit more."

Upon standing up, Scotty pulled Alice in close and kissed her. She smiled and said, "Don't start something you can't finish now."

"Oh I can finish. I just don't want to do it that quickly for your sake. So I'll be good." Scott said as he started to let her go.

Alice went downstairs. She immediately fed the dogs and set about to making breakfast for Scotty. She was glad his kitchen was super easy to navigate. Even though she was competent cook, she was not one to spend more time in the kitchen then she had to. Even when Scotty was away, she would barely cook herself dinner, usually settling for a salad. She started the coffee.

When Scott came down, everything was done cooking but she never got a chance to plate it. He smiled "Smells good, babe. I could get used to this." Then he started to load up a plate with his favorite morning meal.

Alice teased, "Don't get too used to it. You might end up hungry along the way."

Scott grabbed her by the waist and held her for a moment. Alice just inhaled his scent with pleasure since it was a mixture of his woody cologne, soap and just natural scent. Scott nibbled at her neck when he said, "That's no fun. I like having you cook for me." Eventually, he broke away so he could eat his meal. He sat down at the counter and dig into his meal. Alice sat on the counter across from him drinking some coffee. In between bites, he asked, "Have you heard from anyone?"

"Not yet but I expected to hear from everyone later. I know the plan was for people to come in about noon. The one variable was if they got Noelle up and onto the road in time. My dad will be here on time at noon."

"That's not too bad. Plenty of time after practice. Do you need me to pick up anything on my way out?"

"Mhmmm. I don't think so." Alice looked in the fridge and freezer to make sure they everything. "Crap, I meant to pick up some chicken fries from Giant Eagle and forgot."

"Chicken fries?"

"My niece is super picky so she prefers her chicken nuggets to be in the shape of a French fry. I don't get it. But I was going to get the bag and forgot. Would you mind running to Burger King for a box of them on the way home?"

"Okay. That's easy enough. Anything else?"

"Nope, I got everything else covered."

"Just remember to relax today, okay. It'll be fine." Scott said so reassuringly almost to the point of being cocky. It was clear he didn't have one doubt about the afternoon plans while Alice was trying not to let her doubts take control. She really wanted to impress her family and she wasn't sure if she could.

"I'll try. But you are one of the few boyfriends, they have ever met and not only that, I am introducing you to them after we started living together. They have never cared for my boyfriends before so yes, I'm nervous. I just want everything to go smoothly."

Scott put his empty plate in the sink and started to grab Alice to pull her into a romantic embrace. He kissed her and said, "It will. But don't forget, I'm dating you and not your family. I'll always be there for you. Unfortunately, it's time for me to head out to practice."

13

ALICE

Alice was driving herself crazy and she knew it. She was worried about her family not liking Scotty and really any judgement on her relationship. She needed to relax so she threw on Louden Swain's acoustic album on the stereo while she finished the last minute cleaning. Lunch was pretty much ready and the house was more or less spotless. She even had her jersey and purse ready to grab so they could leave for the game at a leisurely pace.

Chloe and Backup started to rush towards the garage door which meant that Scotty was home from practice. When the door opened, he immediately handed her a small Burger King bag as he said, "Hey baby" and started to give the two pups some attention.

"Hey, how was practice?"

"Not bad. Focused on some of the special teams drills mainly today. But I might have a surprise for you at the game this evening." he said with a sly grin.

Alice was instantly intrigued but she knew Scotty was likely to be super tight lipped about what he had planned. He would hold out and make her wait. So Alice would have to settle on being coy and settling for a clue or two, "Really? Should I be worried?"

"Nope. But you will like it and you will know it when you see it."

"Okay. But cryptic much?"

"Yeah. But you know you love the suspense," Scott said with a chuckle. Alice just rolled her eyes. She really wished he would just tell her. Both of the dogs were desperate to go out and play for a little bit. They were keeping Scotty almost pinned in by the door hoping to nudge their dad out. "Let me take the pups out. They seem like they want a walk."

Alice said, "That would be perfect."

Alice put away the cleaning supplies and got a beer out of the fridge. She took a sip straight from the bottle rather than taking the time to put it in a glass. She was hoping to take a few sips before anyone showing up. But of course, the doorbell rang almost immediately.

So Alice quickly headed towards the door and opened it. On the other side of the door, she saw her mom, sister and niece. Her niece looked like a miniature version of her mom with long straight blonde hair who bounced into her arms for a hug saying "Aunt Alice."

"Hey Noelle."

Noelle smiled and was lowered back to the ground. Allison immediately asked "So where's your new man? I would have thought he would be here to meet us."

"He's walking the dogs. I'm surprised that you didn't see him as you were driving through the neighborhood. He should be back any minute now. Do you need to go to the bathroom or would you like a drink?"

Everyone wanted a drink and they went to the living room. Everyone got settled in, and Alice was actually getting curious about where both her dad and Scott could be. Scott should have been back by now and her dad was usually on time. There wasn't any messages on her phone so she decided to make a lame excuse to get something out of the garage since she figured she could look for Scott or give him a call in private. Especially since if Scotty was a no show, her family were going to hate him for not supporting her.

As soon as she walked out into the garage, she saw the most ideal situation ever. Scotty and her dad were talking to each other in the driveway while Chloe and Backup were playing in the front yard. She loved seeing her two favorite men chatting casually and looking extremely comfortable. She walked over towards them.

"Hey. I see you two met without any problems" as she gave her dad a hug before standing close to Scott almost inviting him to grab her around her waist as he so often did. "Everyone else is inside. We probably don't want to keep them waiting too much longer."

Scott called for Chloe and Backup to come to him and the dogs instantly came to him. He took the precaution of putting Chloe back on a leash but he let Backup just go straight up the stairs of the garage. Alice put down the garage door. As soon as they were in the house, the little 4 year old was there to greet them. She was enchanted by the two dogs especially Backup since he was tiny like her and kept saying "so cute" in a sing song voice. Chloe was behaving well and didn't seem to have any of the malice that Scott mentioned when they first started dating. She was wondering if Scott was putting her on about Chloe's behavior with women.

At first, everything felt stilted and awkward. They started to have the lunch that Alice prepared: just some burgers, salmon, salad and pasta salad although Noelle had the chicken fries instead of the other meat options. It seemed like there was a guard up initially by her family despite how charming Scotty was trying to be. But there was polite conversation and things seemed to be okay. It seemed like whenever things got quiet or weird, Noelle would get silly with her food which helped to put everyone at ease.

As per usual, Alice and Noelle were the first two people done eating. Everyone else was talking and taking their time. So as a way to keep things easy for everyone, Alice took Noelle to the family room so they could play while everyone else finished up their meals. She always loved having some private playtime with Noelle as people were finishing up their meals during the holidays. Normally, Alice would do whatever game or toy that Noelle wanted to play with. This time she wanted to pet the dogs especially Backup. So Alice paid attention to Chloe as Noelle was telling her how much she wanted a puppy and how she couldn't wait to go to the hockey game to see Scotty play.

It seemed like at that point everyone started to come into the family room. Scotty immediately sat down behind Alice and she just leaned back against him. He hugged her tightly at first with his right arm but then started to give Chloe some attention too. He whispered into Alice's ear "You seem so good with her. I can't wait until we can have our own."

Alice's eyes went wide for a second. It was something that she wasn't expecting to hear, they never talked about having kids. So she whispered back, "I love spending time with her, that's for sure. I don't do it enough and I see some of me in her. But I've never really thought about having a child on my own."

"Really?" he whispered back to her.

Alice was a little surprised that they were doing this then and there but it worked. They continued to whisper back and forth with each other. She was sure her mom and sister would assume they were just saying sweet nothings or so. "Yeah. It's a ton of work. Some days I feel like I can barely keep myself together and idea of raising a child scares the shit out of me."

"But you want them?"

"One day," was Alice's answer which kind of surprised her. There was something about Scotty that made Alice see having a family together and she just knew he would do everything he could for his children. Scott had to like that answer since he just hugged her tighter and she swore that she could feel him smiling behind her.

From that point on, everything felt less stilted and awkward. Everyone was getting along well and it was nice. Maybe it was because she finally relaxed. It felt like all too soon when Scott said he had to get ready for the game and went towards the bedroom to get changed into the prerequisite suit that he and all the players had to wear in and out of the arenas on game day. As per usual, it didn't take him long to get changed and he came back down in one of her favorite slim-fitted suits that seemed to show off his body. But he also had a little gift bag in his hand.

He knelt by Noelle and handed her the bag. Alice smiled since she knew he got Noelle a jersey since they talked about getting her one and if he should sign it. As she pulled the jersey out of her bag, it was a wine jersey with the gold logo and white accents and had Scotty's 34 number on it. He smiled and said, "I thought you might like wearing the same thing that I will be wearing and I'm sure your Aunt Alice will have one on at the game as well."

"Thanks." She turned to Alice and asked, "You have one too?" Alice nodded and almost as quickly Noelle turned to her mom and asked if she could wear it at the game and her mom said it was okay. Alice noticed that Scott still hadn't stood up and that made Alice curious to see if there was something more in the bag. They didn't talk about doing anything more for the little one. Noelle dug in the bag for one more item and pulled out a tiny Gritty plushie that fit into her hand. She immediately stood up and did her 'Gritty dance' by doing a big stomach circle and shaking her butt as she said, "It's Gritty. He's funny."

Alice couldn't help but smile. She mouthed over to Scotty "Thank you." She was equal parts surprised and happy in that moment. She knew that the only reason Scotty found the plushie was because of her and the fact she taught Noelle about Gritty. Alice loved the fact he picked up a Gritty doll for Noelle. It was the perfect gift to add on to everything.

But then Scott stood up and said, "Sorry that I can't stay longer. But it's good meeting you all. I know Alice said you might head home straight from the game. So if that's the case, I hope that we get together soon."

After he left, it allowed for some more frank talk about their impressions of Scotty. Noelle was smitten and showing everyone her new Gritty toy. Everyone else thought that overall he was a good guy and that they liked him but they weren't thrilled how quickly Alice moved in with him. But she was surprised that she got the overall stamp of approval. It felt like a major win and she could relax some.

Scott

Scotty felt bad about leaving Alice alone but the lunch wasn't that bad. She made it sound like it would be so much rougher than it was. They were perfectly fine and had no idea how good she was with kids. It was actually really cool to see since he was still hoping for a family one day. He knew it was too soon for them, but one day.

Getting to the rink was easy. He immediately got out of the suit and switched into some shorts and a t-shirt to wear as a base layer. He also threw one of his favorite ball caps on backwards where he could feel at ease again instead of a monkey suit. All the guys started to trickle into the locker room which a good sign. He was hoping to start a small soccer ring to help wake up the hand-eye coordination before having to get into his warm up gears.

As Lager entered the room, he sat down next to Scott as per usual. He immediately asked Scott, "How did it go with meeting her family?"

"It wasn't that bad. But I can tell her mom and sister were trying not to like me and now I understand why Alice can be so hard on herself. She gets some intense pressure from her mom and I don't think her mom is fully aware of how much pressure is stacking onto Alice. But it was so much fun watching Alice with her niece, she loves that little one."

"Can't expect much more than that dude."

"Yup. Want to play around?" as Scotty grabbed the soccer ball.

"Sure" as they started to kick the ball around some before it was time to get ready for warm ups.

Warm ups went smoothly. Scotty felt loose and relaxed which was always a good sign before a game. He was looking forward to surprising Alice with the Sound's power play. The music was fun during warm ups and he found himself singing along to a few of the songs as he was playing around with a puck and just doing some stickhandling skills. He looked towards the bench and saw that Alice and her family were sitting in the front row. Both Alice and Noelle were in his sweater and he noticed that her sister was also wearing a Sound hoodie that might have come from Alice's collection of clothes that she got on her birthday. Noelle looked so excited to be at the game. He couldn't help but smile when he noticed how Alice was pointing him out and talking to Noelle. It was cute seeing her teach her niece hockey.

As warm ups were winding down, he lost sight of Alice and her niece initially. But as he walked towards the tunnel, he realized that Alice had to take her to be one of the kids that were hopeful for high fives from the players. So he made sure that he didn't miss giving a high five to Noelle as he walked by.

The change between the warmups and the pregame speech seemed to drag on forever. Scotty just wanted to get onto the ice and play some hockey. He was starting to get antsy and wanted revenge for last night's loss.

He went out and won the ceremonial drop puck. Then it was the national anthem. He was moving his skates a lot.

Scotty, Lager and Dykstman were out for the first shift of the game. Scotty was on the puck and got it to Lager. Lager pushed it up the side boards with Columbus trying to initiate the forecheck and the puck squirted out. Petey got to the puck in the neutral zone. Petey started to yell "stretch" as he pushed it up and got it to Dykstman. The Blue Jackets were trying to get through the defense to stop the Sound. Scotty was shouting "One T, One T". Finally Dykstman took the shot but the puck bounced off of Bob's pad. Scotty was able to get the rebound and went glove high into the net. Scotty just let out "Fuck yeah" as it went in. Scotty skated back towards the bench and gave everyone the fist bump. He couldn't help to toss a smile at Alice.

Alice

Alice was enjoying the game despite the slow pace after the initial goal in the first couple of minutes of play. It was a lot of good checking on both sides with a bit of the chase and dump element. Neither team was letting up one inch. While it was a new and slightly forced rivalry, both teams have bought in on making sure that they were the best team in Ohio.

Alice loved the seats for the view. But she regretted that Noelle was getting exposed to the player's swearing. Sure there was a glass that helped to dampen some of it but you could still hear it. She didn't think about the profanity when Scott said he could get first row seats. Alice was extra careful not swear during the game since she wanted to make sure that she didn't teach Noelle any bad words so she would stay in Allison's good graces even if Noelle might pick up on player's swearing.

It was midway through the third period when the Blue Jackets hooked Scotty on a breakaway opportunity. It was the first power play for the Sound of the game. As soon as they were in the faceoff circle, Alice went "Holy……" and never completed the thought since she knew there was an adorable four old next to her that she didn't want to curse in front of.

Alice's dad asked, "What's going on kid?" He knew that Alice was super into hockey.

"It's the freak line. Wait it's not just the freak line. Wow. That's super aggressive," as she realized it was a five forward power play. It was something that it seemed like that teams were trying more and more.

"I'm missing something," responded her dad.

"Remember how I told you that Scotty had me join for an OTA when he came back from the All-Star break, that front-line is my idea. I swapped Lager over to the opposite side and used Corey instead of Dykstman on the line. Then on the 4-on-4, Dykstman and PK together playing against Scotty's line which is on the outside. Dykst must be quarterbacking this like usual."

"Still missing the aggressive part, kid. Since I'm not seeing any punches or anything."

"Five forwards, no defense. Which means they will be going hard to the net but could be risky if the puck leaves the zone. Although Dykst and Scotty have the speed to go back if need be."

The puck was dropped. As expected, Scotty won the puck cleanly. The line arrangement definitely was giving the Jackets fits since they were playing man coverage for almost all night and they couldn't figure out how to handle Lager flipped to the other side, especially as he wasn't playing the point on the time. Alice just wanted to see the puck settle down and it didn't want to settle whatsoever. It wasn't until the puck battle at the backboards that the puck started to settle on Scotty's stick. Finally, Scotty was able to get the puck free and got it over to Lager. Lager had to pass it off to Dykstman and Dykstman sent the puck to PK. It then went back to Scotty who finally took a wrister towards the net. It bounced off Bob's pads and it was loose in front. Both Corey and Lager were there crashing the net along with two Blue Jackets whacking away at the puck. Then Corey's whacking allowed for a tip-in until it passed the goal line. Sending the Sound up to 2-0.

Everyone was celebrating the goal. Her dad hugged Alice. Alice was just surprised they used a combo that she came up with and in a power play. That wasn't a scenario she thought to use with the freak line but she should have known if Scotty said they were working on the pp in practice. She was elated that they would use it. Noelle tugged at Alice's sleeve to get her attention. Apparently, Lager wanted to fist bump her through the glass and Noelle noticed right away that he wanted Alice's attention.

So that's the surprise. Not the Gritty toy, thought Alice.

Noelle asked, "Who was that?"

"Lager. He's Scotty's best friend."

"Oh cool." Noelle was so nonchalant about Lager wanting to get Alice's attention. As soon as she knew it was Scotty's friend, she was happy. She didn't care who he as other than that.

Alice thought it was cool that he wanted to include her in the celebration. She was still couldn't believe that the Sound used lines that she dreamt up. It seemed too out there to even think it would happen in more than an OTA especially when they only had a few guys they were playing and it meant abnormal lines. Since the power play has been on the anemic side since mid-December, Alice was curious if this was a one-time look for the pp or if the freak line would be the new normal.

The game continued on but seemed to lack urgency by either team. It was a dull third period. The only sustained pressure from the Blue Jackets didn't happen until the very end of the game when they pulled the goalie for an extra attacker. The Sound's defense remained strong. It was almost surprising there was over 43 saves by the Columbus' goaltender despite the score only being 2-0 and it was so much dump and chase.

At the end of the game, Allison and their mom wanted to head back to Erie since it was a long drive with a little one and they wanted to keep Noelle on a regular schedule despite Noelle wanting to spend more time with Scotty and Aunt Alice. Alice would have loved to spend more time with her family but she understood why they were leaving from the arena. Although she was glad that her dad was going to remain in town for the weekend. As Alice gave the three women hugs and said, "Thanks for coming today. It was lots of fun. I'm glad you could finally meet Scotty. Drive Safely. Love you guys." Her dad did his own goodbyes as well.

Alice and her dad already planned to hang out some after the game but didn't have firm plans, so he asked, "So kid, where do you want to go get dinner?"

"Why not Market Garden?"

"Okay. Sounds good."

Alice texted Scott to say: ***Dad and I are going to Market Garden post game. Feel free to join.***

Alice: ***Also, you have no idea how much that I love that you guys used the freak line. That was amazing.***

As Alice and her dad passed some TVs showing the post-game, she noticed that Corey was doing the post-game interview. She was glad for two reasons, Scott might make it to dinner earlier than usual and it was also Corey's first goal in months, he deserved a little extra time with the press.

"So what were you and Scotty talking about when you guys were alone?"

"Which time?"

Alice looked at her dad in confusion, she wasn't sure what he was saying at first and then she realized, he also meant after lunch as well. It was something that she didn't really think of him getting left alone with her dad. "I guess both. I forgot that I did leave you guys alone after lunch. I was more thinking about before you guys came inside."

"Mostly about you. I was trying to see how you were dealing with everything. He gets to see you a lot more. We both know how you've had questionable coping skills in the past and I was making sure you were staying healthy." Alice made a face but she could understand why her dad would ask Scott. She wasn't the most forthcoming about her feelings a lot of the time and even less so when she was stressed. Importantly he was making a reference to how in the past, she wouldn't eat when she was stressed. Her dad continued and said, "He missed seeing your eyes smiling on a regular basis. He noticed and loved it coming back anytime you guys do anything hockey related. I also think he likes that you guys can share hockey together."

Alice nodded, "I'm trying."

"We know and no one is saying you're not. I remember how you were in high school. I didn't see you get really happy much other than on the trips we did. The fact he picked up on how your eyes really shine when you're happy told me how much he actually cares and picks up on the details. He was looking for other ways to make you happy. "

Alice nodded and she asked, "So what about the second time?"

"Saying how you and Noelle enjoy playing together after finishing up dinner during the holidays and how it can be nice that you will help to babysit her or other kids at family events. You let the adults talk it out but it can also be a downside where you can be an enigma to most of the family."

"I guess that's true. I just know that I sometimes feel ill at ease with small talk and I never see Noelle. So it's fun to be with her. I wasn't thinking about it."

"He didn't realize it was normal for you. Don't get me wrong, he didn't mind. In many ways, I think that he liked it. As I said, he was just surprised since he's never really seen that side of you."

"I guess there is still a lot to learn from each other yet. You probably think it's a bad idea for us to move in."

"Honestly, yes and no." Alice tilted her head in curiosity with her dad's comment. "It's too soon if you look at how long you have known each other. He's the first guy you have dated for a really long time. Let alone dated someone seriously. But with the break-in. It's good that you are out of your apartment and in a much safer area. I know you are being smart about things, like keeping the lease. So I see no harm in seeing how things develop. The fact you both care about each other a lot, that is completely evident. But what's it like when he's on the road?"

"Admittedly, it wasn't a big deal before. I would watch his games and if they were playing at the same time as the Flyers, I would watch both games. We would chat after the games. Most of the time it's FaceTiming. It's nice that way. Now, it's the same but I will have the two dogs with me when I watch the games. I barely sleep when he's not around but at the same time I know I am safe. I've noticed that Chloe gets super protective when I get jumpy at night. I know this month will be interesting, we will both be gone a lot for the first time."

Alice and her dad got their dinner at the brew pub. They were both drinking and chatting about the game and then the upcoming prospects for the Indians. All of a sudden in the middle of the conversation about the depth of the Tribe's pitching core, Alice heard the all too familiar joking voice of Scott as he sat beside her say, "Wait, I thought you were a Phillies fan hoping that they sign what's his name?"

She looked towards him, "I am. Also wrong position, babe. But I got raised on the Indians. Since I keep living in their territory, dad always wants to see what the local guys are saying about his team since I get to hear stuff that my dad doesn't. Although I bet you will never guess my all-time favorite baseball team."

Scott looked towards Alice's dad for some help but he was just smiling. Since her dad wasn't giving him any hints, Scott said, "It should be the Blue Jays."

Alice laughed knowing that had to be his team. "No way... Do you want to try again or should I tell you?"

"I have a feeling you should just say it."

"The Colorado Rockies."

Scott literally sputtered at that response. "Wait. What? You never lived there or was even close by. How the hell did you start liking them?"

"They expanded out when I got into baseball statistics and I was looking to claim a team for my own. We already moved to Cali, and I wasn't sure about the Phillies even though they had the best mascot in the world, at least until

Gritty. The Indians were my dad's team and I never lived close to super close to them until after MLB looked to expand the league. I wanted to do something my dad couldn't do, follow a team from their inception. And I liked their team colors."

Everyone started laughing some especially when Scott said, "That's the most girly reason ever."

"Hey I was like 10 and it was never just the team colors."

"I will say, she was always good about following the stats and understanding the game first. The fact they wore purple was what made them stand out from Seattle and Tampa. So you like the Blue Jays I take it."

"Now. But I grew upon the Expos. When they left, we started to root for the Blue Jays since they are the Canadian team. But I will always support the other local teams anywhere I play."

"Good man," replied Alice's dad.

Alice couldn't help but smile when Scott started to drink from her beer. She teased Scott, "Hey, get your own beer."

"I will. But what is that. It seems familiar."

"Bourbon barrel aged feats of strength. My favorite from here."

"Oh right. You had that had that at your place. No wonder it seemed familiar."

"I should get another growler of it to enjoy for later."

After a while, it was time to get going for the night. Alice's dad headed back towards his hotel downtown. While Scott and Alice headed back to his place, "Your family weren't that bad. Everyone seemed nice."

Alice took a deep breath. "Yeah, it was good."

"I like your dad. I can tell you are a bit of a daddy's girl."

"Yeah. As long as there isn't a tournament that required pairing up with a parent. Then Ally always wanted to be with dad. I would play with anyone who wanted to help participate. Also, I'm sorry for abandoning you at the lunch table. I wasn't thinking. I hope it wasn't terrible."

"It was fine. But seeing you with your niece was really cool. I noticed you were teaching her hockey throughout the game."

"Well someone needs to teach her the sport. I'm just making sure she knows who are the good teams and doesn't end up as a Penguins fan like her mom and dad. Although neither of them are real hockey fans so I'm not too worried about Noelle."

Scotty chuckled, "Can't have that. But remind me, who are the good teams?"

"The Sound and the Flyers. But she's all about Her Scotty right now. He's the best one out there, don't you know?"

He couldn't help but laugh as he cupped her face and teased, "Her Scotty? I thought I was your Scotty."

"Yeah you definitely are mine. But she's enamored with you too. I'm pretty lucky that I get to have you. Although sometimes I wonder if I just dreamt you up."

"Everything seems pretty real to me. Do I need to spend the night proving that I'm no dream?"

Alice said rather hopefully "Maybe...."

"Oh you and your maybes. Maybe, I won't make love to you when we get home."

Alice rolled her eyes slightly knowing that he was teasing and just wanted to hear her confirm what they both knew. She also knew, if they weren't in the car, he would be trying to tickle her something fierce. "Okay, fine. No maybe. I just want to make love all night long. Especially knowing that I won't get to see you for like two weeks after tonight."

"About that. I think that is too long to be apart for us to be apart. And a little birdy told me that Philly is always a good place for you and we are playing the Flyers. So why not fly out for the game?"

"I can't afford that."

"Who said you were paying for it? What if it was something that I wanted to do for you."

"But I can't just let you pay for everything all the time."

"Sure you can." He then turned and gave her the most mock serious face possible as he said, "Now do you want to join me for a Sound vs. Flyers game next week?"

"Of course, I do." as if that was the most obvious answer in the world.

"Good. I know you have work so it will just a flyby visit. Basically come in for the game and leave in the morning. But I have a request. Scratch that, it's a demand." he said with a coy smile.

Alice knew he was up to something but wouldn't just reveal it without asking, "Oh?"

"That you wear my sweater. It's good luck thus far."

"Wait, what? Do you want me to get harassed by the natives? This is Philly, remember?" Alice knew that it was a reasonable thing for him to ask for. She didn't actually care about the request in some ways. Sure she might end up with some beer spilled on her if she acted like an asshole but given her love of the Flyers, she would be rooting for both teams and the fans would be fine with her. She just didn't like being told what to wear.

"Oh you will be fine." Scotty said, not once believing for

one second that she would have any issues at the game. Instead he did a coy smile and said, "Now you have to ask yourself, would a trip to Philly and two tickets for the game be worth wearing your boyfriend's sweater at a game?"

"You know I can't say no to something like that and I love wearing your name and number. It's just more it will be weird to do it at a Flyers game. If it were my call, I would prefer not to show any favoritism towards either team. I would end up in something like an oversized sweater and leggings."

"Nope my sweater or nothing," he said teasingly.

"Meanie. You won't let me be impartial. Wait you said two tickets, does that mean I can invite Jenna to the game too. But I know there is no way in hell she would be in Sound stuff."

"I don't care about who you invite or what they wear. But I want to know you will be representing me."

"Deal."

"Awesome, I'll email you the details for the trip and all the tickets."

"Wait, What?" Alice was completely taken off guard there. When or how he could have gotten tickets already when his phone was completely in his pocket. She couldn't believe he had everything already set.

"I might have made all the arrangements for the trip when you told me about the kid getting charged in the case while I was in St. Louis," said Scott so nonchalantly. That's when Alice remembered he asked about keeping a day open, she didn't realize it was the day of the hockey game.

"Scott..." Alice paused as she tried to get a grip over her emotions. She was so elated that he would do that for her but also in utter disbelief too since it was something that she wasn't expecting. "You are amazing. Like completely and truly. But how did you know I would say yes?"

Scott lowered a brow at her as if she was talking crazy in the moment. "Flyers vs. Sound. Then add in not seeing each other for like 3 weeks if you didn't come. It was the safest bet I've made all week."

Alice had to laugh, when he put it that way. She was being pretty dumb about the whole thing "True. But seriously, thank you. I think you are a bit insane, but this time it's insanely sweet."

Scott leaned and kissed her, "You're welcome. Bringing you out to the game is as much for me as it is for you." he said with a lustful look in his eyes. Alice knew that she was looking forward to seeing him and doing similar things together both that night and on the trip.

Alice still couldn't quite get her head wrapped around the idea that Scott planned the trip for her and kept it a complete surprise from her for at least a week. It was amazing. She knew if she planned something like that, she wouldn't be able to keep it in for two days, let alone over a week. She would have wanted to get his reaction as soon as possible so she marveled at his control to keep it in. As they got out of the car, Alice rushed over to his side and practically leapt at him as she said, "You are fucking amazing, you know that right?" She started to kiss him passionately for a second, "I don't know how I could have handled everything without you. I love you so much."

14

ALICE

Getting ready for her trip to Raleigh felt so weird. Normally she was excited to get away, meet new people and learn from her friends. This trip was different. It was the first time since the burglary that she had traveled, and it's been weird not seeing Scott much since their schedules weren't lining up. She felt guilty that she had to put Chloe and Backup at a kennel overnight until Scott got home although he raved about the place and was okay with the situation.

When she got to the airport, she started to relax. She first texted Scott to wish him luck for the game since she was sure that he was most likely napping before the game or doing his warm up routine at the rink and wouldn't be around to pick up the phone right then. She just hoped that she could follow parts of the game while on the plane but she knew it might be a bit iffy.

She called her family to see how things were going with them. Unfortunately, she found out her stepfather had to get emergency surgery. She tried not to worry about them, but it was tough not to be worried about him. So she put on one of her calming playlists, hoping to have some of the anxiety just ebb off through the soothing music.

The flight itself wasn't even ideal. She found herself lacking focus when she was hoping to write. Then when it was time to get to the game on her iPad, the Wi-Fi blocked both the video and the radio feeds for the game. The moment she closed her eyes to get some sleep, she had a massive panic attack. She was glad that she knew it was a panic attack almost instantaneously and didn't freak out more than just getting really really spooked. She knew she wasn't in actual danger but she had to let it run its course before her heartbeat settled down.

Once she finally landed, she texted Scott to let him know that she made it safely to Nashville and sent similar messages to her family. Then she queued up the radio feed of Scott's game. She just groaned to herself when she heard the score, since the Sound were losing. But almost immediately, Scott's line scored. As she continued to listen to the game in the Uber, she heard several quality shots on net that could have tied up the game but they just weren't going through.

Getting into her hotel room, she wasn't any more at ease. The room while large, had a set of connecting doors that would allow it to join up with the room next door. So instead of one door that she was afraid someone would come through on, there were now two. That ill-at-ease effect post a panic attack wasn't going away. So Alice decided to take a warm shower as she continued to listen to Scott's game. Thankfully, Scott made the tying goal. Alice let out a shout for joy and was so proud of her boyfriend.

Alice watched the third period and was so happy when

Corey's line got the go ahead goal and in the end sealed the win for the Sound. Alice also started journaling and writing a story as she was watching the game to help release the nerves going off in her brain.

Alice continued to write well into 2am in the morning resting on the comforter when she got a text from Scott saying that he was glad to hear she got in okay. She sent a smiley face back to him. He immediately called her cell phone.

"Hey babe" he said in a relaxed manner. Alice could tell that he was pretty tired after the game but he normally was.

"Hey. Good goal."

"Yeah. It was no big deal" replied Scott a little too calmly.

"Alright, what's up?" Alice knew at this point in their relationship that if he was downplaying any of his plays, he was preoccupied with something or was trying to ignore pain. Given the timing, it was probably something from the game.

"It's nothing. I could ask you the same thing, since I can tell you are stressed out just by listening to you and you are clearly not even trying to sleep."

"Really? Cause I'm pretty sure something is going on." Alice said as she adjusted her body position and laid back on the pillows on the king bed. "I have no problem saying I had a panic attack earlier today. Not to mention I'm worried about my stepdad who had to get emergency pacemaker surgery on my mom's birthday. Nor did I want to leave Chloe and Backup at the kennel. I miss having you and them in bed with me. So that's enough to keep my mind a wee bit crazy, but I'm laying down in bed."

"I'm sorry kid." Scott said sympathetically. "Seems like birthdays in your families suck this year."

"No lie. But it's not your fault. It's not that bad. If I could, I would be working out or just wanting to be held. So I'm writing it out and I will try to sleep soon. But what about you, what are you up to?"

"Yeah. I would hold you if I could. But we are about to have a quick drink before the flight back to Cleveland."

"Have fun babe." Alice said almost expecting him to want to get off the phone. If he was going out with friends, he should be doing that.

"I'm not getting off the phone with you just yet. I miss you too and I still want to chat."

"Okay. I just didn't want you to miss out hanging out with the guys since you are talking with me."

"It's all good, baby."

Alice decided see if Scott was going to be more forthcoming about what was bothering him. "So will you say what's wrong?"

"Stinger to the hip that won't go away just yet. Also like you, I'm not looking forward to getting home and you not being there. You spoiled me last time when I came back and you were all cute in one of my t-shirts. Now I get to go home to an empty house."

"Aww." Alice was genuinely touched to hear the last part of his comment. She felt bad about the stinger and figured he was going to be sore in the morning after the flight if he couldn't get the stinger to go away soon. "I wish you were with me in Raleigh. Although I may have stolen one of your shirts."

Scotty started to chuckle and say, "You may have? You don't know if you did or didn't steal one of them?"

"Fine, I stole one" Alice with a laugh and a slight eye roll.

"You little thief" but you could tell that he didn't mean it. He was smiling.

"Hey, they are comfy and they smell like you. It's like having a little piece of you when it's on. It's not the same but it's better than nothing."

"It sounds like I should steal something from you for road trips."

"Maybe. But what would you steal that you could actually wear?" asked Alice since she was curious what he would want to borrow of hers so he would think of her. He was so much taller than her and his upper body was so solid that she couldn't imagine there was much in her closet that would even fit.

"I don't know. It's not that I could be all sexy or if anything that you own would even fit me."

In a way, Scott was right, with her being so tiny, there wasn't much that would fit him. So it was silly and it got her smiling and feeling happy. Then Alice realized there was a whole cache of things that he would fit into. "Actually, you could fit in a few things of mine but I don't think you would like it."

"And why not?" Scott first sounded skeptical. Then he started chuckling when it dawned on him what Alice meant. "Wait, you have a crazy amount of Flyer shirts and sweaters that are all way too big for you."

Alice shrugged. "What can I say? Promo shirts are never made for those of us who are vertically challenged. I can't really explain why all my jerseys are all oversized but that's how I buy them. I guess it's because they are comfy. You are always welcome to steal one."

"Yeah not going to happen. I can't wear a rival. I could always steal a bear."

Alice had to shut down that one immediately because she knew he would only steal one of her bears for the very same reason he wouldn't want to steal one of her t-shirts. "True. But no to the bears. You would only steal China and they get jealous. Plus I would miss having China around. I use both of them to sleep when I can't hold onto you."

Alice heard Scott take a deep breath and say "Fine, I won't steal the bears but please promise to send a photo of you wearing on my shirt when you are on the trip."

"Sure thing."

"I should go. But I'll text you when we land."

"Sounds good. I love you."

"Je t'aime."

Alice hung up the phone and laid back on the bed feeling stronger and more relaxed. She didn't realize how much better she would feel after talking with Scott. She looked down at the shirt that she stole with the Sound logo and the little number 34 on the sleeve. After a few attempts to get a selfie that she liked, she sent it over to Scott.

Scott: ***You didn't say you were wearing it now. You just said you stole one.***

Alice: ***You also didn't ask if I had it on.***

Scott: ***Now I wished we FaceTimed***

Alice: ***Next time :P***

Scott: ***I should let you get some sleep but I'm almost tempted to video call you but I know I shouldn't.***

Alice: ***Is this your way of saying I should sleep?***

Scott: ***Sorta. I know it's at least 2am and you should be in bed.***

Alice: ***True.***
Scott: ***Je t'aime. Good night.***
Alice: ***Nite. Je t'aime.***

ALICE WOKE up several times in the night. She was restless and hoping to hear back from anyone. Fortunately, she saw that Scott got home okay but she didn't respond to the text since he knew he would have wanted her to be back in bed. But she hadn't heard back from her mom. Eventually, she just stopped trying to sleep. Finally she heard back from her mom that her stepdad was okay but still in the hospital. Right as she was starting to get into her swimsuit so she could try to burn off some tension before she had to meet up with her colleagues for breakfast, she caught sight of an email notification saying what mail she was to expected to get at home. As soon as she saw the first letter, her stomach dropped.

Out of instinct, she dialed Scott's number. It took a few rings and he sounded groggy as he said, "Hello."

Alice felt guilty realizing that he must have been sleeping in after the flight and she was a bit of a jackass. So she said, "Hey. Sorry I wasn't thinking. I should have waited."

Scott immediately went into the soothing mode and said, "Shh. It's fine. What's up? Is everything okay with your stepfather?"

"Apparently he's okay. I don't know when they are releasing him but he's okay. It's not that."

She heard Scott pushing around the sheets and was trying to get up so he could fix things. She half expected to hear the dogs until she remembered that he wouldn't pick them up until later on today when the kennel opened up.

Alice quickly said, “You don’t have to get up. But I was hoping you could go to my place this afternoon and get the mail. I have a letter from the prosecutor coming and I will go mad not knowing what is in the letter.”

“Sure. What time does your mail come?”

“Around noon.”

“Okay. I’ll grab it after practice. I’ll call you when I get it. Are you at least hanging in there okay?”

“Sorta, not really, but it’s fine. But I was going for a swim before I had to meet everyone for breakfast so my head is on straight.”

Alice could hear the surprise in his voice as he said, “Wait, did I hear that correctly?”

“Probably. I’m going for a swim and then shower and then go meetup with everyone for breakfast.” Then it dawned on Alice why he was so surprised, she was going to get breakfast. He’s been trying to get her to have breakfast every day for a month.

“So is that what you need to do before you will eat breakfast?” he said laughing.

“Basically yes. Now hush.”

“Fine.” but he didn’t actually stay silent for more than a split second. “I still can’t believe you are having breakfast.”

“Yeah I’ve been up for a bit and I won’t meet up with them for at least an hour and a half. My stomach settles down after being up for a couple hours and I then want food. Just most days, people will call it lunch. But yeah, anyway sorry about being an asshole and waking you up.”

“You aren’t an asshole. But if that’s everything, I’m going to go back to sleep while I still can.”

“Okay. Sleep well my love.”

"Night."

Scott

Practice was brutal. He knew that going in since he hated skating without enough sleep but that was the price to pay with late flights back from the west coast and maintaining a strict training schedule. At least, he could relax the rest of the day before the game after doing one last errand, at least until he had to go back for some video sessions. He just picked up the dogs. Chloe was chilling in the front seat and Backup was running around like a mad man in the back.

"Settle down Backup. You are going to make yourself sick." But at that exact moment, he heard the puppy starting to hack up in a high pitched noise which was a telltale sign that the puppy was throwing up. "Oh, I guess, it's too late for that advice. At least, we are almost to Alice's. Just try to calm down and don't lick your throw up."

Almost immediately, he was pulling into Alice's apartment complex. He used her parking spot since he knew today's trip would take a little bit longer than usual and her car was at his place. He got out of the car and he waited for Chloe to jump out the driver's side door before shutting it. While he grabbed the puppy's leash from the seat, he left Chloe unleashed. He leashed up Backup before letting the puppy jump down. It seemed like the puppy kept growing in both height and bravery on each and every road trip. Unsurprisingly to Scott, Backup threw up one more time from his motion sickness. He knelt down and rubbed behind the puppy's ears. Once Scott was sure that Backup was done getting sick, he headed to go inside.

Originally his first plan of attack was to load up his car with a few of Alice's belongings. He knew that movers would come tomorrow to pack and move her stuff over to his place but he figured he could grab some of her stuff like her precious craft beer and some of the artwork while he was at the place. He expected he could get movers booked much earlier but that was something that took a bit longer to get the schedules to work out. It seemed like Alice had most of the things that she required for day to day living but she was still basically a guest in his house. He couldn't wait until tomorrow where they could really have it be their place with a blend of their tastes put together and give her stuff in his place. But thanks to Backup's motion sickness, that changed his plans to cleaning the car first. So he brought the pups inside and just let them explore her apartment as he cleaned the car and took out the box of beers and some of the artwork to the trunk.

After cleaning and stowing everything, he opened up the mailbox to get the mail that Alice was looking for. Right on top was the letter that Alice was looking for. It was a thick envelope and he had a feeling that it couldn't have been good news. He texted Alice to let her know that he got it but she didn't respond right away and he wanted to wait a little bit longer before opening her mail.

Scott realized that he wasn't hearing any noise from the dogs and that was never a good sign. So he went back towards the bedroom to see what they have gotten up to. He wasn't surprised that Chloe was resting on Alice's bed and just being a wee bit lazy. But he was surprised to see that Backup was playing with one of Alice's teddy bears in his mouth.

"No Backup. You cannot play with things that aren't yours," scolded Scott in a very stern voice.

Backup immediately dropped the teddy bear in shock

since he never heard Scott scold him or get firm with his voice while Chloe only perked up her ears for a second. Scott picked up the teddy bear and put it up high on the dresser so Backup couldn't chew it apart. Once the teddy bear was safe, Scott leaned down to Backup in a very calm voice and said, "That's your mama's bear. She won't like if you destroyed it. Let's get you home so you can chew on stuff there." Backup immediately started to lick Scott's hand in a sign of atonement.

That's when he finally heard back from Alice asking what was in the letter. So he opened it up and realized very quickly why the letter was so thick. There was a second person charged in the case and there was another victim impact form for her to fill out.

S: ***Do you want me to call or text.***

A: ***Text. I can't talk talk until later.***

S: ***2nd person charged. This one is in adult court. You need to do another impact statement.***

A: ***Joy. FML since you can't just cuddle with me as I write this one since I'm not bringing that to Philly.***

S: ***I'm sorry but you can do it. I will support you through it anyway I can.***

A: ***I know. You are truly amazing.***

S: ***I try. So how's Raleigh? Feeling calmer?***

A: ***Not bad. Still got a ways to go before will be ready but we will get there. How's the pups?***

S: ***Okay. They have been enjoying spending time in your place.***

A: ***:) but I know they love our place.***

That made Scott smile. It was the first time he heard her call his house their place. It wasn't just his anymore and that was before her stuff was merged with his. Sure, she had barely been back at her place in weeks other than to grab odds and ends but he wasn't sure if she considered it her home yet.

S: ***I should let you be. Will you call when you are done?***

A: ***Yes. But it might be rather late.***

S: ***I will be waiting.***

Alice

Alice was exhausted from a day of travel and work but she couldn't wait to get back home. She knew that Scott left for his current road trip earlier that morning so it would be just her and the dogs at home that evening. She would have normally hated knowing that they would be missing each other if wasn't for the trip to see him play tomorrow night in Philadelphia. But she was excited to see the house especially knowing that Scott had the movers come in and bring the stuff from her apartment over the weekend. She wasn't sure what to expect but she assumed that he would just bring her stuff in and put it in the mostly empty rooms like the guest room and office.

As she walked into the house, Chloe and Backup rushed her at the door as they always did. While it was sweet, it always made it a little tricky to get into the house until she would say, "Hey guys, come on back up a little so I can get inside." Fortunately Chloe was super well behaved and Backup was taking after her but was still a little unsure about commands.

As she was giving some love to the dogs, she couldn't help but notice how some of her Paris artwork was up on the wall across from the TV and her red chair with matching ottoman was in the living room with Scott's sofa. She realized he took the time to mix and match their furniture instead of leaving his design more or less alone. But she knew the dogs wouldn't let her make a full exploration until they got a chance to play outside and do their business. So Alice took them on one of their quickest walks she could so she could get back to explore the rest of the house.

When she got back, she realized very quickly how all her bigger pieces from her family room, office and whatnot were all more or less incorporated together. It was rather amazing how well they all went together like her black dining room chairs with his table. His recliners were in the basement with her sofa along with several of her book shelves. Her office area was more or less unchanged but he did leave all the Flyers signs next to her desk on the ground. She had to smile since he incorporated a lot her achievements like her diplomas on the wall with his hockey achievements. Plus he added a photo of them to her desk area that she absolutely loved.

She quickly texted Scott and said: ***Made it home. You did an amazing job. I can't believe how awesome it is.***

When he didn't text back, she knew she missed the texting window and he was busy with work. He had to be on the ice doing warm ups or listening to the coaches in the locker room. She ran downstairs to prepare a salad for dinner and fed the dogs. Then it was time to turn on the game.

Like usual, Scotty was super easy to find on the ice during warmups since he never wore a helmet and his red hair had a habit of standing out in the best possible way. She smiled since it seemed like he was in a good mood that night and normally that would translate out to a win for the Sound if he kept the good mood throughout. She settled in for the game.

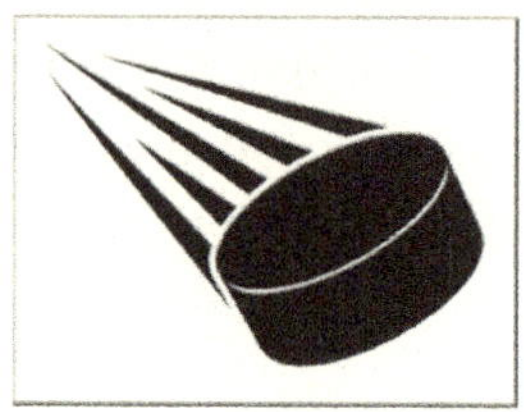

Alice was making her way through the airport as quickly as she could. As she passed the last security marker reminding people that if they exited they would have to go through security again, she saw Scotty waiting for her. He was in his pea jacket, tight fitting suit pants and a beanie which meant that he wasn't going to have much time to hang out and basically had to go straight to the Wells Fargo Center to get ready for the game. But at least he took the time to pick her up.

As she approached him, he had a wide smile showing much he missed her and immediately scooped her up into a bear hug as he started to kiss her forehead. Then he said, "Hey you. I didn't see you come up. Your hat doesn't stand out around here."

Alice laughed. During the winter, she always wore one of her Flyers knit hats. Not a lot of people in Cleveland tended to rock a Flyers hat so it wasn't that popular. It was something that Scotty liked to razz her that she never wore a Sound hat but especially since lately for almost everything else, she would grab a Sound item first. Alice laughed, "It really wouldn't. At least you are easy to spot. So ready for tonight?"

"Yeah. Now that you are here."

"Aww. God, I've missed you."

"I have too. Unfortunately, I have to go pretty much straight to the arena from here. I hope that's okay."

"Kinda figured that with you in the suit and all. I'm just glad that you picked me up. I'll probably going to head to the hotel to check in and get rid of the suitcase prior to meeting up with Jenna for pre-game drinks in Center City."

As Scotty was playing with his phone, most likely to summon an Uber for them, he asked with a coy smile, "So I'm going to have to ask, do you remember our a deal?"

"Of course I do." Alice unbuttoned her jacket to reveal the wine and white jersey with a C on the right shoulder. If it was possible, Scotty's grin grew even wider when he saw the jersey since it was clear whose team it was based on colors alone. "I just make no promises that this will be on when we are at Evil Genius afterwards. You are still good for meeting us there?"

"Yup. I know it's one of your favorite places and I want to meet your friends. Come on, our uber is here."

Scott

The overtime clock was winding down. Knowing that he was going to be sent back out there soon and he needed a bit of a lift, he took a heavy whiff of smelling salts. He shook his head immediately disliking the decision but knew that was half the reason he took a whiff. He just needed to get the last goal before the game ends. As much as Scott hated them, he almost wanted to get to the shootout where he didn't have to worry about getting stripped of the puck on a near constant basis like had happened over most of the night.

It was him, Lager, and Wheels sent out for the latest faceoff against the Flyers top line. Neither team had real possession the whole night and it was driving Scott mad. It was bad enough they only squeaked out the win against the Penguins last night, but there were too many overtimes lately.

He didn't want to lose to the Flyers at all, not again. They were a third rate team.

Despite losing the puck in the faceoff, the Flyers have been damn good at the faceoff all season so that wasn't actually surprising to lose. The key was to take advantage of the fact they didn't protect the puck well. Scott took off and was able to poke check the puck away from Claude Giroux. The puck squirted loose and went backwards and for a moment it seemed like people didn't realize where the all-important piece of rubber was. Fortunately, Wheels was close by and could hear everyone shouting "Behind You" and could scoop up the loose puck.

At this point, the game was on the Sound's sticks. Wheels pushed the puck up towards Scotty. Of course, G was on Scotty immediately in hopes to return the favor and strip the puck back. G was chirping something fierce but Scotty just ignored what he was saying. Scott was able to deke the puck while getting towards open ice but he was still having heavy pressure by G despite Scotty trying to push hard and fast down the ice. Thank god that Lager was open and actually had a good angle on the goal.

"Yo Lager!" as Scott passed the puck hard towards Lager hoping that it would land right on the tape. If centered, Lager would be in perfect shape to use his one-timer. It wasn't a perfect pass but Lager still took the shot while Scotty was trying to crash the net so he could get the rebound. But the Flyers goaltender had been not giving up many of those all night. It was a pad save with just enough kick on it that the goalie wouldn't be able to cover it up. Scotty was trying to get the puck past the rookie and but it wasn't going and it didn't help that the Flyer's defense seemed to be whacking at the puck at the same time. Eventually the horn sounded ending the overtime play.

Scotty was cursing at that point. He should have had the win on his stick. Plus he realized that the shootout might not be so good after all. He wasn't sure how he could trick the goalie. Most of the goalies in the league, he had an idea or three of how to take the shot. Thankfully the Flyers elected to shoot first so he had a little bit of time to talk with the coaches.

Colbert, the special teams coach, said, "Just be shifty. Don't try to freeze him. Make him blink first."

Scotty nodded. He knew that was probably the best thing to do. He just had to make sure he didn't caught in his head. This was his time to shine. But he was thinking through what his options should be so he only paid enough attention to the Flyer's attempt to know when it was time to go to the red line. Then he was reminded his Alice was in the stands.

He used his speed first and then started to shift the puck around, having it go from forehand to backhand to forehand a few times and shot off a wrister that caught the goalie off guard since he was thinking it would be a backhanded shot. It was a clean goal and Scotty was happy about that. He heard the stick taps from the bench and knew his team liked that effort.

Then it was time for him to wait and see what happens after that. He needed Crestie to seal the net and if any of the other Sound shooters could get another goal, they would have a nice cushion. The rest of the shootout was pretty uneventful. Although Scotty knew if Lager was starting to annoy him for the next couple games, all Scotty had to do was remind him how he losing the puck before even getting a shot off. As soon as Crestor caught the last shot in his glove, it was official. The Sound won the game. It only took three rounds in the shootout which was good. The whole bench went towards Crestor to celebrate the win since in many ways, he was the real hero of the night. Scotty had a few helmet taps from his teammates too.

The only thing that he was cursing at that moment was that now he knew he would be required to do media tonight since he had the game winning goal. It always seemed like he always did something in the game that made the reporters want his insights when all he wanted to do was hang out with Alice. She was both a good luck charm and a curse for an early evening. He knew that she was cool with his job and understood all the aspects of the job like talking with the media, but he still felt like a bit of an asshole for always doing that to her.

After an hour of talking to reporters and getting ready, he was finally able to leave. Of course, as they were getting ready Lager, Corey and Petey all found out that Scotty was planning on going to Evil Genius Brewing to meet up with Alice and wanted to join. He let them come along since it was going to be a group meet up and Alice always seemed to have a more the merrier personality. Lager was definitely in the mood to bust Scotty's balls since he couldn't believe that Scotty was going to a taproom. Thankfully, Corey and Petey were more interested in just going to a local craft brew place.

As Scotty was walking up to the doors of Evil Genius flanked by Lager, Corey and Petey. He heard Lager say, "I don't care what you say, I won't believe it until I see it with my own eyes. I still bet that you will only drink a Yuengling or nothing at all. Just watch." Scotty just rolled his eyes and was wondering why he was friends with Lager at that moment.

Scott looked around the bar and realized immediately it wasn't what he expected. The place was bright and open. There were wood tables set up along the wall and in the back but he noticed that his girl was surrounded by a small group of friends spread out between two sofas in the front of the place. All her friends look small in comparison to him and his buddies from the Sound. Alice was engrossed in conversation at first and he couldn't help but notice how happy and carefree she seemed. But almost at that moment, she caught sight of him and the group and came over to greet everyone. The first thing she did was to hug and kiss him and he said, "Nice shootout goal."

Scotty smiled widely and kissed her. She didn't know the other guys were coming so she gave them the quick intro, "Order at the bar, they only bring food to you. When you come back, I can introduce everyone."

Scotty knew about that ahead of time and since he was still very picky when it comes to craft beer, Alice offered to share her flight with him. So he headed over to the couch with her. Everyone else went to go get some drinks.

He sat next to Alice and she whispered, "try E." Scott nodded and went to grab a glasses from the wheel in front of them that was holding five tasters. He was only glancing at the wheel and nearly grabbed the wrong glass. Alice shook her head and kissed his ear before saying, "E, not C. You would hate C." So he grabbed the right beer that was darker and seemed to be more in his wheelhouse.

"Thanks for the tickets tonight," said a woman who was sitting next to Alice. Scott knew that had to be Jenna. He was glad to meet her since he could finally put a face to the name. He's heard a lot about Jenna from Alice.

"Sure thing. It was good to know that Alice had someone to go to the game with." Scott said as he took a sip from the small taster glass.

Almost immediately he heard Corey say, "Dude, pay up." Scott turned around and saw the three guys approach the sofas. Both Corey and Petey had flights while Lager had a hazy beer. Scott wasn't even surprised that there was a bet about his drinking especially for all the shit that Lager was saying on the way over.

Lager was trying to get out of the bet by saying, "He didn't buy it. It doesn't count."

Scott was surprised when Petey said, "No you said drink. Pay him." Petey didn't often disagree with Lager since that was usually his ride and they lived together.

Lager pulled out a $20 and handed it over to Corey as he said, "Fine. It's still weird."

Alice and Scotty just laughed at the whole interaction. Scotty was about to say something to his teammates but he also didn't want to appear to be a jackass to Alice's friends. So instead he turned back to Alice and went, "Okay, I liked that one, so what is it?"

"Nobody Expects a Spanish Inquisition," Alice responded a little too quickly. Scotty blinked a few times, surprised since Alice went from being a bit more flirty than normal when she was a little tipsy but he wasn't expecting to go straight to sass.

He was about ready to ask a question or look for some help. But one of Alice's male friends said, "Look at #12 on the board behind you."

Scott turned and realized that was the name of the drink.

He let out a chuckle and as he was reading some of the other names on the list. He should have known since this was the brewery that always had craziest names in Alice's beer collection. He should have realized that she would want to have some fun with the name.

He turned to Alice and asked if she wanted anything else to drink while he was ordering his. She said with a sly smile, "A taster of the What Are You Wearing, Jake From State Farm." She knew it would make him uncomfortable at the same time and was trying defended herself by saying, "Hey, I've been wanting to try it and it didn't fit on my first flight."

Scott laughed knowing that Alice was telling him the truth. He knew she had been waiting to come back to Evil Genius for a while and was looking up all the beers they had when he called the other night. He couldn't remember how many she was hoping to try but he knew it was a few. But that one was definitely on the list and he remembered teasing her about that name.

Once he returned to the area where they were sitting, everyone was close together but it seemed to be working. Although he was a little curious as to why Petey and Lager were on either side of the group and Corey was sitting next to Jenna on the other side. Normally Petey and Lager were always sitting next to each other, he was half wondering if Alice split them up. Alice then finally did the introductions for everyone. He was a little bit amazed how varied their connections were to Alice. Alice knew Jenna from college, she met Nick at a diner though a college friend, Chris was from a Star Trek roleplaying group and Macy was from game nights that Alice used to host in Philly. Where it was easy to say where he knew his friends from. But he was amazed at how witty and funny the whole group was and how they were super welcoming to everyone.

The only time things got a wee bit competitive was when they started to play Jenga. Scotty knew that they would have been just as intense if the Sound guys weren't there egging them on. They all had that look of concentration and ragged on each other just as much as his friends were if the tower toppled over.

They all drank a little more than they probably should have that night. Nobody was out of control but they were all tipsy. Scotty's favorite thing about the night was that for the first time in weeks, he saw Alice be completely relaxed and her old self again. She was lively and excited with no trace of stress. She was being extra flirty with eyes only on him and it was fun. That was exactly what he was hoping for with the trip after all.

One of the things that he wasn't expecting was for Jenna and Corey to hit it off. Scotty rarely saw Corey be interested in anyone when they went out so he always kinda assumed that Corey was a confirmed bachelor in the making and what he heard from Alice, Jenna didn't date much either. So the fact he was showing interest in Jenna and it seemed like she was having as much fun in return meant that he felt hopeful for the dude. He just wished that Jenna didn't live in Philly.

Before they knew it, it was time to get back to the hotel due to the curfew for the players and the fact that Evil Genius was starting to shut down for the night. Scott hated the idea of them having to end the night since he was having a ton of fun. Alice's friends all walked as a group towards the Septa station or to the one guy's place that was close to the Septa station. Scott almost offered to walk with them and get the

Ubers there but they were going to get in trouble if they did. While the rest of the guys didn't really care about the curfew, Scotty did since he was supposed to be setting the example for the younger guys like Petey and Corey.

They decided to get two Ubers since having four muscular guys who range from 5'11 to 6'4 was a little claustrophobic especially when they add Alice in the mix. Scott was starting to wonder if there was something up since Corey opted to ride with Alice and Scotty instead of Lager and Petey. Since they were joking the whole evening, Scotty wasn't sure. Although it could easily have been because their car would be quieter or he might have been sent by Lager to play chaperone.

As they were riding back, Corey just let out a dejected, "Damnit, I didn't get her number."

Scotty nudged Alice to see if she could help out Corey. She gave him the serious face. "Jenna is one of my best friends and I know you are a great guy, I just can't give it to you. I'll text her and if she says I should share it, I will."

Then Alice started to quickly move her fingers over the keyboard of her phone to send a message as Scott kissed her forehead. It seemed like it was only a few seconds later when Alice was smiling and handing over her phone to Corey. He was taking a photo of her phone to capture all the relevant details and saying, "I owe you one."

That's when Scotty said, "More like a few if you count the fact she is the reason you are on the first power play unit and suddenly the star everyone is talking about this month."

Scotty could feel that Alice was trying to burrow into him and hid the fact that she was blushing. She hated the attention liked that. But Scotty liked to give her the attention she deserved for the awesome idea. He always believed in giving credit to where credit is due. Besides, there was something so cute about seeing her blush and get all shy about things especially when they knew she did good.

The car was silent the last ten minutes of the ride as Corey was texting on his phone presumably to Jenna since he was smiling so hard. Scott was comfy next to Alice and looking forward to the evening ahead with just the two of them. He was trying to keep his hands off of Alice.

Scotty knew that Alice was still going to have a lot of bad days ahead of her, especially as the court cases started to approach. But he was glad to see her just free of all anxiety that had been ruling her lately when they weren't in bed together. That part was as good as ever. As much as her dad hinted at how a trip to Philly would be good for her, he would have never guessed to see how much of a change he would see in Alice. After meeting the friends, he could understand why she enjoyed hanging out with them. He wasn't jealous of that connection since he knew that Alice would be even more adrift in Cleveland if he wasn't there to help support her. He just hated that the two of them weren't going to spend more than tonight together for a little over two weeks.

15

SCOTT

The Sound was playing yet another tough game. It seemed like the entire stretch of games when he was apart from Alice were just tough games but he was supposed to see her in a few more days. He knew that honestly Alice had nothing to with it even though he missed her immensely. He also kinda hated the fact that she wasn't watching the game. It's the first game in the last two months that she wasn't going to be watching or listening too but she promised to follow the game some. He knew the game was tough since many teams were trying to steal whatever points they could so they could have a viable playoff run now that it was late February and the season was ending. Tonight was no exception and it seemed like the Wild were playing with a real chip on their shoulders the whole game. At least the Sound had solid puck possession throughout the night but the hits were starting to add up and cause turnovers.

It was late into the second period. Scott was in for the offensive zone faceoff. He liked taking faceoffs but he was struggling with winning them tonight. After losing what felt like the 12th time that night, he immediately hit into fast hard strides backwards to defend the zone hopefully causing a neutral zone turnover. Fortunately there was a quick steal by Lager. Both of them started to head back to the net hoping to make it cleanly onsides. Lager was getting hounded by Suter so he launched the puck towards Scotty since he had more open room at the moment.

Scotty saw that a Wild player was coming towards him so he deked the puck so he could protect it. His saw that the Wild player was coming after him and he had to protect himself and the puck, so he tried to throw his body to the right so he could avoid the hit all together as he threw the puck to Dykstman. He knew he didn't get his whole body out of the way for the incoming hit, and the next thing he knew, it was a knee on knee hit. Scotty was pissed since the Wild player didn't even try to prevent the hit. Scotty was flipped up into the air and landed on the ice hard. He was cursing even harder since he could just tell there was something seriously fucked up in his left knee. The pain was so searing that he couldn't even pay attention to the kerfuffle going on beside him since hockey rules were taking over.

Scotty wanted to get up but he couldn't. He just clutched the knee in pain and waited for the trainers to come out. It felt like it was taking forever for the doc to come onto the ice but he knew it was more likely due to the fact that he was in serious pain that was making time seem like forever. Then he finally heard both Lager come over to him with Doc Curren in tow.

Doc Curren leaned down and asked, "Can you get up on your own? I won't be able to see how serious it is until we get back for repairs."

Scotty shook his head and said, "I don't think so."

"Alright." Doc moved towards Scotty's left side. "Okay just grab onto my shoulder and lean on me. Let's get you back."

Scotty followed Curren's lead and was able to stand up. He couldn't put any weight on his knee at all. That was a bad sign. Scotty knew the coaches were hopeful that it would be a stinger but the pain Scotty was feeling was too reminiscent to when he tore his right ACL back in juniors. So he was just hoping that his season wasn't over.

Alice

Alice and Jenna were at their second Flyers game in less than two weeks. Unlike the last game, the two of them had been planning on going to the stadium series game basically from the moment it was announced a year ago. The stadium series game was Alice's annual birthday trip to Philadelphia and given the events that actually happened on her birthday, she was glad to have the birthday trip now even though she did have the fly by trip last week.

The first half of the day, Alice and Jenna were catching up on life and were day drinking at some of their favorite spots or new craft breweries to try out in Philly. Alice was excited to hear that Jenna was still flirting with Corey over text. Alice was rooting for things to work out with them if only to give Jenna an excuse to come and visit Cleveland some more. Plus she knew Jenna never seemed to have great luck with the guys she liked and Alice just wanted her to be happy.

Alice and Jenna were pleasantly surprised by the weather so far during the game. Alice had been expecting to freeze her ass off since it was an outdoor game in the middle of February at a football stadium. Both of them were expecting rain since there was talk of possibly having to move the game due to weather. So far it wasn't as bad as it was predicted. While it was misting, there wasn't outright pouring and the temperature wasn't below freezing. The game could go on without any interruptions, although there was a pit in Alice's stomach that if the weather turned, they could call the game and that would mean a Penguins win.

The Flyers were going hard and trying to tie late in the third period. There was lots of pressure on Murray, the Penguins goalie, so Alice was hopeful that her hometown team could pull out a miracle. They had a high vantage point. She was keeping her phone buried in her hoodie pocket that was underneath her poncho after taking a few photos as keepsakes. She could feel the phone vibrate a few times throughout the game and assumed it was updates from the Sound game. But then it started to get a little crazy and she had a bad feeling something was going on yet she couldn't bring herself to look at the phone in case they missed anything on the ice and she didn't want to jinx the Flyer's chances.

Amazingly, the Flyers tied with less than 20 seconds left. It seemed like the remaining fans in the stadium were all a bundle of nerves that just had an eruption of happiness. Given all that was going on the ice, Alice opted to wait until the last 5 minutes or less of sudden death overtime to see find out who would win the game before looking at her phone.

Jenna was taking photos and videos. Alice was just thumbing her Celtic cross hoping for the win for both of her teams and that Scott was okay. The OT Flyers win was super important at the moment and she refused to look at her phone. The first couple of shifts didn't really lead to many chances but there was something about the captain taking the puck, Alice knew that G was going to do something amazing. Sure enough, after finding some open space G scored and won the game.

That's when Alice finally dug out her phone to see a stream of texts from the various players' girlfriends and wives from the Sound and a missed call from Brigitta. She knew that something bad had happened to Scotty. So despite the Linc being extremely loud with cheering the epic comeback win, Alice called Brigitta. Brigitta immediately picked up and said, "Given the noise, I'm assuming that you aren't watching the Sound game right now."

"Yeah. What happened to Scotty? I haven't looked at all the messages yet but I see have a ton."

"Knee-on-knee hit. It was pretty bad."

"Shit" Alice started to chew at her lip as she tried to process everything. "Do you know anything more than that?"

"Not yet. The announcers haven't said anything which means word hasn't left the locker room that he's ruled out...."

"But that doesn't he will return tonight either."

"Exactly. So all you can do is wait. But I will tell you what I know. If the MRI isn't good, they will send him back to Cleveland for treatment unless it's broken. Then that is an instant hospital trip tonight."

This is where Alice was happy that Brigitta was there to help guide her through this end of things. She knew some of the stuff from a fan's perspective but not as a girlfriend. The fact she didn't see it happen made her feel like shit, but she knew that there was no way for her to know that could have happened. Not knowing the ropes, she asked, "Okay. Should I call his phone?"

"Not yet. He won't be able to turn it on until after the

game. Same rules apply even if they are getting worked on by the trainers."

"Figures."

"If you can't reach him, call Lager. He'll keep you updated. He'll be keeping tabs on Scotty anyway."

Alice's stomach dropped at that point. She felt horrible but she needed to get his real phone number. Lager was so ashamed of having to take swim lessons, that he swore her to secrecy and was only setting up lessons through his Swiss sim card in case anyone looked at her phone. Alice had no clue if he confided about the lessons in Brigitta or if he would have his Swiss sim card. So Alice said quickly, "My phone has been acting weird tonight and I lost some contacts, any chance you can send me Lager's contact information?"

"Sure. I'll text it for you."

Alice knew it was a super long shot but she had to ask the question anyway, especially after seeing what happened on the ice earlier tonight to one of the Flyers in the second period, "Any chance it's just a stinger?"

"Doubtful. Scotty needed help off the ice and couldn't put any weight on his leg."

"Fuck." Alice knew Scotty well enough that he wouldn't have liked needing help one iota and if it was a stinger, he would have walked it off. Hell, he would try to walk it off still and have the leg buckle on him. So it had to be pretty bad if he needed help and the fact he couldn't put any weight on the leg only underscored just how hurt he truly was.

"Yeah, exactly. Just know we're here if you need to talk. The boys get so moody when they can't play especially if they think they might be done for the season. Expect a bumpy road ahead."

"I'll keep that in mind. Thanks Bridge."

Alice felt slightly deflated. No matter how epic the Flyers win just was especially with the unreal comeback against their archrivals, she was worried about Scotty's knee and the outlook for his season. She wanted to talk to Scotty and be there for him.

As soon as Alice put her phone in the pocket, Jenna asked, "What's going on? That wasn't a happy phone call."

"Scotty got hurt tonight."

"Is he okay?"

"Don't think so." as Alice shook her head. "Now I just want to get to a place where we can turn on the Sound game and get any updates during the game. But you know how that doesn't always happen mid-game."

"I won't be opposed to watching the game at my place. That way I can see Corey play some more."

"Cool. I just don't know who they will slot into Scotty's spot at center. I guess either Dykstman or PK but neither are natural centers. Also, I still can't believe you and Corey are now a thing and you even care about the Sound in more than them winning will help the Flyers or Scotty makes me happy kind of way."

"I could say that about you. Hell you moved in with Scotty. I still can't believe you guys were practically living together before you told me fully who he was. I should still be giving you shit for having Instagram break the news that your Scott was the one freaking Sound player that you been crushing on since they got a team."

Alice just shrugged her shoulders. She knew Jenna was right. While Jenna always knew she was dating a Scott, Alice never mentioned anything about how he was a hockey player for the Sound until after the puppy video that Scott posted. She was justifiably pissed and gave her shit for not actually divulging it was Scott.

"True. But if wasn't for the break-in, I wouldn't be living with him now. I know it's been going so super-fast but it's been good. This month has been kinda sucky with both of us traveling a lot but it makes our time together better. I actually can't imagine him being out of my life. I love him."

Jenna nodded and was happy for Alice. They rushed towards her place. But by the time they got there, the Sound vs the Wild game was practically finished. They watched the Wild try to force something to happen with the last three minutes. But the Sound looked solid and won with 3-0 giving Crestor his sixth shutout of the year.

Basically as soon as the game ended, Alice texted Scott asking how he was doing. She was surprised when he called back so quickly. She knew he would call when he had a chance since he seemed to love talking on the phone over texting about stuff. So she quickly accepted the call and said, "Hey babe."

Scotty's voice sounded rough and almost angry when he said, "Hey."

"You okay?"

"I will be once the pain meds kick in but it hurts like a mother fucking bitch, right now."

"I can only imagine."

"It's not broke but I will need to get surgery on my ACL tomorrow."

She instantly supplied him with "Oh that sucks!" as she was trying to remember the timeline for an ACL surgery. But

Scotty knew what information that she was trying to dig out of her mind.

"They are hopeful that I will be out 6-8 weeks."

"So at least it's not season ending. You should even have time to play a few games to shake off the rust before the playoffs." Alice was trying to put a positive spin over the injury but knew that was a weak attempt at best.

Scott's voice seemed slightly deflated as he said, "If we still make it."

Normally it was Scotty who tried to build up her confidence or squash the negativity. This is the first time Alice saw him doubt anything or be a little dejected. So she went into her standard coaching mode, "Seriously, you can't be doubting that. You have a solid position in the standings and there's a great team around you. Even without you playing, the Sound will have a playoff berth for you to come back to."

"I knew you would talk sense into him," Alice heard Lager say and laughing in the background. She just shook her head and rolled her eyes, not that he could see it. But it did keep her from saying something rude to Scotty's best friend.

"So should I look for an earlier flight back to Cleveland or a flight to Minnesota?" asked Alice. She knew that her original plan was to leave in two days but she knew that she couldn't be in Philly when he was hurt.

Scott dismissed her out of hand and said, "Stay in Philly like planned."

"Are you sure?"

"Yeah. I fly out in the morning and then surgery at UH in the afternoon. You will just be waiting around. I would rather you to be with your friends since you never see them. It's just going to be one day that you would be missing."

Scotty was clearly forgetting that her flight was late on Monday, so it wasn't like she was just missing him the day of the surgery. She wouldn't be there for two days and she didn't like the idea of staying in Philly that long if he was hurt. He wouldn't be able to put weight on his knee after surgery, he wouldn't make it up the stairs to go to bed on his own.

Lager interjected again by saying "Don't listen to him. Go to Cleveland. Play nurse. Make him less cranky."

"Shut it Lager. I wasn't asking you." Alice said sternly. Alice was amazed at how much he was chirping in. She was starting to wonder if Scotty had them on speaker. There was some background noise but it didn't seem echoey like most speaker calls so she wasn't sure. She just wasn't going to over-think the idea that she might be but she was sure as hell not going to say anything embarrassing either. But she softened her voice again while addressing Scott, "Scotty, are you sure you that you want me to stay in Philly?"

"It'll be fine. I don't want you to miss out on time with your friends just to sit in a waiting room for a routine repair."

There was something about Scotty's tone that made Alice less convinced that she should stay. But for now, she was going to go along with his wishes, "If you say so. I just feel bad."

"It sucks for sure. The meds will kick in soon and that will help. Until then, it's lots of ice to keep the swelling down. I can handle it."

"I know. Too bad the meds aren't already working for you. If you can't sleep, you know to call me anytime."

"You just want him to get loopy," she heard Lager say. Now she was sure that they were on speaker.

But before she could say, Scotty said it first, "For fucks

sake, shut it Lager. We are trying to have a private conversation."

Then she heard a voice she's not familiar with or at least she couldn't instantly place say, "Well next time, don't make calls on speaker."

All of a sudden, the background noise decreased dramatically and there was a very apologetic Scotty saying, "Sorry Alice, I didn't mean for that to happen. I don't know how it went to speaker."

Alice just shrugged her shoulders and said, "Shit happens. It's not like either of us said anything too embarrassing. Besides you are having a shitastic day. You get a pass on any mistakes."

Scotty changed the subject, most likely to take his mind off the pain by asking, "How was your game? I haven't heard anything about the other games today."

"It was dramatic for sure. But the Flyers pulled off the all too important win. But I won't lie, I would be far more excited about that win, since it was basically a dream game, if I didn't learn about your injury. Since then, I've just been worried about you. Okay don't hate me, but I need to know more. Do you have the surgery booked and how long will it take?"

"It's booked at like 3:30pm. As long as all things go well, I will get to go home at the end of the night."

"Okay." Alice was still wanting to make things work to help so she could get back in time. She knew that Scott wasn't fully on board with the idea of her coming home early.

"Don't you have a game night planned tomorrow?" Scotty clearly knew that she was trying to switch out her plans so she could go home to him even if he refused to say that he wanted her there.

"Yeah but it's more of an afternoon thing and I've seen everyone who is going to the game night at least once this trip."

Before Alice could say more, Scott cut in and said, "First, I know you were looking forward to the game night and especially the beer drinking game. You were talking about it too much beforehand and you wanted to win without relying on ABV. Second, have you had a chance to meet the baby of your friend?"

Alice took a deep breath. "Yes, I saw Sierra and her baby. I can play the game another trip. I would rather be there for you and if I stayed, I would feel hella guilty if I didn't investigate the options."

"Fine. It's obvious that I can't stop you from coming home early," said Scott. Alice knew he wanted to say more but he was holding back something. She had the sense it was either to say don't cancel her plans and/or he was stopping himself from a stream of curse words. She could hear him suck in his breath as if trying to control the pain. Then he spoke with a slightly more dejected tone, "Hey Alice. I have to go back to the hotel. I can't stay on the phone and use the crutches. I'll call you back later to see what you end up doing."

"Okay Scotty. Have a better night. Je t'aime."

While Alice was on the phone, she noticed that Jenna turned on a Harry Potter movie in the background. Jenna was furiously typing into her phone. Alice had a feeling that Jenna was talking with Corey. Alice started to see if she could bump up her flight. As she was searching, she found the ideal flight since it should allow for her to do the game night if they moved it up just slightly and she could be back just in time for Scotty to be discharged from the hospital.

Scott

Scott hated being injured. The season was proving to be rather frustrating. Between the concussion and now screwing up his ACL, the season would be eaten up with more injury time then he ever wanted. The thing that sucked the most was that when he was on the ice, he was on pace to have a career season. He thought the Sound had a really good chance for the cup but they needed him, Dyskts and Lager to stay healthy and he was failing at that. He was just hoping he could return before the end of the season and still have post-season play ahead of them.

Scott could barely sleep since the pain meds were barely taking the edge off the pain. It seemed like any time he moved, it would set off a new spasm of pain and jolt him awake. He already sleeping a little less since he was staying up late with Alice after every game.

The only good thing about the prospect of being out of action for at least six weeks was that he could be home with Alice. It would be the longest they had together in one shot. Scott hoped that it was just 6-8 weeks together and not until the next season. He knew that there was a solid chance that he might not be ready in time. While the Sound should make it to the playoffs, it wasn't like they officially had a berth yet. They were already seeing both the Flyers and the Blues dig themselves out of the bottom of the standings and make a run for it.

The flight to Cleveland was uneventful. The trainer kept Scott's knee on ice throughout the flight and that was actually helping big time with the pain and swelling but it wasn't comfortable. He felt stiff and awkward with the crutches.

At least, the Sound arranged a car from the airport and

later on to the hospital. They offered to do a car as well from the hospital but he declined that since Alice insisted on flying back early. The ride was quiet and Scott tried to see if he could get any rest he could. It wasn't until they started to pull into his driveway, the driver said, "It looks like you have company."

That surprised him. Scott started to look to figure out what was going on. As soon as he saw the car, he knew it was his mom's. "Don't tell me she drove all night." He shook his head. Now instead of just one upset woman who would try to dote on him way too much, now there would be two. He wasn't upset that his mom actually drove down but thought the whole thing was overkill.

The driver helped to open the car door and took Scott's suitcase up to the house door. As he opened the house door, he heard his mom call out in French, "Is that you, Scott or is it Alice?"

"C'est moi, maman."

It was obvious that his mom was in his kitchen as per usual since he heard all the noises from that area stop and his mom immediately rushed out. She came with a hug and said, "Are you okay? Where's Alice and the dogs?"

"Why did you come?" As Scott hugged his mom without losing his crutches and gave his mom a kiss. "I will be okay soon enough. I can take care of myself and Alice will be here to help too. She gets home tonight. She had a belated birthday celebration with her friends in Philly this weekend. I already feel guilty enough she's canceled some of her plans there. You didn't have to drive all night."

"I wanted to take care of my boy. I knew from how you couldn't get up on your own, it was more than just a stinger.

Your dad tried to convince me to wait a little longer and not worry but when you didn't come back to the bench in a period, I decided to come."

Scott shook his head. He could see the whole thing play out exactly that way. His mom was a bit of a force who wanted to feed and care for her family. He would prefer just to forget about the whole thing.

"It's just an ACL surgery. I'm not dying." Scott said with a bit of a grimace. The crutches were digging into his armpits. He knew he should be sitting down, so he started to hobble over the couch.

"I can still be there for you. I don't care if you are all grown up and some hot-shot NHLer. You will always be my boy. Now what do you want to eat?"

"I can't eat maman. You know that is standard surgery protocol. I just need to sit down for a little bit."

Scott didn't want the attention. He got hurt like everyone else. He didn't need to be pampered. It's the same reason he wanted Alice to keep her original plans. He'd rather just hide out for the time being and would much rather just get back on the ice.

His mom fortunately didn't try to fight him on the food issue. But he knew that was likely to change as her stay continued. As she continued to do things in the kitchen, she asked, "Alright. But I expect you to eat something afterwards. What time do we need to go to the hospital?"

"A car is coming at about 2:30pm to pick me up. You should be able to ride in the car without a problem."

Scott leaned his head back and closed his eyes. Then he realized he should warn Alice. The last thing he needed to do was freak her out since he knew that if Alice walked in without any warning, she would be justifiably pissed. His mom meant well and wouldn't leave for at least a few days until she knew that Scott was in the clear. So he pulled out his phone. Normally he would have called but after finding out his mom knew more English than she let on, it was more private to just text Alice and she liked it better that way too.

S: *So maman is here.*

A: *That's good, right?*

S: *I guess. Wasn't expecting it and she's already taken over the kitchen.*

A: *Oh boy. This will be a dumb question but hows the knee?*

S: *Hurts like a bitch. Are you doing anything fun today?*

A: *About ready to start Unlabel'd*

S: *Going to kick some butt?*

A: *I hope so but Jenna knows beer better.*

S: *You seem to know your shit too.*

A: *I'm good but beer can be weird. I don't trust my palate to know the styles especially as brewers start to do weird shit.*

S: *Just trust your gut. You know it.*

A: *Are you trying to pump up my ego as a distraction from your mom?*

S: *Maybe.*

A: *Hang in there. I can't blame her for coming. I wish was there.*

S: *Yeah but you would do more than cook and pamper.*

A: *Yeah. I can keep your mind off of things. Oh, before I forget, when I should I pick up Chloe and Backup? I could do it before going to the hospital or we can leave them at the doggie hotel until tomorrow like we planned.*

S: *Tonight would be nice.*

A: ***Okay. Need to talk more or is it okay if I go into competitive game mode?***

S: ***Go be competitive. I should be social with maman.***

A: ***Good luck today and see you soon. Love you.***

S: ***Thanks. Je t'aime.***

"Scott, are you paying any attention to me? I was asking you some questions" said his mom a little bit upset by him being oblivious to the world around him as he was texting Alice.

"Sorry. I wasn't maman."

"How's things with you and Alice? Is it still going well now that she moved in?"

"Things are great but this month has been crazy. We have been like ships passing in the night. The only good thing about the surgery is that we will finally have some real time together after weeks of not seeing each other."

"Yeah. It would be good for you guys to experience life without a ton of road trips. This is when things will become real when you are living together full time. Just remember it won't always be bliss. So what do you want for dessert tonight?"

"Nothing. I still have to be good with my diet. It's a bit of a long shot for me to make it back before the season ends. Staying fit and working on my conditioning will help to make sure I can get back quickly."

"Now, you know that one dessert won't mess that up. I'm only in town once in a blue moon. Let me bake something for my boy. I promise I won't make dessert every day when I'm here."

"Fine. How about angel food cake with some fruit compote?" asked Scott. He knew that if he didn't at least agree to one dessert, she would just go ahead and do it anyway and possibly do something that would be far less healthy.

"Sure. I should have guessed. That's always been one of your favorite desserts."

The time with maman wasn't bad. She was cooking what seemed to be a feast. Scott couldn't figure out who she was cooking for since it seemed like way too much food for the three of them could ever eat. But Scott knew any protests, saying it was too much food would only get brushed off. It didn't matter that Alice wasn't going be getting home until later that evening. The more Scott thought about it, he realized the person who was going to struggle with his mom's desire to feed everyone would be Alice. There was no way his mom was going to let her go to work with just a cup a coffee although he could always wake her up earlier than normal.

As he was waiting for his ride to the hospital, he decided to catch up on yesterday's hockey games starting with the game that Alice was at. It was a safe bet to be an entertaining game since Alice called the game dramatic. But before he made it to the third period, the car was there to pick him up for his surgery. So they made their way to UH.

At the hospital, he did all the necessary paperwork. Then it was all the prep work: getting into the proper clothing, getting fitted for the knee brace that he would wear in a couple of weeks' time. He was already looking forward to when he could be in the knee brace instead of the crutches. Then it was time for the surgery itself.

16

ALICE

Alice felt like she was running around all day but it was all worth it. She had one last day with friends to do some gaming, then it was the flight back to Cleveland. She got the dogs from the kennel and then made the trip to the hospital to await Scott's surgery to be complete. It took a little bit to find the right waiting room inside the hospital. At least she knew that she was in the right spot when she could see Scott's mom sitting in one of the hospital lobbies.

As Alice approached Scott's mom, Alice's nerves started to increase. She realized that she would have to use her imperfect French skills and translate for her. That seemed to be a scary proposition. There was a part of her that wished there was an official translator to make things work. But she knew that she would have to listen to Tim Gunn's catchphrase and "just make it work."

As soon as Scott's mom spotted Alice, she came up and gave Alice a huge hug and asked, "How's the flight back?" Alice wasn't expecting to be so tightly held right away from his mom. Before Scott's mom even gave her a chance to breathe or speak, she said, "You are shorter than I thought you would be. But I shouldn't be too surprised."

Alice smiled and had to think through what his mom was saying since she spoke so quickly in French. As she started through the mental translation she started to speak, "The flight was okay. Any word from Scott's doctors?"

"Not yet. Should be another 30 minutes or so. That's if they started on time and nothing went wrong."

Scott's mom pulled her towards where she was sitting and invited Alice to sit beside her. It was clear that she wasn't going to hold back at all with Alice. She wanted to use the time to get to know Alice without Scotty around. The other thing that shocked Alice was just how calm his mom seemed despite driving what had to be all night.

"You seem to be so calm. Have you gone through this before?"

"Yeah. He tore his other ACL in juniors. I'm just glad that he's been healthy over the years. I know it could be far worse. But missing this part of the season will make him crazy. He's always hated being on the sidelines and prefers to carry the team when he can."

Alice nodded. She knew that Scott loved the action. His drive is what helped to get him into the NHL and then into being a stand out player each and every single night. But she had no idea that he had another knee surgery. She knew that he'd been fairly healthy over the years and even played close to 250 games without missing a game before his first concussion last season.

Alice's phone buzzed so she looked to see what it was. There was a message from Jenna who said that the Wild player got a suspension from the hit on Scott. While she was glad that he was penalized, it didn't help her boyfriend get back on the ice any quicker. She knew she should tell Scott's mom. So she had to google the word for suspension. She just hoped she was pronouncing it correctly as she said, "The guy who hurt Scott is suspended for one game."

"That's something. So I want to know more about you. Do you cook?" as Scott's mom started to shift the conversation again.

"Not often. I can cook and people like what I do make. More often than not, Scott does it since he's home earlier and enjoys it more." His mom nodded and didn't seem surprised by that. Alice knew that Scott and his mom were close so she assumed that he must have told her. But talking about the cooking, it reminded Alice that she saw basically saw a full dinner prepared for when they get home. "I'm assuming you were the one that made the cake and everything else at home today?"

"Yeah. I cook when I'm stressed. It's nice to keep my hands busy and I love to feed the boys. And it was nice when Scotty would help out in the kitchen with me too."

Alice nodded. "I normally write or knit when I'm stressed so I can keep my hands busy. Although lately, I haven't knitted much."

"Scott showed me some of your pieces. They look fantastic. But why aren't you knitting? I know that life hasn't been the kindest to you lately."

Alice took a deep breath. It was weird to put it into words. But she thought that she had it. "Knitting hasn't felt right after the break-in. I think part of it, I mostly knitted and listened to crime stories. I can't bear to listen to the crime stories and it just doesn't feel right doing one without the other. Plus nothing has really been calling me with the designs. So I've been writing short stories to keep me busy."

Scott's mom nodded in agreement but said almost wistfully, "That makes sense but I hope you restart knitting again."

Alice wanted to say I will but she realized that she wasn't quite sure which verb she should use. So she settled on saying, "One day."

Their conversation was interrupted when a doctor came out looking for them. The doctor had a Sound shirt underneath his white coat so Alice was wondering if that was the trainer that traveled back with Scott. Once the doctor determined who they were, he said, "So the surgery went well. He's still coming out of it and once he's cleared by the anesthesiologist, he can go home."

Alice paraphrased for Scott's mom, "It went well. He's waking up some and we can take Scott home soon."

Scott's mom looked happy and said, "Good."

Alice knew that she should say something since it could be a while before they got to see Scott and take him home. But his mom must have had the same idea and she said, "Just so you know, Scott won't want to have too much help after the surgery. He loves to fix things when people are struggling and make everyone smile but he doesn't always like it when people return the favor. He doesn't like to be doted on."

Alice nodded. She could understand that. But if his mom knew that Scott hated the attention, there was a part of Alice was wondering why his mom came to visit. But then she realized it was the same reason that she decided to come home early: she wanted to be of some use and it was a way to calm her own fears.

"I could tell by the way he didn't want me to come home early."

A nurse brought out Scott. He was in a wheelchair with his left leg extended out so it couldn't bend. Scott was clearly under the effects of anesthesia and possibly some pain medication as well. His eyes were sleepy and his head kept rolling around. But once he saw the two of them, his eyes lit up and he said in a very slurred voice, "Hey you."

"Hey," said Alice. "Ready to go home?"

Scott attempted to nod but it didn't really work. Alice was going to take control of the wheelchair but Scott's mom was already there. So Alice stood beside Scott. He grabbed her hand and interwove his fingers with Alice's fingers. Then they started to head over to Scott's SUV that Alice drove over so Scott would be more comfortable on the ride home.

"You're pretty," said Scott to Alice. Alice had to laugh. He looked at his mom and said, "Maman, don't you think she's pretty?"

The one thing that was almost strange was how Scott was speaking in English and not using French to his mom. If anything Alice was almost expecting him to speak more in French then English. So Alice did the super quick translation and his mom just agreed with him.

They were practically to the SUV, Scott looked up to Alice and said, "You're pretty" for the tenth time.

His mom at that point said "Tabarnak de calice"

Alice was a loss of what she actually bit it sounded like was swear word but it also sounded like something from church. And given the way she used it, it sounded like it was more of a curse word then a prayer. Then when Scott said, in a mock seriousness "Maman" that she knew it had to be a curse word that Alice wasn't actually familiar with.

Scott's mom said to Alice "He's worse than last time."

By then it was time to transfer Scott to the car. His mom and Alice had to work together to get him into the passenger seat and make sure he was keeping his weight off the leg. He was mostly asleep again on the drive back to house.

The drive back was quiet. Both Alice and his mom were trying to let Scott sleep. When Alice pulled into the garage, Scott woke up which was helpful to get him out of the car. Scott's mom had the crutches ready but he was still unsteady so they were careful that he didn't fall over as they entered the house. The dogs tried to flock until they realized they couldn't get anyone's attention. Then Scott saw the dogs and he said, "Hey, we have puppies. I love puppies."

Alice just giggled. It was so silly and it was like he was drunk which is something that she literally had never seen. He was always in control. They got him to the sofa and propped up his leg on a pillow. As he got comfy, he cupped her face and said, "Sit next to me. You're so pretty and I've missed you. I haven't seen you in so long."

"Okay." Alice sat next to Scott. She cuddled up next to him but spread out her legs to the side. She missed him too. The dogs were sniffing around the two of them. But since there wasn't any space on the sofa for the dogs, they just placed their heads on his lap. He started to pet the puppies head. He had the same goofy grin from earlier.

Scott's mom went to the kitchen and started to reheat the food she cooked earlier. Alice looked over to the kitchen and asked, "Would you like any help?"

"No, just keep him company. He's happy and that makes things so much easier." Scott's head fell over on top of Alice's head. She knew that she was out again. Alice just stayed still for a few minutes. Scott's mom broke the silence when she said, "He really likes you. I've never seen him like that. He's just so happy with you. After his last surgery, he was so grumpy although he still said anything that came to his mind. I wouldn't be surprised if he would want to get you a ring soon. Do you want a plate brought over to you?"

Alice was surprised that his mom mentioned an engagement ring. It seemed crazy since she just moved in. But she just acknowledged the question about the food and said, "Sure."

Then after a few more moments, Scott's mom came into the living room with two plates. Before she took a plate from Scott's mom, she turned and kissed Scott lightly and said, "Hey sleepy head. It's time to eat."

Scott woke up some but almost as quickly fell back asleep. But his mom was having none of it. She said in a loud, stern voice. "Now Scott Simon Wheiland. You are going to eat right now. I don't care whether you are hungry or not."

That's when Scott woke up fully. Alice had to laugh. She'd never heard Scotty's middle name before. She had a feeling that she would hear that a few more times during his mom's trip. She also took her plate. She noticed a rustic stew and fresh bread that smelled good.

Scotty turned to her and asked, "What's so funny?"

"You babe." He was really a trip any time he was awake. If it wasn't so silly, she would like to see him be under the effects of the anesthesia on a regular basis.

"That's not nice. I had surgery. You should be nice to me." He practically started to stick out his tongue at her.

Alice had to stifle the giggle that was still threatening to come out. So she took a spoonful of stew. It was delicious and something she was craving without realizing it. Scott was eating some of the stew but Alice could tell right away that he wasn't hungry and only appeasing his mom by taking a few bites. He normally would eat his plate and then clean off any of hers if he had any appetite at all.

Once Alice knew that she wouldn't be laughing anymore at Scotty, "How would you like me to make it up to you?"

With no hesitation, he said, "Hockey and kisses."

While laughing, she turned on the TV. It was literally the best answer she ever heard. She noticed that there was a game that was that was paused on the TV and she just hit start. She then turned to kiss his jaw first and then his mouth in a very chaste kiss since his mom was sitting across from them. Once she broke away from the kiss that she realized it was the outdoor game the night before. She was confused if Scott was watching that on his own or if he turned on the game for her. Alice smiled and said, "Is that better?"

Scott shook his head, "Yes." He leaned his head back and got comfy. He took a few more bites of the stew before setting the plate on the coffee table. He then turned to Alice and planted a sloppy kiss on her lips. Then he turned his attention to the game before falling asleep again.

Scott

Scott woke up the next morning feeling groggy and like a mac truck ran over him the day before. He was glad to have Alice in his arms and his knee wasn't bothering him like it was before. Although he wasn't sure where Backup and

Chloe were but he assumed that they were running through the house. The day before felt like a blur and he only remembered bits and pieces thanks to the medicine and he wasn't sure how he got to bed.

He looked at the time and realized the two of them should be thinking about waking up. Since if they didn't do that soon, there was a strong chance his mom would try to interfere and he wanted some alone time with the two of them. He leaned and started to kiss Alice along her neck tracing a line all the way up to her ear. She murmured something but Scott couldn't understand what she said, so he kissed her ear again. She stirred again and said a little louder, "It's too early." He kept kissing up and down her neck until she rolled over to face with a smile and said, "What happened to the silly, sleepy Scott from yesterday?"

He smiled and said "He got enough sleep". He knew that he probably said a few silly things but he legitimately couldn't remember much.

Scotty grabbed Alice into a big bear hug and pulled her on top of him while being careful not to bump his bad leg. He wasn't going to let her go back to sleep. He kissed her passionately and said with lust in his voice, "You're not trying to tell me, you'd rather sleep instead of making love. Are you?" Alice was reciprocating everything he gave her, so while she was protesting that she was tired, he didn't think that she really wanted to sleep.

"Is that what you are after?"

He kissed her nose gently and said, "Of course, that's what I want. It's been like forever."

"True and you are so good." Alice said a little dreamily. Scott couldn't help but smile widely.

"So what do you want to do?" Scott asked he started to kiss some of Alice's largest pleasure centers: her ears and the nape of her neck. He saw her head fall back in pleasure and he helped to stabilize her torso with his strong hands. "More of this or sleep?"

"More of this."

Then Scott was off to the races with tossing her shirt off to the side of the room so he could have easy access to her breasts. He started to kiss her nipples and massaged her breasts. She started to kiss him on the mouth and had her hand on the back of his head. He could tell that she was stiffer then normal, most likely trying to avoid the leg that had surgery on it.

Unfortunately for them at that moment, there was a knock on the door. They both froze and Scott made sure he was speaking in French, "What?" He closed his eyes and hoped that his mom didn't open the door and would leave them be quickly. He wasn't sure if Alice would have locked the door the night before.

"Are you okay?"

"Yup."

"Need any pain medicine?"

"Nope. I'm good," and Scott knew he would be in even better shape with his pain management if he was allowed to go back to what him and Alice were doing.

"How much more time do you expect to be in there?"

"I don't know." Scott took a look at his beautiful girlfriend that was sitting on top of him. He wanted to go back to making love. But he knew that answer wouldn't satisfy his mom so quickly added, "Maybe an hour or so."

"Alright. I'm going to take Chloe and Backup for a walk

then."

"Sounds great. We'll be down in about an hour."

Alice was smiling at him but she remained so silent. They were like teenagers who got caught making out despite the fact they were both in their early thirties. He felt the need to apologize again. So he pulled her close to his chest and whispered, "I'm so sorry. I didn't know my maman was coming. I hope everything was okay with her at the hospital and afterwards."

"Everything was fine. Don't worry."

Scott kissed her with vigor. When he pulled away, he said, "You know my maman doesn't like it when you don't eat. You will have to eat breakfast when she's here."

"You got in trouble yesterday for not eating so I know that I will have to eat if I don't want to get on your mom's bad side."

"I did not," scoffed Scotty even though he wasn't really sure if that was the case.

Alice leaned and teased him with a kiss before saying, "You keep telling yourself that Scott Simon Wheiland." That's when knew he was busted and did get into trouble. He never shared his middle name with Alice and the only way she would have ever known that was if his mom said it. He was almost afraid to ask about the details. He had to know but before he could, Alice was looking at him intently as she asked, "I did want to know, what does 'Tabarnak de calice' mean? Cause what I think it means and how your mom used it were two very different things."

Scott had to laugh and really needed to know how on earth Alice heard the phrase. "It basically means Fuck. It's a Quebec thing. But how did you hear it?"

"When we were getting you into the car, you kept saying that I was pretty and wanted your mom to reaffirm that I was pretty. She just said it and that you were worse than the last time you had surgery." She smiled widely and was clearly amused by his antics from the day before, "Frankly, all of last night, it was like you were drunk. It was hysterical. You would wake up and either compliment me, say that you love puppies, or asked for hockey and kisses."

"Oh lord, really?" Scott hated hearing that. He was always on good behavior and Alice had never seen him drunk. He knew he had to be blushing some.

"Yup. It was fun." The more he heard about yesterday everything, the more he was embarrassed. He reached for his phone that was normally charging on the night stand to see if he did anything silly on social media. Alice leaned in and kissed him before saying, "If you are afraid of posting anything on social media, I hid your phone pretty early on. It's one of the reasons you wanted hockey and kisses since you didn't want to give it up. I knew you would be pissed if I let you end up posting anything ridiculous. It's charging in my nightstand drawer."

At that moment he wanted to roll Alice over and take her right there. But he knew that with his knee, he would have to stay on his back and maybe his right side. But definitely no rolling over to his front or moving the left knee at all for the time being.

"So anything else that I should know about from yesterday?" asked a curious Scott.

Alice hesitated but then shook her head no. But Scott didn't believe her one bit. She was holding back something and he wanted to know what it was. Since she was on top of him at the moment, he started to tickle her torso as he said, "Come on, tell me." She was giggling furiously but her tongue remained silent then Scott leaned up to kiss her. As he pulled back, he whispered, "Come on, you know you want to tell me."

Alice laughed some. "Damn, you are persistent today."

"Like that's a bad thing." He said with a wide grin and was so self-assured in that moment, "I play to win, you know that. So tell me before I really have to play hardball."

Alice started to feign with her hand and said, "It's nothing. Really."

"So if it's really nothing, you should share." Scott was smiling. He decided if he wanted to get her to talk, he should start kissing her senselessly since the tickling wasn't loosening her tongue at all.

Just as he was about ready to make his next move, Alice said, "Your mom thinks you will be proposing one day soon."

Scott knew he was smiling widely at that. "Is that all?" Then when Alice didn't say anything right away, he got a little afraid that she wasn't feeling the relationship the same way as he had. So he asked, "Is that a bad thing?"

"No. It's just me being dumb."

Scott put his hands on her shoulders and tried to steady her. "Okay backup. I need to make sure I'm following. It's not a problem that I would **love** to propose to you one day. But it might be? I don't see how you are dumb since the last time I checked you were brilliant but you aren't making sense. So what's up?"

Alice smiled and said, "Basically that's it. I get all weird planning life with a guy after an ex wrecked me. It's nothing but a damn superstitious thought, well fear. You aren't him and we are living together. Everything is perfect and I don't want it to ever end. So yes, this is me being dumb. "

Scott kissed her carefully. He wanted her to know how much he loved her and this morning was perfect. He reached towards his nightstand and dug around in the drawer for a small box. He had purchased the ring while he was on the road trip and didn't really have full plans on when or how he was going to give it to Alice. So, he stuck the ring into his nightstand until he got a plan but today seemed like as good a day as any. He said, "What would you say if I had a ring for you." Before she could even try to deny him, he was quick to say, "It's not an engagement ring yet. I need to do it right, especially the part about being able to get on bended knee. I can't do that for a while."

Alice looked at him incredulously. She had no idea what he was doing and he loved seeing her face with furrowed brows and confusion on her face. He finally was able to get a hold of the ring box and pulled it out. He opened the box with a coy smile. Inside was a small silver Claddagh ring that he designed especially for her to include a garnet, her birthstone, as the heart and the #77 into the center of the crown since that's the number she wears for hockey and his own #34 etched into the band directly underneath the heart.

"What the...."

Scott took it out of the box and handed her the small ring as he said, "It's a ring, silly. See it even goes with your necklace." Alice took the ring and started to look at it carefully. While her face was still fairly confused, he saw how much her eyes were smiling and she was in awe. "Don't leave me hanging. Say something."

"It's beautiful. I just...." She cocked her head and chewed

her bottom lip some. "But why the 77 in the crown and not your 34? Are you sure it's not an engagement ring?"

"Positive. If it was an engagement ring, it would have a diamond in it and I would do it right. Ask your dad, plan an elaborate day and all that kind of shit." Scott started to play with Alice's hair as he looked intently at her face as she kept looking over the ring. "The 77 is in the crown since you get to rule your heart and who you want to let into it. I am pretty sure that's where you keep me inside your heart, so my number is the underbelly of the ring's heart."

That's when Alice finally slipped the ring onto her right hand and then crushed the both of them into the pillows from the strength of her kissing. He wasn't expecting her to be so passionate or to lean into him like she did. The only way she could have moved him at all was if he was taken by surprise. When she pulled back, she said, "You are so fucking amazing. I love you so damn much."

As she started to pull at Scott's boxers and his athletic shorts. Scott smiled and felt himself getting incredibly hard again and he knew he was getting close so he would have to control himself. He reached over to the nightstand to grab a condom. Then cursed when he realized that he was out.

Alice looked at him inquisitively and asked, "What's up?"

"No condoms. I thought I had more."

Alice pulled back and said, "What do you want to do? I'm not on birth control but I'm clean. We could risk it or we can do something like Plan B. I have to go to the drug store any way for more pads to keep your knee clean."

Scott took a deep breath. He knew that he wanted kids so much but they weren't ready yet. He was letting his hands rub up and down Alice as he thought about it. "Would you hate me if I ask you to take Plan B? I just think we should do it in order: a proper engagement, a wedding and then have kids."

"I wouldn't have suggested it if I thought it would be an issue. I might need to investigate getting some birth control though in case this happens again."

Scott leaned up and kissed Alice as he started to rub her clit as Alice adjusted her body so her legs couldn't accidentally hurt Scott's injured leg. Once he entered, she was tight and wet. They both worked at a quick pace. It felt like he practically climaxed straight away and released into her. He felt bad about getting the orgasm quicker than she did. It was rare when he didn't get her off as well and if he could have, he would have easily switched techniques but it seemed so many of his moves were limited by his mobility. Fortunately, Alice didn't seem to mind as she laid on his shoulder. He was so content at that moment. It was the first time that he could say he was okay with the prospect of not playing hockey for a few weeks due to an injury.

In that moment, he didn't feel like he was screwing up his career by being hurt. In the back of his mind, he was still worried that his season was over but it was it was distant voice rather then something that was front and center. He knew the only reason he was so content was due to the woman lying in the crook of his arms.

After a little bit, Scott was getting restless and he was sure that his mom would be coming back to check on them if they stayed in the bedroom for much longer. He looked down at Alice and realized that she fell back to sleep as they were cuddling. With the way, she was sleeping, he was worried about her lack of sleep, and she must have been trying to catch up from when they were apart. He almost felt bad about waking her up a second time but he knew that he would need help to go downstairs and he didn't want to call his mom to help. So he started to kiss Alice's neck again and woke her up in the same way as he did earlier. Once she stirred, he said, "Hey baby. We should go down for breakfast soon."

"Do we have to? It's so comfy here"

"Come on. I know you like it here. But maman will be looking for us soon. Besides don't you want to spend time with Chloe and Backup?"

"Yeah. I guess you're right." She started to prop herself up some on his chest. "Do you think we would have enough time to get a shower? I would prefer not to make it super obvious to your mom what we were doing this morning."

"Probably not a bad idea. I wish I could join you in the shower." Scott said wistfully as he started to play with Alice's long hair.

"Why couldn't you?" asked Alice.

"Uh the surgery. I can't the get area wet. I would think that would be hard to forget."

"There's an easy solution around that. Tape plastic bags around your leg much like how you use tape to keep hockey socks up."

"Seriously? You think that would work?"

"Yeah. I might do a little extra tape above and below but yeah. It would keep your surgery site dry. I already brought up the skin tape and plastic bags to keep in the bathroom."

The idea of being able to join Alice made him hard all over again and he quickly agreed to going into the shower. Alice got up first and handed Scott his crutches. He moved off the bed and hobbled towards the bathroom attached to the master suite. Alice grabbed some clothing for both of them as he started to prep his leg to keep it nice and dry while they were in the shower. It was nice that Alice wasn't trying to smother him and would only help when he actually needed it. It was a nice balance. He had a feeling that his mom might have warned Alice not to try to do too much for him. Although given her own personality, she might have figured that out on her own.

After a quick shower, they headed down the stairs. Scott felt so unstable even with Alice helping to give extra support at his sides. "How the hell did you and maman get me up the stairs last night especially if I was hopped up on drugs?"

"It took a while. But you were insistent that you weren't going to sleep downstairs. I even offered to sleep with you, thinking that was the issue. But you wanted to be in your bed."

Scott shook his head but it did sound like something he would do. Alice and his mom must have had their hands full by the sounds of it. He was actually glad they were together to help with his after surgery care. Since neither of them were super tall and he was a big guy and basically solid muscle on top of that, having the two of them probably made it so they could control and lift him. As soon as they got downstairs, Chloe and Backup were obviously curious about his crutches but gave them enough room to move around albeit slowly. They headed towards the sofa in the living room so he could stretch out and get off his leg and after he got settled, Alice headed to the kitchen to help his mom with the food prep.

Maman immediately said, "Finally, you guys are up."

Alice smiled, "That was my fault. I didn't want to wake up at all today."

"Well, I assume you guys are hungry by now," said Scott's mom. Scott didn't have to look over to the kitchen to know that his mom had the usual spread of food that she would make daily for him and his dad: eggs, Canadian bacon, sausage, potatoes and even fresh biscuits. He could smell the delicious food waiting for them. The only thing that didn't seem to be ready was the coffee but he knew that Alice would be working on that immediately.

"Do you want any coffee, Mrs. Wheiland?"

Scott tried to hide his snickers, he knew that maman would hate that especially after spending yesterday together. But he didn't know what would be appropriate for Alice to call his mom. Although, his mom said nothing about the formality to the name or that it reminds her of her mother-in-law and instead said, "No, thanks."

Alice made their usual coffee for both of them as his mom started to prepare plates of food. Maman brought a plate over to Scotty and started to look at his knee. "How's the pain? I can already tell you are much more like yourself so you must have kicked the anesthesia."

"Pain's tolerable for now. I will take some medicine after breakfast." Scotty said as he started to eat the food, "You know maman, you don't have to cook anything while you are here. Alice can cook too or we can order in."

"I know but I enjoy it." Maman went to the kitchen to get her and Alice's plate. Alice brought over the coffees for both of them.

He was so tempted to say something as Alice was eating breakfast since he'd never seen it in person. But he knew that would go over like a lead balloon. Sure, every once in a blue moon, he could convince her to take some breakfast into work so she could eat it later. Instead as she sat next to him, and his eyes drifted to the ring that he gave her. He loved seeing how it seemed to fit perfectly on her hand and went well with the casual look that she was wearing that day with a tunic and leggings.

"Do you mind if I turn on some hockey?" asked Scotty.

"Not if it's just hockey," said his mom. "I don't need to know or see everything you want to do with her."

Scotty attempted to feign innocent as he turned on the Lightning game from the previous night but he knew there was a subtle reddening to his skin since he knew that his mom was making a casual reference to how he was requesting 'hockey and kisses' the day before and his desire to make love to Alice.

It was a low key day. It seemed like Chloe was confused by how immobile Scotty was. She kept trying to get him to play with her and she whined some when Alice took her for a walk. She clearly wanted Scotty to come with them. Backup was much more easily entertained and didn't care if Scotty was laying on the sofa all day.

The only time things got a little loud was when he turned on the Sound game that evening. He really hated being at home and not with the team. He saw all the blown coverages and was wishing to be out on the ice to help corral the guys in. Even being in the locker room would have been preferable then watching it at home. The only good thing was that he was watching with Alice although it felt like she was holding back since his mom was around.

Alice

Alice's alarm went off for work. Her alarm was on the obnoxious side with way too many sounds but it was hella effective, although normally she would use a different alarm when sharing a bed with Scott or use his alarm. If was the first time since they came home a few days ago that she set up her own alarm. Alice pulled away from Scott's body so she could silence the evilness and he cursed at her, "Why?!?!? That alarm is evil."

"Sorry. Just go back to sleep," Alice said casually as she turned off the alarm.

Scott reached out for her and said, "Come here first." He then pulled her in for a tight hug and kiss. She loved getting held by Scott but she knew that she should get ready for work and couldn't get trapped in the warmth and comfort of his arms. He pouted some as she pulled away. Initially Alice thought that she would be able to get away from the bed without too much trouble, but as she walked by the bed, he grabbed her hand and kissed.

"Babe, I need to get ready for work. Go back to sleep. Let your knee heal."

"Okay, but I wish you would play."

Alice went into the bathroom to start with a quick shower. She got dressed and slowly worked her hair into braids so she was ready for the day. She noticed that Scott was asleep again and that made Alice happy. The two of them stayed up a little too late the last few nights.

As Alice started to head downstairs, she heard a couple voices talking in French. She immediately recognized Scott's mom's voice but she was having trouble placing the male voice initially. Then after a few words, she realized it was Lager. That's when her plans to go downstairs immediately changed.

What the hell is he doing here this early? I know I'm not

supposed to see him until tonight, thought Alice.

Alice went back to the bedroom. She sat down on the bed next to him and kissed him over and over until he started to stir again.

Eventually he said, "Mmhmm. I thought you said I could sleep a little bit since you had to go to work." Scotty then immediately pulled her down in a hug and a kiss.

"I wanted to warn you that Lager was downstairs."

Scotty's whole demeanor changed. He went from being lusty to downright confused. Alice couldn't blame him. She had no idea why he was there either. "Don't look at me. He's your friend," Alice teased as she started to kiss him. "Might as well get dressed and find out. Do you want any help?"

"Can you just grab some clothes and bring them over? Save me from trying to carry stuff with the crutches."

"Sure" Alice said as she immediately grabbed him a grey Sound t-shirt, boxers, socks, and his favorite athletic shorts for him. She knew that those were some of his go-to clothing when he had time off and they didn't have anything official planned. Scott pulled the clothes on and started to get up from bed. He grabbed crutches that were lying beside the bed and the two of them headed downstairs. Alice supported him on one side while Scott tried to keep his balance with both crutches under the other.

As they made their way downstairs, Lager said, "This is why you should have gotten an elevator installed like I told you."

Scotty immediately fired back with, "Seriously?!?" If I had an elevator, I wouldn't have the perfect excuse to be held by my girlfriend multiple times a day."

Alice rolled her eyes. This was when Lager was just a bad

influence on Scotty. But she knew underneath Lager's bravado, he was a good guy. Plus in that moment, she completely sided with Scotty on this one. She thought they had the best solution thus far, albeit if it was a little riskier than an elevator.

Once they reached the bottom of the stairs, she let go of Scotty's torso. He ushered Lager towards the living room saying, "I've got to sit down. Also what's the deal with coming before practice?"

As they were heading towards the living room, Alice attempted to make a quick exit to go to work. She heard someone, she pretty sure it was Scotty who said, "Where do you think you're going?"

Alice turned around and tried to show some innocence with the failed Irish goodbye. She shrugged her shoulders saying, "Just about time for me to go to work and I wanted to let you guys hang out."

"Not before you eat some breakfast," said Scott's mom sternly. "Most important meal of the day. It's all set so it won't even make you late."

Alice just couldn't help but think this is why Scotty wanted to stop her escape just to make sure she ate breakfast. But instead of making a fuss, she just did as she did as she was told. She got a plate and put a small portion of eggs and potatoes on it and sat down next to Scotty as Scotty's mom was preparing other plates of food for Scotty. Lager already had his. Lager was in the red chair and Scotty's mom sat down in the loveseat across from Lager after she was done handing out the food to Scotty.

Alice remained silent as Scotty and Lager were dissecting last night's Sound game. But as soon as Lager caught sight of her ring he said, "Don't tell me you proposed to Alice already? Do I have to start supervising you anytime that you are away from the Sound to make sure you guys don't elope?"

Alice shook her head and said casually, "Wrong hand for an engagement ring. But, yes Scotty did get me the ring."

Scotty pulled Alice closed, tipped her chin as he started to kiss Alice's lips softly. Then he looked towards Lager and said, "Is it such a bad thing that I got her a ring especially since I know for a fact that you got Bridge those fancy shoes and a necklace from Tiffany's the last time we played in New York City and in Vegas."

"I guess not. But you already blindsided me with having Alice move in over the All-Star break, so I wouldn't put it past you to propose or do an elopement now that you are on IR for a few weeks. Just remember if you are thinking about doing that, please tell me about it ahead of time. I want to be there."

Scotty's mom asked what was going on since they were speaking in English and Scotty did the quick translation to what was being said. Once she understood what was being talked about, she said, "I want to know before you propose to her too." Scotty just shook his head in disbelief.

Alice was quickly trying to eat what was on her plate. She didn't want to be late to work and she wished like hell that the attention was off of her. She felt on the spot with the conversation. She didn't hide the ring or even play with it but she was trying to hide a little bit by leaning into Scotty. He just put an arm around her for a second before kissing her. He said, "I'm glad you are wearing the ring, don't listen to Lager." Alice just nodded.

The kiss comforted her but she still hated being the

center of attention. Once she finished her plate, she stood up and said, "Sorry I have to get to work," as she started to put her finished plate into the dishwasher.

She grabbed her favorite travel mug and was about ready to fill it when she noticed that it was already full. That's when Scotty's mom said, "Don't forget to take your coffee. Scotty told me how he normally preps that for you in the morning."

"Merci." Alice was tempted to say Mrs. Wheiland but Scott mentioned that his mom typically didn't like to be called anything super formal and that it was okay to be relaxed around her. So Alice was trying.

Alice started to head out through the garage door where she attempted to make the failed get away when Scotty looked towards her. He got off the couch and gave her a quick goodbye kiss. Before heading to the door, she looked towards Lager and said, "Take care of him while I'm at work."

"You don't have anything to worry about. He's even going to practice today," said a confident Lager.

Scotty looked slightly flabbergasted and said, "That's news to me."

"Yeah. It was decided last night on the plane back. Coach and doc wanted me to drag your ass to the rink. Why the hell do you think I'm here this early?"

"Dude, I don't have time to hear this. Settle it after I leave. But if Scotty is injured even more, I will throat punch you Lager," said Alice.

That made Scotty laugh hysterically and Lager just scoffed. As Alice was closing the door, she could hear Lager say, "As if you could reach." All Alice could think at that moment was how much Lager needed to learn yet about how scrappy a Philly girl could really be.

Almost at the moment that she started her car, her dad called as he did most mornings. It started as an emergency alarm for her in high school but it just continued since it was a convenient time for both of them.

"Hey dad."

"Hey kid. How's it going at home?"

"Not too bad."

"So I take it that Scotty is recovering okay." Her dad knew about the extent of the injury and actually helped her to make new flight arrangements. He didn't call the last couple days since they both thought she would be busy taking care of him.

"So far so good. But I suspect that it won't remain this easy for much longer. The past few days it's been more about being together after being apart for so long. I don't think it's really hit him that he can't play hockey yet so I keep waiting for that to happen."

"At least, it's good now and you never know, it might stay easy."

"Yeah."

"Everything okay? You seem a little quiet this morning."

"Yeah. There's just been a lot of talk about Scotty proposing between his mom and Lager this morning and the other day. It didn't help that he got me this beautiful Claddagh ring that Lager mistook for an engagement ring. But it's all good. Scotty said, while he wants to, it won't be for a while yet. He wants to do it right and do the whole thing. I know that I'm just overthinking it."

"Okay. That's why I like him thus far. But his mom is there? How's that going?"

"Yeah. She came for his surgery as a surprise. But it's been fine. She's been cooking a ton. Having her immediately after the surgery was a godsend for sure. Scotty was either asleep or severely punch drunk that first day."

Her dad laughed and said, "Sounds like you after your surgery."

"I guess so but I would bet that I was much easier to handle. I knew he was strong but damn dad. He was pure dead weight at times. Thankfully, the next day and was like his old self and seemed to fully kick the meds. For as amusing as he was when he was punch drunk, I was so glad to have him be aware enough to help with his body weight."

"That's good. So is everything still good for me to come this weekend? I know things might be a little bit busier now that his mom is here and he's pretty immobile."

"Yeah I think so. I want to see you anyway. So dad, I have to get off the phone. I just pulled into work now and I was already running a smidge late."

"Alright kid, I'll talk to you later."

Alice quickly got out of the car and dug her phone out of the top pocket to her bag. She saw that she had missed a text from Scotty that made her have a giggle fit as she was trying to scan in to the gym so she could open it.

S: ***Do I have to worry about you throat punching the guy who took me out?***

A: ***LOL! Nah. I don't think I would ever run into him and even if I did, I don't see that working out in my favor.***

A: ***On the way to practice with Lager?***

S: ***Yeah. The more I work with doc, the quicker I can get back on the ice. But I think this might be something different.***

A: ***Just keep me in the loop and have fun. Love ya.***

S: ***Will do. Je t'aime.***

17

SCOTT

As Alice left, Scotty was still laughing at the throat punching comment from her. He'd never heard her say something even remotely similar to that before. Even when they watched games together and her hockey mouth came out, she never called for violence. Then when Lager was trying to say she was too short to reach his throat, that just made him laugh even harder since he could envision a couple different ways she could do it and all would be sneaky as hell. "I don't know Lager. She's scrappy and damn stubborn."

"I'll take my chances. Besides, we all know you aren't going to get hurt more. Mainly Doc wants to see how your knee is healing and to get you into a solid conditioning routine. The usual on that front. Now coach has something else in mind but I've been sworn to secrecy. I promised that I would get you to the rink."

Scotty chuckled and said, "Well look at who's all being a good acting captain. But at the same time, some friend you are for not telling me why coach wants to see me."

"Sorry coach and his habit of making you do herbies until you puke scares me more than most things out there. So we better head over. I don't need to actually piss him off. You okay if I drive your car? I wasn't thinking this morning and I forgot you would be on crutches yet."

Scotty laughed. The thing was Lager wasn't kidding. Berman would make Lager do that many herbies if he told Scotty and might even try to make Scotty do the same thing despite the fact he couldn't even put weight on his knee, let alone skate. "Yeah. That's fine. But don't get used to it."

Scotty turned to his mom and said in French, "Do you mind if I head out with Lager? Apparently, I have practice today. Do you need anything before I head out with him?"

"Go. I'll be fine," replied his mom. Then she turned to Lager and said, "Good seeing you again. Take care of my boy." Scotty had to laugh, Lager always seemed to be the charmer and could always get the trust of anyone. Lager charmed his mom a long time ago.

With that, Lager and Scotty headed off to practice. The ride was friendly but Scotty couldn't help but wonder what Berman wanted to speak to him about. While he pissed off coach a few times when he first met Alice, he and Coach were usually on good terms. They had to be since he was the captain. He knew it couldn't be a concern about his post-surgery protocol since if anything they both knew he would be trying to get onto the ice as soon as possible. He just hated not knowing what Berman wanted him there for.

Once the two of them made it to the rink, Scotty relaxed some. He loved being there and hanging out with the guys. He wished that he could be lacing up with them too but at least he was there. Everyone was being nice and saying that they hoped he would get off the crutches soon. The only person he knew that likely didn't want him to heal super quickly was the rookie they pulled up from the AHL to fill in until he got healthy.

Doc was in the locker room as Scotty and Lager were chatting, checking in on the tape of Andy's leg. He addressed Scotty saying, "Talk with Berman first. I'll get to you when everyone's out on the ice."

"You got it."

Scotty headed to the coach's office. He never minded talking to Berman as long as he wasn't going there to get chewed out. He knocked on the doorframe to the open office door like he always did.

"Come on in Scotty. Let's get you off that damn leg. I need you to have a speedy recovery and get back on the ice as soon as possible. I know the guys will be fine without you but they don't have your talent."

Scotty nodded and sat down keeping his left leg extended so he could keep the pressure off his leg. As he was sitting, "For everyone's sake, I hope the guys play cleaner since the last game. That was way closer than it should have been. Lager said you wanted to speak with me."

"Yeah. I know you got plenty more years in you yet but what do you want to do after you retire?"

Scotty was surprised. While he was on the wrong side of 30 in many people's eyes, he was playing some of the best hockey of his life. To be approached with retirement questions seemed so odd. He shrugged and said, "I always liked the idea of being a coach or scouting then maybe a general management job. There are so many guys with potential out there. I know I couldn't just abandon the game."

Berman smiled widely, that probably scared Scotty more than the retirement question. Scotty was now wicked concerned where the conversation was going since he wasn't ready to retire anytime soon. Coach leaned forward on the desk and propped his elbows on the desk. "That's what I was hoping to hear. We are going to be in a bit of a jam for a few weeks and we need an emergency scout. With you on IR, Parks was hoping we could maybe use you as a scout if you were interested. I still need you to be religious about doing your PT and getting healthy for the ice since that's paramount. What do you think?"

Scotty's jaw dropped. He was surprised that he was even being considered as an option. It seemed unreal and he had no idea what to think. "Honestly, not sure coach. I always thought it would be down the line."

"Well are you interested or not?" Coach Berman said shortly. That's when Scotty knew Berman was hoping for a more definitive response.

Scotty said quickly, "Interested." He left out the part of being in shock and wondering if he was a little less sure of his capabilities in that moment.

"Good." Berman said, and then he picked up the phone and said, "Come on down. He's interested." Then he hung up the phone with a bit of a slam. Not out of anger but because he was rushed. He said, "I have a practice to run. Stay here until Parks and Doug arrive. I'm not risking you on the stairs. As I said, I want you back on the ice sooner rather than later. This scouting thing is NOT and will NOT be your primary focus. Getting back and playing hockey is."

Scotty just nodded. With that Berman grabbed his whistle from the desk and left the office. Scotty felt weird being alone in the office that wasn't his. He tried to look around nonchalantly but he had a feeling it was coming off as awkward.

After a few minutes, two men in suits came down. He immediately recognized GM Parks. The man controlled the day to day operations and would travel with the Sound when he could. He was the one who gave the media the injury updates and would address potential rumors if needed. Then there was a person that was tall but on the stout side that Scotty wasn't familiar with that he assumed to be the Doug who Berman mentioned. He'd seen the name from scouting reports and once in a blue moon from a video session but he'd never interacted with him. Scotty was about to stand up to shake their hands when his GM said firmly, "Don't get up." So Scott stayed put while Doug sat beside him and his GM sat behind Berman's desk.

After the perfunctory greetings, Parks got down to business. "So I think Coach Berman gave you the gist of what we need. This is a busy time for scouting between the upcoming college finals, getting a look at kids coming up for the draft and then reevaluating teams after the trade deadline has passed. If that wasn't bad enough, one of our scouts needs to get heart surgery taking him out of the mix. So we need someone to step in and your name came up since you will be on IR the whole time that we are short."

Scotty nodded his head. He was still wrapping his head around everything. "So what do you need me to do exactly?"

That's when the guy next to him spoke up. "So we are thinking about having you go to professional games and watch them to look for the trends of the games. Basically list out things you boys can do on the ice to counter those trends.

Pay attention to the players that have been recently pulled up from the AHL or acquired in the trade deals. Even think about moments of the game which can be used for video review sessions and then look at talents that could work for or be problematic for the Sound. Also pay attention to those who might be entering the free agency market and if you think they might be someone who makes sense for us to acquire. There might be a practice or two in the same area as a pro game that we will want you to scout some of the undrafted kids prior to the pro game."

Scotty nodded and thought that all seemed pretty straightforward, "Okay, that sounds good. Do you have a schedule in mind?"

"Ideally we would like you to do these games," As Doug passed a sheet of paper to him with a list of dates and games. These were games that Scotty would have watched regularly just to keep up with his hockey sense. They were all mostly eastern conference games. It was ideal aside from the fact that he would be on the road a lot and he wouldn't be watching the Sound play live like he would prefer. Although after the other night, it might be better to watch games that weren't going to make him angry. But he would catch games at least a day or two before the Sound would be playing them. He even saw a Philly trip at the tail end of the first week where he was hoping he could bring Alice to but he didn't want to mention that right away. "I would go with you the first week for training and then the rest it will be on your own."

"That seems pretty straightforward. But would this interfere with my contract at all?"

"I checked with your agent already and there would be no

issues as long as you want to do it. But you can call him yourself to confirm. I wouldn't expect anything less." Then Parks paused for a moment before continuing on with a slightly lighter note almost like he was dangling a bonus, "I know you brought your girlfriend out on the last Philly trip and that she's from that area, we can make arrangements to have that happen again."

Scotty blinked his eyes in shock. It seemed to be too good to be true. It was really surreal. He ran his hand through his hair and said, "You are sure that this isn't coming from the pain meds? It seems literally too good to be true."

GM Parks immediately said, "Well I can't say anything about the meds affecting you. If you are thinking you are hallucinating from them, I would stop. I can say that this is quite real. We need an extra scout and we all know how strong your hockey knowledge has always been. It won't be a cake walk. Knowing Philly, they will probably want you to help promote Gritty in exchange for the tickets and having you at the game in a dual role. Not to mention, we want to keep as much of your rehab with our in-house doctors so we will be flying you back and forth between the games."

Scott knew that it was all reasonable. He didn't expect to have his rehab be cut down at all. He liked knowing they were trying to keep things in-house which meant he will get to see the team a fair amount too. But he knew he had to be smart about the whole deal and couldn't just accept the offer. "Can I get back to you later today? I think it sounds awesome but I need to think and talk to my agent to make sure he's on board."

"No problem. But the sooner, the better. That way we can get all the arrangements set for flights and etc."

Scotty nodded and said, "Will do."

With that both GM Parks and Doug started to get up to leave. They shook Scotty's hand and Parks said, "Go see Doc and do what you need to do there. As I'm sure Berman said, you are more valuable to us when you can actually play, so we don't want any setbacks. Call my number with your decision."

"Got it." Then Scott gathered his crutches to go to the trainer's office. He wanted to make a few phone calls to get the opinion of his mom and most importantly his agent. Also on the list was Alice. He was dreading talking to Alice about the offer. Even though he knew that she would be supportive and love the opportunity for him, he felt like an asshole for dangling the idea that they had several weeks together only to snatch it away from her. He didn't like getting her hopes up only to take the offer away even if it included a trip to Philadelphia for her.

Scotty moved on to see Doc Curren in the trainer's room. Doc seemed to be waiting for Scotty. Then again, he was one of the few guys not out on the ice. Sure before and after practice, doc had his hands full with guys who needed ice, taping and etc. But typically, he wasn't really needed too much while the team was out on the ice. So doc pointed to an examination bench and said, "Come on. Let's see that leg. How's the pain?"

Scott sat on the bench and pushed himself back enough so he could extend out his leg. He let the doc examine his leg. Scott said, "Pain's been manageable. Nothing super crazy for the most part."

Doc just nodded his head at first and then asked, "Been doing the quad sets like we discussed?"

"Yeah. Making sure that I keep them strong and getting things to straighten out properly between each set. That way the knee will be as good as new."

"Good. Now let's see you try to move your left knee for me."

Scotty did as he was told but it was incredibly painful. He cursed under his breath and gripped the edge of the table with considerable force but never gave up on the moving his knee. He didn't stop bending the knee until he heard, "That's enough. Now get it nice and straight again." Scotty could relax so much by the simple command to straighten his leg and he almost instantly let go of the table's edge.

"Not bad. Still got a ways to go but it seems to be healing okay. I think we should still be able to go to the brace next week. I do want you keep the cardio up as much as you can. Until you can put weight on the knee, I would recommend swimming. This week it can be traditional swimming with arms only but we might be able to add the skating motions next week."

Scotty nodded and asked, "So when do you want me to start that?" Scotty wanted to do some more exercise then his just arm workouts in the gym but he knew that he couldn't rush things if he wanted to return in time before the end of the season.

Doc paused a moment before saying, "Could start as early as today. Do you want me to prep the leg? You won't be able to bend it for a while and it might be a little uncomfortable while you wait."

"Yeah. Sounds good. It will be good to see how you prep it so I know how to do it on my own for next time."

So the doc started to change out the gauze pads first and

then taped those in place. After that, they wrapped the knee with lots of plastic. It was almost as if he was getting it iced up after a practice. Then doc paused to say, "So this is should keep things nice and dry with the leg. Are you going to straight to the pool or will you be hanging around here yet?"

"I'll be around be round here for a bit."

"Okay. I will be putting the ice on the knee then. You can take off this top layer with the ice after 20 minutes but leave the rest on until after you swim. It will help to keep the swelling down."

Scotty nodded and said, "Good stuff."

Scotty looked down at his watch and saw that practice would be going on for like 20 minutes more. He went towards the ice to watch the guys practice. Out of habit, he started calling everything as if he was on the ice himself despite knowing that for the most part, no one could hear him on that side of the boards really well.

Once they were done, everyone headed off the ice and passed Scotty on the way out. Lager and Dykstman were almost the last two off the ice. Dykstman said, "Apparently old habits die hard."

"You know you can't teach an old dog new tricks. But at least it was useful, if you could hear actually him." fired off Lager.

Scotty rolled his eyes and said, "Maybe if you talked more on the ice, you wouldn't need help from the gimp from the sidelines."

"Yeah but we love that gimp. Going to the video session today?" asked Corey as he got off. Scotty noticed that Corey's been practicing more lately and trying to put more effort in which he applauded.

"Definite, maybe," said Scott. He smiled realizing how much of Alice's maybes were slipping into his vocabulary. He knew he should tease her over that later in the evening. But in this case, he wasn't using a maybe to couch his response even though he was really leaning towards yes like Alice would do. Instead, he really wasn't sure if Lager planned to bring him back for the videos and he didn't know if coach wanted him there. So Scotty gestured over towards Lager and said, "I don't know. Depends on what that asshole has planned for me today and I'm relying on him for the ride." He probably could get a ride with no issues since it wasn't his right knee if Lager gave him back his keys.

They all laughed and headed towards the locker room. Scotty loved being with the guys. The team was still on a high from the road trip and happy to be at home for a while. They had strong confidence despite so many close games and the early sloppy play that allowed for the forced tight games. What most of the guys cared about was finding a way to get things done to force the OT and often winning in OT. Scotty would love to have that confidence and have clean play the whole game though.

Scotty just talked with guys as they were all getting changed. It was normal locker room banter. Nothing super memorable but a good time. Then Lager and Scotty headed out towards the SUV. The moment the doors shut to the SUV, Lager asked, "So are you going to do it?"

Lager had to be dying to ask Scotty that question. But it was a pretty big secret that he was keeping in and it would be nice to discuss it. "Yeah, I think so. You know that was something I've hoped to do when my career was over and it will make me less useless while I'm out. But it will mean a shit ton of travelling. Not sure how that will be for Alice. I know she will be supportive but she will be disappointed." Scotty paused for a moment and said, "I assume I should say thank you for the opportunity."

"Well Berman was already recommending you as an option to Parkey. I overheard the conversation and just reaffirmed what coach was saying."

"Still, thanks," said Scotty appreciatively. It wasn't pure cockiness about the thanks.

Lager shifted the conversation some when he said, "You really think Alice will be against you scouting while on IR?"

"No. But both of us were looking forward to having time together. Now I'm just going to be leaving again. Sure, I'll be in town for rehab like every other day but what does that mean for our time together? I'm sure there will be days that I will barely see her when I'm home with her mad hours and then my own crazy schedule. Okay, it might be more that I'm the one who hates the idea of leaving her."

Lager just laughed at the last admission from Scotty before saying, "And you wonder why I'm worried that you two might just elope when no one is looking."

"We aren't that bad." Scotty jested back. Elopement was the one thing he would never do with Alice. At worst, it would be a city hall ceremony and a proper reception with their friends. But then Scotty turned serious with, "Besides, I need to talk to Matty before anything is fully decided."

"Yeah. That's why you do have agents in the first place. Make sure he gets you a good deal. Although I'm surprised you haven't done that yet."

Scotty shrugged, "I didn't want to do it at the rink. I

figured it would be better to do at home." Lager said, "That totally makes sense."

Lager pulled into Scotty's driveway and then into the garage. Scott couldn't help but notice that his mom wasn't home at the moment. Scotty felt that was weird but assumed that she must have gone to the store or something. She had to use up most of the baking supplies he had on hand since he was always fairly minimal with the amount of food he kept in the house and Alice was pretty similar.

As soon as he entered the house, he was greeted by Chloe and Backup. He tried to play with the puppies some despite his crutches. Chloe seemed to be glued to his side much like she was when he first got her. He had a feeling it was because she hated seeing him so immobile. He hobbled over to the couch where he'd been living out during the daytime. Chloe climbed up to put half of her body into his lap and the other half was on the sofa as he pulled his cell phone out to call his agent.

"I've been waiting for you to call," was the first thing he heard Matty say.

"Why hello to you too," said Scotty slightly taken aback. But he also knew that was Matty.

"Hey you know me, I'm your agent 'cause I get things done and I get straight to the point. The Sound already faxed over a contract amendment for the scouting. Basically it's some extra money for you but it won't hit the cap. The deal is solid for three maybe four weeks."

Scotty was petting Chloe's head as he grappled with what Matty was telling him. He knew there would be some extra money but he honestly never thought about the cap or even the figures. At this point, he almost thought about money as an afterthought since he had plenty. Instead it was more about the details to the amendment. So he asked, "Any downsides that I need to consider?"

"Besides the increased travel time for the PT, not really. The Sound are the ones who are hamstrung in. If you get off of IR early, you return to play regardless of how many more games you are supposed to scout for with 0 repercussion but no bonus for getting healthy early on your end."

Then Scotty asked, "There was a mention of potentially working with the Flyers on a PR thing."

"Yeah. That's in part for supplying a ticket and travel for Alice during the game. You will pay nothing and if she can't go to the game, then there is no media required. Plus I'm pretty sure that if you go to that game, you won't have to worry about any suits since you will be under the guise of just going to a game with your girlfriend but Sound legal is still double checking if that is allowed."

"Damn you thought of almost everything," said Scotty amazingly. He never even thought about how he might be able to wear normal street clothing to the rink since for all the professional games and even for travel, they had to be dressed up. He assumed that the same rules would apply.

"Pretty much but that's what you pay me for. I'll email the amendment to you now." Then Matty paused for a second. Scotty knew that had to be him working on the computer since anytime Scotty had seen him in the office, Matty would pace until it was time to sign something or send out a document. "Sent. Let's get it signed and I can get it faxed to the Sound. This is a no brainer man."

"Thanks" and the moment he said that, the line went dead. Scotty knew that his agent would be working on something else. But he was happy to get the green light for the opportunity. Scotty knew that he had to talk to Alice and he would rather do it in person but shouldn't drive on his own, he knew that would have to call her instead. He kinda hated how impersonal it felt to do it on the phone but both Matty and the Sound wanted to get the deal done sooner rather than later.

Alice

Alice was surprised when she got a call from Scotty. He rarely called her during the day when he was in town. Sure, it would happen when he was on a road trip but never when he was home. "Hey babe, what's up?"

"'Um we need to talk," said a hesitant Scotty. It didn't sound good and that phrase usually was the start of a break up speech (hell, one time that was the entire break up speech she had) but Scotty caught himself by saying "I'm not trying to break up with you."

Alice was glad to hear that, it wasn't like they had a fight or had anything weird happen. Instead things were pretty normal on that front. So she said, "Okay?" She wanted to ask him to spit it out and just tell her what was going on, rather than dancing around the subject. But she didn't want to rush him so she said, "I'm listening."

"Don't hate me. But this is an amazing opportunity and I have to take it."

"What in the bleeding...." Alice wanted to throw in a f bomb or say hell but since she was at work and a co-worker was beside her, that it would be highly inappropriate. So she watched her language and said, "I know you couldn't have gotten traded and you just surgery so babe, what are you even talking about."

"The Sound want me to be an emergency scout for them for a few weeks," said a slightly more excited Scott.

That surprised Alice for sure. She basically let out a string of consciousness when she said, "Woah, that's amazing baby. Why would I hate you for doing that?"

Scotty seemed to be instantly relieved by her reaction. This was a huge shift in their dynamic. Thanks to the burglary, Scott was the one who would calm Alice down with a simple conversation or a hug. She was glad she could do the same for him. He said, "Cause I'm going to be travelling a ton. Like literally all the time for up to four weeks."

Alice was a little puzzled by why it would it matter. If Scott wasn't hurt, he would be travelling a fair amount. Okay for the next two weeks, the Sound had like five games in a row at home but still travelling was part of the routine as much as she hated it. But she kept a level head about her, "Okay, no big deal. We will make it work. What are we talking about then?"

"Like every other day, I'll be away."

Alice knew that was going to get old real quick. It would put some wear and tear on Scotty, but in terms of their relationship, it wasn't so bad. Alice was quick to say, "So every other day you will be here. That's not terrible at all."

"You sure? I don't know how much I'll really be here. They made it sound like it might be town for rehab only. But I will ask for as many nights at home as I can."

"Babe, I don't want to stand in your way and besides, you said you always wanted to scout or coach at the end of the career. Talk about a good way to see if you actually would enjoy scouting and to keep you busy with hockey."

Then she heard Scotty say something to his mom but she

couldn't quite catch what was being said. It was clear that Scotty pulled the phone far away from his mouth as he talked to her. If it wasn't for the rapid French, she wouldn't have assumed that it was his mom so quickly. After a second, Scotty came back to the line. "Sorry Alice, maman just got home. There was one more thing that came with this offer and it relates to you. The Sound offered to have you come with me on the Philly trip. Can you get off next Thursday and Friday?"

Alice laughed in delight. "Another Philly trip? Yeah, I think I could swing that. I won't book any lessons on Friday but I will have to ask my boss about Thursday. But typically I can get off on Thursdays since we aren't usually shorthanded."

Alice could tell Scotty was practically smiling through the phone when he said, "Oh that'll be awesome. So you are okay with me scouting for 3.5 weeks?"

"Yeah baby. This is a great thing for you. This is a great way to spend your time on IR, helping out your team and learning a new skill. I am proud of you."

"So you will be okay not having me 24/7 during IR like expected?" asked Scotty obviously trying to make sure she wasn't angry or faking her excitement for Scotty.

"Yes baby. I won't always like how you are gone but hey I will get to see you for a fair amount of time too. So we will make for whatever lost time we have when you are home. Besides you are seriously spoiling me rotten with Philly trips. You know that right?"

"Yeah but you are worth it. I just hope we have lots of time in Philly together so you can show me your favorite sites."

That's when Alice knew she had to throw up a roadblock.

What he was talking about seemed to be a little too unrealistic. Philly was a city that required lots of walking usually. Sure there were Segway tours but she would never do that. "Babe, won't you still be on crutches next week?"

"Probably but also I will have my brace then. I will be more mobile and can put some weight on my knee. If it gets to be too much, we can just eat our way through Philly. But I was hoping to see some areas of the city that you always talk about."

"We can work it out when we are in Philly. But how do you feel about this other than being afraid that I would hate this opportunity?" Alice asked being curious to what he was feeling especially now knowing that she was on board with it.

"I am in shock but happy about it. The main thing keeping me from being super excited is the idea of not sleeping next to you each and every night of this IR as we thought."

"Yeah. That part will suck but still, they are having you come back for PT so it won't be 3.5 weeks away straight. It's already better than the past few weeks. Too bad you won't be playing at all during that time."

Scotty just chuckled and said softly, "I would kiss you right now for not only saying that but understanding the need to play."

"Trust me, I would love for you to be here to kiss me," said Alice slightly wistfully.

"Later mon cherie, je t'aime," said Scotty tenderly in the way that always made her swoon some.

"Fine plutard, mon cheri. Je t'aime aussi," said Alice trying to be just as romantic.

Unfortunately, that wasn't the direction that Scotty took

the conversation and said with a laugh, "Sorry, your accent is absolutely horrid mon cherie."

Alice just laughed and said, "So you keep reminding me. At least, I've never said I can speak French well. I just try to speak it and I understand you."

"Thank you for that. I should let you get back to work."

"Okay. I'll see you later tonight. Love you."

"Je t'aime," said Scotty. Then the phone went dead and Alice was filled with a mix of emotions. She was happy for Scotty but she knew she always slept ten times better when he was holding her. She hated the idea of him being run ragged by travel but she wasn't going to share that with Scotty even if he suspected that idea.

Work was a pretty normal day for the rest of the day. There was a mix of cleaning, swim lessons, and catching up on the news. She was surprised to get a call from Doc Curren from the Sound. He was inquiring about her capability to provide water therapy for Scott. She said it would be possible but there were two major problems: the pools that she ran were at a temperature that was better suited for lap swim and she wasn't a PT. Sure she's shadowed and watched PTs train people all the time but she was a classic swim coach only. So she figured the idea was dead in the water.

Late in the day, she was getting ready for masters swim. Her jaw dropped when she saw Scotty come into the pool areas in a pair of jammer swim pants and plastic wrap completely sealing his surgical site off. It was like sex on a stick even with the injury since all his muscles were on full display especially his abs and his legs which were always a weakness for Alice.

"What the......?" asked Alice.

"I'm here for practice," said a very nonchalant Scotty.

"Okay," Alice said trying to shift into coaching mode and didn't want to be openly ogling her boyfriend. She wasn't mentally ready for him to show up to masters practice. "What strokes do you know?"

"Freestyle.... Maybe some breast. Although probably a bad idea with the knee"

"Okay. Oh yeah, you are to stay away from breaststroke. Just grab a lane. I normally assign 200 swim, kick, pull. But you are going to be doing strictly pull tonight."

"200 lengths?" asked a fairly concerned Scotty. He was clearly not used to how swimmer's talked. But that was fairly common and Alice just smiled.

"No yards. Eight lengths. Each length is 25 yards," said Alice really reassuringly.

"Okay," said a relieved Scotty.

"I'll get you the pull buoy" as she was already grabbing the piece of foam that would fit into the legs. Scott started to slip into the water in the first lane.

Alice wasn't sure what to expect with Scotty's swimming skills but she was hoping that he didn't completely suck. She didn't want to get into the water until Lager showed up for his lesson after the masters. But the mere mental mention of Lager got her cursing since his secret was going to be blown tonight since she wasn't sure if she could get a message to him in time.

As per usual, her masters group was on the small side with only four people swimming that night. Her attention was drawn towards Scotty most of the workout. He wasn't the best swimmer. In fact, he was kind of awful. Thankfully he was extremely coachable and improved throughout the workout. The rest of the group were regulars so they were pretty decent swimmers and she could fix most of their stuff on memory without having to focus on their form too long. Alice felt bad that she wasn't paying equal attention to each swimmer like she normally did, instead she was focused on her boyfriend and his terrible swimming.

At the end of practice, Scotty was the last one in the water in part due to his slow speed. He also seemed to relish being the last one to leave practice in any sport he did since Alice knew he would do the same thing with hockey. Watching him push himself up onto the pool deck made Alice think all sorts of naughty thoughts. Instead of acting on any sexual desires, she grabbed Scotty's crutches and his towel that were off to the side.

Scotty said slightly out of breath, "Damn, that was way harder than I thought. You would swear I'm out of shape with the way I'm breathing."

Alice shrugged and said, "You just need to come regularly and stamina in the water is different than on land. Plus, a lot of it will get way easier as your form actually improves. But you did good for your first time."

As they were chatting, Alice was prepping for her lesson with Lager that was going to happen in a few minutes. She grabbed two kickboards, two pull buoys and some hand paddles. Scotty wasn't in any rush and just trying to breathe normally on the deck and seemed to enjoy watching her move.

"Will you be coming to more masters?" asked Alice. She was hoping he would come to more but she knew she couldn't just focus on her hockey hottie each and every practice he was there.

"Yeah. At least until I can skate again," said Scotty. Alice grinned. She pulled her shirt off to reveal a one piece swimsuit that had Sound colors throughout. That's when Scotty said in a teasing voice, "Hey, no fair. How come you didn't get in with me?"

With a deadpan voice Alice said, "You didn't purchase lessons."

"Wait, you have a lesson yet?" asked a disappointed Scotty. That's when Alice realized that he must have been dropped off by either his maman or an uber and was hoping to get a ride with her and wanted her to come home.

"Yeah, just a half hour one. Nothing crazy." Alice said as she tugged off her leggings and folded up next to her bag and placed them on top of the t-shirt that was already on the bench.

Once she was undressed, she sat down next to Scott. He immediately pulled her close to a cuddle. She initiated a quick kiss while they were beside each other. She half expected Lager to see them and give them shit for being too coupley but it was nice to be alone with Scotty. Almost as soon as Alice pulled away from the kiss, Scotty asked, "Do I get to see you swim at all?"

Alice shrugged her shoulders and said, "Sure." Alice slipped into the water quickly. While she didn't think Scotty was the type to push her into the water, she always preferred to be able to enter the water on her own terms. She grabbed her pair of goggles that were on the wall and put them on.

She headed towards the wall so she could have a real start. She decided to throw a 100IM just to show off in front of Scotty since it showed off a length of each of the four stokes. The water was one of her elements and she was a thousand times more capable than he was. As much as she loved being on ice, no matter if it was hockey or figure skating, she was never as fearless as she was in the water. In the water, she would only get in her head when she was injured and couldn't break a time barrier. The first length was a clean butterfly, which was her event. Her rhythm was smooth and quick although she was a little splashy and knew she got Scotty with her arm spray. After she touched the wall, she went onto her back. She was keeping her head still and arms locked as she just rolled through the water. Then it was a turn into her slowest stroke, the breast stroke. But compared to most people's breast strokes, she was fast and light with her pulls but she knew she probably should be keeping her head down more on the breath. The final 25, she sprinted with the freestyle.

When she was finished, she went over to Scotty. As she pushed herself onto the deck so she could get to be about eye level with Scotty and give him a kiss, she asked, "Wanted to see something like that?" before she went in for a wet kiss. He helped to hold her up by wrapping his arms around her waist.

Alice heard the pool door open and shut, followed immediately by, "Ah man. Get a room you two. Although what the hell are you doing here?" asked Lager.

Scotty dropped Alice into the water in surprise. At that moment she was never so glad to have a wet landing into the water since she was laughing so hard. The look of surprise on Scotty's face was absolutely priceless and she was sure that Lager had a similar look on his face. She got her giggles under control and stood back up pretty quickly to hear Scotty say, "What the fuck? You are taking lessons with Alice?"

"Yeah," Lager said as if he wasn't pulling any punches.

"But isn't Bridge like a world champion swimmer, went to the Olympics and that shit?" asked a very disbelieving Scotty. Alice wasn't actually surprised that Brigitta could be the superstar swimmer Brigitta Fenster. She knew that Brigitta retired from swimming but didn't realize she got married or that Alice now had a personal relationship with her. But then again, she couldn't name what happened to most Olympic swimmers after they retired unless they got arrested.

"Yeah, but there are some things you just don't do with your wife. She does have not patience with me, trust me. It got ugly the couple times she tried. So we let it go."

Scotty clearly not letting the subject drop said, "But you always go to beaches and shit on vacation time. Including this past all-star break."

"For her man. I stay where I can stand. Just get off my back. No one was supposed to find out." Lager pushed back his hair and said, "We have been doing lessons for a while."

That's when Alice decided to say something, "Sorry, I should have texted but I got distracted when Scotty showed up for masters and I wasn't sure you would see it time."

"Yeah, Doc wanted me to get some swim training to help with the cardio. I knew she coached it on Monday and Wednesday nights and it was free. So it seemed like a perfect time to see my girl in action."

"Uh huh, likely story," said a skeptical Lager. Alice wasn't sure if he was fronting and just messing with Scotty. In many ways, Alice didn't care what the case was. She was just staying quiet.

"I won't say anything promise." Scotty said as he held his hand out for a fist bump which Lager did return.

"Thanks," said Lager sounding more than a little distrustful of his best friend. Although Alice was sure that Scotty wouldn't mention it to anyone on the team. That's where Scotty was always awesome when it came to living up to his word.

Alice shifted modes and went back into the instructor mode rather than the girl playing around with her boyfriend by the poolside. She said, "Hey Scotty, why don't you go get dressed. I'll meet you in the lounge upstairs. We did pick this time for the privacy factor and that includes you too."

Scotty immediately said, "Ok" as he started to get up from the pool deck.

"Thanks babe," said Alice.

The lesson with Lager didn't go as smoothly as Alice would have liked. Lager was distracted for the most part. Alice tried to keep him on point so they could make some progress. Unlike the previous lesson, they stayed strictly in the shallow end. Between the break during the month of travel and Scotty's finding out, it was just a slow moving lesson. It seemed more mental than just trying to shake off the proverbial rust off.

Alice knew she should have said it earlier in the lesson but she waited, hoping that if she didn't mention anything that Lager would get out of his own head. But he really wasn't so she said, "You know that Scotty won't say a word."

"I know. I just hate that he knows now."

"I get that. But he does, so we have to move on. On the plus side, you know he couldn't have faked that sort of reaction when you caught us on the pool deck."

Lager actually started to laugh and let loose again, "Yeah. That was pretty funny him dropping you mid-kiss like that."

"Yeah. And out of anyone, he was the best person to find out from the team. He always has your back."

"True. I know a few people would be a douche about me taking lessons and use it as a way to get under my skin. I know Scotty won't be a dick. I just hate anyone knowing about any shortcomings that I might have."

"We all suck at something, I suck at hockey." teased Alice. "But seriously. Don't let it get to you. We have lots of time to work on your swimming with the homestand and we all have bad nights where we just don't move as smoothly as we like. You know that. The big thing is to just keep trying. On the plus side, I've noticed that your transitions while skating has really improved lately. I would think part of that is the extra core workout from swimming. Who knows, now that Scotty is out of the lineup, you could steal the team MVP award from him if you keep up the scoring and whatnot."

That was the first time Alice saw Lager smile all evening since he caught her and Scotty kissing a half hour earlier. He was the overly confident guy that she was used to when he said, "Oh you know I will." While his bravado could get annoying since it was always a tad extra, it was good to see that spirit return. "Also I'm so telling Scott that you think that I will be team MVP now."

"Hey, that's not what I said. I said you could be the team MVP not that I think you will be the team MVP."

"That's not what I heard," said Lager.

Alice just rolled her eyes. She knew that there would be little to convince him much of otherwise but she still said, "Hey, don't be a jackass. You know I'm Team Scotty."

"Yeah, yeah. That's what they all say."

Alice shook her head with a laugh. As she pulled herself

out of the pool and started to dry herself off with the towel, she said wearily, "Go home Lager. Scotty is upstairs waiting and I can't leave until you do. Don't make me wait longer than I have to."

Lager fortunately didn't give her any more problems and just headed out the door. Alice followed closely behind him taking the time to lock up and take a quick shower in the locker room to rinse off the chlorine. Eventually she finished getting changed and just threw her damp hair into a swimmer's bun without taking the time to really brush it or take care of it. She felt bad for keeping Scotty waiting for as long as she did.

When Alice made her way upstairs, she saw that Scotty and Lager were chatting. The college students seem to be oblivious to the two professional hockey players around them. As Alice approached, Scotty just seemed to light up and immediately went to stand up. He almost instantly pulled her close into a loving embrace, clearly not caring about the bad knee or the fact he was on crutches. Alice asked, "Ready to go home?"

"Almost," replied Scotty. Alice quirked her head to the side in confusion and looked up towards him to ask for an explanation. He just smiled and said, "I ordered us some dinner, so we have to make a pit stop for that."

Alice was actually really happy to hear that. She was starving and while she was loving his mom's cooking, it was nice to break up the home cooking a little bit with something different.

Lager teased and asked, "What about me?"

Scotty said very quickly, "You can get your own dinner."

The three of them headed towards the parking garage.

Lager even joined him on the elevator ride to the level where Alice parked her car. Alice couldn't believe how at peace she was standing between two professional hockey players who were both so much taller than her. She didn't feel too short. The only weird thing was at that moment, she wasn't holding Scotty's hand when they were walking next to each other. She didn't realize how much she liked him either holding her hand or resting a hand on her lower back. Alice was surprised that Lager got off on the same floor as her and Scotty but they quickly parted ways since Lager parked on the other side of the parking garage than Alice normally did. Once they reached her car, Alice asked, "So what's for dinner?" as Scotty was tucking his crutches in the back seat and taking a seat in the passenger seat. At that moment, she was glad one of the few things that Scotty didn't tease her about was the size or age of her car. She knew that one day she should get something like larger so he could be more comfortable.

"Kenko. I know you always enjoy that."

Alice couldn't have been happier at the sound of getting sushi and teriyaki. She was tempted to kiss Scotty in appreciation but she was too afraid of knocking him off balance. So she just said, "Thank you. That sounds perfect right now."

Kenko was around the corner from campus and Alice was very familiar with the location. They even got lucky and got a space right up front of the restaurant. She ran inside to go to the register to find out there were three bags of food and a mango bubble tea. Alice was eyeing the mango tea since she knew that had to be for her. The last time she ordered it, she found out that Scotty thought bubble tea was just too weird for him and he teased her endlessly.

As Alice was approaching the car, Scotty made her life so much easier by opening up the driver's side door for her. She was glad she didn't have to do the awkward balance while trying to open the car door. Alice teased as she was sitting down, "Did you order enough food? I think we could feed a couple families with the amount of food that you got."

Scotty just had a sly smile on his face, "Well I didn't know what you or my mom wanted. So I ordered all your favorites. I figured that you could take any of the leftovers for lunch over the next few days."

Alice kissed him. It was one of the most thoughtful things someone could have done for her. "This is so awesome but also slightly insane. Thank you."

It was a quick drive home. When they got home Scotty's mom was in the living room and said, "Good you guys finally made it home. Sorry, I won't stay up later with you but tomorrow will be a long day of driving."

Scotty picked up on the last line, "Going home maman?" Alice couldn't tell if Scotty was happy or disappointed by the news. It was one of the few times that he was really a clean slate with his mood.

"Yeah. You are up and about. I've seen how Alice won't let anything happen to you while I'm away. I know you are in good hands with her. Besides, you are about to get back to work with the scouting. So it seems like a good time to go home. I'll be a phone call away and I expect you to call frequently."

His mom hugged and kissed her son. Alice had a feeling that she would be declined but she figured it was worth asking, "Are you sure don't want to any food first? Scotty order a ton."

As his mom was starting to head up towards the guest room, she said, "Yup. I ate before Scotty went to the pool and I'm tired."

Alice started to unbag the feast as Backup was playing by her feet. Most likely hoping that Alice was going to drop some food. Chloe was still hanging around Scotty for the most part. Alice couldn't help but marvel at how Chloe knew who protect and needed a little extra loving in the moment. Alice was glad that Chloe accepted Alice into the family.

She looked over towards Scotty and asked, "So what did you order for yourself, babe?"

"Gyoza, the poke bowl with avocado, Surrito and Ohio rolls."

"Okay." Alice had only gotten into the first bag. It had one order of gyoza, two poke bowls, a teriyaki shrimp and chicken meal and a Kenko Roll. Since she knew that walking over with four of the takeout dishes would be problematic, she decided to walk over the gyoza and the poke bowl with a set of chopsticks to Scotty since he was already reclining on the couch with his leg out.

Scotty pulled her into a hug and wouldn't let her get her own food. "Not so quick." He hugged her and looked at her with such love and compassion. He then took a gyoza and dunked it into the sauce and fed her a piece since they both knew she loved gyoza as much as he did. Alice greedily took a bit leaving half of it left on the chopsticks. He took the other half and said, "Je t'aime. I know I say it a lot but it's not enough to really convey how I feel about you."

"I love you too." Scotty let go of Alice and let her get the rest of his food and some for herself. She also found another plate of gyoza, and several other sushi rolls in the other bags.

She decided on the gyoza, a poke bowl and a California roll for the evening. But Scotty wasn't kidding he did order all of her favorites.

Alice sat beside Scotty on the couch. He pulled her close to him as he turned on the Sharks game. It was a moment of pure bliss. She looked at him and said, "You know, I would have been just as happy with just this. Why all the food? We could have easily had Lager over with it all."

That's when Scotty got lustful with his tone and look and said, "Cause I wanted you all to myself." Alice half expected him to kiss her in that moment but he didn't as they ate their food. After a shot by one of the Sharks players that was reminiscent of Lager's style, Scott said, "I still can't believe you never told me that Lager was taking swim lessons with you."

"Do I really talk about any of my lessons?"

"True but it's still a bit surprising that you are teaching my best friend and I never knew. But it also explains why you are a little bit mouthier with him lately."

Alice just giggled. She never really thought about it but Scotty was right. She had been a bit more willing to let her sarcastic side out and wouldn't let him get away with much anymore. When she was first around Lager, she would be quiet rather than say much. "Really? You think that it's just the lessons?"

"I think it's some of it. But I also think it's the Philly in you. Even after that first trip back to Philly, you were more yourself. But you have done a few trips now and let me just say, you aren't letting people get away with bullshit as you were when you were first burglarized. I'm glad you aren't so quiet and detached anymore."

"You think I have Philly in me?" asked Alice.

Scotty started to laugh at Alice's feigned attempted at naivety. He said, "Oh yeah. I know that there's a lot of Philly in you. You don't suffer fools or bullshit and I love that about you. I still remember how that first day you didn't give an inch about me mocking the Flyers. You were proud of your team without being blinded by their talent. You didn't care if you were impressing me or not. You were just you. I think my favorite part was when you cussed over the fact I was playing again."

Alice started to blush. She never thought about it that way. There were times when her mom would complain about her sarcastic side and she would try to dampen herself. Then just being in Cleveland also meant having to monitor her directness so she wasn't coming off as rude. So she was glad to hear how Scotty liked to see that side of her.

The two of them ate so much food. Alice was feeling seriously stuffed after the first round that she knew that there was no way they could indulge in more. At least, she would have lots of food to pick from for when Scotty was away. She looked at him and said, "So come on, tell me more about the new gig. When do you leave?"

"Sunday. Then it's a lot of going in and out of cities. Doc was pretty strict with the rehab regime and he wants to supervise it."

"Okay. That makes sense. Just so you know, I think it's a bloody amazing opportunity and I would have been pissed if you didn't take it."

Scotty kissed her on the nose and said, "That's what I love about you. I will miss you when I'm gone." Then Chloe started to butt her head into Scotty's leg, fortunately it was above the surgical site.

Alice said, "I think Chloe is going to miss her daddy too."

Scotty was rubbing Chloe's ears and said, "Yeah. She's a good girl like that. But she didn't like it when you were away either."

Alice was touched and surprised to hear that. She leaned towards Chloe to give her a quick rub too. Chloe's tongue was out and rolling from the pleasure she had in all the attention that she was getting. Then Backup noticed how he was getting left out and jumped up into Alice's lap to ask for his own tummy rub.

18

SCOTT

Scotty woke up fairly early and he noticed it was still pre-dawn. Not that he would really tell Alice, although he was sure that she was suspecting it, that he wasn't sleeping well. The two of them agreed that until Scotty was in the brace and not so sensitive to pain, Backup should stay out of the bedroom since Backup never stopped moving, even in his sleep. Chloe had been in their bedroom basically since his maman left since she would be a relatively still sleeper but she would bump his leg while she was asleep which always would cause shooting pain. But he missed having his whole family in the bed. This morning he knew would be the last morning where he could sleep with Alice before heading back out on the road.

Scotty couldn't keep himself from touching her for too long. He lazily traced a finger along Alice's body with one hand and was playing with her hair in the other. He would have propped himself but Alice was snuggled on his shoulder and had him pinned down to a certain degree. He knew he could easily move her, but he wanted to let her sleep as much as possible since he knew that she had her own sleep issues when he traveled. Even though it seemed to be getting better, he wanted her to get as much sleep as possible before his trip. Alice started to stir. It never ceased to amaze Scott that Alice could stir in the morning and still avoid knocking into his bad leg. Half the time, she would just burrow deeper into his upper body so instead of risking her pinning him down even more, he gently lifted up his body so her could get some better positioning and kiss her on the forehead.

"Hey there sleepyhead," said Scott with a teasing smile. He was half tempted to call her beautiful but he knew that she would deny it and make a sour face. Teasing her always brought out that the beautiful smile that he loved seeing.

"Hey," said a sleepy Alice who was smiling but also clearly trying to decide if she was going to roll over and go back to sleep.

Scott moved her hand away from his side and started to play with the ring that he gave her. He said teasingly, "It's nice to see you wear this constantly, but I'm starting to wonder if I should have given you a ring with a smaller stone or something with a smoother setting."

Alice quirked her head and smiled sleepily but was clearly paying attention to him. She asked, "Why do you say that?"

"You dig it into my side when you try to go back to sleep." Alice looked slightly ashamed. Scotty laughed and said, "But I'd rather have that if it means you are sleeping in my arms."

Alice leaned up and started to kiss him passionately. When she pulled back she said, "I will try to remember that. I'm sorry. I don't want to hurt you. I can't wait to hear all about your first night."

Scotty nodded, "It's a big day for sure. I'll just be glad to get my brace and have more mobility. At least, Doc thinks I'm ready to have that so I can put weight on the knee again."

"I can understand wanting that mobility back." Alice was staring up into his eyes as she rested her hands on his chest. She asked, "Do we have time before I have to get up?"

"What do you have in mind?' Scotty teased knowing quite well what she wanted. She always seemed to revel in morning sex or the very least morning cuddling. But Scotty enjoyed it just as much as she did. Hell, it was why he woke her up.

"Whatever you like."

Scotty raised an eyebrow. It was all too easy for him to ask for something utterly ridiculous or something that he knew that Alice wouldn't like. She then bit her lip slightly once she realized how that might have been a little too open-ended and could end up being a little kinkier than she intended. He chuckled as he started to tickle Alice's sides forcing her into an eruption of giggles. It was always hysterical to hear Alice giggle and to see her squirm when he tickled her. It wasn't until she was squirming towards his leg that he realized that was probably a bad idea, so he stopped before he set himself up for a world of pain. "How about some hockey and kisses then?"

Alice laughed and said, "Only if we start with one of my two favorite teams." As she started to lean up in such a passionate kiss in a way that he knew that there wouldn't be any hockey watching. It was going to be all love making and that was perfect.

Scotty had a feeling that hockey and kisses would be their code for sex for a while. But it was perfect for them. It was so much more fitting then Netflix and Chill if you asked him, especially since he almost never used Netflix. Alice started to tug down at his pants when her alarm went off. Immediately Alice reached out for her phone and said "merde" as she was silencing her phone.

That surprised Scotty big time. Alice didn't often speak in French unless it was absolutely necessary or when he insisted upon it. Although while his mamam was around she was speaking it much more. "En francais? Pourquoi?" Alice looked at him like he was crazy but he knew he heard.

"What? I did?"

Scott kissed her on her nose. "You totally did. It was pretty adorable even if you can't pronounce anything correctly."

"Maybe it was to impress you?" Alice said amazingly unconvincingly. While her words sounded like there was some forethought, her questioning tone completely undermined her words.

"Given you don't even remember saying it, I highly doubt it was intentional," joked Scotty.

Alice just shrugged and looked to see if he was sure of what he heard. But he was positive. Then she said, "Too much French lately?"

"That sounds much more likely," Scotty pulled her in close. He knew she had to get up soon and their hopes for more than a quickie were going to be dashed if they didn't get to it soon. But he still wanted to use all the time they had together before they had to get to the doctor and for her to go to work. He still really wanted to know why she started to swear in French. "Should I be flattered that you are watching and listening to things in French?"

Alice leaned up and kissed him before saying, "Yes and no. Yes, I want to impress you. But the major reason is because several of my favorite shows that I used to study for my Paris trip just came out with new seasons on Netflix and I've been watching them when I can."

Scotty smiled. That made so much sense but he couldn't imagine when she was watching those shows since they had been spending a lot of time together since he was injured. She's never tried to watch them with him. They just mainly watched hockey together.

Chloe was pacing by the door and was starting to whine for food. Scotty was glad she was behaving this morning and was letting them cuddle before insisting that she needed to be fed or walked. But Chloe's patience was wearing thin. "Chloe. Wait a minute. I'm coming." Scotty said as he was grabbed the crutches lying beside the bed. Although he kissed Alice before he left. "Get your shower. I'll be up in a minute."

Scotty took his time getting downstairs to feed Chloe and Backup. Backup was waiting on the other side of the door waiting for everyone to come out. Scott leaned down to scratch the pup's ears. The pup was close to Chloe's size now, he was amazed at how quickly the pup was growing. The three of them headed down the stairs, Scotty got the food bowls filled and headed back upstairs hoping he could catch Alice either in the shower or at least still undressed. But he was still super slow going especially on the stairs.

He got to the bathroom and the shower was already turned off. He saw his girlfriend was still wrapped up in a towel with wet hair that she was trying to brush out. She smiled sweetly at Scotty. He pulled her close to him and smelled her deeply. He noticed that there were two piles of clothes on the sink top. So she was thinking of him when she was getting her stuff and likely was hoping to get him in the shower but didn't feel like waiting for him.

Alice spotted him eyeing the clothes and turned her head towards Scott's before saying, "Come on. I can get breakfast ready as you get your shower."

"This is good too." Scotty knew he should pull away but he liked hugging Alice especially since she was basically naked yet. He knew that he needed to get ready for their busy day. Alice was smiling and leaned back into him, clearly enjoying herself being wrapped up in his arms. They stood there together for a few moments. It wasn't until the crutches that he was using to help balance them started to dig into his sides he eventually let go of the hug so he could get into the shower. They got ready for the day. It was an unremarkable morning other then it was his ideal.

The doctor's office was quiet. Alice was reading on her iPad while Scotty played a game on his phone. It felt like it was taking forever to be seen by the doctor but since no one really came up hoping for autographs he didn't think it was taking that long. But even thinking that, he realized that he should take some time to go over towards Rainbow Babies to visit with kids with far worse than his own health issues. It was the one time he loved to use his celebrity for his own good.

Scott leaned over to whisper into Alice's ear. "Hey do you mind if we make a pit stop before dropping me off at the rink?"

"Sure, we can do that as long as we have time."

Then Scotty was pulled to the back. From there things went quickly with the doctor. He was fitted with a brace and allowed to do some walking without crutches. Not a ton yet but it would be nice to get around without having to keep weight off his bad leg. He was looking forward to walking the dogs and getting around a hell of a lot easier again.

Unsurprisingly, Scotty walked out to the waiting room to find Alice engulfed in her iPad reading. He wanted to scoop her up. Instead, he just headed over to her and kissed her forehead almost scaring the crap out of her. It was one of the few times that she literally jumped when he initiated contact with her. He immediately said, "Sorry. I didn't mean to scare you, baby."

"It's okay," said Alice.

"Good book. I take it," said a teasing Scotty. He knew that she normally only got that absorbed when she really liked a book.

"Yeah. I'm glad to see that you are walking without both crutches." Scott was leaning on one of the crutches yet but he wouldn't need both for a bit. Alice smiled and asked, "So what's the pit stop?"

"Visit a few kids at Rainbow Babies. I know I didn't bring any swag for the kids but they always love when they get visitors. I figured if they wanted to have anything signed and/or take some photos. I promise I won't be too long but there are a couple kids that have been here for a while for awhile that I would love to check in on. They might not even let me in since it's not a planned visit."

Alice seemed to really like the idea since her face lit up with a wide smile. Scotty wasn't sure what to expect but that wasn't it. He liked that she was okay with wanting to spend time talking to sick kids. He liked the fact that she gave her time to the Sound's various charities. So they were able to spend about 20 minutes brightening up some cancer patient's day. Being in the brace actually seemed to make him more relatable to the kids but they wanted him to be playing on the ice again.

Scotty came home from the scouting trip absolutely exhausted. He was looking forward to being able to sleep in his own bed. He was surprised that only Backup greeted him downstairs by the door. At the very least, Chloe would normally be at the door too. While he didn't expect it, there was a part of him hoped that Alice would be there to greet him while the other part of him wanted to her to be sound asleep.

Scott climbed up the stairs so he could enter the bedroom. Immediately upon entering the room, he saw his two missing girls. Alice was curled up in the fetal position with her two teddy bears in her hand. He didn't like that one bit, he hadn't seen her bears in her hands since the burglary. In his normal spot on the bed was Chloe and between them both was Chloe's puck. He wanted to rush to the bed and find out what happened but his speed was still pretty slow. Chloe must have caught Scotty's scent and jumped off the bed and then she was trying to push Scott towards Alice. Scotty looked down at Chloe and said, "I know girl, I'm getting there. The stupid brace won't let me go much faster."

Scotty moved to the bed and as he was sitting down, he

pushed the puck away from him and Alice. The bed sunk slightly with his weight. While Alice didn't stir, he noticed that she must have fallen asleep not too long ago and was crying rather profusely since her eyes were red and puffy and he could see there was some dampness on the bed. Scott needed to know what shook her so much. He leaned over. First moved her hair away from the nape of her neck and ears, he then kissed her ear softly. Alice started to stir and then woke up. She wearily said, "Hey"

Scott probably asked the dumbest question possible but he asked "Everything okay?" They both knew that she wasn't okay but he couldn't think of anything else to say.

"Hard day," as she started to tug her two bears closer to her chest and then dropped her head onto the top of the bear heads.

"Need a hug?" asked Scotty. Alice nodded her head. Then Scotty moved in and scooped her up into a tight hug. Almost as if the tighter he could hug her without hurting her, the safer she would feel. After a few moments he guessed that Alice just immediately fell back to sleep but he looked down, and he saw she was still awake. She was just being super quiet and still. He played with her long, loose brown hair and then asked, "What happened?"

"Court date was set for the adult who broke into my place. I ended up emailing the prosecutor after talking to my sister. I just wanted to know some of the details for the court date and etc." Alice said. She was starting to cry and she was trying to silence herself again.

Scotty pulled her into him even closer. That was something that he could understand could shake her. He felt bad that he was travelling while she was dealing with that. He just couldn't understand why she didn't call or text him at all during the day. He was never too busy for her especially if she was having a problem. She had to know that he thought she was so incredibly strong and wouldn't care if she was crying. Besides, he wanted to know what was going on with the court stuff and wanted to always help her.

She said after getting herself collected again. "Then the prosecutor called back. I will say he reminds me of a bulldog. So that fairs well." She steadied herself again before saying, "I learned a lot in that call. Plus side, not gang related, although it was related to drugs in a sense. It's Cleveland, I never thought of it as a gang hotspot so I wasn't thinking that in the first place. He also said that she will remain in jail and is unlikely to have a plea deal."

"That doesn't sound so bad," Scott said trying to comfort her but he had a feeling she didn't share what was really getting her upset and he noticed that her heart was starting to race much faster.

"He also said that there as a third person to be charged and they haven't been able to locate that kid. Oh yeah, and I will have to testify at least three times since each hearing will be different."

"Fuckkk....." Then he really understood why she was so upset. He kissed her forehead since that was the closest thing to him. He just wanted to shield her from the pain and fear that she was feeling. He laid his head on hers and asked, "Why didn't you call or say anything?"

"My mom." That didn't make any sense to Scott but he didn't want to push Alice when she was clearly feeling fragile. He was just trying to share his calmness with her. He was glad when she started to say more, "I talked to her almost immediately after the calls with the prosecutor. She kept telling me how I needed to get over it. That I was letting the criminals win and I was only going to push you away if I keep acting like this. I just needed to suck it up and I couldn't let it get to me. I was just trying to hide away before you got home."

Scott found himself having to steady his own breath and keep his own anger in check but he was actually pissed off by her mom's statements. He wanted to be there for Alice and her feelings were normal. It was absurd that her mom would tell her that she was being weak. It was just wrong. Alice was one of the strongest people he'd seen. It was a quiet strength but even he knew that she couldn't bury everything nor think she should have to. He said quietly and surprisingly calmly, "No offense but that's the dumbest thing I've ever heard. You are many things but weak isn't one." He then pulled away slightly and tilted her chin up so she was looking directly as his eyes. "Also don't EVER be afraid to tell me anything no matter what. I'm not going to push you away, ever. I don't care what your mom says but you're bloody amazing."

"Okay." Alice closed her eyes and gave a nod. "Sorry that you found me like this. I meant to be more put together and have the bears put away before you came back. I must have fallen asleep."

"Hey, what did I just tell you?" asked Scotty. He didn't care if she was holding her safety bears. He knew she would sleep with them when he was away. It was kind of cute.

"Don't be afraid to tell you anything."

"Yeah. That includes having your bears around when you need them." Scotty then started to finger the teddy bear hands. He was amazed how soft they were.

"Okay," as Alice started to burrow into Scotty's body again. She went very still again and her breathing started to slow into the normal sleep pattern. He just stayed still for a little bit making sure that Alice was in a deep sleep before moving the two of them into a lying position. He was just glad this all this happened before the Philadelphia trip. He had everything to make sure that Alice could smile and at least he already planned a surprise for her. Then he fell asleep himself.

Alice

Alice woke up in Scotty's arms. She was already feeling much better than when he woke her up during the night. She was still not feeling a hundred percent normal but she didn't feel like she was an emotional wreck or on the verge of tears anymore. That was a win in her book and she was glad they were going to have a few days together. She moved to put the bears back in their normal home when Scotty was home in her nightstand drawer and checked the time on her phone but she was stopped before grabbing her phone. Scotty gripped her tighter and said sleepily, "You aren't going anywhere just yet."

That's when Alice realized that he was still more or less dressed from the night before. He had the suit pants, the belt, and the business shirt still on. She didn't see his suit jacket or tie but she knew would have ditched those two immediately when he left the arena. She felt like an ass because he wouldn't have slept in those clothes if he wasn't worried about her. He rushed into the bed without taking any time for himself. While it was an expression of true love, she felt bad for making him so worried about her.

Alice said, "Who said I was going anywhere?"

"More just making sure that you know that I wasn't ready for you go anywhere until it's absolutely necessary;" she smiled and he kissed her. He pushed some of her hair away from her face and gazed lovingly into her eyes. "You seem better this morning."

"Why wouldn't I be? You're here. I woke up to you holding me. We are going to a Flyers game tonight" Alice was smiling and calm. She was ready to put yesterday's news fully behind her even if she was still stressed out underneath it all. She wanted to avoid some of the fears attached to the fact that she could have easily been killed, raped or had lots more taken so easily that night if there were three people in her place. Besides, she had been looking forward to their little trip ever since it was booked.

Scotty propped himself onto his elbow. "Babe, you seemed so upset last night and that was after god knows how long you were dealing with it solo. It's kind of amazing to see how much calmer you seem. Hell, the fact you even were crying yesterday is a big deal."

"Yeah, it was a bad day." She hung her head low and didn't want to admit how badly it shook her. He knew how badly it shook her. But this is when she had to use her compartmentalizing skills. She liked how she could push some things down when they were getting to her especially how other things, she will dwell on. "Sorry to worry you so much last night. You didn't even take any time to get undressed or get ready for bed either. You should have changed before or after checking in on me."

He was still running his hand along her arm. "Not before. Even if I wanted to, which I didn't, Chloe was going to let me." Alice frowned. She knew that she came home and finally let herself cry and get out the emotions that she was holding in all day. She basically tucked herself into bed with the teddy bears and let her emotions out. She hated knowing that she caused everyone to worry. Scotty must have picked up on her self-hatred. He ran his finger along her jawline and said, "Hey don't be so hard on yourself. We all have those days and it's okay to show your sad emotions."

" I know." Alice nodded her head and said, "I'll try not to be so hard on myself."

Scotty said, "There is no try, only do." and then he broke out into laughter knowing he was doing an absolutely terrible Yoda impression just to make her smile. Which totally worked on Alice. She then started to kiss him passionately. She was still trying to avoid hurting his leg while they were making love. They continued to make love until his alarm went off. Then it was time to get to the airport.

It wasn't long before they were touching down into Philadelphia. Scotty was looking damn sexy in his jeans, black t-shirt, his ever present Sound ball cap and sunglasses. Alice was dressed casually in a pair of leggings, one of her Philly Phaithful shirts celebrating the Flyers and a black flyaway sweater. She had one of her Giroux jerseys in her bag for the game that she was waiting to put on until right before the game due to a silly superstition. Almost immediately, Scotty was on the move and said, "Come on, we have to get going."

Alice was taken aback by that, she said, "Wait, what? I thought we were going to take it easy this trip."

"Yeah, we will. I scheduled something and we don't want to be too late. If we hurry, we can check into the hotel and then get to the meeting."

As the two of them were waiting for their Uber, she asked, "What's the meeting?"

Scotty gave her a knowing smile and shook his head, "Not saying anything just yet," as the two of them got into the car.

Then they went to their hotel that was in Center City. They literally just dropped their stuff off and they were off for another Uber.

Once they were on the way to the surprise, Alice was hoping for some clues. She knew right away they were heading towards Old City, one of her favorite areas of the city. They stopped at a residential complex with a professional dressed woman with a folio in her hands standing out front. As soon as they got out of the car, the woman said, "Mr. Wheiland, I assume. I'm Tammy. It's nice to speak to you in person."

Scotty said with a wide smile on his face, "Thanks for meeting with us. This is my girlfriend, Alice. How many places will be able to visit today?"

"I got three places that I think you might like."

"Does that include the Elfreth's Alley place?" asked Scotty.

That's when Alice realized what was going on. She mentioned how she knew one of the places on Elfreth's Alley was up for sale and how that always seemed like a cool place in Philadelphia. She grabbed Scotty's arm and asked in a harsh whisper, "What do you think you are doing?" as the realtor said that it was too late for the place that he initially mentioned but they were going to look at a rental that was available on the alley.

Scotty smiled and said in a whisper, "Thinking about getting us a place in Philly."

Alice shook her head. It seemed so insane to her. While she loved the gesture, but it seemed like a silly decision. She even voiced the one thing that was mainly going on in her mind. "Um. I work year round and you already have a place in Canada that you live in during the off season. When would we be here?"

Scotty said so nonplussed, "Holidays and weekends. Baby, let's just look at the places for right now. I thought you would love the idea."

Alice shook her head. He was asking for a reasonable thing and she did love the idea. She knew he was doing it for her and she couldn't believe he had this all set up just for her. Scotty was literally amazing to her. Just being able to have someone to lean on and be there for her in town after the burglary was more than enough. But he continued to surprise her and show how much he wanted to provide and protect her. She knew damn well that he wouldn't be considering a place in Philly if it wasn't for her.

While Alice was excited to hear that they were going to look at a place on Elfreth's Alley, she was going to dismiss it out of hand. No way she was going to live on America's oldest continuously lived in residential street. People would be coming to their doors and looking into their house every day. Plus she thought she remembered hearing about how there were various restrictions on residents of the street since it was a tourist attraction. She knew that they couldn't just be free to make love at any time of the day the way they had a tendency to do. But Tammy told them that would be the last place they would visit that day.

The first two places that Tammy showed them were condos in the Old City area. The outsides always looked old and fit into the characteristics of the area with brick walls, tall windows, and tree lined sidewalks. But the insides were so sleek and modern. It was like everything that she absolutely loved. Nothing was like a model home and the condos all had some cool features or room shapes due to the old architectural trends.

It was the second place that Alice did fall in love with. It was perfect. There was a library that had a view into Center City, a huge kitchen by Philly standards for Scotty and just a nice airy atmosphere. It was hard not seeing the two of them having a great life in that condo. She was having a hard time trying to find reasons not to get the home other then it didn't make any sense to get a place in Philly. If Scotty was going to insist on a home in Philly, it was the second place that she wanted.

The place on Elfreth's Alley was charming but even Scotty saw how the visitors could get more than a wee bit annoying. The home was charming and modern but it didn't wow them like the second place did. After seeing the Elfreth's Alley place they parted from Tammy and they decided to head back to the hotel.

While they were in the car, Scotty turned to her and asked, "So you hate the idea of getting a place here?"

"More, I think it's impractical. I loved that second place and I love Philly, we both know that. But our lives are mostly in Cleveland right now and you already have a home in Ontario that I've never seen. So why would we need a third place?"

Scotty held her hand and said, "I liked the idea of having a place here for when you need to get away and recharge. I won't lie, I've been thinking about this for awhile. I thought you might like having a place to go for a weekend away after each court date. This was even before I saw the effects of the call with the prosecutor."

Alice smiled and said, "I won't stop you but what about a weekend to your Canadian home? I still want to see it."

Scotty kissed her on the neck. It was only a quick kiss since they were coming up on the hotel and didn't want to get too frisky in an Uber. They weren't really in the hotel for long at all, they were just freshening up before dinner and the game. They decided to get dinner at her favorite dim sum place in Chinatown where they could feast on soup dumplings, various small plates and other treats.

Then it was time for the Flyers vs. Isles game. They had club level seats by the aisle. Alice sat in the inner seat. She was relishing the idea they could go to a game together. Alice wasn't imagining it could be possible, at least not until Scott retired from playing. Until then, they could be at the same place but always be separated since he had team commitments. So she wanted to savor every moment of the game.

Alice knew that Scotty was technically working the game. He wasn't taking many notes outright but he was definitely taking everything in on ice. She didn't want to interrupt so she was pretty quiet for the first five minutes. Scotty leaned over and put his arm around her body and said, "This isn't my Alice. You are way too quiet. What happened to the animated fan girl?"

At least she could say, she wasn't actually dwelling on her problems and said, "I thought you needed to concentrate."

Scotty started to nibble at her ear sending fire through her system and setting off her zones. She really did adore him kissing her. He then pulled away said, "You know so much about your team and your little verbal explosions are always entertaining and sometimes insightful. Besides, you have no idea how much I love watching you get into the game. So tell me, two things that I should know about your other team."

"My other team." asked Alice teasingly. "I thought the Flyers are my team."

Joking around just as much, he said, "What am I? Chopped liver?"

"You're mine and I love you. But I'm only rooting for the team you play on. It's not like they are my Flyers."

"As long as you're mine, I guess I can deal with you still calling the Flyers your team. So come on, tell me what you know."

Alice shook her head. It was an old joke between them. "Whoever scores the second goal in the game, will usually win. This has been true since November. Also Sandy is a beast who has really blossomed this year. He's been producing offense out of nowhere and has been doing some decent checking. Not to mention, he's a good skater."

Right as Alice said that, it was like the defenseman heard her and pounded an Isle offensive player hard. The play then shifted down ice with the Flyers on a breakaway opportunity with Raffl taking the lead.

"Okay then, what's his fault and why don't I remember him from when we played them?"

"He's still a newbie. He makes mistakes and usually at the most inopportune times. And I think you gotta play mostly against Gudi, Ghost and Provie. While Sanheim is his partner, it seemed like Gudi was gunning for you the entire game especially when you got nailed into the boards by him."

Scotty's face lit up. She was a little confused, there was

nothing that she said that he didn't really know. He just pulled her closer, "You have no idea how sexy it is to hear you remember shit like that."

"Why? You know it's super easy. That was the first time you broke my focus from a Flyers game."

"I did?" Scotty said seemed genuinely surprised by her comments. But instead of asking for details, he just teased her instead. "Wait the Flyers game? I thought it was a Sound game."

"You totally did. That hip stinger when you got crushed into the boards. I was afraid it might have been more than a stinger. It was dumb, I know."

Scotty kissed her and pulled her in tight. They were enjoying the moment. The game was semi-lackluster thus far in the game. Mainly it was a give and go with strong hits on both sides. But unlike earlier in the game, Alice was reacting to the hard hits being delivered. It was a chippy game. When the first period ended and the Mites on Ice were being set up, Alice asked if Scotty wanted anything. Unsurprising he wanted a Yuengling. He then tried to give her his credit card which she promptly declined and he said, "Take it."

Alice just shook her head and said, "No, I got it." Scotty gave her a look. He obviously wanted to treat but she just ignored him. She just kissed him as she moved past him. She said, "I may be a bit. I need my crab fries."

Scotty nodded. Alice made her way to the Chickie and Pete's stall for the crab fries and Scotty's beer. While the lines were moving quickly, Alice decided to save time and nixed the craft beer by ordering two Yuenglings. So she quickly moved her way back to the seats.

When she sat down, almost immediately, Scotty snagged

a fry and dipped into the cheese cup. Alice teased, "Hey. Who said you can have one?"

"I did." Scotty said with his cocky smile. "That's pretty good, but it's not as good as poutine."

"Okay seriously? How can you compare the two? Both are amazing but so different." She took a bite of her own fries. Then she did a small pout before saying, "Now I want poutine to go with the crab fries. I only know a couple places in the city that does it and none of them are here in the arena and I don't remember the name of the places that do them either. Fuck."

That made Scotty chuckle and they shared the crab fries. Alice's eyes were pulled down ice with Coots on the breakaway opportunity with G on his tail. Alice was muttering, "Go, go, go." Some of the fans were starting to yell shoot but Alice was still waiting for her guys to get fully set up so they don't waste the shot on Isle goal. Alice was so focused on the ice that she didn't really notice the men in black start to come down. When Coots missed the shot and Giroux wasn't in time for the rebound, Alice just said, "Damnit" while throwing her head down and Scotty just started laughing.

Next thing Alice knew, Gritty was standing beside Scotty. Scotty was focused on the game as he had an arm around Alice. They looked like the perfect couple. When Gritty stole Scotty's hat, Alice saw red for a moment. Scott must have noticed her tense up and whispered, "It's cute, but don't do anything stupid." Alice knew that was his way to remind her that there were cameras on them. So she just relaxed into Scotty's torso. With a grand flourish Gritty replaced Scotty's red hair with a Flyers hat. Scotty immediately moved the hat to Alice's head as he kissed her. He looked at Gritty with a smile and a shrug, "While I'll root for the Flyers today with my girl, I'll always be rooting for the Sound first." Gritty threw his hands up in defeat and walked away.

Alice just hoped that the little stunt wouldn't cost Scotty his favorite hat. It was clear that the fans all knew who he was at that moment and they gave him a mix of boos and cheers. Then a man in black, Gritty's security team, gave Scotty his hat back. Scotty smiled and affixed it back on his head. Then he went back to cuddling with Alice and they watched the game. Alice was just getting comfortable watching the game when Scotty turned to her and said, "See, that didn't seem too bad."

"I guess not but why do I think that this might go viral?"

"Cause it will," said Scotty causally. "On the plus side, that hat does look better on you then it did on me."

"You seem way too happy about that," said Alice. He was cocky although he wasn't usually smug like he was in that moment.

"Why wouldn't I be? I just told both the Flyers and Sound bases that you are my girl and you didn't do anything to ruin Noelle's love for Gritty. Although she might be a bit jealous."

Alice glared at him for a moment although it quickly turned into a giggle. He was right and she knew it. In all honesty, she was happy that he proclaimed his love for her and they all knew how she was a Flyers fan. She was also coming to terms with how she has a bit of a protective streak with Scotty. At least he always seemed to be amused by it, especially since he didn't actually need her to protect him and it stopped her from being crazy.

Alice took a sip of her beer. That's when Scotty must have realized that she wasn't drinking one of her normal beers. It wasn't dark as sin and looked much like his drink. He asked, "Are you drinking a regular beer?"

"I am, so?" Alice said making light of the situation. She knew it was pretty abnormal, that she would drink the lager all the time at home. Long ago, she would drink Yuengling all the time before getting into craft beer. But Scotty only ever saw her drinking lagers.

Scotty took the teasing even further by feeling her forehead to check to see if she had a fever. Since she was feeling just fine, he said, "Okay, so no fever. Who are you and have you done to my girlfriend?"

Alice busted out laughing and nearly sprayed her beer that she was sipping on. "I'm right here. You know a Yuengling is a perfectly serviceable lager. I didn't want to miss any of the game. I would have if stood in both the crab fries and craft beer lines. So I got a beer from Chickie and Pete's to save time. It's not like you are the only one who drinks a lager in this relationship. I just drink fancier lagers 95% of the time. Oh and fuck sakes with the turnovers."

Scotty gave out his own laugh. "Okay that's my Alice. Although it's still weird to see you drinking my beer."

Alice just shrugged and didn't say anything as she drank her beer. At that moment Alice's attention was drawn towards the ice. The Flyers were pressuring and got fully set up on the cycle. Alice was hoping it would get through Lehner but the puck ricocheted off the crossbar prompting Alice to say, "Oh for fuck's sake."

Scotty teased her some as he nuzzled into her neck while he said, "What, you disliked that?"

"Ya think?" asked Alice all sarcastically. They both knew she wanted the Flyers to score early and often.

Scotty leaned and said, "You know that shot was just enough off the tape that he wasn't going to get the goal. He barely had enough control to fling it on net. It wasn't ever going to be accurate."

Not wanting to be schooled in hockey knowledge at the moment despite knowing that Scotty was right. Alice teased, "What team are you even rooting for then?"

"Yours. I was just talking about that shot, babe. But I see the cap has the opportunity now."

G was on the puck and had a great line for the shot after winning the face off and getting the puck back from Coots. G pulled the puck and got through the five hole and got the first goal of the game. Immediately Alice launched to her feet cheering the goal like much of the stadium. Scotty stayed put since it was too hard to get resituated with his leg injury but as Alice sat down again, he wrapped his arms around her and asked, "Do you smile this much when I score?"

"It's probably way more, babe." He just started to kiss her passionately and she let her eyes close and have her breath be taken away with the kiss. She didn't care if the whole arena could see them in that moment. Both of them knew it was just going to be just a kiss until they got back to the hotel. After that, it would be a lot of fun and a lot more purely adult activities then a simple passionate kiss.

19

SCOTT

The game swiftly turned towards the Isles' favor. Lehner just kept swallowing up the puck with his body and the Isles got lucky. Scotty never heard Alice swear such a blue streak in such a short time period but he had a feeling that was a common occurrence when she was watching her guys lose. He understood that it was not a good turn of events but he couldn't help but laugh at her reactions. The worst thing in his book so far was how stiff the seats were even with being able to extend his leg out into the aisle much of the time but when people were walking by, he would have to fold up his leg way more than he wanted to.

Scotty had to meet with Doug to discuss what their insights were. Alice decided to wait over at the Victory at the Xfinity Live Center that was nearby. He was actually glad to hear that she was heading over towards the bar, since that meant he could talk with Doug for as long as was needed and Alice wouldn't be bored.

After a full hour of discussion, Scotty felt like he had a good grasp on what was expected of him and a good feeling that his observations were being paid attention to. He was feeling confident with the expectations of scouting.

He didn't have any problems finding Xfinity Live or the bar that Alice was hanging out at. It was filled with hockey fans and he was greeted with a mix of insults and cheers which was to be expected in that type of environment. He did give out a few autographs and selfies to some of the fans as he made his way towards Alice. Fortunately, Alice caught sight of him before he knew it and headed towards him. She was a bit of a ninja cutting through the crowd and made so much more progress than he was. Once she was next to him, she gave him a hug and said, "Why didn't you text? This place is always packed with people post game. I would have met you outside."

Scotty scoffed, "I'm not a local, remember? How am supposed to know where Flyers fans hang out after games?" Although given the proximity to the rink and the other Philadelphia sports complexes, it made sense that is where people would hang out before and after the games. He then asked, "Would it be okay if we headed back to the hotel?"

"Of course, baby."

Scotty started to help create a path back out of the doors of Xfinity Live that he came through. He ordered an Uber in hopes that it would be there when it they got out of the packed center. They were able to make it out of the area without too many problems but it was definitely interesting hearing the colorful language the fans tossed their way. They did have to wait a few minutes outside with the Uber.

It was a quick ride back to the hotel, they collapsed onto the bed. They didn't immediately start trying to peel each other's clothes off. Alice did peel off the jersey that she had on for the game. But they cuddled on the bed and turned on one of the west coast hockey games, neither of them were saying much to each other.

As they were laying down, Scotty was surprised how Alice wasn't more excited about the idea of getting a Philadelphia place. That was something that he wasn't expecting. He knew she was trying to be practical and he liked that side of her. Denise would have jumped at the idea of another place for them especially if it was in one of her favorite cities. Hell, Denise would have definitely used his credit card at the game. He liked how Alice was just wanting to be with him but he was still surprised, so he turned to Alice and said, "Do you seriously want to go to my home in Canada? It's not exactly close to anything or super exciting."

Alice looked up at him like he was crazy and asked, "Why wouldn't I want to go to your happy place? You keep taking me to one of mine."

Scotty cocked his eyebrow. This is now the second time she had mentioned there was another place that could make her happy that wasn't Philly. He knew it wasn't Cleveland. While she didn't mind Cleveland, it didn't instill that lightness in her eyes like being in Philly did. Scotty grabbed Alice by her sides and asked, "One of your favorite places? Where else should I take you?"

"Any place you are," said Alice knowing that it was a cheesy answer. Scotty tickled her side to get the real answer. "Fine, fine" in between tickles and she said, "Lake Placid."

"Really? You like it there?" said Scotty, surprised. He always thought of Alice as being a bit of a city girl and needing action. He's been to Lake Placid for countless tournaments and he knew it was a pretty sleepy town. In many ways, it wasn't much different from his Ontario home. His other home was so quiet and secluded, he figured that Alice would hate it there and kept putting off any trips to that home even though he loved spending time by his lake or in his own personal rink.

"More like love it. I love the history there. You know me. I adore Olympics and the skating history that happened there. I loved skating on the 1980 and 1932 Olympic rinks but the Lussi rink was slightly tortuous or maybe it was only tortuous since that meant doing figures only. You have the OTC there. I used to do figure skating camps there in high school. Yes, it's a quiet place but I like it there. I've always had so much fun there."

Scotty laughed. That actually made sense to him and gave him hope that she would love his summer home. He really didn't think that she would love being so far away from city life but if she liked Lake Placid, then she would likely like his place. Especially since he had a lakeside property. He pulled her in close to her. He liked the idea they could spend some quiet time by a fire at his other home and be more or less isolated from the world.

After a few moments, Scotty realized that he didn't get a proper workout for today. He knew if he wanted to get back on the ice sooner rather than later, he couldn't just sacrifice his workouts. He groaned and said, "Hey want to join me for a workout?"

"Not really." Alice said but Scotty could tell there is a chance she might still do it since she started to move off of him. He held her in a hug hoping she might still join. "Sorry, but I have no desire to do anything tonight."

"Come down with me at least, you don't have to do

anything, but I need to do stuff and I want to spend as much time with you as I can. Please?" Scotty gave her a pleading smile and waggled his eyebrows. Unlike when he tried to lay the charm on early in the morning for her to eat breakfast, she seemed to be susceptible to it.

Alice agreed although both of them started to get into their swimsuits and gym stuff on top. Scott was amused that while she had no interest in working out, she joined him in both strength training and swimming. She didn't push hard as she could but she did train with him and kept him company. While Scotty wouldn't tell her, he thought that it was super sexy of her to workout with him. Plus he was hopeful that with her joining him, she wasn't upset with him over the idea of getting a Philly home.

As the hotel room shut, Scotty desired to get Alice naked of both the towel and the swimsuit that she was wearing. He was kissing her feverishly and she wrapped herself around his waist. They were like cats in heat. He could hear Alice groan and purr with pleasure. They headed towards the shower, he lowered Alice to the floor.

The shower sex was hot and wet. He loved it more than he should have but it was fabulous. He was allowed to touch Alice anywhere he liked. They were like jack rabbits in the shower. He had to catch Alice from slipping when she got off and then he started to shampoo her hair. He loved to shampoo her hair, it was soft, long and beautiful. Hell, he loved playing with her long hair especially since it was always tightly pulled back until she was ready to call an end to the day.

After the shower, they headed for the king size bed as she said, "Hey, we should talk."

"Talk? Now? Really?" asked Scotty. He didn't know what was going on in Alice's mind. Normally they would cuddle or get ready for their next round. Instead, he was trying to figure what she wanted to talk about. He thought they were in a good spot. Sure, she surprised him earlier in the day about not wanting a place in Philly but she didn't seem that upset, just quiet.

Alice curled up beside Scott and looked into his eyes. She continued so resolutely and he knew he would have to let her say her piece if there was any chance to get to round two quickly, "So we need to get on the same page about things. Sometimes it feels like you want to make big changes and you try to fix everything anytime I'm having a bad day, especially if it's burglary related. I don't need you to always fix things." Scotty wanted to interrupt her but she caught him and put a finger over his lips. "I know you love me and are trying to make me feel better. But I want to be consulted on making life decisions especially if it includes looking at a new home. Sometimes I just want to be held."

"I didn't mean it to be like that." Scott said feeling bad. He hugged her tightly and said, "I'm sorry. I just wanted to make you smile and I thought you would like it."

"And I know that. But sometimes it's too much. I mean seriously babe, a place in Old City. That's even pricey for your contract especially when you consider how often we can use it.."

"So it was too much?" asked Scotty. He was starting to see where Alice was coming from.

"Yeah, it was too much. I don't need everything. Hell baby, you have no idea how powerful your hugs are. Most of the time, I just want to be held, especially when I'm scared. It's weird but I don't want to be fixed all the time. "

So Scotty started to readjust his body and held her carefully. He was looking at her like she was the only person in the whole world. "I know baby. I am just sorry. I didn't mean you to think you didn't matter. I really was just trying to give you something I thought you would love. So what did you want to get on the same page about because I thought we were for the most part?"

"Well I thought we were." Alice was fingering her ring from him. She started to say almost a stream of consciousness. "I know you said you wanted to do the engagement right and that automatically means marriage after. We live together already but the one piece that we never really talked about was kids."

Scotty smiled and was playing with end of Alice's hair, as he started to daydream about the perfect scenario and happy life. Then he said, "I see us having some kids after we get married. It's one, maybe two kids. I don't know if I'll still be playing when we have them. But I do know that we will be happy and we will be together. I know you would be a great mom thanks to how you treat Noelle and Klaus."

Alice seemed to make herself super comfortable in his arms. The warmth from her just seemed to radiate and she said, "That sounds about perfect. But you know what, I can tell you would be a great dad although you will spoil any kids that we have."

"For sure. That's the best part with having money," he said with a laugh. He laid his head back on the pillow but turned to look at Alice, "You will let me spoil them, Right?"

"Within reason." Alice said like it was the most obvious

thing in the world. Scotty gave her a look asking what she meant. She caught on and said, "So no ponies unless they have been in lessons for a couple years. Nothing super absurd like a miniature playhouse that is an exact replica like our house."

"What about the best hockey camps in the world and tournaments every weekend?"

"Given as long as they want to play," said Alice without skipping a beat.

Scotty had to laugh. Alice was so practical about it all but it seemed like a fantastic life for them both. He wanted it so badly. He wanted it to happen sooner rather than later. He kissed Alice lightly on the temple and asked, "So besides spooking you with the housing search, did you have a good day?"

"Yeah. It was with you. We got to go to an actual game together. That was special and awesome. Everything has been good. I liked looking at those places but now isn't the right time. Plus we got to go to one of my favorite places for dinner. It was a great day."

"So we're good?"

"Of course we are. I just wanted to make sure we are on the same page about the big things. That way I'm not too surprised."

Scotty smoothed down Alice's hair and then kissed her. He said, "I'm sorry about that. But it wasn't your bad day that prompted the viewings with the realtor. It was you saying how you always wanted to get a place like the one on Elfreth's Alley in Old City. That does take more than a few hours to get that stuff arranged. I think even realtors sleep during the wee hours of the night. I just thought you would love the idea. I wasn't trying to cut you out. Are you sure there isn't anything more on your mind?"

Alice shook her head then she started to move. She climbed on top of him and started to kiss him rather passionately. She smiled and said, "Nothing right now except what I would rather be doing after delaying it for both our sakes."

This is when Scotty realized how damn lucky he was. This could have been a major fight between them instead it was just a normal conversation. Then they could get back to the love making.

Alice

Alice had awful dreams all night long. Not helping her lack of sleep was that she couldn't get into a comfortable position. All of a sudden, she felt Scotty's lips along her neck. She turned and saw that his face looked a bit pained. It was far more pained than when they had their talk before going to bed. Hell, it looked like he took more than a few hits and she realized that she wasn't still while she was sleeping like she was most nights. She must have been moving a lot in the night and hurt Scotty. She knew that was probably why he was trying to wake her up.

"You okay?" asked Alice hoping she didn't end up hurting him with anything serious.

"I could ask the same of you. I've haven't seen you move like that before."

Alice's face dropped. She felt guilty and said, "I'm sorry babe."

"It's okay. But what's going on in that pretty head of yours, at least when you were sleeping? You had to be running from something in your dreams," asked Scotty as he started to relax.

"It was weird. We were all living underground and taken over by the Nazis. There was a search for art supplies for a crazy scavenger hunt project which included trying to get miniature goats in a pool. The Nazi leader looked like Mark Ruffalo and somehow related to me. When exploring his office for the scavenger hunt, there was a letter that said the Mark Ruffalo guy was actually the Hulk and then running away to make sure that no one suspected that I knew that secret. It was one of those secrets that seemed like it was dangerous on all sides and you had to run away if you wanted to live. So run away from the Nazis and run away from the Hulk. Basically run."

"What the hell? How does that even come to mind?"

"I don't know but that was my dream. Again, I'm sorry if I hurt you. Are you okay?"

"Yeah. You got the brace and there was a wild arm to my goods so I figured that it might be better to wake you up." Then he did a boyish smile and said, "Besides it's always so much fun to wake you up that way."

Alice just tried to make herself small and curled up into a ball as she tried to clear her mind from the dream. She put her head onto her knees. Scotty rubbed her back some trying to give her some comfort while giving her some space. Alice said quietly, "I'm sorry. I haven't had dreams like that in a while."

Scotty lifted her head up and looked at her lovely eyes, "Hey it happens. We all have dreams like that. I would be running and turning in my sleep too if that was my dream. Come on and lie back down with me." Alice didn't move at first. She wasn't crying or wallowing, instead it was her form of meditation to clear her mind and body of the nightmares.

It was the best thing for her but Scotty wasn't having it, he said, "Come on Alice. Let's go back to sleep."

His hands were waiting to envelop her and she leaned back towards them. She felt safe and warm in his grasp. It was amazing how much comfort he could provide. Almost instantly, she fell back into a deep sleep. It was a sleep filled with no memorable dreams to think of.

Alice woke up to her breasts being massaged and great warmth spreading across her body. By the mere fact that she wasn't getting kissed along her neck, she knew that it wasn't Scotty's normal MO for waking her up. So she just enjoyed the warm embrace and loving sensations that were going over her body. He started to move his hands south and got past the panties and started to play with her. She was starting to think he was awake since the movements were too perfect and pleasurable. It wasn't until he started to mount her and she saw his closed eyes that she knew he was still fast asleep.

"Crap." Alice groaned since she was going to need to wake him up. So she leaned up to kiss Scotty and he pushed her back onto the bed. She decided to try a second time. This time she did it faster and more passionately. Alice pulled back once she realized he was awake and smiled saying, "Morning, baby."

Scotty smiled but Alice could see a tinge of regret on his face. It's one of the few times where he didn't have his easy smile and cockiness. Even with his injury, he was still cocky most of the time since he knew he was going back to hockey (it was just whether or not the Sound were still going to be in the playoffs this year). He was worried about his actions and Alice couldn't blame him. He asked, "I didn't...."

"Not yet. I figured you wanted to be awake for that stuff.

At least you were clearly having better dreams than me." Alice said with a smile. She wanted to give him the reassurance that he should have and needed. "Besides, look at what you are wearing."

"And I didn't hurt you? I remember swatting something away," clearly a concerned Scotty.

Alice smiled and said, "I'm good and happy." She held onto Scotty's strong and muscled arms. Trying to give him some strength and love with her grasp. "Trust me. There are worse ways to get woken up than by being pleasured. You didn't hurt me at all. We could continue or we could get some breakfast."

"Okay, what's the deal? You never want breakfast especially this early. What is wrong?" asked an even more concerned Scotty.

Alice just laughed and said, "Nothing. Philly has great breakfast and brunch places. I thought you might like to try one of them since I know you love breakfast. If we walk there, I should be ready for food. Plus I love walking the streets of Philly."

"Okay. But what would you want to do? This is your trip. My stuff is done and it's all about you until we have to go to the airport."

"Honestly, both would be grand. You had me so close."

"I see" said Scott with a pleased look on his face. He said, "I know I say it a lot but je t'aime." as he started to nuzzle at her neck. Alice loved each and every movement he was doing to her body. He whispered into her ear, "You weren't kidding when you said, you were close. Let's see if you can last a little longer." And the low huskiness and lust over his voice wasn't helping her. She wanted to submit and be one with him. He gave the best morning sex in a long time.

"That was amazing." Alice said, as she was enjoying the moment. Scott laid beside her again. He cuddled her like she was a spoon that he wanted to protect and love her. Alice knew that his emotions matched his movements. Before they met, Alice wouldn't have believed how easy it was for her to just let herself be protected and loved by someone else. She had all of her walls down. It was something she hadn't truly done in a long time and she just hoped that she didn't get hurt in the process.

Eventually, they both got ready for the day rather quickly. Both of them were dressed casually.

Alice led the way to Green Eggs Cafe on South 13th St. It was a quick walk from the hotel since it was just a few blocks south. Scotty held her hand throughout the walk. There was something different about the walk. Alice just felt more exposed. While she was home in Cleveland, Scotty was recognized but she would get looked past. Now it seemed like some people recognized both of them, it wasn't a lot but a few. Alice tried to ignore things. Fortunately, once they arrived at Green Eggs Cafe, they were sat immediately.

As they were getting sat, Scotty whispered towards her, "It's still so weird you want breakfast. You even blew past several coffee places without even a longing glance. Are you sure you are okay?"

Alice just smiled and said, "Of course I'm okay. Can't I take you out for breakfast?"

"Of course you can. But I might just keep saying how it's weird unless you do it more often" said Scotty as he started to look over the menu. He started to lick his lips in pleasure and

Alice knew that her suggestion was going to go over well even if he thought it was weird. He said, "Okay. If this tastes even half as good as it sounds on the menu, this could be a wonderful meal."

That's when Alice laughed and she leaned over on the table and said, "Babe, it won me over. Don't you think it would be good?"

"Not sure. You skip breakfast all the bloody time. You might not know what a good breakfast truly tastes like."

Alice was rolling her eyes. She didn't care that he technically had a valid point. The server came up to the table so Alice didn't feel like it was a good time to defend her taste in breakfast places. Scotty surprised Alice by ordering the short rib benedict. She wasn't sure what he was going to order but for some reason, it seemed like a weird order. Alice got the pecan pie French toast.

They made small talk while they waited for their food. Most of the conversation was about how the hockey world was talking about the interaction with Gritty and who his girlfriend was. His phone was blowing up with notifications all morning and he already had a phone call with his agent while she was showering. Alice was almost afraid to see what the other parts of the internet were saying about her but Scotty kept telling her everyone loved it.

Then the two plates were dropped off on the table along with the two coffees that they ordered. Alice wasn't even the least bit surprised that he pulled out his phone and started to take photos. He loved taking Instagram foodporn photos. So Alice held off on taking a big bite of her French toast until he was done since she knew he would want to take photos with both of their plates. He then smiled as he pocketed his phone again.

Alice then took a bite of her decadent French toast but instead of closing her eyes to truly savor that first bite, she kept them focus on Scotty since she wanted to see his reaction to his first bite. When he took a bite of his meaty eggs, he looked like he just reached climax. Despite knowing full well his appreciation of the meal, she asked, "So you like it?"

"Dude, this could be the best thing ever. You might need some dynamite to get me out of here."

"So you would give up your career to just eat here every day?" asked Alice with a cocked eyebrow. She took another bite of her French toast. She knew that he wouldn't give up hockey. While he would move, he will be involved with the sport. She knew that. He lived and breathed hockey too much. She cut off another square of the French toast, speared it and held the fork out for him as she asked, "Want a bite?"

"Okay, I won't stay here forever. I love hockey too much but this is so damn good." He then took a bite from the outstretched fork and he then again savored the food. "Are you sure you don't want to have a place? We could come all the time."

Alice was amazed at how blissfully he was eating breakfast. He even started to steal a couple more bites of her French toast and she let him since there was no way she could finish it all by herself. By the way he was eating, she wondered if that was the look of excitement and contentment she got from an expertly crafted beer.

She shook her head and said, "I think we are good for homes. We can still come back a lot. Although if you like this place, there are at least two other brunch places that I think you would like just as much."

Scotty gave her a wanton look. "You shouldn't have told me that." Alice was just amused. She knew he would like it here. He said with a pointed fork, "If you don't tell me about those places before the next trip, there will be consequences."

That made Alice giggle. She was really curious what kind of consequences he would have against her. She couldn't imagine him doing anything then trying to tickle her to death or maybe a hard check when they were playing. But she also knew he could defend himself on the ice and she was petite and super tiny compared to the guys Scotty fought so it wasn't worth testing the beast. "Don't worry. I'll tell you all about the Red Owl and Sabrina's. Hell, there's even the Dutch that's pretty good. I'm just glad that you don't want to go to one of them today after we are done here."

"There's a part of me wants to do that but I know that we can't. Between the time constraints and being mindful about nutrition. This is sooo decadent and without playing..."

"You have to be careful." continued Alice.

"I'm still surprised that you didn't try to meet up with friends on this trip. We could have easily met up with them at the brewery last night."

"Well we didn't have much time. Besides, I loved the company that I was with. Next time, we can do something with them. The only thing that I would change about this trip was the Flyers score. I even liked seeing those places even if I think it's a dumb idea at this point."

20

SCOTT

Things have been crazy lately. The Sound were inching out games and stacking up several injuries. Fortunately, Lager and Dykstman were still healthy. But over the past four weeks: Corey had a concussion, Wheels strained his hamstring and Crestor tweaked his hip. Scotty just wanted to play again and help the team. He knew there was still a ways to go before he could get cleared. The scouting trips made the three weeks of being on IR so jammed pack, he barely had time to think. It was nice seeing Alice at the end of most nights but he never felt truly at home.

Last week, he got the okay to do some skating practices in addition to the off ice training. He thought there was a good chance of him getting cleared for tonight's game but he got ruled out due to the inflammation on the knee after yesterday's skating practice. At least, he was getting on the ice for some of the stuff.

It was a rare day off for Scotty. Okay not a full day off, he still had rehab time with doc, a video session with the team and he'd been more active with those using the scouting that he got from each of the previous games that he was sent out to. But since he wasn't allowed to play in the game tonight, it felt like an off day.

Scotty and Alice were lying in bed for a lazy morning. Chloe was waiting at the foot of the bed as per usual. Backup was playing with a toy beside the bed. This has become his new normal since the pup was almost always moving and liked to chew on toys a lot more than Chloe. He was sustainable on his own and was happy to wait for them as long as he had something to play with. Scotty loved the lazy mornings mainly because they were so few and far between.

Scotty was about to wake up Alice for morning sex since they both always seemed to enjoy it. Alice just looked so peaceful sleeping that he couldn't wake her up. He noticed that since their trip to Philly, she seemed to be sleeping through the night completely without stirring. If she stirred at all, it seemed to be due to a weird dream and Scotty was learning, she would have some really weird ones like the one in Philly. So he just watched her sleep in her peaceful state. It stayed like that for like ten minutes before her phone started to go off.

She groggily but quickly answered the phone. She said, "This is she..." She started to push herself up into a seated position. She said, "Yeah, I can talk." Scotty tried to scrutinize her face to see who could be on the other end. But then she just crashed into his chest which he knew wasn't a good sign and she wanted to be held. He started to hold her close and rubbed her arms trying to give her any comfort he could. From there he heard that she was on the phone with a prosecutor who wa\s giving her an update on one of the juvenile defendants from her burglary. He was looking down at her to see how she was holding up since he knew how rough previous calls with the prosecutors have been. Other than wanting to be held, she seemed to be okay. She was asked straightforward questions towards the prosecutor to find out which of the two juvenile offenders this was about. Then she was answering questions about what happened the night of the burglary. It was the most he heard about the burglary in one go since her birthday. He was amazed how she seemed to even joke some about the weirdness and the craziness of the people to do it during a snowstorm to be tracked and to take the time to eat snacks. Scotty just stayed very quiet throughout the whole exchange.

When she dropped the phone on the bed, he scooped up Alice and turned her so she was facing him. "You continue to utterly amaze me."

"What?" asked a quiet Alice. "Why?"

"I know that wasn't an easy call for you. But here you are nice and strong. There's no tears or anything. Last time, I found you in the fetal position hours later."

Alice just shrugged. She clearly didn't believe him. "Dude, I'm not that strong. You are the strong one. Not crying over a phone call is a super low bar in most people's books. It's not like I had a bunch of surprises like there was a third person who was charged or that they broke in multiple times that night. Besides, how do you know I won't break down later?"

Scott tipped Alice's chin up so she would look at his eyes. He delicately kissed her lips. "I know you well enough to know that you won't just break down later. You aren't using one word answers as a way to keep yourself together like I have seen you do in the past. Besides, don't you notice how relaxed Chloe is, she hasn't come to comfort you. I'll say you are doing pretty damn good."

"I guess I'm just getting used to it. Besides, it's much better when you are holding me. I know I'm safe when you do that. The last time was just so much harder since I had to handle it completely on my own." He was so close to pointing out how she didn't need to handle it on her own, that was her choice since her mom got into her head. But that would only piss her off and wasn't worth spending the energy.

"Hey, I'm here for you always." He kissed and searched her eyes to see if she was believing him at all. He wasn't sure she if she did. He just saw that her eyes were darker than normal. "You know that right, kid?"

Scotty didn't know why he called her kid at times like this. They were practically the same age, sure he was six months older than she was. He heard her dad call her kid before and it was something she seemed to like. There was always a slight smile on her lips when someone called her kid but treated her like an adult at the same time.

"I do..." Scotty had a feeling that Alice was hiding something but it might not do anything to really push her to talk more or ask her about what was going on in her mind.

Scotty pulled her into him closely. He loved his girl so much and wanted her to feel safe instead of making her dwell on the negative stuff. So he changed topics and said, "What's your day like?"

"The usual. A mix of everything: lessons, guarding, managing and catching up on my inbox."

Of course, with her schedule, he knew that could really mean anything for her day. "What time will you be done."

"Just before puck drop."

"Still want to go?" asked Scotty. He pretty much knew the answer but he had to ask anyway. Alice looked at him like he was crazy. Then again, maybe it was pretty crazy to ask if she wanted to skip out on the Flyers vs. the Sound play for their final matchup of the year (given they won't get matched up in the playoffs). Sure the Flyers weren't at the bottom of the rankings anymore, but Scotty still didn't think they had a real chance of making the playoffs no matter how much Alice believed they could. He just hated that he was going to be watching the game, especially as he was so close to being healthy enough to play. He smiled and said, "Okay, I know it was a dumb question but I had to ask."

Scotty was tempted to ask her what team she was rooting for but he knew she probably wouldn't answer him. Plus if she did answer, there was a good chance of her saying it would be for the Flyers since he wasn't healthy yet and he didn't want to hear that. There was already enough speculation about her fan support for the game already. He didn't need to add to her stress.

Alice surprised him by asking, "So now that you had a chance to relax a bit and be home for a full week. Do you miss the scouting trips?"

Scotty had to think for a moment. He liked the actual task of scouting but he hated how much it kept him from home. "Conflicted. I loved watching the games and assessing the talent. But I could barely keep up where I was at. I'm thinking a role that would bring me home more often might make more sense for the two of us. But even coaches and GMs travel a lot and a lot of coaches spent time as a scout too."

Alice quirked her lips in a smile. It was clear she was

thinking something. But she was staying mum. With her eyes twinkling, it only made him want to know even more about what she was thinking. He knew that she would resist his tickles and could possibly withstand his kisses although that was less likely. So he just stared at her and much like the result from their first date, she blurted out, "What?"

"I'm trying to figure out what you are thinking right now."

She dismissed, "Oh it was nothing."

Scotty wasn't going to accept that. She always seemed to select her words when her guard wasn't up. The call from the prosecutor made sure she had her guard up. But there was too much in her facial expressions to be nothing. "It wasn't nothing. So come on, out with it."

"You won't like it." That she said with certainty. But he wasn't so sure.

"Try me."

"I was imagining you as the next Clarkie or Homer."

Scotty just laughed. Of course she would equate things to the Flyers. Then again Bobby Clarke and Paul Holmgrem were both well-known players who turned into GMs. Hell, he was half surprised she didn't mention Ron Hextall since he knew how much she liked him. It was probably only because Flyers recently fired Hextall that she didn't. They made some good teams but they both had a checkered past with some of their signings.

"Oh I would hope I could do better contracts then Holmgrem," teased Scotty. A clear jab at some of the oversized contacts that Holmgrem seemed to favor.

"Oh you better. If you do anything like Bryzgalov contract, I would personally kill you for the sake of the franchise." she said with so much conviction that Scotty was pretty sure she might live up to that threat. That only made him laugh even harder.

"Is someone still bitter?" teased Scotty. He kissed her to let her know that he was just teasing her.

"Only slightly. I love the baby, you know that. I know the Flyers are set up with few other elite goalies in the prospect chain. But damn it, it's hard to know that we had Bob. We all knew he was going to be getting better and better. Instead we sign a crazy Russian to a crazy contract which no one in their right mind would want and so we had to trade Bob. Look at Bob, he's a stonewalling asshole especially against the Flyers and the Sound. Hell, we wouldn't have needed to use seven goalies with an eighth one ready to start any day now if we kept Bob." She was barely breathing since she was talking so damn fast. It was like she when she watched Gilmore Girls recently and started to talk super-fast.

Scotty wasn't going to argue with her, she was right. Scotty just kissed her on her lips. It was probably the easiest way to get her to slow down and breathe again. Once he broke away, he said, "Breathe. I can promise you I won't do anything that crazy."

Chloe started to whine at the end of the bed. She apparently had waited long enough to be fed and possibly even be let outside. It was always the dogs who prevented them from lying in bed all day long. Since Alice already had to deal with legal crap related to her break in, Scotty pushed back the covers to take care of the pups. Before leaving the bed, he grabbed Alice's wrist and kissed her hand, "I'll be back shortly."

"You better." she said with a teasing smile.

"Have I let you down yet?"

Alice shook her head and said, "Never."

Alice

Alice was feeling a tad anxious all day long. While the morning phone call weighed on her mind, she was more anxious about the game tonight. Ever since the Flyers game, she felt way more self-conscious about her actions especially at hockey games. She liked being fairly anonymous. Plus she was sure that everyone would make a big deal about what team she was wearing. She knew she told Scotty that she would behave at the game with something appropriate. She thought about wearing something Sound related but then she knew her dad and the Flyers fans would give her so much shit for abandoning her team.

She pulled out her phone and texted Jennifer on WhatsApp: ***Help. I can't decide what to wear to the game tonight.***

Jennifer: ***Why not team colors?***

Alice: ***What team? It's Flyers vs. Sounds. You know anything I wear will garner attention***

Jennifer: ***That's your fault. You did fall for him and he took you to the Flyers game where he told the world everything.***

Alice: ***Can you blame me? He's seriously hot. And he's so wicked awesome to me. How could I not?***

Jennifer: ***True. Is he playing yet?***

Alice: ***Not yet. He's practicing some but the knee is still bothering him. So he's not cleared just yet.***

Jennifer: ***So why not just look cute without any team colors?***

Alice: ***That's not a cop out? I was leaning that way but I needed to hear it from someone else.***

Jennifer: ***Nah. You'll be fine.***

Alice: ***Thanks!***

Alice went over to her side of the closet and got out one of her favorite pairs of leggings and her favorite oversized grey sweaters. It was a go to look of hers. She felt cute and knew that it would be a safe option. Not showing a fan girl side would irk some people but it was true to what she was thinking.

When she stepped out of the closet, Scotty was on the side of the bed playing with Backup. It was clear that Scotty got distracted from getting dressed for the game since he was shirtless and it looked like his suit pants were still unbuttoned. He was tousling Backup's ears and rubbing his belly. As soon as Scotty spied Alice coming out from the closet area, he smiled widely and he teased, "Copping out on choosing a side?"

Alice dropped beside the two of them. Scotty grabbed her close and they both started to play with Backup's ears together. It was a great moment and there was a part of her that wanted to take a photo of it. She said with a teasing smile, "You know the internet will likely lose its mind if I took a picture of you and Backup playing just like this."

Scotty kissed her and said, "It might. But you will still be the focus of people's attention tonight despite that. I know the guys on the team have even taken bets."

"Stupid Gritty," muttered Alice as she gave Backup a belly rub. "Should I know which way your bet went?"

Scotty chuckled and laid his forehead towards hers with a wicked grin on his face. He kissed her slyly as he was starting to play with the ring he gave her with his finger. "Just this. Besides I know you have my number on right now."

"Yeah, true but that's not the only number I have on. Do you know why I wear 77?"

"Oh I bet there is a Flyers connection," he said with a

teasing smile. He seemed to expect it. Then again, he always teased her about her love of the Flyers and how it interlaced with so much of her life.

"There's one but it's not the real reason." That had Scotty's attention and he pulled her close to him. "I used to be a bit of a card shark in high school. My favorite game was five card stud with deuces and sevens wild... When I needed to select my hockey number, I figured why not incorporate my favorite team and my favorite wild cards."

"So why not Hextall's number?"

"I'm not a goalie. I didn't want it to be too obvious of a Flyers connection."

"So your own twist." with a smile and said. He started to rub her arm lovingly. "And it's not like there hasn't been players who wore 77 for the Flyers."

"Yeah, Coffey for one. So that's my number."

"What will happen if there's a guy who wears 77 on my team?" asked Scotty.

"There's a guy who wears it," said Alice simply.

"And if I do?" asked Scotty with an impish grin. Alice was taken off guard by that suggestion. He was always number 34. Something dating back to when he was a kid. He never had to switch except for maybe a development camp. It seemed crazy he was talking about changing numbers but he would for her.

Alice just started to giggle and asked the obvious, "Now why would you do that? You've worn 34 for like forever. In international comp, juniors and everything."

"For you." He kissed Alice softly. He then fingered her chin line and asked, "Are you okay from earlier?"

"I guess." Alice said with a dismissive shrug. She was

actively avoiding thinking about it all day and Scotty seemed to expect that from her but he still would ask how she was holding up. She always fared better when she did things on her own terms but he wanted to help anyway he could.

"Don't fret about it. I know it sucks."

"I'm not fretting. It's just..." Alice was struggling to put her feelings into words. But she knew if she couldn't tell Scotty, she wouldn't be able to tell anyone and she should talk to someone about it. "Sucks. It brings that night back to the front of my mind. I feel raw. So raw where I just struggle to stay myself and to be strong. This call wasn't bad. It seems like both prosecutors are good and want to get it done right. I want it to be done and not to have to relive that night longer than I have to. I like the days where I don't think about it so much."

"I understand." Scott kissed her and pushed her back so he could climb on top of her and do some more passionate moves. But before he could the pup came up between them to get some more loving action from the two of them. He literally nosed his way between the two of them and broke them apart with his demand for attention. Alice started to give Backup a belly rub. Scotty took that as his cue that he should finish getting dressed and peeled away from the bed. Which meant it was too late for Alice to snap a photo of him playing with his pup shirtless and possibly distract people from what she was wearing to the game.

Alice was continuing to play with Backup on the bed when Scotty came out of his closet with his shirt, tie and jacket on. He was still fiddling with his cufflinks as he asked, "Ready?"

"Almost." Alice picked up the two necklaces that she had

with charms from each of her favorite team. She carefully slid the Sound charm off the one necklace and then she placed it on the necklace that had the Flyers charm. She then put on the necklace with both charms.

Scotty laughed, "You really aren't picking sides tonight?"

"Maybe," said Alice knowing damn well that she wasn't picking an actual side unless she was absolutely forced to do so.

Scotty just laughed and grabbed Alice by the waist. "What am I going to do with you?"

Alice said with a sly smile, "You could love me for being me."

He kissed along her neck and said, "Oh that's an absolute given. Come on, we are going to be late."

21

SCOTT

Scotty hated being in the press box. He wanted to be on the ice so badly. He knew he was getting closer but it still felt so far away during games like this. Plus he hated how he wasn't watching the game with Alice. He's gotten so spoiled watching games at home with her cuddled up on the couch drinking a beer a few nights a week so being forced apart to their separate viewing areas sucked.

He felt bad about the increased attention on Alice during the game. Ever since the thing at the Flyers game, it has been a constant distraction with the speculation of who she would support at this game and the debates if she was a true fan if she supported her boyfriend or her team growing up. He almost wished she snapped the photo she mentioned earlier but she didn't. The whole thing was nonsense in his eyes and he wished they would focus on the game itself since there were so many playoff implications for both teams. They had enough to talk about with the game itself, they didn't need to involve his girlfriend especially since he wasn't healthy enough to play.

He will admit, he was amused by how far Alice took it when it came to showing no favoritism between the two teams. But that was Alice. He's seen her be equal parts crazy about both teams for long enough that he knew she wouldn't find it easy picking between the two. If he was playing, he wasn't even sure there would be much of a difference in her behavior other than her being a nut if he scored. She went all in for The Sound the moment they met at the rink back in January. He was surprised how the media seemed to love zooming on her facial reactions when it came to key plays by either team. She held onto her cross for both teams and her eyesight was focused in on the ice. The only thing Scotty noticed was that she wasn't cursing which was probably his favorite part about watching games with her. Much to her credit, she wasn't tipping her hand in any way and he knew that she probably wasn't kidding that she was a card shark. He almost wanted to put together a poker night to see her in action.

As he got keyed into the game, he realized that Lager was off. Lager was starting to get testy and reckless. He practically high sticked a Flyer on purpose. It was a miracle that the high stick didn't draw blood and Lager didn't get ejected. Scotty knew he needed to get his friend to cool off during the intermission since the Sound needed Lager for his scoring capability. The moment there was less than a minute left to go in the first period, Scotty turned to Corey, "I'm heading down to see if I can get Lager to settle down. Wanna join?"

Corey didn't say anything but unsteadily got onto his feet. Scotty knew that the concussion was more severe than the team wanted. Corey's absence on the power play unit was just as devastating as Scotty's absence. For the month of March, the Sound pp production dropped as low as 22nd in the league. Corey had already been out for nearly a week yet he was just as symptomatic as he was when he got boarded into the wall head first. The unknown timeline to concussion sucked big time. At least, Scotty always had a more or less defined timeline for his injury. But seeing how unbalanced Corey was standing up, Scotty regretted asking him to come down.

Corey quickly stabilized himself and the two of them headed to the locker room. The timing was perfect where they could high five the players as they entered the locker room. Scotty looked closely for Lager as he went by and like usual, he was one of the last people off the bench. As Scotty suspected, Lager was wild eyed. So Scotty grabbed him by the shoulder as he was walking and asked, "What the hell is going on?"

"Just sick of the assholes" said Lager.

Scotty looked at his friend and said, "Come on, man. Get your shit together. You are the team leader right now."

"That's part of the issue. Everyone thinks I'm the fucking sub!"

Corey spoke up and said, "Dude. You aren't a fucking sub. Scotty is the team captain but you are the team's dad. It's always been the two of you that we turn to for leadership."

"Gee thanks. That really makes me feel better. You all think I'm the old dude of the team."

Corey spoke again, "No! Ask any of the guys who they can go to for help off the ice and they will say you. All the guys know that you are the one who will open up your house and look after them until they are settled. You have to know that there is a reason Petey hasn't even attempted to look for a place despite being given the go ahead. It's because he loves hanging out with you. You teach without teaching. Sure on the ice, we look towards Scotty since he has you beat in hockey IQ."

Scotty hoped that would settle down his friend, "Dude, I couldn't be captain without you. You aren't a sub. You are the only A that I think can carry the team and I rely on. You know the best ways to silence the assholes?"

"Score on them."

"Exactly and grind them down with hits. But you have to stay out of the fucking box and start drawing the penalties. Not taking them. Did you forget who you are playing?"

"Your girl's other team," said Lager with a deadpan voice.

"Yeah. They have a bunch of chirpers who are looking for a way to get under your skin. You know this. So why are you taking their bait."

Berman yelled at the three of them to get into the locker room. So they went in and listened to Berman go over what they already knew needed to be done. They need to stop the dumb penalties, get some offense going and to keep the pressure off of Crestie as much as possible.

Scotty watched out of the corner of his eye how Corey slipped out of the locker room. It was a quick escape. It was clear that Corey was going over towards the quiet room and needed the concussion symptoms to get under control again. Scotty felt bad but didn't alert the Doc about Corey's needs.

Scotty didn't say much in the locker room. He was always a quiet leader in the locker room. He wasn't the cheerleader. He would give tips and play ideas but most importantly of all lead by example. Once in a blue moon, he would say something that needed to be said to hold the guys accountable. But other times, he would at least give incentives to play their asses off. So before the team went rink side, he said, "Guys you got this game. Let's prove to them how they are just a group of upstarts. Be shifty on the rookie and shoot the crap out of the puck. If you win, we'll party tonight on my dime."

That got everyone cheering. It wasn't often he offered to treat the guys. Especially lately, he barely went out since he preferred being at home with Alice. He would explain it to Alice later but at the same time, he knew she wouldn't mind.

Lager then stood up and said, "Come on and let's make Scotty pay tonight. You know he doesn't offer to pay often. We need to take advantage of it." Lager seemed looser and calmer. Lager also showed to everyone that he was just as much of a leader himself and Scotty hoped that Lager was a team leader regardless of what was going on with Scotty.

The two of them were the last ones out of the locker room as per usual. Scotty turned to Lager and said, "You got this. Don't be an idiot."

"Quit being such a nerd," said Lager.

"Only if you keep your head on straight."

"You really noticed I was off?"

"Yeah I did, it was obvious, even before you attempted to use your stick like a 2x4."

Lager shook his head. "It was a fucking slash."

"If you say so. But most slashes happen at the stick, not the head area. Regardless, it was a wild swing 'cause what's his face said something to get under your skin. You are too good and experienced to let some punk get to you."

"Fine, I'll get my shit together."

"Good 'cause you are fucking leader of this team with or without me in the lineup."

"You know, you kinda suck at pep talks. Stick to analyzing and creating plays. That suits you so much better."

Scotty shrugged his shoulders and said, "I know but someone has to talk sense into you."

"Yo. What the fuck are you guys talking about? Lager get your ass to the bench and Scotty get your ass back upstairs," yelled Coach Berman.

The two friends went to where they were supposed to be. Scotty hoped that the game would go back to the Sound's favor. By the time that Scotty was in the pressbox, the puck had already dropped. Dykstman had the puck so the Sound most likely won the puck. Scotty looked over to see if Corey made it back up from the quiet room but no sign of him yet.

Scotty went back to watching the game, Lager seemed to be much calmer. He definitely was hitting harder than normal but he wasn't being reckless. Hell in the first play in the second period, him and Dykstman did some tic-tac-toe passing until Lager was on top of the rookie goalie. But instead of shooting backhand he shot it through the legs. Scotty was impressed by the moves of his friend since it was an inspired move. He saw that the cameras were on Alice as she was celebrating the goal.

Oh good, she's being like herself thought Scotty.

Then the teams started to line up the puck drop. Almost immediately, the Sound had control of the puck and were rushing the net. They were testing the theory that the second goal of the game mattered against the Flyers. This time the pressure was by PK's line. PK was being just as shifty as Lager was deking the puck back and forth. At the last moment, PK passed the puck to Wheels who fired a one timer onto the net that went in. So just like that, it was 2-0 Sound.

Scotty texted Alice. ***Hey looks I'm going out with the guys tonight***

Alice: ***No worries. For fucks sake!***

Scotty laughed. He knew that was just a stream of consciousness for Alice. While she wasn't showing the world he loved how she would just react to anything going on in the game sometimes mid-statement. At least, this time she completed her thought before cursing so he knew it was okay to go out and he couldn't blame her for being pissed about how the Flyers took a dumb too many men on the ice penalty. Unsurprisingly, she fired back with ***Sorry but you know better than to text me mid-game.***

S: ***Lots of swearing and game related thoughts. It's cute. Besides, you could just be excited that we can make it 3-0.***

A: ***I would be happier if the Flyers didn't take dumbass penalties all the time. Other teams can go through whole games without 1***

Scotty couldn't help but laugh. It was a common complaint and she had a reason. But he said, ***Yeah but not the Flyers. I would have thought that you would be used to it by now.***

A: ***Fuck you***

S: ***Anytime, Anyplace.***

Alice sent over the eye rolling emoji and ***I walked into that one didn't I?***

S: ***Love you babe. You are handling the media attention great so far. It's a shame they can't see this side of you.***

A: ***Thanks. Oh for fucks sakes. At least, I get so see how good the baby is.***

Scott just snorted. Dykstman had a solid shot on net and the rookie netminder for the Flyers did an amazing save from behind to keep the puck from going in. It was an amazing save. But the sheer fact that Alice was giving her opinion to him with complaints on both sides, he knew that she truly was torn on who she wanted to win and that was because of him. At most, he would just tease her just to see the reaction.

A: ***Still not quite ready for the interview***

S: ***Interview?***

A: ***For the charity event. But I would bet they will ask more than just the event details. I wish that Diane didn't ask me to do the interview with her.***

Scotty cursed himself for forgetting about the event. Everyone is required to do go to the charity event and Alice had been helping out a lot for it. He forgot that Alice mentioned that she might have to join the promotional interview with Diane.

S: ***Shit. I forgot that was today.***

Scotty too got distracted by the game and let his emotions get the best of him. He started to text him quickly, saying that he could help out but there was a breakaway by the Flyers penalty kill unit that ended up with a Couturier goal. So his message ended up being: ***Let me know... ffs that was awful... if you need me to help.***

A: ***Looks like I'm a bad influence***

S: ***Lol. I love you for that. But why didn't you also swear?***

A: ***Cause I didn't mind it all that much. It's okay if the gingerbeards scored. Just as long as the Sound scores more.***

Scotty just shook his head. He should have known that Alice didn't care it was 3-1 Sound. But he wasn't expecting a comment about the gingerbeards especially since Alice didn't seem to care when he started to grow a beard and then shaved it. She never said a word but did she prefer it when guys had beards?

S: ***Why do I think you added that last line to spare my feelings? Also is this your way of saying you rather see me with a beard?***

A: ***I didn't. I want your team to win, kinda, sorta, maybe. I don't know. But no to the beard unless you are in the playoffs. A little scruff yes. But you look amazing the way you are.***

Scotty had to laugh with how Alice responded. It was typical Alice. At least she didn't dodge the facial hair question. Of course she was okay with the idea of a playoff beard, that was one tradition he wasn't going to give up but he also knew she was way more superstitious than he was.

Alice

Alice loved texting with Scotty. He just knew how to make her laugh and make her heart feel so light. He also was one of the few people who knew how she was having problems rooting for one team and not get too much crap for it. Sure he would tease her if she went too pro-Flyers but he really didn't care. He had been teasing her about the Flyers since the day they met. Alice knew that she probably shouldn't be texting too much during the game since she didn't want him to get into trouble. But their back and forth was the closest to what it was like when they would watch games at home together.

Diane came up to her and asked, "Ready for the interview?"

Alice shrugged and said, "As ready as I'll ever be." She held back on asking if Diane was sure if she really wanted Alice be in an interview with her. But the two of them had really worked hard together to get the charity events planned and done right.

"You'll be fine." reassured Diane. "I'll do most of the talking."

Alice nodded and she knew that Diane was right. She just disliked being center stage and wanted to be behind the scenes. But even without the charity event, she knew that cameras have been on her on and off all night since they were still playing on the "who is she rooting for?" drama. Scotty even confirmed as much with the one text.

Diane led the way to the little area that had been set up for the interview. There was some pipe and drape and some lights at the back of the box with three stools. Diane choose the middle stool while Alice sat on the right. Within a minute, Kylie one of the Sound's Commentators came into the area with a camera man and few mics. They got both got wired up. It was done with precision, with no chitchat or small talk as Kylie waited for her cue. Suddenly the petite blonde said, "We're here with Diane Karlsson and Alice Kercheck to discuss the Sound Wives Charity Gala. So why don't you ladies explain a little about the event."

Diane immediately said, "The Sound Wives Charity Gala is a fantastic night where we blend some of our favorite things by raising money for cancer research and hockey education. People will have a chance to do a private meet and greet with the players, get some autographs and even the ability to play some games with the players."

That was when Alice knew it was her cue, "We also added a silent auction this year where you can bid on baskets that contain our significant other's favorite things."

"That sounds like fun. But will there be an opportunity for fans who can't attend the gala to bid on items in the silent auction?"

Diane answered Kylie by saying, "Yes. If you go to Sound-wivescharity.com, there will be a few of the baskets available online only."

"Can you name the baskets that will be available online only?"

"Not at this time. But the basket auctions will go live over the weekend and run for a week."

"Awesome. Are there still tickets available?"

"Yes, you can go online and get tickets. But we are close to selling out so be sure to get your tickets before it's too late." replied Alice.

That was the end of the preplanned information. But to no one's surprise, Kylie didn't end the interview right there. She asked, "So before I let you go, I have to ask you Alice, who are rooting for tonight?"

"The Sound. It will help the guys get home ice in the play-offs. But I won't lie, I'll still be very happy if the Flyers win." Alice shrugged and said, "What can I say? I will always want Scotty's team to win but I'm a Philly girl at heart."

"That feels like a very political answer," responded Kylie with a smile and nod.

"I know I'm going to upset someone regardless. But my dad always taught me to root for the team you love no matter what. We went to Browns games in LA and Baltimore since he never stopped loving the Browns. He taught me to add teams to follow but never turn your back on your teams. He wasn't going to raise a bandwagon daughter and he hasn't. So I while I will root for the Sound tonight, it's only 'cause both teams can't win but I want the Flyers to get at least a point."

"Well thank you for your time. When we return, it will be time for third period action for the Sound."

Then they all went quiet for the moment. They started to undo their mics and such. Kylie was more talkative now saying, "Great job. I think that went really well."

Both Diane and Alice nodded their heads. Alice also said, "Thanks."

Kylie started to leave the room but turned to tell Alice, "If I was you, avoid social media for the next few days."

"I'm already private on most of my accounts but I was planning on avoiding it anyway. I know how vicious people will be."

"Good. I know it's not always easy. I have to remind myself of that all the time. You were true to yourself and you are straddling the line but it won't make everyone happy."

"Thanks for the advice."

Then it was time for the final period of play. The Sound had to maintain their two goal lead for one more period. Alice just kept her phone in her pocket and tried not to pay attention to it for the rest of the game. She knew she might miss some texts from Scotty and her friends but the game seemed more important. She just watched the game go into a relatively boring 3rd period where the score remained 3-1 Sound. There were chances at both ends of the ice but both goalies kept coming up strong.

Alice was woken up by a loud thumping noise that

seemed to be coming from the front door. It wasn't that long ago, she would have freaked out thinking that it was another burglary. But between knowing that Scotty would be coming home soon and the dogs rushing towards the door, Alice knew that there was absolutely nothing to be afraid of. She left the bedroom and headed downstairs.

As she was coming down the stairs, she heard a very loud and very slurred Scotty say, "Where's my pretty girl?"

Alice smiled as she said, "I'm here."

Scotty was playing with the two dogs and was bent over as he was rubbing their ears. He smiled and immediately looked up at her. That simple act of looking up while being bent over caused him to lose his balance and he fell down to the ground. That actually made Alice rush to Scotty and go "Are you okay?" Although he didn't seem to mind the fall since he just started to laugh and he let the two pit bulls lick his face.

"I'm good." As he sat on the ground and with how super happy he was, Alice knew that he was super drunk. He was similar to how he was immediately after his surgery and this time, she didn't have his mom as backup. He held her hand and pulled her towards the ground towards him.

"So I take it you had fun tonight," said Alice as she sat beside Scotty. He was trying to caress her as he normally did, but it was less gentle than normal.

She was curious how much Scotty had. She knew he could drink a few beers with no affect, much like she could. So she knew it was more than a couple beers. It just seemed unusual to see him so drunk but she wasn't all that surprised when he said, "Yeah. We did lots of shots."

Since she knew that he would have practice and that he couldn't be completely hammered and/or hungover when he got to practice, she needed to get lots of water into Scotty. She had a feeling he would turn her down for a glass of water, so she used the old trick her and her friends did on each other. "Really? Want me to make us a cocktail?" Alice asked.

"Yeah."

"Okay." Alice started to pull herself up from the ground. But Scotty wasn't quite ready for her to get up and he pulled her in for a sloppy, wet kiss. After the kiss, he let her go.

Alice immediately pulled out two glasses. She poured water in both of them but for the glass for herself, she threw in a little bit of silver rum since she didn't want to be completely sober while hanging out with Scotty. Before heading out to the kitchen, she texted Lager.

Alice: ***Any clue to how much Scotty drank tonight?***

Lager: ***No clue. Went home early. Left Petey and Corey in charge. Didn't he get home?***

Alice: ***Yeah. He's just got home and I'm trying to figure how much water to give him so he's good for tomorrow.***

Lager: ***Lots! Feed him too!***

Alice: ***Already on it.***

Alice started to look at the glasses. They still looked way more like a glass of club soda rather than a proper mocktail. So she decided to add a little bit of lime and some mint to both of their drinks. While she had a proper mojito, Scotty's looked like a good enough to be a fake drink.

Unsurprisingly, Scotty was still sitting on the floor and rubbing the dogs' bellies rigorously. He smiled so sweetly when he saw her coming into the hallway. She couldn't help to know how he was completely in love with her. She just hoped that he knew that she felt the same way. She handed him the glass without the rum before sitting down.

Scotty practically pounded his water. Alice now understood how the night went. If he was doing that with shots all night long, it was no wonder why he was lit. At least, he was a friendly drunk. Although she was curious if he was someone who would end up dancing on the bar or something like that.

Alice was making small talk when she said, "So did you have fun tonight?"

He ended up leaning his head on her shoulder and said, "Yeah. I haven't been out with the team for a while. It was good to be with the guys but I was missing something."

"What was that?" asked Alice trying her best not to move her head too much so she bump heads with his.

He then lifted his head and looked at her like she was the dumbest person in the world. "You silly! You should have your hair down, it's so pretty down." Then he started to tug at the elastic holding her hair back into a messy bun that her hair was in since she got home from the game. Once the hair released, Alice subconsciously shook free the the hair. Unsurprisingly, the moment it was down, Scotty was starting to play with her hair some.

"Wouldn't I stand out like a sore thumb if it was a guy's night out?"

"Nah." He placed the empty glass next to him onto the ground and started to kiss her again. While the kisses were sloppy, they were passionate. Eventually after breaking off from the kiss, he said, "I love you so much. You can't leave."

"I love you too but where would I go?" asked Alice incredulously. Why was he thinking she would leave?

"Mhmmmm." Scotty was trying to figure out where she would go. So apparently he didn't truly think she was going anywhere. He was trying to be romantic with the logic of a drunk. He decided to come up with an answer, "To bed."

Alice couldn't help but to bust out laughing. That got Scott's throaty laughter to fill the room. It was amazing. Once she stopped laughing so hard, she asked, "Would bed be so bad?"

As he continued to laugh, he shook his head no and said, "Nah. We share it."

"That we do. And we do so much more than sleep there." Alice was about halfway through her poorly made mojito. She knew she should get more water into Scotty before they did too much. "Would you want another drink?"

Scotty nodded his head. Alice was glad he was so compliant and easy going. While the floor might not be comfortable, it worked and Scotty seemed happy where he was. As Alice was refilling his water and adding some more lime to it, she could hear the sound of dog nails running across the hardwood. She knew that Scotty had to be throwing a puck since they still didn't have any balls for the dogs. At least, she got some chew toys for Backup so the puck wasn't the only thing the pup was chewing on when they weren't around.

When she returned to the area, he gladly accepted the drink. Much like before, he just chugged the drink as if it was a shot. She sat down beside him again and picked up her drink that was left behind. As she was taking a sip, he leaned to put an arm over he and nearly tipped the both of them over with his lack of balance. He just chuckled and Alice thought that they probably need more water but the day was catching up to her.

Alice kissed him as she said, "We should go to bed soon."

"Why?"

Alice laughed. "We have work in the morning."

"Bah. Sleep is for the weak."

"Well I like it. But I didn't say sleep, babe. I said let's go to bed."

Scotty cocked his head and was trying to work out what she meant. Then it clicked and he started to kiss her again. He took control and started to lift the two of them off the ground. Alice was a little afraid that he might drop them but he controlled the situation by using the wall for support. Once they were upright, he started to lean her against the wall as he started to hit some of her favorite pleasure zones. That's when Alice started to feel something bulky and hard in his front pants pocket.

When Scotty pulled back from the kiss and she could breathe comfortably again, she asked, "What's that?" as she pointed towards his pocket.

Scotty didn't even looked at her hand. Instead he asked, "What's what?" as he started to work his hands under her shirt and kiss her lips again. Alice was half surprised, he didn't try to push back her hand at all.

Alice broke back and said, "That bulky thing in your pocket that is jabbing into my hip." He started to get a little rougher with his breast massage. Scott didn't have his normal finesse and control but that didn't matter since she knew she was getting just as aroused. In a lust laden voice, she said, "Come on, what's in your pocket?"

Alice was about to reach towards the pocket and investigate for herself and get the object away from her hip. Scotty caught her and grabbed her arms and started to raise them above her head. He effectively pinned her to the wall with one hand on the walls and his thighs on hers. Then he used his free hand and pulled out a ring box from his pocket as he said, "You mean this...." with a sly smile.

Alice saw the box and went wide. She had a pretty good idea that the box wasn't for a new pair of cufflinks. Now she really wanted to know what was in the box. She was at a loss for words and just shook her head yes.

Scotty held it further away not that he was allowing her to move from being pinned to the wall. This is when she hated how he was basically a foot taller than her and had about 40lbs of pure muscle on her. She could only let him nibble at Alice's neck. He said, "What if you aren't ready for it?"

She flinched at that. As soon as he said, you aren't ready for it, she knew it had to be an engagement ring. He already gave the Claddagh so there was a part of her trying to tell her that it wasn't an engagement ring. But the fact he wasn't ready to give it to her also made her nervous. What if she wasn't good enough for him, she already had that happen once with her ex-partner. "Not ready for it? What do you mean?'

He stuck the ring into his back pocket and he said, "You heard me."

"Why wouldn't I be ready for it?" She pouted and said, "That's not fair."

"Life's not fair. Anyone who says differently is selling you something."

"Don't you quote the Princess Bride at me. You are being mean."

"As you wish," said Scotty knowing that he was still doing it. Which only served to delight and frustrate Alice. He kept kissing her and making her feel like she was the only one in the room. He just wasn't going to let her see what was in the box. He broke away from the kiss and asked her with all the seriousness he could muster, "Am I really being mean?"

"Yes and no." said Alice. "Why won't let you let me see what's in the box?"

"Cause I said so." with all the force to prove why he was a team captain of the Sound. He was resolute without being mean. His s' were so slurred that it only served to remind Alice that he was still very drunk. She knew, she could peek at what's in the box if she got him off balance. But until she got him off balance, she would have to let the issue go for now.

Alice leaned over and started kissing Scotty very passionately. Massaging his tongue and starting to really have some fun. That's when Scotty released her hands from over her head and she just settled them on his neck and started to put them through his soft hair. He started to ease to a wider stance and ended up shattering one of the glasses they left on the ground.

"Fuck." said Scotty. "I didn't mean to do that."

Alice kissed him softly and then said, "I'll take care of the glasses if you can keep the pups away." She took control and grabbed the box from his back pocket as she brushed past him. Scotty did grab her for one more kiss before letting go but didn't seem to notice that she palmed the box. She walked to the hall closet as he walked to the living room to occupy the dogs by throwing the puck again.

Once Alice went into the hall closet, she immediately opened the box instead of grabbing the broom and dustpan. Inside sat an absolutely beautiful engagement ring. The diamond was unreal: it was so clear and cleanly cut. It wasn't a huge diamond, in fact it was understated other than the fact it was a beautiful rock. There was a trinity knot on either side of the diamond and it was smooth with no hard edges. Then she saw the two small black wedding bands with lovers knots etched throughout. It was like he read her dreams on the ideal engagement ring for her. The only thing she now hated was the fact she would have to pretend she never saw it both tonight and if and when he actually gave her the ring. She kicked herself, she had to start cleaning the glass up or Scotty would catch on to the fact that she pulled the box out of her pocket. So she quickly cleaned up the glass shards so nobody had their feet/paws cut up by the glass.

As she entered the living room where Scotty was throwing a puck for the dogs, she hugged him and slipped the box back into the pocket that she stole it from. He swatted her hands away from her and said, "Nice try baby."

Alice shrugged her shoulders and casually said, "You can't blame me for trying."

"Sure I can. I told you, it's not the right time for it."

"So you keep telling me." Alice said with a pout. She knew she had to act like she never saw it.

"You'll see it soon enough."

"But I would rather see it tonight. I'm not very patient, you know that."

"You'll see it soon enough."

"Rather see it tonight," said Alice almost petulantly.

"Maybe" as Scotty pulled in close. He started to sway them both in a silent dance. It was nice being in his arms but Alice was positive that he wasn't going to give the ring to her that night. After a few minutes, he stopped the dance. He kissed her forehead and said, "Let's go to bed."

"Alright."

Scott

Scott was waking up with a raging headache. He heard Alice's alarm go off a little bit ago. She silently pulled out of bed and was trying to let him sleep. While she was being quiet, everything was just pounding and he couldn't fall back asleep. He hated how she just disentangled herself from his bed without giving him a kiss or hug. Hell, most mornings he would get up with her so they could have more time together.

Scotty listened to how Alice took the dogs first and got them situated downstairs. She came back upstairs and went to the bathroom to get ready for work. She didn't get a shower, which Scotty knew meant she had a lesson first thing. He was glad that she didn't take a shower since he wasn't sure if he could handle the noise from the shower. He was surprised to hear her come by his night stand. She put a couple things down on his nightstand. That's when he grabbed Alice's hand. "Attendre. Sorry. Wait."

Alice smiled and sat down beside him. She did as he asked. Scotty still cursed himself for asking her to wait twice: once in French and once in English after he caught himself thinking in French first. At this point, he was good about thinking and talking in English even when he was tired. In a soft voice, "Hey, how are you feeling?"

"Like hell" Scott said.

Alice pushed some of the hair off his forehead that had flopped into his eyes. Her eyes were shining which made him happy. She said, "Kinda figured, so I brought up some hang-over survival kit items." She leaned over and kissed him lightly. She didn't seem mad or anything.

"Thanks babe. How's your day looking?"

"It's not awful. Just boring. Will be guarding a lot and most of that will be solo. Think you will get cleared today?"

"Yeah. It's a longshot but I should be allowed to go on the trip and play at the end of the week."

"Well good luck. I hope you can get cleared. Let me know how it goes."

"Of course babe," with a slight groan he pushed himself up onto the pillow so he could swallow the aspirin and the water. He was definitely paying for last night's partying. He had fun at least what he could remember but there were holes in his memory.

"I'll let you get some rest," said Alice with a smile. He pulled her in for a hug and a kiss before she left for work. He didn't want her to leave without getting in their proper morning time. He was already starting to feel better just because he was able to touch and be with her. But he did let her go to work without too much issue after getting in his morning hug and kiss.

As he rolled over, he felt something in his pocket dig into his leg. He pulled out a ring box. He remembered picking up the rings late last night on the way to the bar with the guys. He was excited to pick the rings despite knowing it would be a while before he would give Alice the engagement ring and even longer before they would have the wedding rings. But what he couldn't figure out was why he didn't take it out of his pocket before bed or even try to hide it. The only thing he could think of was Alice found out about the box and he was afraid that she would try to look for it when she woke up. He placed the box in the night stand and hid it in the same spot as he hid the last ring he got her.

He commissioned the rings before the Philly trip since he

wanted to have a special ring just for her and he knew it would take some time to have everything made for him. After what happened in Philly with the apartment search, he wanted to make sure he wasn't moving too fast for her. He wanted to know 100% that she was ready for it before he actually gave it to her. He just hoped he didn't have to wait too long before he could give her the ring.

When he heard his phone go off he groaned at the noise. He knew it was going to be a long morning. So he pushed himself up to drink some Gatorade as he looked at the phone.

Lager: ***Morning asshole***

This is when Scotty would question why he was friends with Lager. Lager had to know that Scotty was hungover and that wasn't a good time to text. Lager just didn't care. Scotty put his phone on do not disturb mode so he could sleep. He was going to ignore the text from Lager except for the fact, Lager decided to text again before he had a chance to put the phone on the nightstand so Scotty knew he would have to converse with his friend.

Lager: ***Heard you went a little crazy last night.***

Scotty: ***Ugh. You left early because of course you would leave early.***

Lager: ***Yeah but left I Petey and Corey in charge of your ass. Petey isn't even hungover.***

Scotty: ***Bastard***

Lager: ***I haven't heard from Corey but I'm assuming he's hungover. Still can't believe he came out with the concussion.***

Scotty: ***Who told you I went crazy***

Lager: ***Alice texted last night.***

Scotty: ***Really? That had to be bad. Did she seem mad?***

Lager: ***Nah. She was trying to figure out how much water to give you.***

Scotty: ***She didn't give me any water last night. She made some cocktails.***

Lager: ***Water ones I'm guessing. But seriously, she's good for you. When do you plan to give her that ring?***

Scotty: ***End of the season at the earliest. Dude, I need more sleep.***

Scotty shook his head and instantly regretted it. So he decided to down the glass of water and the remainder of his Gatorade. He couldn't believe that Alice reached out to Lager about him last night. Now he was concerned that he did something stupid or dumb last night that he couldn't remember. She didn't seem upset and he remembered they were making out before going to bed. So she couldn't have been mad but then again, why would she reach out at all if it was nothing when he got home. He might have to ask Alice about last night.

He knew he had a couple of hours where he could sleep so he tried to fall back to sleep and fortunately this time, he could actually fall back to sleep. It was a dreamless sleep.

When he woke up from his alarm, he was feeling a lot better. The headache was gone but he could still feel the dregs of the hangover holding on. But he was happy that he could function and he wasn't close to hurling anymore. He knew he should keep things light for the next hours in terms of food but he could be functional at practice.

Once he arrived at the practice facility, he immediately went to the trainer's room which was his new normal. He was hoping that Doc would give him the all clear and at least grant permission to travel with the team. Being hungover was not the best idea when hoping to get cleared but it was a little too late.

As per usual, the Doc had him doing several exercises testing his knee strength. Scotty didn't have any problems performing them. He wasn't as comfortable doing the exercises compared to yesterday but he didn't want to share that with the doc. He just tried to keep a poker face and it seemed like that Doc was satisfied. Curren said, "Go out there and skate. No contact but you're good to go. But report back when you are done so we can evaluate if you are ready for an actual game."

Scotty didn't need to be told twice. He jumped off the table and rushed to get into his gear. The ability to play was great and he didn't want it taken away. While it wasn't too surprising, he has been allowed to skate for the past week but the inflammation after each skate was what was holding him back from full contact games.

He rushed into the locker room. It was pretty sparsely populated at the moment. Lager was there. Lager was practically dressed and almost ready to go out to the ice. He immediately greeted Scotty by saying, "You don't look like death warmed over so you are doing better than some of the guys. Toli really looks like shit."

"Toli is hung over?" asked a clearly shocked Scotty. The Russian could drink a ton and nothing ever seemed to phase him. Hearing that Toli was hungover made Scotty wish he had a better grasp on what happened last night. Seeing Toli drunk had to be a trip but he couldn't remember anything abnormal from him. "I got to get onto the ice. I'll see you in a few."

"Go." Scotty said. He didn't want to delay Lager. Hell, he

knew he needed to quickly get his stuff on so he wasn't late himself. Scotty knew that he would have liked to have been there a little earlier but he was moving slower than usual this morning.

As Scotty was putting on his shoulder pads, Dima stumbled in and grunted at Scotty. Dima looked positively gray. Scotty had to give Dima credit for getting there and suiting up. As Dima was putting on his gear he muttered, "No shot ever with you. You dangerous."

"Don't worry, I just want you to do shots on goal."

"Deal."

Scotty then headed off to the ice. It wasn't really pretty, nearly everyone was hungover. Everyone was made to do suicide drills followed by lightning drills. Berman claimed it was because the guys were slow through the neutral zone against the Flyers but everyone knew it was a punishment for the post-game party. It was rough. Scotty's left knee was crying out in pain with all the work but he knew he couldn't give up or play it easy. He just had to keep going. Despite the pain, he could tell his knee was probably the strongest since the surgery. He knew that if he didn't do these drills to the best of his capability, he wouldn't get his speed back anytime soon and he needed it for the west coast trip.

Might not be such a long shot after all.

After practice, Scotty got changed and reported back to the Doc. They did the same exercises as before. There was a little decline in movement but it was minimal. There was some inflammation but all in all things felt pretty good. Doc seemed to be pleased as he started to ice down his knee.

"Looks like you are good for the road trip. I am still

advising minimum contact in practice. But you should report to the coach."

"Sounds good."

Scotty had a light step. After six weeks, the doc said he was finally ready to play again. Any tinge of hangover evaporated due to his excitement. Scott reported to Berman's office. As per usual Scott knocked on the door frame before he entered.

Berman shouted out with, "For the love of god, please tell me it's good news."

Scotty smiled and leaned against the doorframe. He said, "Yup. Doc said I'm good to play in the next game but he wants to minimize contact in practice."

"Thank god. But I should bench your ass for getting everyone drunk last night."

"I just wanted to make sure that everyone was loose and enjoyed themselves. I didn't realize how we overdid it until it was too late. At least, we all showed up today and I will make sure they play their asses off in California."

"As long as you also play your ass off. I won't bench you. Mainly, because we still need you."

Alice

Alice was working in her office trying to catch up with the paperwork and figure out a good time to schedule some lifeguard courses. She was staring at the computer screen with extreme focus and barely heard a knock at the door. It wasn't until she heard a familiar voice say, "Hey babe" when she looked up from the screen. She saw Scotty standing at the door holding two very large cups of coffee.

As she got up from her desk to hug him, she said, "Hey, what are you doing here?"

"I would think it's pretty obvious," he said with a chuckle as he gave her one of the coffees. He kissed her as soon as the coffee was secure in her hand.

"Really? You almost never come here when it's not for some PT. Unless..... Do you have some news?"

Scotty smiled and sat down in one of the office chairs making himself comfortable with a wide leg stance and slouching in the chair. She walked back to the desk as she took a few sips of her coffee. He said, "I don't know what you are talking about. Can't I just bring you some coffee?"

As the coffee worked its way through her veins, she realized that he was toying with her. She knew he had morning skate and would have seen the doctor. He was smiling too much and enjoying the moment too much. "Yeah but I know you are lying. So come on, spill. What's the real reason you came here. I know you should have you talked to Curren by now. Soo...."

Scotty's smile changed slightly. It went from adoring to being cocky as all hell. He was enjoying the fact he knew a secret. Hell he was technically hiding two secrets from her, although he didn't know that she knew about the spectacular engagement ring and wedding bands since he was so drunk last night. She knew there was no way in hell that he would be proposing to her at work. He was too much of a romantic to do it on a whim. Hell, he wouldn't even show her the rings last night when he was drunk since he wanted to do it the 'right way'. Alice just continued to stare at him and drink her coffee until he finally said, "I'm cleared to play tomorrow. Although, I still have to worry about the swelling."

Alice immediately broke in and said, "That's awesome! But when do you have to leave?"

"This evening before you get home from work."

She nodded in understanding realizing that if he didn't come out now, he wouldn't be able to see her for a few days. She did a mental rundown of the Sounds schedule. "So it's the Sharks, Ducks and Kings this trip?"

"Almost. Sharks and Ducks only."

She shook her head. "That's not too bad. So you will be back before the end of the week. Do you know how much you will play?"

Scotty shook his head in the negative. She knew that it would be a decline in some of his ice time. Scotty would want to play as much as possible. She knew if he was allowed, he would probably try to play the whole game despite what the skating could do to his knee. But the team needed him throughout the rest of the season in order to make a real go for the Stanley Cup. Not surprisingly, Scotty switched the topic and asked, "Do you have time to get some lunch?"

"Just enough if we go to either Subway or Einsteins."

"Let's do Einsteins, then."

The two of them headed towards the building with the bagel place. At first, the two of them were fairly quiet. Then all of a sudden Scotty noticed how there was a swing attached to a tree. He grabbed Alice from behind and swung her towards the swing. With a light, playful voice, he said, "Do you really have a swing on campus?"

"Yeah," said Alice with a laugh. Then it dawned on her, "You want to play with it don't you?"

He nodded. The two of them sat on the swing together. Alice was in his lap. He pulled out his phone for a selfie. Alice posed for it like a good girlfriend. Then Alice whispered and said, "I don't care if the photo goes on Instagram but I want one for just us too."

Then he took another photo when he started to kiss her ear. "That's the one for just us." They felt the swing start to groan under their combined weight. He immediately slipped out from underneath her and said, "Come on. I'll push you for a bit."

"I didn't know you were a sucker for swings." As she got comfy on the swing seat, she turned back to Scotty and said, "Not going to try and push me around the world are you?"

"Not today. Too many branches to go through," teased Scotty.

It was fun and childish and she couldn't stop giggling. It didn't help that Scotty kept catching her to either kiss or tickle her with each and every push. After a few minutes, when he caught her at the end of the one push, she asked, "want me to push you some?"

"Sure." Scotty said. They swapped spots. While Alice couldn't push Scotty nearly anywhere as high but Scotty was laughing just as much as she was.

At the end of one push, she noticed the time when it flashed up on her watch. "Fuck."

"What is it baby?" asked Scotty. He was clearly concerned by her tone of voice.

"I need to go back and reopen the pool."

Fortunately, Scotty understood what that meant. He immediately stopped swinging. Alice half expected him to jump off mid-swing but was happy when he didn't since she didn't want him to screw up his knee after getting medically cleared to play again. But when he did get off the swing, he said with a fair amount of disappointment in his voice, "You didn't get any food."

"I'll live," said Alice as she started to head back to the gym.

Scott grabbed her by the wrist stopping her in her tracks. He said, "Nope. You skip too many meals as it is. I'll bring you something to the pool. What do you want?"

Alice should have known that there wasn't going to be a way to deter Scotty. So it would be easier to just have him get her something and she was hungry. "Nova lox from Einsteins sounds good."

"Okay. Do you want anything else?"

"Coffee."

Scotty just started to laugh. They both knew how she loved to drink caffeinated products, especially coffee. "I should have known. But didn't you have enough with your first cup?"

"Not even close. Babe, I need to go."

"Okay." Scotty let her go but snuck in a kiss before releasing her.

Alice rushed towards the gym. She quickly tested the chemicals for the pool and opened everything up. It was a quiet start to the open swim so Alice was sitting at one of the two desks. The first person to walk into the pool area was Scotty. He immediately said, "I feel bad for your heart sometimes," as he handed her an iced coffee.

Alice rolled her eyes and said, "I'm not that bad."

He kissed her forehead and said, "You are addicted to caffeine. Like totally addicted, babe. Also they didn't have the nova lox for you. So I got a sandwich for you instead. I hope it's okay."

"Thanks. I'm sure it will be fine." She sat down and invited Scotty to sit with her. She said, "You're the best. Thanks for coming today and for the food. You could have easily just texted me the news."

"But then I wouldn't have gotten to see you. That would have sucked for both of us. Besides you are now on your second espresso drink now in a span of an hour, it seems like you needed me to be your supplier."

"It's not a full need. More of a pure desire for the second latte."

"Babe, I saw your face. It was your moment of bliss. Okay not pure bliss in the sense of how you get in the bedroom but that momentary kind." Scotty was babbling. He almost never babbled. She was the one who would do that, typically 'cause she was excited and over caffeinated. She was starting to think something was up with him. She wanted to know what was on his mind. But he was self-assured as ever and she had a feeling he would deny it. He asked, "What?" when he noticed her staring at him.

"Something seems off. You sure everything is okay?"

"It's nothing," said Scotty trying to brush her off. She wasn't surprised by that response. She cocked an eyebrow as if to tell him that she was far from convinced. That's when Scotty let her in, "I'm just a little nervous about the game tomorrow. That's all. I will get it settled down by the time the puck drops. The best thing will be me getting out there and playing. But I will do my little secret ritual of getting a haircut. I know I'll be fine. The Sharks won't know what hit them. Literally."

That surprised Alice. He was never nervous about playing. He just carried himself like he owned the ice and hell, he normally did. But after six and a half weeks away, she knew he would be a bit rusty and it will take him a few games to be back to normal. They both knew he would be fine. First, she said, "As long as you don't try to take on Jumbo Joe, you will be fine in the hit department. But I know you will rock it out there. You always do. But why the haircut?"

Scotty pushed a hand through his shaggy hair. It's gotten long in the past few weeks but it was never clean cut like some guys. "Old superstition. If I get nervous before a big game, I always get cleaned up before. Works like a charm for me. Plus mom always liked how it got me cleaned up."

Alice laughed. It was such a simple superstition but Scotty never seemed to have them. Instead, he usually used his hockey IQ and studied the game more. She was the superstitious one in the relationship. But the haircut sounded no different than how she would apply makeup before any big presentation. Then she realized something. "Wait a minute, you didn't get cleaned up before that first game against the Flyers. That means you weren't nervous about the game or trying to win me over?"

"Yeah. I wasn't nervous at all that game. I knew I could impress you. Besides, I didn't have that much rust to shake off. It was an easy matchup. You were trickier but I was confident" said Scotty with a sly smile. "I just want this return to be just as easy."

"Well I have faith in you. I know how awesome you are. You will kick some ass." If she wasn't working at the moment, she would totally have hugged him to reassure him but she felt like it would be crossing a line that she shouldn't do. The pool wasn't closed like the first time he came to the pool for PT.

Then Scotty looked at her and asked "Are you sure you can't get off of work and fly out for one of the games?"

"Yes, I'm sure. Especially since the day you play the Ducks, I have to be in court testifying against the adult who got charged and tomorrow I have to meet with the prosecutor to go over my testimony and whatnot."

"Oh right. Sorry, I won't be there to support you that day. I wanted to be there for you," Scotty said super apologetically. The look on his face said it all at that moment. She honestly wanted him to go to court with her but she had been purposefully downplaying that day in her calendar so she didn't get scared. She would never ask him to give up a game for that especially after sitting out so long with an injury.

Alice smiled and said, "Its okay. I will let you know if I need anything. While I can't go west, I promise to be at the game on Saturday. I seriously can't wait to see you back in action again."

"Sounds good." Scotty said with a forced smile. Then he changed the conversation to "You really should eat your food."

With a groan, Alice said, "I'm not going to starve to death."

"Yeah, 'cause I won't let you." Scotty said with a laugh as he pushed her sandwiched her way. She shook her head but took the sandwich. "Eat."

"Fine," she said with an exaggerated eye roll. She unwrapped the sandwich to see one of her other favorite orders: a BBQ chicken sandwich. Scotty knew her so well and nailed the impromptu sandwich order. She quickly took a couple bites: both because she loved the sandwich and to get

Scotty off her case about not eating enough food. Scotty also pulled out a sandwich for himself.

When a swimmer came in. She quickly put the sandwich down on the wrapper and took her place on the lifeguard stand. She could feel Scotty's eyes on her looking at her disapprovingly and her eyes were focused on the pool straight ahead. She said somewhat defensively, "What? I will eat more later."

"You better. I'm going to need to head out." Alice could tell by the tone of his voice that he was disappointed in her not even trying to eat more.

"Have an awesome trip! Also thanks for my stopping by and getting me some lunch. I'm going to miss you this week. I love you."

"Je t'aime." He came up and hugged her from the side but didn't kiss her. As he got closer to the door, he turned her way and shouted, "Eat your food!"

Alice shook her head but she responded the only way she knew how. "Go play hockey!" The way Scotty's face lit up, she knew she said the right thing. It was absolutely priceless.

22

SCOTT

The trip to San Jose was uneventful. It was just long but it felt good to be on the road with the team and to be in the lineup. The only downside was that Lager wasn't allowed to play in the game against San Jose thanks to that reckless high-stick against the Flyers. The Sound would still have only two of their top three guys for one more game. At least, it was only a single game suspension.

The morning practice was mostly uneventful for Scotty. He wasn't allowed to do much since Doc was concerned about Scotty being slightly stiff after the plane ride out. But he felt pretty good with the few skating drills he was allowed to do.

While he was travelling, he reached out to Joey, a pal from juniors who was now based in San Jose as a goalie coach at one of the local universities and the Sharks standby, emergency goalie at games, to find out a good place to get a haircut. Fortunately, he was able to get slotted into an appointment almost immediately after practice.

Apparently, the hairdresser was a big hockey fan and had no problem making time for Scotty although the guy couldn't stop talking. Scotty didn't say much and just let the guy carry on a conversation. But he had to give it to the guy, he did an awesome job with the hair although his hockey takes were basic at best. He wasn't sure what to fully expect for the cut since he didn't walk in with a real plan. In the end, it still had some length up top where it could swoop to the left but was short along the sides. In some ways, it reminded him of Lundqvist's hairstyle.

As he was walking back to the hotel, he sent a selfie to Alice so she could be one of the first people to see the new look. Almost immediately, she texted back: ***Pantydropper.*** That made him laugh so hard and he couldn't let that slide.

So he immediately dialed her and said, "Pantydropper, you say?"

"Oh you are. You were gorgeous before but that looks damn super sexy on you."

"So you like it?" he said knowing that she did. He was hoping to get one of her classic maybes and hear her get all shy and coy.

"Dude. I love you no matter what. But yes, you are looking really good that way. I promise I won't ever question your superstitions again," she said quickly. He was surprised to hear how she much she liked it.

He decided to take it up a notch and said, "Mmmm. So if I was there, what would you be doing right now?"

He was hoping to take her down the familiar path of their more sensual calls but she replied with such a flat tone, "Still at work, so drooling from afar. Would at most, ask you to bring me some coffee so I could see you."

"Boo. That's not how you are supposed to play the game," teased Scotty. But that was his Alice. A little too literal at times and he knew that she wouldn't do any sexy talk while at work. In some ways, he was amazed she let him hang out while she was at work yesterday and got on the swing with him.

"Oh really? What should I be saying then?" she asked somewhat inquisitively and showing off her naivety or at least taking the bait.

As Scotty got back to the hotel, he had to dodge Crestie in the hallway but after that everything seemed pretty quiet. But he took a few seconds to get his hotel door and then he could try to make Alice fluster and blush, he loved doing that. Hell, it was why he decided to call her rather than text just to hear it in her voice. If he was willing to wait, he would have tried to do a video chat. "It should be something like I would undress you, caress you, and tease your body through my touches."

"You expect me to say something like that when I'm work?" asked Alice with a laugh.

"Yes. It's not like I said anything super naughty. Not like how I would totally lay you down on the bed, flick my tongue across your clit, tease it for a second and then come back for more of your sweet, sweet pussy," he said with his full sexy voice and he flopped back onto the bed. It was all the things he was dreaming of doing to her at that moment.

Alice was silent. He looked at his phone to see if she was still there. She didn't hang up so he got her to the point where she was shocked and completely blushing. Scotty started to laugh and asked, "Too much?"

"Maybe," said a quiet Alice.

"Maybe my ass," said Scotty. He knew her well enough to know that was indecision on her part. "So do I need to stop?"

"For now. After work, we can get carried away. Hell, I will give you my best response although I still really am nowhere near as good as you are."

"Are you sure?" asked Scotty. He was hoping that it wouldn't be the case but he knew deep down there wasn't any real likelihood that Alice would continue.

"Yes. For now."

"Fine. But you are no fun."

"And you're incorrigible."

"You keep telling me that but I think you like it when I talk dirty to you. Even when you are at work."

She laughed and said, "What if I do?"

"I could keep doing it." he said with a laugh and a smile in his voice.

"Don't you dare!"

"So should I get off the phone?" Scotty asked, hoping that he wouldn't actually be told to get off the phone but he knew she would want to get back to work sooner rather than later. Hell, he should be napping before the game.

"Nah. I can talk a little bit longer. So feeling better about tonight?" asked Alice.

"Oh yeah. I wish I could have played against Philly and have you there for my return. At least this time, my knee isn't super stiff from the flight. It's already loosened up plenty so that should be fine. Only thing left to do is get my pre-game nap."

"While I totally get that," Alice said with a yawn, "There's a part of me that is totally jealous that you are expected to take a nap as part of your work day."

Scott smiled, he knew she had to get up early and she hated when she had to be at work at 7am. She would just do it but her actually admitting that she was super tired to even to him or her dad was pretty rare. "Jealous, you say?"

"Yeah. I could use a nap."

All this talk about sleep was making Scotty miss having her lay beside him. He was alone in the bed. So he figured, "What's your Friday like?"

"Friday?" Alice said clearly thrown off guard. He loved how her voice would go up high on the last syllable when she was thrown. He didn't manage to do it very often. Sure, he could surprise her with a gift but it wasn't the same.

"You know that day that's the end of a traditional work week and the morning that I get back from the road trip." He knew that he was teasing her.

Unsurprisingly, she threw it right back at him, "Right. Friday. If I recall, it ends with a y too."

"Yeah, I was hoping to hear how I will get to sleep with you when I get home."

"It should be a lazy morning. I won't have work until late afternoon. Although, I will be on kid duty when you get home."

"Kid duty?" That was surprising. While he loved envisioning Alice with his child, she didn't always spend that much time around kids. When she did, it was always amazing and he was sure that he would have remembered it if Alice mentioned it.

"Earlier today, Bridge asked if I could watch Klaus until you get back on Thursday night. Something about a research project for school. I didn't ask too many questions."

"Cool. That'll be nice." Scott was trying to figure out if he would get to see her interact with the 3 year old or if he would miss it completely. But he didn't want to spook her thinking that he wanted kids right away and scare her off, so he didn't ask for too many details.

"Did you really ask about Friday to find out if we can sleep together in the morning?"

"Yup." He looked over to the empty spot on the bed beside him where she would normally be. He said with longing, "I miss having you beside me."

"I miss you too. I should let you get to your nap." At least, Alice didn't point out how she never napped with him which he half expected.

"Alright. Je t'aime. Call me after the game."

"Je t'aime." Scotty smiled. He loved hearing her tell him that she loved him in French. He never heard it enough and normally he would have to say it first. Even then she would often respond in English. Probably to avoid him making fun of her jacked up accent but he still loved how she said she loved him in French.

Scotty sunk into the bed and was feeling comfortable. He was happy. He also had so much to look forward to - the game tonight, the Ducks, and getting back home to Alice.

There was a knock on the door. He cursed and opened up to see it was Lager on the other side. Scotty let him in and asked, "What's up? I was about to get my nap on."

"Dude, you look like one of the pretty boys." Scotty just rolled his eyes at his friend. Scotty wasn't even surprised by Lager's reaction. He wasn't going to fight it. He just stared at his friend. Scotty could practically see Lager put two and two together. "Wait, don't tell me you are nervous about playing tonight."

"I'm good now."

"But you were," accused Lager. Scotty still wasn't going to dignify that with a response.

"Did you have a reason why you came over?" Scotty said with a bit more force.

"Yeah. PK stopped by earlier and you were out. He wants you and some of the other guys to have dinner with his girlfriend when we get to LA. It'll be some fancy place and he needed an RSVP. So I told him that I would pass along the message."

"Yeah sounds good. Wonder why he didn't text me."

"Cool. I'm glad you are back. It will be good to have you back as center again. Sorry we couldn't reunite the 3 amigos until Thursday. Stupid suspension."

"Whose fault is that? But until then, I'll just have to remind everyone how lethal my wrister is and how I don't need to have you by my side to pass up the puck."

"Don't be an asshole, you know you love it when I give you the puck."

"True."

Alice

The work week was a whirlwind but she was glad that Scott had a killer game against the Sharks. He had a goal and two assists which was amazing given how they had limited him to about ⅓ less minutes then normally played. She knew he had a maintenance day yesterday to help keep things happy and avoid any unnecessary setbacks.

Alice was dreading her day. This was the first of her court dates related to her burglary and she was a bundle of nerves. The building was huge and she wasn't sure where she needed to go other than what was on the letter from the court. Fortunately, a person who was familiar with the court, likely a lawyer, took pity on her and helped to direct her to the 22nd floor. Once there, she was directed to wait in a lobby. At first, Alice was the only one who was there. She had her headphones on and was trying to read a book on the new iPad in hopes to stay calm but it wasn't working at all. She also had her teddy bears in her purse and would rub a paw or ear for comfort by slipping her hand into the purse. She couldn't focus on her book no matter what and kept looking at her phone to see if she had any messages or new lives in the game she was playing. All of a sudden she saw a text from Scotty.

S: *Good luck today. Sorry I'm not with you.*

A: *Thanks. What are you doing awake?*

S: *Checking in on my girl. What's going on?*

A: *Just waiting for the prosecutor*

S: *That's no fun.*

A: *Yeah*

Just texting with Scotty made her relax a little bit in the lobby. It was good since he was the one person who could make her relax when her anxiety was high. Sure her dad called in the morning to wish her luck but at that point she wasn't that nervous yet. As each person started to occupy the waiting area, she got more uncomfortable. It seemed like most people there were seedy and just not the best crowd. So anything to temper her nerves was a good thing.

After a while, Scotty texted again:

S: *You seem quiet*

A: *Yeah. Waiting sucks.*

S: *You got this. I know you do. You are awesome.*

A: *Thanks*

Alice was also warned that Scott wasn't getting enough rest for the game. It didn't matter that Alice had the same amount of sleep if not way less since she was awake, dressed and at the courthouse while Scotty would be texting from bed. But she didn't want to be the reason he wasn't well rested for the game so she thought screw it, and texted him her thoughts.

A: ***Get some rest***

S: ***I told you I wanted to be there for you.***

A: ***Sleep. Don't add guilt to my anxiety***

S: ***Fine. Only because you asked but ping me if you need me***

A: ***Je t'aime***

That's when the police officer who was also the receptionist at the waiting room asked Alice to go into the next set of doors since Alice's prosecutor hadn't shown up yet and it was already two hours after the time listed on the subpoena. She was glad to get away from the waiting from and the guy sitting next to her who was clearly on drugs. So she tentatively walked ahead.

When she walked into the next waiting area, she saw a deputy at a desk and several lawyers all talking around the table. She was still nervous but maybe she would have answers. She was asked by the deputy why she was there and she handed over her subpoena. The deputy asked the lawyers if they knew where her prosecutor might be.

One guy said, "He's downstairs in court." The deputy took her subpoena to talk with the bailiff for the courtroom she was assigned to. Alice waited what felt like forever when she knew it was likely five minutes. The deputy returned and immediately asked, "Didn't anyone call?"

"No. They didn't." Alice knew how she waited for such a call the day before.

"It's been continued. The bailiff signed this and take it to the cashier's office so we can at least reimburse you for parking. The new date is here."

Alice was livid but tried to mask her anger. She couldn't believe it. She wasted so much time and stress for nothing. They didn't have the courtesy to let her know that she didn't need to come in. She made her way to the cashier and got the reimbursement.

Alice: ***Wasted my fucking time. Got to let off some steam and do some pick up***

Almost immediately Alice's mobile went off. She saw the photo of her and Scotty on the swing. She smiled and she instantly felt happier and better than she did moments before, "Hey you."

"Hey. You okay?"

"Pissed but okay."

Scotty chuckled and said, "I would be too."

"You seemed tired. I should let you sleep." Alice said, trying to be considerate and make sure that she didn't screw up his gameplay.

"I wouldn't have called if I wanted to sleep." Alice heard the sheets rustle around so she imagined Scotty was still in bed. That made her feel more comfortable, especially as she imagined him half naked since he never liked wearing much to bed. "So you're going to play some pick up?"

"Yeah. I figured between the ice and just shooting the puck, I'll be calmer and/or exhausted."

"Want any company for that?" asked a curious Scotty.

Alice didn't hear anymore movement from the bed so she didn't think he was actually getting out of bed.

"Aren't you in LA?" asked an incredulous Alice. She knew Scotty had guilt about not attending court but there was absolutely no chance he would be allowed to miss another game especially after missing 6.5 weeks with his knee injury. They had less than a week before the end of the regular season and the Sound didn't have their position fully locked in so they needed their best player on the ice every single game. But Alice could see Scotty trying to make it work out that he was there doing both.

Scotty just started laughing. It was a full throttle laugh rather than just the chuckle she normally elicited from him. But hearing his laughter helped her relax even more. "Sorry babe, I didn't mean with me. Coach said no to trying to spend half the day with you and flying back before the game, remember. But Corey isn't on the trip. He said he is starting to feel better. I bet he would let you go to his house to play and would like some company."

"Maybe. I still can't believe he has an ice rink at his place and you don't. If I thought only one of you on the team had an ice rink at his place, it would be you."

"Tried. The foundation wouldn't support it and that was if I got the permit. That didn't seem super likely. At least for the summer, I got ice at home."

Alice laughed. That made so much sense.

"I like hearing you laugh again baby." He took a deeper breath. "I'm sorry that today didn't go smoother."

"It could have been worse but thanks for always being there for me."

"Of course, I will be there for you even if I can't physically be there."

"I love you too. Kick some ass tonight. I'll see you when you get in. But I need to run inside and grab my gear."

Scotty laughed, "So you aren't going to call Corey."

"I don't know. Maybe if I need to do more after the pick-up."

"Well, have fun and don't overthink it. Keep the puck on your stick for longer than you would like but don't over handle it. IE don't just pass the puck."

"Always passing works for Voracek." Alice knew Scotty would be telling her how she shouldn't be passing the puck around nearly so much. It was something he always told her. This was one of the few times she actually had a bit of a retort.

"You aren't him and you're too afraid of the puck. Besides Jake will shoot on net occasionally."

"Fine. Any other advice?"

"Call Corey."

"Fine. Call me later?" Alice asked.

"Of course, baby. Je t'aime."

"Je t'aime." Then the phone line went dead.

Alice did as Scotty asked and talked to Corey. It was going to be hard to make to her normal pick up time. So in the end, she headed over to his place to play.

Corey was happy to have someone to play with and it was good to actually know someone on the ice rather than playing with random guys. He took it easy on her but that didn't stop him from trash talking the entire time. She realized how much he was a chirper on the ice. He was the one who probably called her a nerd at the OTA. He definitely called her a nerd four times during their game.

As Alice was heading out of the hockey rink, she got a message from Jennifer with a news article link asking if everything was okay with her and Scotty. Alice responded first going how things were great without even looking at the article. The moment she did, she laughed her ass off. It was a photo of Scotty next to PK's girlfriend and they were trying to link the two as a couple. Their evidence was his new haircut.

Alice: ***That's PK's gf. It was a team dinner. Hell that tattooed hand is PK's. Scotty doesn't have any.***

Not to mention, we were sexting most of the night shortly after the dinner. Trust me nothing is broke. That's just some puck bunnies' dream.

Jennifer: ***But they are saying his new haircut was to impress the girl.***

Alice: ***He got it before the Sharks game because he's slightly superstitious like me.***

Jennifer: ***Just glad to hear things are still good.***

Alice: ***Yup and he gets to come home tonight :) Today might have been a shitshow but I don't have to worry about Scotty.***

Scott

It was late. He just wanted to sleep. The game against the Ducks ended up being brutal. He had several fresh bruises all over. The Sharks game was downright easy in comparison and he was expecting the rough game against the Sharks. He was also just pissed off about the day. Between the puck bunny rumors and not being there for Alice at court, he just wanted to be done with the day and snuggle up with his girl.

When he opened up the door, he was greeted by both Chloe

and Backup. He tried to keep quiet with them as he rubbed both the pup's ears. Out of the corner of his eye, he noticed that there were kid shoes next to Alice's shoes. That reminded him that Alice was taking care of Klaus that night. On the counter, he noticed there was the flowers he ordered for Alice. He was actually surprised Alice didn't come downstairs to greet him. She might actually have fallen deeply asleep like he hoped.

He climbed the stairs and into the bedroom. He quickly changed into athletic shorts and a Sound Tee. The moment he started to climb into bed, Alice rolled over and gave him the widest smile as she said, "Hey there, sexy."

Scotty smiled. He knew he had to look like hell and yet all she saw was him looking sexy. He leaned forward and kissed her as he said, "Hey, I thought you were still asleep."

"I heard you moving about."

"Sorry," said Scotty as he kissed her forehead. "I was hoping to avoid that."

"Nah, you're good. You know, your new haircut is soooo sexy." Scotty had to smile. He knew that she was exhausted. She almost never let herself get drunk but she would get punch drunk every once in a while and seemed like tonight was one of those nights when she was punch drunk from staying up too late. There was a huge part of him that wanted to keep her awake to have her say something silly like his hockey and kisses.

"You keep saying that babe."

"It's trueee....."

All of a sudden there was a burst of energy that came through the bedroom door. "Miss Alice, Miss Alice" said the little boy. But the moment the little one saw Scott, he said, "Uncle Scotty!" Klaus launched himself into Scotty's arm and landed near one of his bruises. He tried not to cringe. The boy loved all the guys on the team but probably loved hanging around Scotty the most.

"Hey there, buddy," said Scotty trying to keep things light in his voice.

Scotty was going to set Klaus in between him and Alice. But before he could, the little boy whispered in his ear as only a little kid would, half hushed and yet perfectly audible to everyone in the room, "Uncle Scotty. If you sleep with Miss Alice like how mommy and daddy sleep, does that mean I should be calling her Aunt Alice?"

Scotty smiled and wanted to laugh. That was something he wasn't expecting but it made so much sense knowing kid logic. Scotty whispered back to the little one, "You are going to have to ask her."

Klaus then pulled a smile that was so much like his dad's, complete with the charm turned fully up. He was way too young to know how to charm someone but it seemed to be an instinctive trait for the Lagerfield guys apparently. Klaus said, "Miss Alice, can I call you Aunt Alice?"

Alice smiled and said, "Sure, but why are you awake?"

"I heard noises. But now I see it's Uncle Scotty. Does that mean I have to go home now?"

"Not yet but you should be in bed asleep. The sun is still sleeping," said Alice with a yawn.

"And I should be asleep too. But I can stay up if hockey is on." said Klaus as if he heard it before and was repeating the obvious. Turning to Scotty with Lager's smile again, he said, "Is hockey on?"

"Not yet, buddy. Even hockey players are sleeping or going to bed." said Scotty with a laugh.

Alice grabbed Klaus from Scotty's arm and started to get up from bed. Backup jumped back off the bed to Klaus and Alice. As she was grabbing him, "Come on, let's go back to sleep. Before you know it, we can all get up."

"Okay. Night Uncle Scotty," said Klaus from Alice's shoulder.

Scotty loved seeing Alice's maternal side. She just took over in that caring way. It was the perfect thing to see them together. The only bad thing was that Alice was alert and no longer punch drunk. Within five minutes, she was coming back to the bedroom but Scotty was surprised that Backup didn't come back in. Scotty rolled to face Alice and said, "You know, you will make a great mom one day."

"Well given he jumped up for you the moment he saw you, are you sure that it's not you who will be the good parent?"

"When you put it that way, it will be the both of us," said Scotty. He laid his arms on her shoulders in a loose hug. He was glad to hold his girl and look in her eyes. He leaned his head on hers and said, "Are you okay?"

"Yeah. What about you? That was a chippy game."

"Been better. Have I ever mentioned I hate LA? Sorry about not being there for you today."

"Given all the shit you have been dealing with today. It's no wonder you hate LA. Don't worry about me being alone at court today. Literally, all you missed was the courts wasting my time and energy."

"I hope you didn't see all of it," muttered Scotty under his breath as he thought about the super reports of him supposedly hooking up with PK's girlfriend.

Alice started laughing. That's when Scotty knew that she

heard about it. But he was also relieved to hear her so relaxed and knew he didn't need to worry. Alice looked at him and said, "I don't know what's the most ridiculous part about the rumor: the fact they think you cut your hair for her despite the fact you clearly had it done when you were in San Jose or the fact you can clearly see PK's hand on her waist. Unless you have been hiding a third arm with tattoos on it, I know there is nothing to worry about. Not to mention all the Face-time'ing we did, when would you guys have done anything?"

Scotty had to kiss Alice passionately with full tongue. He was just so relieved to hear that she saw the report for exactly the load of rubbish that it was. He was so glad to see that she wasn't a tiny bit jealous or worried that he might stray. He's seen similar reports blow up a seemingly stable relationship with teammates over the years. While he couldn't imagine straying from Alice, he knew that there is always a threat of an easy lay since there were always girls who threw themselves at hockey players. It just seemed a bit crazy to be linked to PK's girlfriend since PK and half the team were present at the dinner that night. He was never even alone with her.

"I can't tell you how glad I am to know that it didn't phase you."

"Dude compared to the court crap and seeing you manhandled by the Ducks, I didn't have room to worry about nonsensical rumors."

"I get that. At least, we showed the Ducks who's the best. Beating them 5-1 was pretty ridiculous."

"Yah. You did pretty damn good" said Alice a bit coyly.

"Pretty damn good? What should I have done better?" asked an incredulous Scotty. He had two goals and two assists that night. He played almost his normal amount of minutes too. His numbers were even back on track to be a very strong year for him even with the injuries.

In the most blasé fashion possible, she said, "A hat trick. Dykstman had one."

"Oh you." He rolled Alice over so he was on top of her. "What am I going to do with you? Don't you remember I did just come back from surgery and even by your own words, I was getting manhandled out there tonight and you are saying I should have a had a hattrick?"

Alice just laughed and leaned up to kiss him. It was that moment that Scotty realized that she was just trying to rile him up and didn't really think he was only okay in the game. He knew that they were both exhausted and should be sleeping but it was just fun fooling around and his bad mood was almost fully dissipated at that point. He kicked himself for so easily falling for her ploy to get him on top of her so she could have an easier time to give him kisses.

Alice was still smiling and seemed satisfied with just getting him on top of her. She keep leaning up for more kisses. Alice was careful with her hand placement by keeping her hands around his neck or fisting through his hair. While he would have loved for her to caress his body, he was glad that she didn't touch any of his bruises at that moment. While he was loving her actions, he knew they couldn't get too loud with Klaus being down the hall but fortunately, she seemed to be thinking the same thing.

Thinking about how Klaus was down the hall, he realized that the two of them probably watched the game together due to the boy's earlier comments. He loved how animated she was during games but it wasn't usually kid-friendly. He pulled back from the kissing, "Babe, did you watch the game with Klaus?"

"Yes, babe and before you ask, I was on my best behavior and it was tough. Although if we have kids, I won't make any promises about my language during hockey games. They will probably learn how to swear way too young."

Scotty shook his head and laughed. He could see it going both ways. Her being really good at finding creative ways to swear without swearing or just letting it go like she does whenever she watches a game. "As long as you didn't teach Klaus any, I won't care. Lager and Bridge would probably kill both of us if you did."

Alice smiled and asked, "How has Petey not sworn in front of Klaus?"

"No clue. Probably fear of death if he did. Come on baby, let's go to sleep like the sun is."

Alice threw her head back and groaned, "Ugh. You are going to tease me over that for a while aren't you?"

"Probably. Just like you love to bring up hockey and kisses."

"You use it as much as I do," accused Alice. "Besides Klaus said it first. I just realized it worked and it was something his parents must say to put him to bed after games."

Scotty pulled Alice close in a spooning position, how he usually held her right before they went to sleep, "Maybe I do. But come on, let's go to sleep. It's been a long day." Much to his surprise, Alice didn't put up a fight on the need for sleep. He looked down to her and realized that she was already practically asleep in his arms.

Wow. That didn't take long thought Scott.

He started to fall asleep almost as quickly. But he loved

having Alice in his arms as they slept. He waited all week for that moment.

A few hours later, he thought he heard the doorbell but by the time he actually woke from his sleep, there was no more noise. Chloe was alert although she never actually moved off the bed which was odd since she normally went to door anytime there was someone there. So Scott was unsure if he really did hear anything. Then he heard Alice's phone ring which was weird since she always kept the phone on silent other than her alarm clock. So Scotty grabbed to phone to silence it and saw it was Brigitta. So he answered it.

"Hello." He knew he sounded sleepier then he would have liked. Not only that, he was tired and stiff. He knew he should do a couple soaks today.

"Hey, Scott. I thought I called Alice's phone. Sorry to wake you but I'm here to get Klaus."

"You did, she's still asleep. Okay, I'll bring him down."

Scotty carefully disentangled himself from Alice, somehow she remained asleep. He carefully padded his way down to the guest room. He smiled when he saw Klaus and Backup both sprawled out in the middle of the bed. He wished he had his phone to take a picture but he left it in the bedroom. Instead, he grabbed the kid's backpack and the little boy. The little boy remained passed out in his arms. Surprisingly, Backup and Chloe remained upstairs. Chloe actually made a lot of sense since the she kinda hated Brigitta but normally Backup would love to get up. Scotty opened the door to pass off the sleeping three year old wordlessly.

Before getting back upstairs, he filled the dogs' bowls so he and Alice could stay in bed longer. Then he noticed that he forgot to grab Klaus' shoes. He made a mental note to give Lager the shoes at practice and climbed back to bed.

As he started to grab Alice, she said, "hey sexy" with her eyes closed. While he was tempted to say something about being called sexy it was clear that she was basically still asleep. He figured it wouldn't get the reaction he was hoping for so he remained silent.

23

ALICE

Alice heard Scott's alarm going off. She stirred and he turned off the alarm. She was surprised his alarm went off first. She thought Bridge was going to pick up Klaus at 6:30am but it was clearly much later than that. Also it was weird that neither dog was in the bedroom.

"What time is it?" asked Alice rather sleepily.

"About 9:30 am"

"Really? Why didn't Bridge pick up Klaus this morning?"

Scotty nodded and said, "She did." That shocked Alice big time. She couldn't believe she was out like that. While she barely slept when Scott was gone, she was shocked to catch up on sleep in one go and in his arms.

"Really?"

Scotty kissed her and pulled her in close to him. He stared at her reassuringly. "Yup. At about 6:30 am this morning. It's all good. Everyone was passed out even the pups when she came but I took care of it."

"I didn't wake up at all?" which was shocking to her. Given

how fraught her sleep had been since the burglary, it just seemed completely unreal.

"Well when I climbed back into bed. You did say 'hey sexy' without even looking. So not sure if you woke up or not on that one. But if you keep saying that without looking, I'm going to start thinking you say that to everyone." He kissed her nose.

Alice shook her head. She couldn't believe it. "You know that I only have eyes for you."

"For that I'm grateful."

Scotty got on top of her and pulled off the t-shirt she was wearing. Then things had to be reciprocated and she pulled off his shirt. She said, "Fuck," as she saw that his torso was littered with several black bruises along his sides in-between the shoulder pads and the shorts. She forgot how much Scotty got beaten up in games even despite the pads.

"What babe?" he looked down at her with love trying to figure out what made her swear.

"You really got really beat up yesterday."

"It's fine," he said absolutely nonchalantly as he pushed into her body and brought his warm body on hers. He caressed her with kisses and nuzzled his neck onto hers. She was almost afraid to touch anywhere on his body. He pulled back and looked at her, "If you don't start showing me some love, I'll stop."

It was so easy to forget how many bruises would form anywhere the padding was missing. He wasn't in pain and he wanted her to act like it was normal which it really was. She wasn't going to risk him stopping especially since her dad was coming to visit that weekend and they would have to be quiet each and every day he was over.

So she started to press against his torso and caress his abs. She nuzzled into his neck as he started to massage and play with her breasts. She continued to move her hands down his body, paying no mind to his bruises. She pulled at his shorts and boxers so she could have free access to his goods. She was panting in pleasure. He then pulled her shorts and underwear off. She kept craving to get closer and closer. They moved quickly and it was good for both of them. She just hoped they didn't have a present in a little over nine months' time. Scotty rolled off of her and pulled her close. She knew she should go to the bathroom to clean up but she just wanted to be next to him. She felt him start to play with some of her natural curls. "God, I've missed you," said a quiet, lusty Scotty

She looked at him and said, "Me too."

They continued to embrace each other for about five minutes. He kissed her ear and whispered, "We need to get up."

"Are you sure?" asked Alice. She knew he was right but she didn't want to. She was too comfortable exactly where they were at.

Scotty lifted her chin up and kissed her as he continued to finger her chin line. She reached up and pushed her hands through his hair. Before they got too sensual, he pulled back and said "Oh yes, baby."

They slowly made their way to the bathroom. Alice showered while Scott used the toilet. He didn't get into the shower until she was done so she put on a pair of leggings and a Sound t-shirt. She quietly went downstairs to start some breakfast for Scotty.

Once downstairs, she started to make Scotty's omelet

and some toast. She also started the espresso maker so they could have their morning coffee. For as addicted to coffee as she was, Scotty wasn't far behind her for his need of a first cup. She was happy to see that Scotty was wearing an ab hugging tee as she was sneaking a bite of toast off his plate.

As she took a bit of toast, Scotty teased, "Did hell freeze over?"

"What?" Alice said as she gave him the food. But he didn't immediately go to sit down, instead he snuggled up against her with an arm snaked around her waist. She practically purred as he hugged her with his free hand.

"You just ate something and you haven't been up."

"Shhh. Don't tell my stomach that." Alice said as she moved away from his grasp so she could pour coffee into their usual cups. Scotty sat down at the island across from her as she passed him a coffee.

"Thanks for breakfast," he said with a smile. As he was digging into his omelet with his fork "Your dad is coming tonight for the weekend, right? Did you want to do dinner here or go out?"

"I was thinking of dining in, but I accidentally back ended my day so you and dad will be here before I'm done. But I'll be here around 8:30 tonight."

Scotty flashed a wicked smile before going back to a more neutral one. It was almost as if he caught himself from revealing too much. He said, "No problem. I'll make dinner tonight. Is there anything that your dad doesn't like?"

Alice had to think and shook her head. "Not that I can think of. And before you ask, I don't know what to make for dinner. Everything you cook is fabulous."

Scotty just nodded with a cocky smile, "I'm sure I can come up with something."

Alice leaned over the counter so she could kiss him in appreciation. "Thanks babe." Alice took a moment to savor her coffee. Before she opened her eyes from sipping her coffee, Scotty was hugging her and kissing in her ear. Mornings like this were always just perfect. She couldn't believe how easily mornings became their thing especially since she used to hate mornings. Okay, most days she still hated waking up even if Scotty was making love to her.

"Time for me to go to practice."

Alice said quickly, "Okay. I'll take care of the pups." Scotty kissed her ear once more, then he headed out the door. Alice got a pair of booties on and grabbed the two leashes. Both Chloe and Backup sat to get leashed up. Alice took the two for the walk. She was glad that Backup was so easy to walk and well behaved, especially now that he was the size of Chloe. Alice knew that Backup wasn't even close to being done growing yet. But it had to be amusing for people to see a petite woman taking care of two pretty large dogs.

Scott

Scotty was starting to get anxious, a feeling that he always hated. Keeping his hands busy preparing dinner was a godsend. When Alice mentioned that her dad was arriving before she was done with work, he knew that he had the perfect opportunity to talk her dad about his intentions. As his arrival was drawing closer, he just worried that it wouldn't go his way. Although he couldn't imagine a reason why her dad would say no.

Scott was just putting the fish packets into the oven when the doorbell rang. Both dogs started to rush the door. He grabbed Backup's collar to prevent him from trying to run over Alice's dad when he opened the door. Seeing Alice's dad, Scott smiled and said, "Hey, Mr. Kercheck." As soon as Alice's dad came in the door, he let go of Backup. Both dogs just sniffed both Scotty's and Alice's dad's legs but when they didn't get any attention, they scampered off.

"Hey there, Scott."

"How was the drive in? Do you want anything to drink?"

"It was fine. A beer would be good."

"Any particular kind? Alice has a large selection although she said, she's sorry about the lack of pils." Scott was still nowhere comfortable talking about beer. He knew Alice and her dad enjoyed it way more than he did. He was basically repeating the words that Alice texted him. Scotty said, "I should let you pick out the beer for tonight rather than listing out what she has..."

"Sounds good." Her dad followed Scott to the fridge. Scott pulled out his standby beer as Alice's dad pulled out a craft beer. "I bet you are glad to be playing again."

"Yes, sir. It sucked not being able to play." Then Scott instantly regretted his choice of words. He knew her dad was way cooler about swearing than Alice's mom but he still wanted to impress her dad. Her dad settled down in the living room on the couch.

"Relax Scott. I know Alice won't be here for another twenty minutes."

"It's not that. I have to ask you something and I don't want you to get upset."

"Given what I know about you and how much you care about Alice, you have nothing to worry about."

"Okay. It's not just care for her, I love her very much.

Which is why I wanted to ask if I could marry her. I know she's not quite ready for an engagement and I won't rush that. But I do want to ask her for her hand one day. Possibly after the end of the season but maybe Christmas. I don't know the exact time frame, something that feels right."

"Breathe, Scott." Alice's dad started to chuckle. "You are as bad as Alice when she's nervous." Scott took a drink of beer and he waited for what felt like forever, although it was probably seconds. Finally her dad said, "Yes. You have my blessing. Honestly from the moment you asked her to move in, I've been waiting for this. I always took it that you would be man enough to ask."

"Of course, sir and thank you."

"Stop calling me, sir. Just keep treating my daughter the way you do."

"No problem. I wouldn't dream of treating her any other way," said Scotty instinctually.

"But, she's probably more ready than you think." replied her dad. That surprised Scotty. It made him happy and her dad continued on, "First, she knows about the rings. Don't ask me how, I'm sworn to secrecy. But the idea of that makes her nervous as much as it excites her." Scotty had a feeling that she had to see them the night he got the rings ever since he found the box in his pocket the next morning. He was surprised she hadn't said a thing or even tried to find out more about them which was so unlike her. Although that might have been on the advice of her dad.

"Nervous?" That didn't make much sense to Scotty. While he's seen her start to shut down emotionally when stressed, it seemed like she took comfort in him and never seemed to turn away. Scotty had to get up and check on the food.

Alice's dad then said, "Yeah but it's not really about the two of you. Rather she's nervous from what happened with her previous relationships. Has Alice told you anything about her exes?"

"Not much. Just that there were a couple bad break ups and she's still friends with a couple of her exes."

Alice's dad smiled and took a sip of his beer. "Well that's Alice for you: understating the facts. Okay. I'm actually not sure if it's true about Davey but she seemed to be too hurt to have that happen for the first time when Nick broke up with her. But it would explain some of the shutdown after Nick. But I know her and Nick were talking about marriage before they broke up. They seemed good for each other and the only real flaw in their relationship that she saw was that he was an asshole about her hockey knowledge. Always downgrading her opinion since she was a Flyers fan and he was a massive Penguins fan. And yes, I know you tease her about the Flyers but you respect her, the way it should be. But it all ended suddenly. Ally was there, witnessed it all and told me about it first. It took a long time before Alice said anything about it. Nick literally broke up with her for not promising to smile when they were going out to a club and not having the right clothes for the night."

Scotty was dumbfounded. He couldn't believe it. "But Alice doesn't like to go to clubs. They give her migraines from the strobe lights. So he literally wanted her to be happy about getting a migraine? Sure, she would go for him if he wanted and would try to fake it. But she would never promise something she couldn't guarantee."

"Oh it gets better. Alice was having a terrible day already. Several of her plans fell through including a lunch with Ally.

So she was genuinely not in a smiley mood. So in the end, he really put the icing on a really bad day. After that she got so guarded with relationships. Probably fearing for a long time. Even when she did date some, she didn't open up to anyone until she met you."

Scott felt his blood boil. He knew it wasn't going to be a good story but this was ridiculous. If he knew who that Nick guy was, he would want to kill him. No wonder she had more than a normal amount of hatred towards the Penguins, they were a constant reminder of that asshat. But he knew that he had to keep his temper in check. So he focused everything on, "So let me guess, she's worried that we might end over some bullshit reason especially if I wait too long."

"Yup. And that's why I think she freaked out about getting a place together in Philly. It was just another piece for her to lose if things went south for a nonsensical reason."

"So you heard about that too." Scotty shook his head marveling at how much Alice confided in her dad. It seemed like they were the only two people she would say anything and everything to. It was good to know that she was talking to him when he wasn't around. He said, "I thought she would love that idea."

"She did. But it was too much. Maybe if you guys get married she will open up to an actual place in Philly. But I know she wants to spend time in your summer place too. All I can say is got to see what happens. Until then, just continue to love her hard and keep being you."

Scotty smiled and he was thinking about everything that her dad told him. It was a lot to process. He nodded, he was about to say something but then her dad shifted gears, in a manner that was similar to the way Alice would just switch things around, "I know you were on the road but you talked to her a lot, how did the court stuff go this week?"

"Okay" Scotty traced the bottle opening with his thumb. "She was fine with the prep stuff but I could tell it brought that night up for her and she was pretty quiet about things. Then yesterday was....." he was going to say a clusterfuck but he caught himself since he still didn't want to swear too much so he changed it to, "a mess. I could tell she was nervous waiting but then she was so pissed off after she found out that the case was continued and no one told her. Not that I could blame her. I was glad that she decided to play hockey as a way to work off the emotions and she was much better afterwards. This morning she was basically her normal self again, like she wasn't that stressed or angry."

"Yeah, I got through to her shortly after playing hockey. She gave me an update when I was in a meeting and then I hit her voicemail. I just couldn't tell if she was putting on a front or what. But I'm glad that things weren't that bad."

Scotty continued bouncing back between the kitchen and the living room. He turned on the Flyers game. He thought her dad might like the game and knew Alice was going to want to turn it on when she got home. Besides, he wanted to know what was going on with them anyway since they still had a chance to make the playoffs given the outcome of tonight's and tomorrow's games around the league. But Scotty felt much more relaxed talking to her dad at that point.

Scotty heard the garage door open and close along with the nails of dogs coming around the door to be there. He wasn't surprised at all when Alice opened the door. Chloe and Backup were greeting her. Once she was able to get past the two dogs, she came towards Scotty as he was putting the finishing touches on dinner in the kitchen. She went up to Scott and hugged him as she said, "That looks and smells amazing, babe."

He kissed her forehead. "Hey baby. How was work?"

"It was good. How was practice?" Alice didn't even given him time to answer as she noticed her dad sitting in the living room saying, "Hey dad, was the drive in okay?"

"Practice was good." Scotty smiled. "Come on, dinner's ready."

Alice's dad came up to the kitchen. He hugged Alice. Then the three of them of them started to head to the table. Alice did make a detour to grab a beer from the fridge. As the three of them started to sit down, that's when Alice seemed to notice that the Flyers game was on and saw the score.

"For fuck's sake." Alice said under her breath as she saw the Flyers score. It was early into the second period and they were only down by one.

Her dad shook his head as Scotty chuckled, "Hey, they aren't doing that bad. It was an unlucky break."

Alice smiled and teased Scotty knowing that he seldom roots for her team, "Don't tell me you are rooting for the Flyers tonight."

"Yup. You know that I hate Columbus on principle. Even I didn't it would be better for the Sound if the Flyers win their next two games and Columbus loses."

Her dad asked with curiosity, "Still not a lock for the playoffs?"

"Well the Sound is, it's more who they have to play through. It could be the Penguins, the Canes, the Blue Jackets, and possibly the Flyers," explained Alice.

"Obviously, I want to go through the Flyers. It's an outside chance of it happening," said Scotty. Alice made a face. She had to be one of the few fans who didn't want that match up, not that Scotty could blame her. "Sorry, babe, but they are the least evil team to go through."

"But your record against them was 50-50. Wouldn't you rather face the Canes? You swept them."

Scotty should have known that was the match up she would have rather seen for him. While both of them were in agreement that even though the Sound swept the series against the Penguins that was amongst the worst matchup possible. He couldn't argue with her logic. "Touché. As long as week the Pens stay exactly where they are in the standings, I'll be happy."

Alice just started to laugh. The two of them knew that it was only a matter of time before the Penguins got hot like they do almost every year in the playoffs. The Scotty turned the conversation away from hockey before they got too colorful and asked, "So what are your plans for tomorrow?"

"I was thinking of taking dad to Platform Brewery or maybe one of the breweries nearby before the game. Did you have a preference on which one?"

"Doesn't matter, it's your day, kid."

"Please tell me you'll be okay for the game," said Scotty. He remembered how drunk he was right before the trip and he didn't want Alice to get that same wicked hangover and he wanted to make sure that her swearing didn't get too excessive since he knew her tongue was looser when she drank and when she watched the Penguins.

"Seriously? You think I won't be good?" asked Alice incredulously.

Scotty kissed her temple and said, "Babe, you're going to

at least one brewery and it's the last game against the Penguins. Can you blame me for thinking your cursing might go next level? I know you won't get drunk with your dad and will be fine on that front." Alice seemed to accept that explanation.

After dinner, the three of them settled into the living room and watched the remainder of the hockey game. Alice cuddled up with Scotty on the couch and he had his arm around her. Alice was trying not to put too much pressure on Scotty's torso but he loved holding her in that moment. Watching hockey with her was one of his favorite times of the day especially with how creative she was with her cursing for and against the Flyers.

Alice continued to swear and react to the game. Almost all of her swearing was out of happiness since the Flyers were winning. Midway through the third period, Scott turned to see her dad who was doing some work on a laptop but he was still following the game. When her dad didn't react to a Flyer's goal, he realized that her dad wasn't really reacting to anything at all. But that's when it dawned on Scotty, "Wait, you aren't a Flyers fan too?"

Scotty just assumed that Alice learned about hockey from her dad. He knew that her dad taught her most of the love of sports. That's when he said, "Hockey isn't my sport. I loved college ball, baseball, even football. Hockey was something she learned all on her own."

That stunned Scotty some. Hockey always seemed like a sport you got raised on by your family. It also filled in the holes as to why he didn't seem to know the full playoff picture options for the Sound at dinner. He just shook his head and said, "So it will be good that we can enjoy the Indians game on Sunday then."

"Yeah. I'm definitely looking forward to that game but any time I get to spend with my girls, it's good. Hockey is a good sport, I just don't know it all that well."

At the end of the game, Alice's dad went up to bed. Alice and Scotty stayed on the couch a little longer. They started to watch a west coast game. By that point in the evening, the Flyers were statistically eliminated from the Playoffs. So that meant the Sound were going to face a slightly more difficult team, no matter what Alice thought. Eventually, they moved their way into bed.

Alice

Alice woke up in Scott's arms as per usual whenever he was home. Scott immediately started to kiss her lightly. He held her tight in a spooning position. He was clearly trying to savor the moment.

Alice looked up at Scotty and asked him, "Ready for tonight's game?"

Scotty looked down at her and was brushing her chin as he said, "You know it. It's time to finish the sweep. Last game of the season. Besides, you are going to be there and I have to impress my baby."

"You already impress me every day on and off the ice. Was everything okay with you and my dad yesterday?"

"Yeah. I told you that last night." Scotty said while shaking his head. "You're dwelling. You need to quit worrying."

"I'll try." Alice just genuinely felt bad for leaving them alone for a little bit.

Scotty pushed her hair to the side and started to kiss

along her neckline. Then he pulled her up onto his torso so they were both in a sitting position. He then started to run his arms along hers. "That's all I ask. Je t'aime."

As per usual, she echoed his words saying, "Je t'aime. I wish we can stay like this all day."

"After the season ends. I promise you at least one day of anything you want. I would promise you more of those days but you like to work so much that I don't think you would let me do it more then one day." Scotty said with a wink, "But unfortunately we can't do it today. I have to go to practice and you will have to go drinking with your dad today."

Chloe got off the bed and headed to the bedroom door. Alice knew it was time to get up and out of bed. Alice ran her hand along his jawline before kissing him one last time before they had to get up. She liked feeling the roughness of his scruff in the morning even though there was barely any stubble."I'll take care of the pups and start breakfast. You go get ready."

"Sounds like a plan."

As Alice started to get up, Scott grabbed her wrist and then pulled her in tight for a second time that morning. Both of them wanted to stay in each other's arms even longer. Chloe whined again and Scott let her wrist go since they both knew that Chloe would only get more insistent to get fed.

Alice opened the door and both dogs rushed downstairs. Alice followed behind at a slower pace. She immediately filled their bowls and she heard her dad say, "It's about time you guys got up."

Alice wasn't ready for her dad's teasing just yet but at the same time, she still enjoyed it. She said, "It's not even that late. We still have plenty of time before Scott has to leave for practice. Ready for some food?"

"That sounds good."

Alice started to make a couple omelets and Canadian bacon. It was an easy meal to make and it was Scotty's favorite. He always loved having the Canadian bacon over sausage or bacon. She also got the coffee started. As she was starting to make some toast, Scotty snuck up from behind and hugged her tightly around her waist. She should have known he was going to do that. He loved to come from behind and surprise her with a hug and an ear nibble. He held her for a moment and laid his head on top of hers. He then whispered in her ear, "Please eat a little bit, for me."

Scotty almost never asked her to eat in such an intimate fashion and her dad was there. She knew it would just be easier if she had a plate and would make Scotty's day. She put an omelet on two of the plates and everything else on all three plates. However, her portion was much smaller than everyone else. Scotty helped to bring the plates to the kitchen table. She was actually surprised when he didn't say anything or make a move for her grabbing a plate.

It wasn't long before Scotty had to go practice. Alice and her dad took the dogs out for a very long walk. Then the two of them had a lazy morning.

It really wasn't until Alice and her dad were at Platform before she was truly relaxed around her dad. They both got different flights so they could sample a bit of everything before even thinking about a larger beer order.

It was her dad who said, "I can't believe how domestic the two of you are."

"What?" Alice said. She knew that her dad was clearly

talking about her and Scotty but the comment seemed to come out of nowhere.

"You and Scott. You are so cute and comfortable with each other. You make each other meals and have a great home together. You take care of the dogs together. It's wonderful to see it happen. I never thought I would see you settle down after Nick."

Alice laughed and shook her head. She said, "You make it sound like I was so wild."

"Definitely not wild. More closed off and working all hours of the day. You barely dated for what? Ten years? Then not only did you date Scotty for the first time in like forever. But you didn't just date Scotty. You got fully settled in as if you have been together for so much longer. It's good to see how open you are with him. He's just been so good for you in every sense of the word. He's so protective of you too."

"Yeah. He's definitely been doing that for me. He even hates it when I don't eat."

"And I love that about him," replied her dad.

"You would," which came out slightly more barbed then she would have liked. But her dad didn't seem to mind.

"Yeah, cause I love you. I don't need you or Ally giving into that demon of yours again." Her dad made a pointed reference to the fact that both her and her sister had bouts of anorexia at various points in their lives. Alice knew that she used not eating as a coping mechanism to give herself the illusion she was in control at stressful times in her life. It was why she didn't give Scotty too many issues when he was on her to eat and went into counseling after the burglary. Alice kinda groaned since her dad was the one person she could talk to about that particular part of her past. But she would prefer to act like it never happened. She never even told Scotty that was an issue. He just picked up on her eating habits.

"Dad, I've been good. You know, I have other ways to cope, now. If I was going to relapse, it would have happened immediately after the burglary. Even if I wanted to relapse, I wouldn't be allowed to."

"Which is why he's so good for you."

"I just hope it stays that way."

"Why would you even think that it wouldn't?" asked her dad. He was clearly astonished to hear her have any doubts about her relationship.

Alice said, "Cause I keep worrying that I will do something dumb and push him away. Or he realizes that I'm nothing special. It just seems to be too good to be true. Any other time it got to be like this, it got screwed up."

"Alright, just stop right there, kid. He loves you so much. You just have to see how he looks at you. You told me that he got you rings that seemed to be custom made for you. He won't just pull the plug on you. He's just wanting to make sure that things are good and that you are 100% ready for it. I probably shouldn't tell you this, but he asked for your hand in marriage yesterday. So you need to stop worrying."

"Wait, he did?" Alice wanted to ask more and her dad's reaction. But if he was angry or had concerns, he would have said something. She knew she should listen to what her dad was trying to tell her. "I'm being stupid but I can't help it."

"Hey given what's happened the last time you got almost this close with someone, I understand. But we both know Scott's different. He's not Nick and he's gone so much further than Nick to create a stable relationship that will last."

"You're right." Alice closed her eyes. She knew that as much as she wanted to argue with her dad, she knew he was right. It was her that was being foolish in the moment. She took a long sip of her last taster and looked down at her watch and realized they were at Platform much longer than she anticipated. "Want to try out a different place or catch warm ups?"

"Up to you."

"Let do warm ups."

"Okay. This is where I know you are my daughter." While her dad wasn't the same level of hockey fan as she was, they both loved going to games and enjoyed catching all the action. He wouldn't ever let her skip part of a game even if there was a blow out going on.

"What can I say, I love warm ups. It's when you get to see everyone so relaxed. Besides, it's the only time I can see Scotty on the ice without his helmet on."

Her dad just laughed. He knew that she had a huge thing for redheads. The two of them took the rapid over to the stadium since they were both drinking and it was cheaper to keep her car parked by Platform.

24

SCOTT

Scotty was on the blue line for the opening game ceremonies waiting for announcements and the national anthem. As per usual, Dykstman and Lager were on either side. It felt good to be on home ice again. He knew that Alice and her dad were in the stands and that helped to get him hyped up at the game. Once they were done with the national anthem, it was time for the first face off.

Lager was chattering nonstop to one of the Penguins' guys. Scotty just focused on getting low and winning the face off. He had to beat The Kid and traditionally Scott struggled to beat him. He looked up to the family area and he saw some extra incentive after the talk with Alice's dad and a better understanding as to why Alice hated the Penguins so much. The puck dropped and Scotty scooped it towards Dykstman and the game was on.

The first shift was filled with crazy hard hits and speed by both teams. The Sound had the finesse and if they kept with the hard hits, it should be a really strong game against the

Penguins. It was almost as if they were on the power play on the first few plays since the forecheck was so strong. It wasn't long before Scotty was able to force the puck past the goalie. The horn sounded. Only bad thing, Lager had contact with the goalie. So both him and Crosby were skating by the linesman trying to argue their points. Lager barely touched Murray and it was accidental movement at best since he was pushed by the defensive man. Crosby of course believed that Lager hindered Murray's ability to stop the goal.

Of course, the Penguins challenged the goal. They had to wait for the final determination from the instant replay. While he couldn't say for sure if there was enough to get the goal overturned, he did notice that throughout the year the refs were less likely to overturn a goaltender interference call without clear evidence and Scotty just didn't see it in any of the replays he saw on the iPad.

Finally, the lead ref went out to center ice said, "Ruling on the ice stands. Good Goal."

Scotty looked over to the bench to see if wanted his line to stay out there for the power play since the Penguins lost their challenge and had a bench minor. Berman yelled for the Freak Unit. Now that Corey and he were healthy, they only had people who were banged up from the season rather than any key guys actually out and people haven't seen the full Freak unit in a while.

Scotty approached Corey and said, "I'm going to try and send it to you but be ready to run through them if I don't get it."

"Got it."

Scotty knew they would really only have a chance or two and it would be a short shift for the first unit. Berman was still being cautious using Scotty. So they will have to play it quick. Plus he was already out for a long shift after being on the ice for the goal.

Unsurprisingly, the Penguins MVP got the puck. But true to his word, Corey stripped the puck as he made contact with the Penguins forward. Corey then passed the puck to Scotty who was up on the left hand side. He rimmed it off the boards and behind the net towards Lager. They then had it set up and Corey was by the net. Lager sent the puck back towards Scotty who had pulled all the eyes away. Scotty sent it to Wheels who fired a wicked hard shot on net. Murray got the block but it was loose and Corey cleaned up the trash. Everyone tapped Corey's helmet. Just like that it was 2-0 Sound. Scotty and Lager finally got to take a rest and let some of the other lines onto the ice.

Lager looked to him and said, "Someone is fired up today."

"Let's just say I found new reasons to shut Pen fans up as much as possible."

In the background, he heard Dima shouting for a whistle. Scotty loved the chatter that was always ongoing. It was a crazy mix of people following the game and having their own side conversations.

Lager said, "Okay, I'll bite. What is it?"

"Apparently Alice's ex was a major fan who thought she didn't know jack about hockey."

Lager just shook his head and said, "What a clueless asshole."

"Yeah. That's not the only reason he was an asshole. Since this will be the closest I will get to take it out on him, why not embarrass his team completely? Besides it will help to pad our statistics."

"You and your statistics." Lager loved to tease how Scotty could tend to pull out the team statistics on a drop of the hat.

"Get out there: Scotty, Lags and Dykst," shouted Berman

As Scotty was going over the boards he said, "At least, I'm not telling everyone my current NHL rankings during faceoffs."

"Hey those tools need to be reminded just how good we all are. Besides he started the chirping, I needed to set him straight on who's better."

The game continued to an offensive field day for the Sound. It ended up being a final score of 7-1 in the Sounds favor. The Penguins never stood a chance in the game. The Penguins were slow and the entire Sound seemed to follow Scotty and Lager's offensive lead in scoring.

After the game, Scotty headed home fairly early. He wanted to hang out with the boys to celebrate the end of the regulation afterwards but with Alice's dad visiting, he knew that he had to get back home. While Alice would be cool if he went out, he wanted to be on her dad's good side, so he should spend time with them.

When he got home, Backup and Alice greeted him at the door. Two things were odd. Chloe didn't come to the door. His Pitbull always came to greet him and Alice didn't always come up to greet him with a kiss. She was a bit flirtier since the California trip and he wasn't complaining as he kissed her back and then held her in a hug. He was about to ask about Chloe but then he noticed that she was laying down by Alice's dad and was getting her ears rubbed so he pushed any concerns that he may have had.

"You were amazing today. I can't believe how strong you have been since your return. But today was unreal."

"Yeah. I told you that I wanted to impress you. Besides, I thought you might enjoy seeing someone hand it to the Pens. The right way."

She leaned up and kissed him one more time. "Don't tell me that my Philly is showing again."

"Only a little bit but I love that about you." He smiled quite cockily. He kissed her since he knew that he was going to get a reaction. "Besides, isn't it more fun to watch a team thrash them rather than the close calls from another team you love?"

"You are going to get yourself in trouble mister."

He kissed her once more. Given the smile on her face, he knew he wasn't even close to being in trouble. She just wasn't going to tolerate him giving her too much shit about the Flyers OT wins against the Penguins. He rubbed her shoulders before stepping into the kitchen for a beer and post-game snack. Alice returned to the couch and was drinking a beer. For a change, he actually saw her have knitting out but it was weird to see that basketball was on TV instead of hockey. She never watched basketball.

Alice must have read his mind as he sat down beside her, she said, "Dad wanted to catch up with the action."

"Ah." Scott just tried to make himself comfortable. He could feel his knee wanting to get cranky after such a hard game. So he stretched out his leg on the table.

Alice asked, "Need more ice?"

"Nah. I did that before leaving the rink. Just trying to look after myself. That way we are all set for the playoffs."

Alice leaned in towards him and he put his arm around

her. It was quiet that evening. All that could really be heard was the squeaking of sneakers on hardwood and the game commentary. Scotty looked down to see Alice was asleep in his arms. He was glad that she was sleeping soundly but he knew he would have to take Alice up to bed eventually. He was debating on the best way to deal with his sleeping girl. He didn't always trust just lifting her up to bed in fear of waking her up since she was back to flinching and waking up with a start.

As Alice's dad was starting to get up for bed, he said, "If you want to wake her, I would try turning off the TV."

Scotty just did as he said. He turned off the TV, almost immediately she woke up with a start. She didn't hit anything but she was definitely surprised by the sudden burst of silence. But once she realized it was just the TV being turned off, she was calm. Scotty was surprised it actually worked. Alice shook her head and her dad started laughing. Scotty wasn't quite sure what was going on but it had to be some sort of inside joke.

"See, not that different from your old man," said her dad to Alice. With that the three of them went up to bed. What was weird was that only Backup went upstairs with them to sleep.

Alice

Alice was woken up by a kiss from Scott as he leaned over her. It was still dark out so it had to be before dawn. She blinked out the sleep and asked, "What's going on baby?"

"I got to take Chloe to the vet. Just sleep some more. It's early." Scotty was moving away from the bed already. She shook her head and started to get out of the bed. She wasn't going to stay put if he thought that Chloe needed to see the doctor at that hour. She turned to see him looking at her disapprovingly. Scotty said, "I didn't wake you up for you to come with me. I just wanted you to know where I was going."

"But it's Chloe. Just give me a moment. I'll meet you downstairs" Scotty took a deep breath. Alice could tell that he wanted to argue with her and tell her to go back to bed again but she could be just as stubborn as Scotty and he knew he wasn't going to win the argument. She rushed to the closet so she could grab a bra and a loose fitting top. While the pj leggings were a little beat up, they were totally fine to be seen in.

Alice was yawning as she went downstairs. She noticed that Scotty was carrying Chloe into the garage. That had Alice super concerned since she's never seen Chloe be so immobile. Alice grabbed the keys from the dish that Scott kept his keys in.

"What's wrong with Chloe?"

"She's not moving around much. I've never seen her like this. So I want to get her checked out sooner rather than later."

That's when Alice realized Chloe didn't come up to bed like normal and how sluggish she seemed last night. She was kicking herself for not seeing the signs sooner. Just in case her dad woke early, she wrote a quick note saying they were taking Chloe to the animal hospital. Scott seemed so worried that she was glad that she was coming with Scott. As Scott was putting Chloe into the back seat, "How about I drive? That way you can sit in the back with Chloe."

"Yeah, okay." Scott climbed into the back seat. She slid the driver's seat up massively forward so she could reach the pedals. She also realized it was 4 am. She was surprised that it was so early.

"I assume we are going to the animal hospital instead of the normal vet."

"Yeah." Scott said a bit wearily. "You know I really hoped that at least one of us would get some sleep."

"It should be you. You have the fucking playoffs starting in three days."

"Your dad's here right now."

Alice felt herself groan. She knew he was just trying to be nice and how he wanted to protect her and it wasn't even a real thing that she needed protection from. "Babe, I slept so much with you home. My insomnia is under control. The court stuff didn't mess up my sleep this week any more than jump starts. So no need to be all ultra-protective of me."

"But..."

Alice looked back into the rearview mirror, she saw him rubbing Chloe's body. Alice cut him off. "Scotty, I'm not going to break."

She heard him sigh again. "I know you aren't fragile. You are so damn strong. But you are my girl just like Chloe. I would do anything for you guys."

"You know it's reciprocal, right?"

"Yeah."

"You tell me not to worry so much all the time. Now it's my turn." Alice pulled into the animal hospital parking lot. "Need help getting Chloe out of the car?"

"No. I'll be okay. Just get the doors for me."

"Kay."

The two of them rushed into the hospital. Almost immediately they were greeted by the reception. Scott sat Chloe down on a chair and Alice sat next to Chloe. Chloe laid her head on Alice's lap which is the most movement that Alice had seen since last night. After Scotty finished up the paperwork, he sat on the other side of Chloe. He was petting Chloe's backside.

It didn't take long before they were called back to the examination room. Alice wanted to get out of the way and hang out in the back corner but Scotty stopped her almost immediately by grabbing her waist and pulled her close to him. He held her that way for a bit.

"So what seems to be the problem?" asked the vet as she was starting to look at Chloe's face and do the examination.

Scotty spoke up with a calm fashion but Alice could tell by how he was holding her that he was more nervous than his voice indicated. "Chloe wasn't acting like herself last night. Super sluggish. Then this morning, everything seemed worse."

"Any changes to her diet or anything of that sort?"

Alice spoke up. "None. At most, we had a couple new toys around for our other puppy but she never had any interest in them. Although come to think of it, I haven't seen her favorite toy around since the other night."

"Well, let's do an x-ray to rule out any obstructions."

Alice stayed still in his arms and tried to give him any comfort that she could by her proximity. She knew that Chloe was his baby. In a way, she was hoping it was an obstruction instead of something like cancer. They brought in a mobile x-ray machine.

They had to wait for the tech to come back with the results. But finally, they were told that Chloe swallowed her hockey puck and it got stuck in her intestinal tract. They were going to have to do surgery to get it out and Chloe would have to spend the night at the hospital.

They were moved to the waiting room. Scotty was quiet at first. He just held her and it was weird to see him so quiet. Alice was tired and she wasn't super talkative. But she knew she should say something, "Scotty...."

Alice was stopped immediately when Scotty said, "Don't. Not now."

"Don't tell you I love you or that it will be okay?" Alice looked up at him in confusion? She wasn't sure what he was thinking. When she saw his eyes, she realized how she caught him off guard. Then she thought back to their talks about if the puck was a good toy when she first moved in or if they should switch out her puck to a new one since that one was getting pretty beat up. He must have thought she was going to chastise him.

He pulled her closer and said, "I'm sorry. I thought it was going to be something different."

"It's okay. I know you are worried about Chloe and I am too. I know if this was a romance novel, this could be something that would mess everything up. We have a dumb fight and break up before we get back together. I just want you to know that I love you and maybe see you smile some since it's such a pretty smile."

That got Scotty laughing and she loved hearing him laugh. She knew that he was finally starting to ease up. He was immediately more relaxed and he kissed her in a less than chaste kiss in the lobby. When he pulled back, he just laid his head on hers and they waited. From there they waited until they heard that Chloe was in great shape after the surgery but would have to spend the night for observation.

The two of them were pretty quiet for the rest of the morning. The Indians game wasn't as much fun as they thought it would be 24 hours ago but Alice was just happy Chloe would be fine after a few weeks of recovery. She knew Scotty was definitely being more subdued than normal. Alice couldn't imagine what Scotty would be like if anything actually did happen to Alice or Chloe.

25

SCOTT

The Series against the Penguins was going better than he anticipated. The Sound were up two games in a best of seven series, which was a bit unexpected. But just because they were up, it didn't mean they could get complacent. They were going to Pittsburgh tomorrow for games three and four.

Scotty spent far longer trying to figure out why he was losing face-offs to The Kid. There wasn't much to go on from the video replays from games one and two. But he wasn't going to settle that it was bad luck. He could be just as quick as The Kid.

The other thing that was starting to gnaw at him was Alice's dad's words. He was hoping that her dad was right and that she was more ready for marriage then he thought. Her dad practically told him that he should propose sooner rather than later. Scotty knew he wanted to do it soon but he wanted to do something elaborate and special.

Since Alice was supposed to work until late, he decided to use the office to help create a perfect proposal idea. Alice had a habit of leaving her computer on and even leaving some of her browser tabs open. He knew where he wanted to do it, but it was the when and who he wanted to be there that was more difficult. He knew her closest friends weren't here in the area but he wanted to make sure they were involved. The easiest that he knew about were the friends he met in Philadelphia and her family. But he knew there had to be more people she would want to be there. It couldn't just be guys from the Sound and the way she talked about her time at conventions, she knew there had to be more people there.

He looked to see if he had access to her Google calendar. It was obvious, only automatic schedule blocks were on it. He just wished that her calendar was up to date but he knew her schedule was always in flux and she preferred to use a paper schedule that she kept on her. So he would be out of luck on booking the ideal venue and things until he took a look at that one night when she was sleeping.

So he spent a few hours spying on her Facebook page. It was invaluable. While most people she chatted with were people he knew of, there were a few new names that he wanted to follow up on. The only thing he felt guilty about was how he was invading her privacy and spying on her.

Scotty knew that the time was getting late and Alice would be home soon. He wanted to continue to investigate her computer as much as he could before the road trip and he knew she would be suspicious. So he needed a way to distract Alice as soon as she came home. He called up Corey to see if he would loan out his ice space for an hour or two. Like usual, Corey was going to help him out.

Alice

Alice came home from work and was surprised that

Scotty wasn't in the living room or the kitchen. He was almost always in one of those two spaces when she came in. Alice peeked downstairs to see if he was lifting but the basement lights were off so he wasn't there. So she figured he had to be napping upstairs.

Alice went upstairs to switch out of her work clothes. She was surprised to see that the office door was closed. Scotty almost never used the office. Since she moved in four months ago, he was in the office like three times total and the door was always open. It was weird.

Alice knocked on the door, "Hey babe. You okay in there?"

Alice heard some rustling and she swore she saw heard a chair scoot across the room. "Just a moment baby."

Alice leaned against the door frame. She would have normally just continued on to the bedroom to get changed since she was just checking in. But Scotty was clearly up to something and wanted to talk a bit. The door swung open and he lifted her into a hug. She swore that the chair was moved out of the way but Scotty seemed content on distracting her. He then seemed to be pushing and carrying her to the bedroom. Scotty pulled back with a smile and he said, "You're home early."

Alice laughed and said, "What? It's practically 8:30pm. It's not early. So want to try again?"

He laughed and said, "Are you sure?" As he pulled off her work shirt and even tossed her bra off. He continued to kiss along all her pleasure points. He was distracting her pretty good and so she might let him get away with anything.

Alice nodded and said, "Very." Before letting Scotty get her too worked up and fully distracted, she asked, "What's going on? Have you lost your mind?"

He pushed her into the bed and started kissing her madly. He was smiling like a Cheshire cat, "Oh. Nothing. Just waiting for you."

"But you never are in the office and why was the door closed?" asked Alice in a moment of clarity.

"No reason." Scotty must have decided to switch tactics or something since he pulled her practically off the bed. Alice wasn't expecting it. He seemed to be full of all sorts of surprises today. "Come on. We are going to be late."

"Late for what?" Alice wasn't expecting to do anything tonight. Well they were probably going to do one more night of hockey and kisses before his road trip. But he just stopped the hockey and kisses. "Babe, you are being weird."

"I'm not being weird. But you need to put a shirt on and we need to work on your shot."

"And who's fault is that I don't have a shirt on?" Alice smiled but couldn't understand what was going on. If he wanted to work on her shot, why would they be late? They would just go downstairs and use his stuff. She walked to the closet to put on a shirt and a new bra. As she was pulling the shirt over her head, "We? The royal we or are we meeting someone?"

Alice looked towards Scotty. He still had the crazy sly smile on his face. "We are going to Corey's rink."

Alice just shook her head said, "So you aren't going to tell me what's going on."

Scotty shook his head and said, "Why are you so curious about everything? Can't you leave it be?" Alice knew he was up to something but he wasn't going to be forthcoming if she didn't try to distract him as well.

Alice came up to Scotty and kissed him. She left her

hands on his broad shoulders. "Cause I know you. You never do work in the office and it's weird. You are up to something."

"It's nothing that you need to worry about. Come on we need to get going."

Alice shook her head. She knew that Scotty wasn't going to tell her what he was doing. But she had to admit he was doing everything he could to get her mind off of his mystery stuff. Scotty started to direct her downstairs. She said, "So we need to work on my shot?"

"Yes. You have a game this week. I told you we would work on it and I can't promise we will have time to work on it beforehand since I'll be in Pittsburgh. So it has to be tonight."

Alice was surprised. It was a touching gesture. He was right, she wanted to work on her shot before her next game. But with him being busy in the playoffs, she figured that it would have to happen later on. She was just playing in a recreation league. It's not like her games mattered.

Scotty loaded up the SUV with their skates and sticks. Alice was surprised he even put her hockey skates and her figure skates in her bag. They never took her bag. He drove the short distance to Corey's house.

As soon as they got to his house, Corey greeted them with, "Hey. I didn't think you guys were coming." Alice thought that odd that she didn't remember anything about Scotty wanting to work on her shot tonight but Scotty clearly had it all lined up. In many ways, she really thought Scotty was aiming for more than a simple distraction for the night.

Instead of heading down to the ice surface right away, Scotty said, "So I want to run some ideas by you before we get going on Alice's shot practice."

"What kind of things?" asked Corey.

"Ideas for game three."

Alice wasn't honestly too surprised by that. Scotty was obsessing about his game lately. She'd never seen him be so intense before but she figured it was playoff stress. If she didn't know how much he hated working on a computer screen and would rather watch things as large as possible, she would have thought he was doing that in the office. Maybe it was just to get a different perspective. At least, Corey could provide a different sounding board to Scotty's ideas and worries.

Alice knew that might take a little bit and she wouldn't mind getting as much time on the ice as possible. Since she knew the boys would be talking a bit and she had her figure skates with her, she wanted to use them. She asked Corey, "Do you mind if I skate while you guys talk?"

"Nah, as long as you don't tear up the ice with that damn toepick of yours." It seemed like ever since she brought her figure skates along with the hockey stuff after the bad day in court, Corey kept teasing her about the figure skates. It was amazing how it only took one time of bringing figure skates despite not even using them to get an endless supply of teasing.

"As if you don't tear up the ice on your own."

It seemed like that was the only thing that always united hockey and figure skaters, the mutual hatred of the other one's skates tearing up the ice. Since she did both styles of skating, she's complained about the skates herself. While she wouldn't admit it to many, she liked how the hockey skates actually improved her figure skating since she learned how to control the blade better without relying on a toepick and got a better sense of freedom and flight with her hockey skates on. Now she needed the toepick for jumps and that did gouge the ice. But since she wasn't doing anything over a single rotation, she didn't dig in the toepick into the ice and knew Corey couldn't complain.

She led herself downstairs to the rink and put on some music from her phone. It was peaceful and fun to just skate along to music that she choreographed in her head.

Alice was feeling pretty warmed up by the time she saw the boys watching her while she was skating to "All My Friends" by Dermot Kennedy. At first, she continued to skate as if she never noticed them. That was until she realized that Scotty was filming her. From then on out, she started to skate safely and only did jumps she could safely land. She still tried to put herself into the music.

When the song was over she skated up to the two boys. Almost immediately, he said, "You looked amazing out there. You should figure skate more."

Alice scoffed, "You obviously know nothing about skating. Those were all single jumps and I even two footed a jump." She leaned up on the toepicks so she could kiss Scotty. "But thanks for thinking it was good. Let me switch boots."

Alice grabbed her phone and turned off the music. Then she walked off the ice so she could swap out her skates. As she was tying up her laces, she watched Scotty and Corey skate on the ice. They were passing the puck around in a drill to work on their skating skills and the stickhandling.

As soon as she stepped back out onto the ice surface, Scotty came up to her. "Come on Al. Let's work on your shot now."

After an hour and a half of working on her shot, Alice was more comfortable trying to make a shot. She didn't think it was still super strong but it was definitely better than it was and she needed to continue to work on it. But one of the things that stuck out that night, was how comfortable she was working on her shot with Scotty and Corey. Even a couple months before, the mere thought of playing with Scotty would scare her shitless. Now she was just wanting to learn from him. Sure, he would always outclass her in so many ways and she didn't want to play a game with him and his buddies. But at least, she was improving and not letting her head get in the way from learning from one of the best in the game.

By the end of the night, she had more or less forgotten about the incident in the office. Instead she was just happy to spend time with the love of her life.

Scott

Scotty had fun playing around with Corey and Alice. He was still glad that Corey provided them the perfect distraction to keep Alice from prying too much.

It was cool to watch Alice figure skate, since it was the first time he saw that side of her. They talked about it a few times but Alice always wanted to work on her hockey or tried to stay completely off the ice around him. Despite hearing how she wasn't very good, he thought it was pretty and that she was practically dancing on the ice. The song that she was skating to seemed to be the embodiment of her feelings. He was also glad that Corey took video of him and Alice working on her shot. He couldn't wait to share the two moments since he was so bloody proud.

The next few days were going to be a grind. But it would be worth it in the end, especially if The Sound won the two games in Pittsburgh. A clean sweep. Then he would have a few days off and could spend more time with Alice at home. The next round wouldn't be as hard by the looks of it.

The only thing Scotty needed was to finalize a day or two for the proposal and he wanted to do that before the trip to Pittsburgh. He knew who to invite for the most part after the afternoon on Alice's computer. He wanted to take a look at her planner. He knew the only two ways he could do that: do it while she was asleep or when she was walking the dogs.

When they came into the house, both Chloe and Backup were anxious for love and for a bathroom trip. Scotty knew that he had his opening thanks to those. He kissed Alice's ear and asked, "Can you take the pups without me? I can start making some food for the two of us."

"Sure."

Alice smiled as she grabbed the leashes and went outside with the two dogs. She didn't seem to suspect anything but he waited for a minute before he went into her work bag.

He found her planner and looked out to the month of June. She seemed to be mostly free except a couple weekends. That didn't seem too bad and he could work with her schedule. Afterwards, he put the planner back into her bag nearly in the exact same spot he found it.

As he put the planner away, he grabbed a bottle from the fridge and started to make a quick meal for the two of them. It didn't take too long before Alice opened the door and the dogs went straight towards Scotty's legs. He rubbed Chloe's ears as he started to get some food for the pups as well.

Alice wrapped her arms around his torso. That was something he normally did. He smiled as he turned towards Alice. He thumbed her lips as he asked, "What do you think you are doing?"

"Enjoying my time with you."

"Uh huh." Scotty said with a smile. He wasn't convinced that Alice had forgotten what that he was up in the office in an unusual manner. He was just glad that she wasn't pressing the issue or working too hard to find out what he was up to. At the same time, he was enjoying her doing his move on him. "Dinner is almost ready."

Alice leaned up and kissed him. "Okay. It smells good."

They sat down and ate dinner. Alice did the dishes afterwards. When she was done, he started to hug her from behind. He said, "We should go to bed soon."

"Fine." Like so many times she used the word fine, her tone of voice didn't match the settlement. She wanted to stay up a little bit.

He leaned down and kissed her. She always seemed to fight him on sleep whether it was going to sleep or to wake up. He knew he needed sleep before flying out to Pittsburgh. "Come on. You know we should sleep eventually but we still have plenty of time to play. We just should go to the bedroom.

Then he got her sensual smile and he knew they were on for more hockey and kisses.

26

ALICE

Alice was anxious and she hadn't even left for court yet. She was still at work until 9 am. Then she had to change and rush over to the courts. She wasn't ready for it. Not helping things was the knowledge she had to do it solo and basically do everything all over again the next day in juvenile court. Scotty was away yet with the Stanley Cup playoff games. It was round two and the team weren't able to get out to Carolina on time thanks to some severe weather. She wouldn't see him until after court today but at least he was on his way home for a few days. While she knew she could do it on her own, she wasn't looking forward to it. She was hoping that Scotty would get to stay home until the next series without a return trip to Carolina. She got a little spoiled there by him being home for a bit between sweeping the Penguins and having the home ice advantage for the series against Carolina.

It took longer for her to get to court then she would have liked. It felt like things were just getting in the way. At least this time, she knew where she was going and went straight up to the 22nd floor. Unlike the first time, the waiting room was packed. Alice walked towards the desk to check in. She was immediately sent back to the prosecutor area. She saw her prosecutor.

"Sit here. The defense lawyer went to get a coffee. Then it'll be our turn."

Almost as quickly as Alice sat down, her prosecutor left to take care of something downstairs. She opened up her Kindle app on her iPad and buried her head into a book while she was trying to keep her nerves at a steady pace. She couldn't help overhearing the other prosecutors talk about their cases including whether it was easier to try a murder or a rape case and why it was dumb to lend out your house to a heroin addict. It was a lot to take in but she wanted to stay quiet to learn what she could even if some of the conversation seemed to be a bit more morbid then she thought. Eventually her prosecutor came back but he immediately got up and moved around to see about the court status. It was almost as if he had ADHD.

After about an hour of waiting, it was their time to go into the courtroom. Alice immediately picked up her stuff to follow her prosecutor to the courtroom. There was wood paneling everywhere. The sound of the judge's voice made it clear that the microphone was in use based on how it echoed off the wood. Alice sat down in the chair where the prosecutor indicated that was close to the aisle. She put her head back in the book that she was reading since there was someone else's case was being heard. From what Alice gathered it was probation hearings of some kind. Then, there was one more quick probation hearing and then they called up Alice's case to be heard.

Almost immediately, three people from the back of the room stood up and made the table on the right side. Alice's prosecutor went near the table on the left side but then carried his laptop over to the railing of what looked to be a jury box. He placed his laptop on the railing and Alice closed her tablet and slid it back into her backpack.

The judge read out charges that the woman pled guilty to felony two burglary which carried a sentence of two to eight years, a felony three burglary with a sentence of nine to thirty-six months, a misdemeanor of the first degree petty theft with up to six months in prison and/or a fine, and a misdemeanor charge of contributing to the delinquency of a minor with up to a $1000 fine and up to 180 days in jail. Nobody contested the charges although the prosecutor pointed out how you really couldn't do both a felony two and a felony three at the same time but it was clearly a throwaway comment not meant to pay attention to. Plus the defendant made it clear that she understood the charges and the potential crimes.

Then the prosecutor pointed out how the victim was in the audience and put Alice on the spot. She was asked if she wanted to say anything. While she was presumed she would have to speak, she expected to be warned to have a statement ready or she would be led in questions. Her eyes went wide and she was terrified and unready. She was completely taken aback and was under prepared. The prosecutor said she didn't have to speak so she shook her head no. She knew should say something but she didn't know what to say at that moment. She was more ready for the next day's questioning in juvenile court.

The defense lawyer spoke next. He said how the defendant made the biggest mistake of her life that night. She was a child that had issues at home with a mother who couldn't care for her due to drugs and mental health issues. Her adoptive family wasn't much better. She was homeless that night and desperate so she made the worst choice of her life.

The prosecutor interjected by saying how she broke in twice, it wasn't just one mistake. The defense continued saying how she never meant to hurt the victim and they fled the moment they realized that someone was in the apartment. Since then, she was able to reconnect with her biological mother and grandparents and things were much better.

Alice just steeled herself. She wasn't that surprised. Of course, the defense lawyer would try to make the defendant sympathetic. That was his job.

What Alice didn't expect was for the judge to address the defendant, "How good you look, and I can see there's been a real change in you. You are a different person."

After one of the judge's comments, the defense lawyer said, "It's not just on the outside either. She's made a real commitment to changing her life."

Alice closed her eyes for a second. She needed to stay strong. She pushed her hands into her lap and refused to let herself to cry. She knew things weren't going to be easy. She just hoped she didn't blow it by not saying anything. But she saw clearly that the sentencing was going to be much harder than she expected.

From there, there were two letters presented from the defense lawyer. The judge was pleased that she had a job at Burger King and letter of reference from her manager there. Alice couldn't believe what she was hearing. It seemed like the judge was saying that flipping burgers was a way to erase the fact that the defendant decided to break into her apartment and because the defendant got a job, the whole crime wasn't a big deal. Alice was starting to get upset and was really kicking herself for not speaking initially since this was absurd. They were downplaying the price of the burglary to a degree that she couldn't even comprehend.

Alice was given a second chance to speak and she wanted to take it this time. She knew if she didn't speak, things were only going to get worse for her. So she jumped at the chance to make a statement. She didn't care if the statement wasn't going to be very strong.

There was some confusion about who was going to speak next since the defendant wanted to give an apology to Alice. The defendant was granted the apology before Alice's statement.

Alice tried to listen to the apology but the girl was reading it from her phone and it felt, well, empty. Alice wasn't even sure if she was willing to forgive the defendant in the moment but she tried to listen. It didn't help things that the court reporter kept interrupting the apology every few words. So the defendant had to repeat the same words over and over again since the defendant was speaking too quickly and the court reporter couldn't understand it. But with all the interruptions, Alice couldn't really follow what was being said. The only thing that stuck out was the girl used a stronger vocabulary then Alice anticipated. Alice thought maybe that's why it lacked conviction, the defendant was trying to impress rather than to write something in her true voice. It seemed to Alice that if the defendant was that educated, wouldn't she have known better than to break into someone else's apartment and steal stuff? Alice knew she was being petty and awful since she was being so judgmental. She tried to remind herself to be forgiving and to attempt to listen but it sounded like the parents from The Peanuts movies.

Then Alice had a chance to speak. She had to stand in front of the judge between the two lawyers tables. She knew she would have to speak carefully and slowly. First, she had to spell her name for the court. Then in a carefully measured voice, "The burglary was easily one of the worst nights of my life. There was talk about how harm wasn't done or even meant. That's just not true. Everyone seems to underestimate the mental anguish that is associated from having your privacy violated and from seeing an intruder in your home when you were sleeping. I'm still having panic attacks whenever I hear noises of an unknown origin. I never feel safe at home alone, especially at night. I moved out of the apartment almost immediately. Invading someone's privacy isn't a thing that should be taken lightly and it leaves mental scars that don't easily go away. The fear and discomfort stays a lot longer than it takes to replace some stolen items. This isn't something that should be taken lightly." Alice knew she was battling to keep her voice steady towards the end.

Alice was becoming uncomfortable as the emotions were welling up. She kept things in control but it wasn't just the fear and discomfort of being around someone who broke into her place twice. She hated public speaking especially when she didn't have time to practice it. But she spoke her truth and at least it didn't seem to be all over the place and maybe it was halfway eloquent. She was relieved to sit down.

The prosecutor said, "The receipts for the victim was $940. The victim did request for remand but we will defer to the court."

The judge spoke almost directly to Alice. "The woman who is standing in front of me is a completely different woman from the woman who was here six months ago. While I acknowledge your mental anguish and I'm glad you spoke to us today, I have to find that the defendant receives no jail time and will remain on the community bond program that she's been on." Then the judge turned the attention to the defendant, "Now if you are to mess up in anyway, you will have to go to jail for all the charges you plead to. I do find that the defendant owes $940 in restitution to the victim."

Alice started shaking and knew she was going to cry sooner rather than later. She always would do everything in her power to keep people from seeing her cry. The prosecutor immediately pulled her outside the courtroom. He immediately told Alice how he hated the pilot program that the defendant was in since it was too willy nilly with those who were on it and the defendant would have gotten prison time if she wasn't on it. Alice was barely listening in a way, she hated the pilot program despite the fact she barely knew anything about and really wanted to get away.

She stepped onto the elevator to go down the 22 flights. The only small justice she got that day was not having to share the elevator with the defendant, her lawyer and the damn friend of the judge. She tried to pretend everything was normal and didn't feel like her sense of justice just fell apart. She checked her phone and got ready for work. Unsurprisingly, she had messages from Scotty, her sister and her dad. She knew that the moment she called someone back, she would start crying and everything was real and she was hoping to keep it to a minimum. So she knew she had to call the one person who could probably comfort her the quickest.

Scott

Scott was still on the team bus after landing in Cleveland. He was waiting to hear how Alice made out in court. He was half tempted to meet her at the courthouse but he would get so many fines and likely miss the next game if he tried to skip practice. So he would have to wait to get her call and hope it came soon since they were going to have to head in for practice as soon as they got into the rink.

He felt his phone buzz in his pocket. He figured it was Alice texting back since that seemed to be her preferred method while he was more prone to call her first. So he was surprised to see it was Alice calling. He picked it up and said, "How did it go babe?"

He barely heard anything at first except for some sighing breaths. He knew Alice well enough at this point that she was trying not to cry. So his heart dropped. Today was supposed to be a formality and easy. It clearly wasn't the walk in the park that she thought it would be. She said in a low broken voice, ".... prison." She gasped some and Scotty had a feeling she was actually crying now. "Just restitution."

"I didn't catch what you were saying."

"Gasp... prison. Just restitution." This time the word restitution was breaking up as well. He was no closer to understanding why she was so upset. She should have got prison and it would be okay.

"What?"

"No prison. Nothing at...gasp... at all."

Scotty instinctually punched the seat in front of him, forgetting that someone was sitting there. Corey immediately stood up to find out why his seat was just punched in the back. Scotty put up a finger to say one moment while giving an intimidating stare. He didn't have time to explain himself until he got off the phone with Alice.

"I'm sorry, baby. That's not right." He was trying to be supportive. He also wanted to punch something more than a seat in that moment. He hated how Alice was crying especially since she didn't cry often at all. He couldn't hear much from her either which wasn't helping things. "All I can say is that at least it's over."

"For today," her voice sounded defeated. He hated it and felt so useless being on the bus back to the arena. She continued speaking through her tears, "I still have tomorrow and that's just to decide if the kid is getting moved to adult court. Besides, there's that third kid who is way behind the other two. I'm nowhere near done."

Alice's tears continued to flow and were getting faster and harder. "Hey, hey. It's going to be okay. "Scotty knew that he couldn't bear to hear her tears, he was about to say consequences be damned and go to her. Just hold her until she stopped crying. "I'm upset too. Do you want me to come and get you?"

"No. I need to get back to work. I'm going to get coffee before I get back. I didn't plan for this and I don't have enough vacation time left especially if you guys decide to make it interesting in the next round."

"Alright. If you say so, but call if you need anything. Je t'aime."

She surprised him and only said, "Moi aussi." She always echoed the words, never just said, me too. Scotty hated hearing her cry but he couldn't blame her. The whole thing was terrible. He wanted to hold her and comfort her. Do something to change the day around.

Then Corey and Lager turned to Scotty. Lager was the first to ask "What the hell happened?"

"One of the people who broke into Alice's place was sentenced today. They didn't get any jail and Alice is upset."

"Ah shit man," said Corey, "No wonder you needed to punch something."

"Wait, I thought you were going to court with her tomorrow?" said Lager.

"Different defendant. She had to go in today too. But she was convinced it would be easy: the person was getting sentenced after a guilty plea and they would get jail. Tomorrow is a hearing. That's where wanted me for sure since she's afraid she might have recognized the kid and there is a chance it won't go well. I just wish I knew what to do for her."

"I can't help you. Normally, I do flowers when I mess up with Bridge but I don't think this is a flower occasion. Plus you didn't mess up here, the courts were just weird. Are you sure she said no jail?" asked Lager.

"Definitely. Took a few times to hear it since she was upset and barely audible."

The bus turned into towards the practice facility's parking lot. As they were heading off the bus to get ready for their morning workout, Corey said, "You can bring her over to the rink if you like after the game. Jenna is going to be in town so it could be the four of us."

"That might work. I didn't realize that Jenna was coming for the game."

"Yeah. She decided to come in after a lot of debate last night."

"Good for you guys. But are you sure that we wouldn't be intruding on your private time?"

"Yeah, it will be cool. Besides I'm pretty sure she has beer for Alice yet again."

That got Scotty laughing. "She almost always does. Jenna is practically Alice's supplier. On the plus side, Philly beer does make Alice happy. I just hope for Alice's sake, she's bringing some EG or Form for Alice." Scotty was starting to use Alice's nicknames for her favorite breweries in Philly.

"I have no idea what Jenna is bringing. I can't keep up with what Jenna is drinking or picking up at a brewery."

"I know the feeling. At least you drink craft beer more than me. Even after six months, I sometimes swear that Alice is speaking in a different language when she talks about her favorite beers. But I will run it by Alice if she wants to come over to use the rink."

It was good for Scotty to have practice after that call with Alice. He needed to hit some things, although he probably went a bit harder in practice then he should have on some of the d pairings. But it kept his mind busy and he liked the freedom he had on the ice.

27

ALICE

Alice woke up in Scott's arms. She was dreading the day especially after what happened yesterday. As she stirred, Scotty hugged her tighter and tighter. She knew she was going nowhere but she really wanted to pace the room some to burn off some excess energy. Hell, what she really wanted to do was a full blown workout. But Scotty was trying to calm her in a way that she normally loved, he was just holding her. He whispered in her ear, "Alice it's going to be okay." She swore he held her even tighter at that point.

"I know it will be one day. Although you might squeeze me to death if you aren't careful."

Scotty didn't loosen his grip at all, but he at least didn't hug her any tighter. Despite her desire to move around, she felt safe in his arms. He then rolled the two of them so Scotty was on his back and she was facing him. He kissed her first. As he pulled away, he bit her bottom lip before saying, "Now why would I want to do a thing like that?"

He seemed to be in a good mood and was trying to make

sure she was smiling too. While she hoped she had a fraction of his good mood, she just hoped that her day wasn't a repeat of yesterday. On the plus side, she was going to the hockey game tonight and that was likely to be an amazing game if Scotty's mood remained the same all day long. Even the most casual Sound fans knew that if Scotty was in a good mood, the team as a whole usually played much better. She blamed herself for screwing up Scotty's mood yesterday and taking his focus off the game and the Sound losing.

"I didn't say you wanted to silly. Just that you might."

He smiled and hugged her tighter, "Nah, I got you right where I want you."

Alice giggled and said, "You do that a lot."

"It's how you win and you know I love winning."

She was laughing so hard at that point. That was probably Scotty's whole goal. On the plus side, she was smiling. If it wasn't for his love, she would be struggling way more than she would have ever thought. Hell even with him, she was still struggling a fair amount. She said, "You make it seem so easy."

Scotty tipped her chin. "It is. I know you have had it rough lately but that part was out of your control. Today will be different. Just say your truth and you will rock this. You can't control what the judge decides but you are so damn strong. Remember that," Alice smiled and wanted to believe him but she didn't say anything. She just looked into his eyes. Scotty's alarm went off for the morning. He continued to hold her with one hand as he silenced the alarm with his right hand. He said, "We need to get going soon, babe."

"I know." She gave him a quick kiss. She took a deep breath (well as deep as she could get in his tight hug) to focus her thoughts. The two of them started to get up. "At least, you are coming with me today."

Scotty nodded. For a change, he didn't ask her about breakfast. "I'm assuming it's just a coffee morning." asked Scotty as Alice was grabbing some clothes so they were ready after her shower.

She picked out a blazer, cami and leggings. As she was pulling out a belt, she said, "Yeah." She was glad that Scotty was trying to help out and didn't want her to stay stressed out. She knew that he wouldn't love the idea of just the coffee but he was going to try and get her to eat today.

"Okay babe," Scotty said as he was taking the dogs downstairs.

Alice got into the shower slowly. Alice was surprised when Scotty came into the shower a few minutes later. He didn't usually join her if he started to make breakfast in the morning. She immediately grabbed in him into a wet hug and closed her eyes. He lifted her up and breathed her in as he said, "Hey you."

"What are you doing?" asked Alice incredulously. She wasn't expecting him to join.

"I thought you might want some extra support today."

She laughed and said, "But in the shower?"

"Yeah, don't you like having a bit of fun? Besides, we haven't done it in a while," said Scotty with that odd combination of a sheepish grin and being totally satisfied with himself that she would see when she called him out.

She laughed and said, "I'm not complaining. I was just surprised."

He caressed her throughout the shower and even washed every part of her. His touch was making her stay as relaxed as possible. In a way, it nearly made her happy. She knew that deep down, he was still trying to make her feel better after yesterday's tears. She was just glad that she was in a better spot today then she was yesterday. She still hated herself for not actually being able to control her emotions and crying on the phone so much but the court case hit her extremely hard and by surprise.

Scotty was just so attentive and wanted to keep her as happy as possible. While he offered to take her to hang out with Corey and Jenna after the game, she wanted to go home. If she wasn't over exhausted, she might have actually gone over to Corey's, so they could skate.

After the shower, she got ready. There was something about seeing Scotty in one of his pre-game suits minus the tie that made her very happy and relaxed. As soon as she was done pulling on her blazer, he grabbed her into a hug from behind. He said, "You look good. I like seeing this side of you all dressed up and professional looking."

Alice smiled, "Thanks. You look good too but it's weird seeing you like that and knowing we aren't going to a game yet."

"Don't worry. It's not like this will be the last time you see me in a suit." Scotty then kissed her temple before getting his cufflinks. He was keeping close to her throughout the morning probably waiting to see if she needed the extra support.

The two of them went downstairs and got their coffee. He made himself a small meal. Scotty drove them down to the juvenile court center.

Alice led the way to the fourth floor to go to the prosecutor's office. Unlike the adult court, the hallways were wide and bright. It was definitely a newer building. It also felt less oppressive and scary. It wasn't hard to find the office. She checked in with the receptionist. Then the two of them sat down in the small waiting room. Scotty held her hand and she felt stronger with his strength beside her. Just having someone let alone someone who loved her beside her made things seem easier to handle. His thumb rubbing her hand and the constant contact let her know that he was there. The two of them were quiet.

In about ten minutes, the prosecutor came out and introduced himself. The three of them went to the elevators. Alice was somewhat distracted by her nerves at the prosecutor's presence but she pretended that things were normal. The prosecutor was asking about her job and education. Alice wasn't sure if he was making small talk or if it was meant to serve an overall purpose. As they walked, he said that he was going to ask questions like that or from the preparation call like on Sunday. That sounded fine from Alice's standpoint. Nothing sounded hard. She just hoped that she didn't break down on the stand.

"Alright. So go ahead and have a seat over here. The courtroom is down the hall. I'll grab you when it's time."

Alice nodded. She and Scotty sat down on one of the benches lining the hallway. It seemed like many people were waiting but it didn't have a waiting room feel.

"So that doesn't seem so bad," said Scotty.

Hearing his voice felt good. Scotty had been so quiet since they left their house. But having him there to hold her hand and sit next to her made everything seem easier even if he wasn't talking much.

"Hopefully it stays that way. I just wish I knew how long we have to wait. I could go for a coffee."

Scotty grinned and asked, "Already?"

"Yeah. If only to steel my nerves."

"So not looking for another caffeine fix?" Scotty was obviously teasing her and her caffeine addiction. Ever since he visited her at work before his California road trip, he been teasing her about how often she wanted coffee. But he understood that sometimes she wanted a coffee purely for her addiction needs and sometimes it was just wanting to have a cup to keep her calm. Now it was truly to have something in her hands and the ability to calm herself down.

"Not quite, yet."

They were silent for a little bit. Normally, they would have both pulled out some devices to occupy themselves but neither of them did. Alice just leaned into his strong frame and rested. She knew he had to be looking down at her as he asked, "They like to make you wait, don't they?"

"You don't know the half of it. I think I waited over an hour yesterday and that was after being told they would be quick to see us," she said with the distinct impression that they were going to be waiting for a while yet again.

"Ugh. No fun." As Alice learned when he was injured, Scotty hated waiting. He was lucky that he seldom had to wait for anything. Even doctor appointments, he didn't have to wait much. Not that Alice could blame him. She hated it as much as he did, she just showed it far less than he did.

"None at all. At least you are here today." Alice held her tongue. She wanted to say how much it really meant that he was beside her, as much as she could do it by herself, it was better to have some support. But she felt dumb for even feeling that way since it made her seem so damn weak. She hated showing him any more weakness then absolutely necessary, not that he actually cared that she had moments of weakness.

The court dates were tough. It was at court where she was forced to put faces to the names that were given to her. The police never told her much of anything. Hell, she stopped hearing from the police altogether basically since the first two weeks after the burglary. The two juvenile cases scared her the most since she feared she would actually recognize the person who entered her bedroom door. While she couldn't place a full ID that night, she was pretty sure it was a male person and the only two male names she saw were the two charged in juvenile court. As if the fear of recognizing someone wasn't bad enough, the judge held the overall outcome in their hands and she was dreading yet another crappy outcome.

Scotty looked at her and was probably suspecting that she was holding back a lot. He didn't try to pry which made Alice really grateful. He did ask, "So what do you normally do during the wait?"

"Pretend to read."

"Only pretending to read? Aren't you a pro at reading?" asked Scotty with a teasing voice. It was clear that he was trying to distract her and keep her mind off of dwelling on things.

"Let's just say when I'm waiting outside of any courtroom, my mind basically becomes like a rave thrown by a bunch of squirrels. I'm lucky to read a page or two in an hour and a half. I keep reading the same lines over and over again. I was hoping to get done pretty quick today but it doesn't look like it. Are you sure you are okay with missing practice and game prep?"

Scotty kissed her temple and whispered, "I will never confirm this to anyone but my body is okay with a little extra rest today. Although I should be watching video from last night's debacle."

Alice wanted to ask him if his knee was acting up but she knew he wouldn't confirm anything right now. She wasn't going to dare and tell him the game wasn't a mess since it was. Instead she said, "It's okay to watch it as long as we have it on headphones."

Scotty nodded. Alice pulled out her iPad as Scotty pulled out his ear pods. He immediately started to access everything from his email account. She looked over his shoulder, he offered one of her his ear pods but she didn't take it. Alice knew he probably didn't even need the sound at all. They were quiet as they watched the video breakdowns until the prosecutor got them over an hour later.

Scott

They walked into the courtroom together. Scott was directed to sit in the area behind the prosecution but Alice was told to go all the way to the stand. Before walking up there, she handed her bag to Scotty as she continued towards the box beside the judge.

Alice looked small in the box but she was sitting erect. She zoned in on him although to most people it would look like she was looking at the people asking questions from the podium. While he was glad that she was in a better mood than yesterday, he could see that she was still hiding a lot. He was hopeful that he could get her to turn green and gold again.

Alice gave the oath to tell the truth and then spelled her name for the court. He really wanted Alice to have his last name. Every time he heard hers, he knew what he wanted to. While he ordered the rings a while back, he still had to wait a few more weeks before he could propose to her and he had no idea how long of an engagement she would want.

"What is your occupation?" asked the prosecutor.

"I'm an aquatics manager for Cleveland Technical University. I make sure the pool is properly staffed with lifeguards, run our swim lesson program, and masters swim program."

"Do you often travel for work?" Scotty knew the prosecutor was trying to get Alice to explain how uncomfortable she was with traveling and rooming with anyone but him. Hell, he knew how bad her panic attacks were on the first two trips after the burglary.

"I do not. At least not for that job. But I do for my other job. I work with a convention company."

"What is your role at a convention?" asked the prosecutor.

"It depends on the convention itself. I'm usually part of the tech team. I used to run the camera for the stage projection but I've been recently moved up to the show manager position. I keep the panels on time, run the various contests throughout the day and I am the karaoke DJ. Last weekend, I ended up doing the sound." Alice's voice gained a bit of lightness to it. You could see the joy that she got from doing those jobs. Scotty loved to see her relax and talk about one of the things that she enjoys the most.

"So it's safe to say you travel for that job," stated the prosecutor as if he was asking a question.

"I do. Since the burglary, I haven't been able to room with

people working the convention. So that's been an unexpected expense since I'm now footing the full hotel bill myself."

"So you used to room with people?"

"Yes. For the last six years, I would share rooms with friends from the conventions. But since the burglary, the slightest sound that I can't place at night can trigger a panic attack. So it's not always easy since some hotels you can hear a lot more noise than others. But add in the noise from friends coming in and out of the room on their own schedule. Really the only person I feel fully comfortable with at night has been my boyfriend since I know his habits and he does everything he can do to make me feel comfortable and safe at night."

Scotty hated how he could hear the shame and fear creep in her voice when she talked about how she gets panic attacks and the discomfort she felt. It wasn't something to be ashamed of. He just wished she could see some of the strength she was projecting. He gave her a smile to help reassure her.

"Have you had any other effects?"

Alice took a deep breath and rubbed a couple spots along her hairline, especially close to the widow's peak and the temple. That was something Alice often did when she was particularly stressed and didn't have anything to occupy her hands. "Yes. I'm still having panic attacks. I actually had one the other night after my hockey clinic."

That was news to Scotty. He knew the other night when they skyped after his game, she seemed quiet but she said that she was tired. Now he wished that he pressed harder but he was so tired after the game that he just let it go. Alice continued saying, "The panic attacks are getting better for the most part, but they do happen. I entered counseling to help deal with the trauma and the lack of sleep. I've never done that before."

Scotty nodded his head subconsciously as he thought about the counselling sessions. She stopped going to the counsellor since she didn't think it was helping. To be honest, he didn't think they were helping much either.

"How often were you going for counselling? Two days a week?"

"I was going once a week or so for like seven sessions." Scotty could tell that she was holding back something. He assumed it was her thoughts on talking about everything. She didn't like talking about that stuff but would rather write out her feelings and it allowed her to deal with things.

"Are you still living at the apartment?"

"I do not. I moved out shortly after the burglary. I tried to stay but it was too hard to spend the night even with installing additional locks and keeping the bedroom door barricaded."

Alice was back to rubbing her hair again. She was nervous again. Scotty knew it wasn't related to their relationship. It was the fact that she was telling people that she wasn't strong enough to remain independent.

The prosecutor stopped his questions. The frumpy balding defense attorney stood up. Despite the one sign of nerves, Alice was still sitting upright and was maintaining a steady voice. Scotty was proud of Alice for maintaining her cool.

The defense attorney asked, "Have you ever sought counselling before the alleged burglary?"

Scotty hated that and saw something in Alice's eyes that

said she didn't like it either but it wasn't the anger he felt. While he understood the attorney would try to distance the kid from the crime, it was a bit of an insult to call the event itself an alleged act. But Alice just said plainly, "No, I have not."

The defense attorney ended his questioning. Then the judge asked Alice about the night of the burglary. She gave the details. Scott noticed the judges eyebrows go up when Alice said it was her birthday. He hated hearing the details as much as Alice hated talking about them. Hearing about that night always made him feel like he failed her even if it brought Alice to his home each and every night.

Then Alice had to discuss her living situation. She talked about how she moved in and was living with him. She didn't bring any attention to his career or that kind of thing. She emphasized how it was more about safety and being around someone who made her feel safe and loved. Scotty didn't realize how much safety he provided her. It's not that he didn't know that about Alice, it is more about the power of hearing her express it outright. Now he understood why sometimes Alice thought there was so much power in voicing fears.

Then Alice was done with the questions. She got up from the question box and walked towards the table. She looked towards the prosecutor as if to find out what she had to do next. Something was exchanged between the two of them. Then Alice came over towards Scotty and said they could go. Scotty grabbed her bag as he stood up. As soon as they were outside the courtroom doors, she grabbed his hand. He said quietly, "You did great."

He was still concerned with why she didn't tell him about

the panic attack. Their relationship was so open up until that point, so he didn't get why she didn't say anything. Once they were alone in the elevator, he hugged Alice but asked in a soft voice, "Why didn't you mention your last panic attack?"

Alice melted in his body before saying in a quiet voice, "I wanted to forget that it happened as quickly as I could."

Scotty had to ask, "Was it your mom getting into your head again?"

"Nope. Just my own fucked up head, this time around."

Scotty hated when she put herself down like that. But it wasn't as malicious as he's seen her do it in the past. He wanted to ask for details but the elevator doors opened revealing the ground floor and he knew she wouldn't want to say much until they were in the car. So he didn't push the issue until then. But as soon as he shut the SUV door, he said, "You really need to stop being so hard on yourself. Your head has been fine from what I've seen. So what happened?"

"It was sooo dumb. I was in the shower and I heard a weird noise. I got spooked 'cause I couldn't identify what it was and then scared to death that someone would walk in on me when I'm naked in the shower. Once I found the courage to get dressed and investigate, I realized that one of the pups, most likely Backup, knocked over our hockey sticks. So then I felt so stupid for getting spooked by nothing. I wanted to forget it. I turned on what was left of your game. You were killing it, so it was easy to push my stupidity aside. At least for the most part. I still hate how I got spooked in the first place. I just want everything to be normal again, you know."

"Aww baby. It'll take time but you are doing pretty good all things considered. Besides it seems like you had an actual trigger, it's not like you are afraid of the boogeyman." He kept rubbing circles with his thumb over her hand trying to be as reassuring as he could. While he wished that she would have shared that when it happened, he understood where she was coming from. So not to dwell on it any longer, he asked, "Still craving coffee or do you want to head straight to work?"

Alice looked at the time and pursed her lips together. "Work. It's getting close to the open swim time and I don't want to be too late. I can always get a Pepsi or a coffee later. Plus I'm sure you need to get into regular game prep mode."

Since they were at a red light, Scotty turned to Alice and said, "I would rather make sure you were okay any day of the week than go to a practice that I'm not expected to be at. You know that right?"

"Yeah. But today was much easier than yesterday. Between you being there and the fact I only was there for my testimony, I don't feel so shaken up. Hearing all the defense's stuff was so much rougher yesterday. I know they were doing their job and then to have the sentencing be so ridiculous, it was just another sucker punch to the stomach. I just hope the outcome is better today but I don't even know what better would be. I just know that the prosecutor said he would call with the outcome later on today."

"Okay. But are you sure about the coffee? I could always get you one and then head over."

"Yeah I'm good. But thanks. You are literally the best."

That surprised Scotty. He thought she would have jumped at the offer of her picking up a coffee. She was more shaken then she was trying to let on but he knew he couldn't push her.

28

ALICE

Alice was getting things ready for Scotty's road trip. At least it was only one game in Carolina. Regardless of the outcome, it would be the last trip to Carolina for this year. She just hoped that Carolina didn't force a game 7 with their surge. As she finished putting in the last pair of socks into the suitcase, she felt a tight hug from behind and smiled. She knew right away who it was even before he said, "If I didn't know better, I would think you wanted me to leave."

Alice turned and rested her hands on his shoulders. "Nope. Never. But I needed to keep my hands busy and I thought this was better than me reading."

"Things still stirred up?"

Alice nodded her head. Scotty's hug immediately tightened around her as if he was trying to protect her from everything including her own thoughts. She hated how vulnerable she felt since the moment she found out the first defendant got off with just probation. It also didn't help that it's been two days since she appeared in court and she still hadn't heard the result even though the prosecutor told her that he would call her that afternoon. She was trying to be super quiet and even packed the suitcase with little more than a cell phone flashlight. Now she was regretting not going into the office or even downstairs to read a book. "Sorry I woke you."

"You didn't." It was the most unconvincing thing Scotty had said to her in a while. She made a face knowing that he was giving her a white lie but she wasn't going to call him out on it. But he picked up on the idea and started pulling her towards the bed, "Alright, I woke up the moment that I realized you weren't there. Come on back to bed." He started to pull her back to the bed.

"Alright." Alice said. Not that she was given a choice.

As they got closer to the bed, he asked "What was it this time?" as he pushed back a strand of hair behind her ear.

"Just me being a freak." Alice said lightly but the frown on Scotty's face told her that she said exactly the wrong thing. She knew that he hated when she was hard on herself but that was what it was. She was just being truthful to herself. "Truly. It's nothing. No panic attacks or nightmares."

"You sure?" Scotty was clearly unconvinced about why she was up at 3am. Then again in the last five months, normally it was something tangible that kept her awake. Waking up from a noise or a touch, a panic attack or even from a nightmare. They were both used to her having some sort of trigger rather than just normal insomnia.

"Yup. Honestly, I just can't sleep. I'm okay. I'm sure it's because things are stirred up but no triggers. It's nothing."

That's when Scotty pinned her to the bed. He said with almost need in his voice, "Come to Carolina with me."

As much as she wanted to say yes, she knew that she

couldn't. She was counting on the Sound winning the series and she didn't want to miss a single game in the Stanley Cup finals. She'd already used up so much vacation time. Plus she was starting to feel like she was taking advantage of Scotty. She knew half the reason he was asking her to come was to provide her security and warmth. He hated how upset she's been the whole week thus far. "You know I can't. You are just going to have to kick some ass in Carolina to finish it up without me. I will be watching from home. Not like you need any luck."

"Alright. But if you change your mind, I'll book everything faster than you can blink. Hell depending on when you tell me, I'll even pack a bag for you too."

That had Alice laughing. He wasn't kidding. He would do that for her in a heartbeat. Scotty placed on hand on her neck and he was running his lips across her neck sending pleasure waves across her body. He always knew what spots she wanted to be touched. It felt amazing. He pulled back with a hushed voice, "Don't run away next time. I hate waking up alone."

Alice couldn't lie to him or make a false promise. She knew that more than likely she would leave the bed and do something else just to allow him to sleep when she couldn't. She yawned out a "Maybe".

Scott stayed on top of her and looked at her sternly. It was a look she would see all too often when he was up for face-offs. She clearly said the wrong thing. Scotty wasn't angry but he was going to be firm with her. "No maybes on this one. You need...." He then paused and seemed to be second guessing things. She wondered what was up. It wasn't like him to just change tactics like that before even finishing his thought.

With the way he would look at her eyes, there must have been something there that he didn't like. He was pleading with her, "At least for tonight, just promise me you won't run away. Let me help."

"Okay. I won't run away." Scotty kissed her forehead and immediately swallowed her up in his arms as he rolled over to a spooning position. He was still holding her tight as if afraid he might wake up a second time to find out she was missing from the bedroom. But it was comforting and inviting her back to sleep. "You do help me so so much." She said, "Je t'aime."

"Je t'aime aussi. Dors maintenant." He said in a hushed voice. While the two of them always said I love you in French to each other, it was unusual for him to tell her to go to sleep. He must be tired or just really reinforced the idea that they should go to sleep.

"Okay." As Alice drifted off to sleep, she couldn't help but to wonder why it was so important for her to stay in bed until the morning.

Scott

Scotty's heart broke for Alice as he read her message. ***Court didn't go well again. Going to stress swim for a bit.***

After what happened on Tuesday, he knew it had to be the juvenile case. He was about to call Alice for details, but she wouldn't pick up if she was swimming. So he grabbed his trunks and headed to her work. He also grabbed one of her favorite lattes. If she wouldn't kill him if he did so, he would have thrown a splash of Baileys in it.

Once Scott got to the pool, he was surprised to see that Alice was the only one swimming. She was really pounding out the laps. He couldn't help but notice the occasional sobs when she was breathing to the side and that means she had to be crying for at least 15 minutes. He knew she was holding things in and it was only a matter of time for her to crack. Apparently, today was that breaking point. He put the coffee down by her bag and took off his flip flops and T-shirt.

Scotty lowered himself into the water. Alice continued to swim. He was about ready to try and grab her the next time she got to the wall, but she naturally stopped. Scotty didn't know if it was an end to one of her sets or if she saw him. When she stood up, Scotty grabbed her and held her close. She didn't say anything but she was crying. He didn't say anything at first and just laid his head on hers as he held her tight. Eventually once she calmed down some, he asked, "So what happened?"

"He's staying in juvenile court."

Scotty felt bad. He hated seeing her cry. That was probably not the outcome she was looking for. Before the hearing on Tuesday, he knew she wanted the kid to be in adult court. But she felt slightly more protected in juvenile court despite the fact the minor wouldn't get a tough sentence. With the adult getting no jail time, she felt like everything was just being taken away from her and it was just being all wildly unfair. He had a feeling no matter what he said, he couldn't really make her feel better. So he did the only thing he could do, "Aww, baby. It's okay."

Scotty just felt her shrug her shoulders. "Thanks for coming but you didn't need to." She looked up with tears in her eyes and said, "Do you mind if I swim some more?"

That actually stung him. It seemed like it was the first time that him holding her wasn't enough but he knew she liked to move as much as she could when she was stressed.

He figured it was so she could release as much hormones as she could so she would stop crying. Scotty knew she would just push off the moment he stopped holding her, so he didn't let go just yet and asked, "Want me to swim beside you?"

Alice laughed and said, "Yeah but can you keep up?"

"Probably not. But I can try. At the very least, I can be there to help support you when you need a break."

"You're here. You don't know what that means for me." He let go of Alice. She kissed him. She did move over to the right side of the lane before pushing off quickly.

Scotty tried to keep up but after a single lap, she was much further ahead. It was the reverse than when they were on the ice together. He knew there was no way he could keep up so he continued on at his own pace. He took a break at the wall. He was glad when Alice joined up with him. She wasn't even breathing that hard but at least she wasn't crying. He pulled her close again. "What are the next steps?"

Alice shrugged. "I don't know. I am supposed to get a call from the prosecutor to go over the next steps."

"I'm assuming this was the same person who was supposed to call two days ago."

"Yeah, so I'm not holding my breath." Alice just leaned in close and buried her head into his chest.

He just held her and said, "I know you don't like not knowing and having any sort of control taken away from you." Alice just looked away. It was the best he was going to get from Alice at that moment. She hated to have some of her flaws pointed out to her. It was when she didn't fight back, that was her form of acknowledging him without saying that he was right. He held her and said, "How long do you plan to swim?"

"Until a lifeguard shows up or if I can feel okayish in the next 20 minutes."

Scott kissed her lips and let her go. She stayed close for a couple minutes. She then pushed off and swam more laps. This time, he didn't try to keep up. He grabbed her kickboard and did a few lengths while Alice easily did double the amount.

He watched her stop at the wall. This time she threw her goggles up onto the wall. She dipped her head back and tried to relax. She looked sexy doing that without any realization of what she was trying to do. So he tried to get back to the wall as quickly as he could.

When he got to the wall, she turned and hugged him. "Thanks for coming. You have no idea how much I needed you today."

"No problem. I wanted to make sure you were okay. I know this week has been rough." Scotty could tell that she was calmer but nowhere close to her normal personality. He hated seeing her like this but he couldn't blame her for being upset. All the cases have taken a real toll on her. The mere fact the adult got completely off with no jail and the juvenile might not be much behind wasn't helping a damn thing and he couldn't do a thing about it. He wished he could have talked her into going to game 6 with him but he knew she needed to go to work. "Don't be afraid to call if you need anything when I'm in Carolina."

As they headed for the edge, Alice noticed the large coffee and forced a smile. "Thanks baby. I'm glad I get to see you before your trip."

"Of course. Although I probably should have gotten you an iced one. I didn't realize you were going for a long stress swim." He hugged her and saw how dead her eyes looked He was just glad she seemed to be better at that moment. "Let's go get dressed."

He looked up at the time and cursed, he knew it was almost time to fly out to Carolina for the game. Since Alice already turned him down for going to the game earlier that morning, he didn't ask her join the team so he could keep an eye on her.

29

SCOTT

"Yo. Are you going to watch the game or not?" said an exasperated Lager.

Scotty looked up from his phone. He knew that Lager was right. He asked Lager over to watch the game and he wasn't being a good host. Over the last hour, he was swamped with messages about his plan for the proposal. He wanted to get the messages answered and cleared from his phone before Alice got home.

"I will. I'm just trying to get through these messages."

"You should have hired a party planner if it was going to be this big of a deal. I know you want it to be special but yeesh."

"It's fine. Really. It's just more, people having been responding now there is a confirmed date. I promise I'll be done soon. Just give me a few more minutes."

"Yeah. Yeah. Can't we just watch the game?"

The garage door started to go up. Scotty finished sending the one last message before Alice walked into the door. He wasn't thinking and he tossed his phone towards Lager. Lager immediately said, "Finally" as he caught the phone.

Scotty looked towards Alice with a smile and said, "Hey baby. How was work?"

"Not too bad. How about yours?"

"Tiring."

Lager buried Scotty's phone in the couch seat. Scotty was just glad that Lager didn't try to break or sit on the phone since he knew that Lager was getting frustrated with Scotty's constant phone usage lately.

Scotty got up from the couch to help Alice with dinner. While normally, he would have started dinner while Alice was at work, earlier that day she said she wanted to pick up some sushi on the way home.

Almost immediately, she said, "Go hang out with Lager. I got this. But why does Lager have your phone?"

Scotty smiled trying to play it off, "Oh it's nothing. He was getting whiny about how I was on my phone too much tonight. So I figured I would shut him up if I gave it to him."

"Uh-huh." Alice said with some slight hesitation. She then said, "Seems like a trend lately."

Scotty grabbed her waist and turned her towards him. He wanted to reassure her and said, "Not you too. It's nothing, I promise." He then lowered his head onto hers.

"That's what you keep saying." But there was a noticeable edge to Alice's voice.

That's when Scotty knew he wasn't being as discreet as he thought with his phone usage and she was getting concerned. Much like the night when she caught him in the office, she was starting to suspect something. Sadly, she might be thinking that he was cheating on her which was the furthest thing from the truth. He knew he would have to be more careful during the next week and a half. He wanted to reassure Alice as much as he could.

"If it was bugging you, why didn't you say anything?"

He was staring into her eyes and continued to hold her waist. She just shook her head, "Cause I know you won't tell me that it's nothing and won't tell me the truth."

Scotty nipped at her lip. She was right. That would be exactly what he would say. He just said, "I promise, it's just a short term thing and when it's done, you will love it. Honestly it's something for you. "

"If you say so."

"Hey, don't be concerned. I promise, you will love it. Okay?"

"Okay. Go back to watching the game. I'll join you in a minute."

Scotty wasn't sure if he fully reassured Alice that all was well. He hoped that she would just believe him.

30

ALICE

Alice knew that something was up with Scotty lately. He was being so secretive and constantly hiding his phone in her presence. At first, she chalked it up to playoff stress but it's gotten worse lately. She had seen him stress out about games before but this it felt different. If anything, he tried to talk hockey to her and he would watch just as much video with her. He also was super confident about the games. It seemed like it was something else.

Then she got a text from Scotty that only seemed to highlight her worry more.

Scotty: ***Be ready at 7pm. Wear something comfortable but don't ask any questions.***

Alice: ***Um, what?***

Scotty: ***You can read the message again. See you at 7. :P***

Alice's mind went into overdrive. Being told not to ask any questions for a date was going to drive her batty. Why was he being so damn secretive about everything lately even their date tonight? She knew that she was starting to think the worst and needed to talk about it with someone. Alice snapped a photo of the text exchange from Scotty and sent it over to Jenna. She dialed Jenna's number but it went straight to voicemail which was weird.

So Alice decided to reach out to Jennifer. Alice knew it was getting late for Jennifer and she would be going to bed soon if she hadn't already done so.

Alice: ***Help! I'm going mad and seeing this doesn't help.*** She also sent over the screenshot of the message from Scotty.

Jennifer: ***Looks like you have a date.***

Alice: ***Yeah. But I know something is up with Scotty. He's been weird for a while now.***

Jennifer: ***Weird how?***

Alice: ***He's clearly planning something or talking to someone. He keeps hiding his phone when I walked into the room and it seems to be getting worse. Now this cryptic message***

Jennifer: ***Okay. That's not good. Think it could be another girl?***

Alice's heart sank for a moment. She was seeing exactly what she was fearing the whole time. While she could never imagine Scotty actually cheating on her, it's what she suspected and in a way was hoping to be talked out of. Cheating was the only reason Alice could see for hiding a phone so often. But Scotty only seemed to care about three things: hockey, her and the pups. She wrote back:

Allice: ***I don't think so but it's the only thing I can think of. I'm not sure I want to look on a hockey forum for any speculation. I don't want to see some of that stuff.***

Jennifer: ***Let me look then.***

Alice: ***Thanks. I was hoping you might.***

Alice was honestly grateful for Jennifer looking at everything. She knew from looking in the past at the forums, any rumor would be there and there was a lot of hate. She had been avoiding the blogs for that reason.

Alice: ***I'm being dumb, aren't I? He's probably just stressed by the playoffs.***

Jennifer: ***We all get that worried from time to time. Good news: you are the only girl in his life by the looks of it.***

Alice: ***That's good. But the bad news?***

Jennifer: ***You get a lot of hate.***

Alice: ***Over what?***

Jennifer: ***Basically they aren't you and you weren't a Sound fan first.***

Alice: ***Should have guessed that. It's why I don't look at that stuff.***

Jennifer: ***I got to go. Early morning. But I don't think there's anything to worry about.***

Alice: ***Sleep well. Thanks for helping.***

Talking with Jennifer was a comfort. It was good to know that there was nothing on the web about a new girl. Scotty was still hiding stuff but at least it wasn't a girl. But she was still concerned and she still hated knowing nothing about tonight's date or as to why he was hiding his phone so much. She knew she would only get worked up if she kept thinking about it. So she decided to take a swim to burn off some of the stress. Before she knew it, she swam over a mile and her break was over, she quickly had to go back to work and pretend she wasn't going a bit crazy trying to figure what Scotty had planned.

She tried to focus on the work day. She got the schedule done for June and July. She realized she was going to be guarding a lot more in June than May. If she didn't fix that, she might not be able to get away to do any Cup celebrations with Scotty if he won the cup, which seemed to be closer with each and every win. Then again, at the beginning of May she was even thinner in the coverage so it might not be that bad in the end.

She rushed home. She wanted to get out of her work shirt and put on comfy clothes. She was surprised to see that Scott's SUV wasn't there. When she pulled into the garage, she noticed her hockey bag was gone. That freaked her out more since she was always worried about getting burglarized again. She was trying to temper her nerves and think logically. So she tried to think who would take her hockey gear without saying anything. There was one obvious person who she immediately thought of. So she shot off a quick text to Scotty.

Alice: ***Did you take my hockey stuff?***

Scotty: ***I thought I said no questions. ;)***

Alice: ***I just got home and it's not in the garage. Trying not to freak out.***

Scotty: ***Shit. I wasn't thinking. I thought you might like to get your skates sharpened and it was just easier to grab the whole thing.***

Alice: ***As long as you have it, it's okay. See you soon.***

Alice was confused. She figured that Scotty wasn't sharing everything since there was no way he would have taken all her pads to get her skates sharpened. Plus his first message made it sound like they might be doing hockey. But he wasn't going to be more forthcoming, sending another message would be worthless. At least, she knew where her stuff was and she could enter the house without being completely afraid that other stuff was gone.

Alice was greeted by Backup and Chloe. Poor Chloe still

had the cone of shame on. Alice looked at Chloe's incision, it was finally healing. Alice wanted to take the cone off but she knew they needed to wait a little longer or else Chloe would start to irritate the wound again which is why she was still wearing the cone since she would lick it at any chance she got.

Alice went upstairs and got switched into one of her favorite Sound tees. It was heather gray and only had accents of the gold and wine. She threw on a gray plaid blazer to dress it up. She knew that Scotty said to be comfortable but she didn't want to look like a complete bum. She then did some makeup to hide any of her skin imperfections. Then it was time to mess with her hair. At first, she thought of keeping her hair down. But something told her that she might want to keep her hair out of the way. So she just did her hair in her usual style although she did end it with a braided bun. Right as she put the finishing touches on everything, she heard Scotty call out, "Hey Alice, are you up there?"

She shouted down, "Yeah, I'm coming."

She rushed downstairs after throwing her phone into her purse. She saw Scotty at the bottom of the stairs. He was looking good in a simple black T and a pair of tight jeans. His playoff beard had gotten really full as it should be at this point since they were about to play game 7 in the series against the Sharks. It suited him. The only downside of the beard was that she couldn't see his smiles as easily before unless they were wide. But with the way his eyes were shining, she knew he was in a good mood.

As soon as she was downstairs, he scooped her up and started to kiss her passionately. He pushed her up against the wall. His hands quickly pushed up the t-shirt and he was feeling up her breasts. Alice was going breathless with the sensuality of the kisses. He then pulled back and shook his head almost as if to clear his mind. "Je t'aime. You look amazing tonight. Sorry, but we have to go, we're going to be late."

"Late?" Alice knew he wasn't going to give her much but she still had to ask. "Late for what?"

He just grabbed her hand and led the way to the garage. "Nice try, Alice. But you will see soon enough."

"Ugh. You're killing me smalls."

"Look at who you are calling small. Besides, I really doubt you will be saying that soon," he said with bravado that she normally saw on a game when he was going to light up the lamp multiple times. "It won't be a secret much longer, just be patient."

Alice laughed but she had to try. She knew that Scotty wasn't going to give away his secret plan for the night. He could be a sealed trap when he wanted to be. Plus he enjoyed reminding her that she was so short and he was right.

It didn't take long to realize that they were on their way to the practice rink or the sushi place near the rink that he loved. But Alice knew that if she were to tell Scott her instincts, she wouldn't get anywhere so she stayed silent.

Unsurprisingly, he pulled into a parking spot along the back of the practice rink. That's when Alice knew he had to have rented out the rink again. She noticed several SUVs and trucks by the door to the rink and several of them were familiar. As they were getting out of the SUV, Alice said, "Why do I think you planned to do more than have my skates be sharpened today?"

Scott just kissed her. He shook his head as he said, "Seriously Al, you gotta wait."

"Babe, I'm more just stating the obvious. If it was just for the skates, we would have pulled up to the front to pick them up from the pro shop."

Scotty just said, "Come on," as he laced his fingers with hers.

He led the way to the rink doors. Once inside, he pulled her into the locker room where they first met. She smiled since the last time they came to the rink together, she was kept out of that locker room. Once inside, she saw her gear was hanging up right next to Scotty's. The only thing that seemed out of the normal was how her normal pinnies weren't hanging up. Instead she saw the alt Sound jersey in grey with only using the gold and wine as accent colors. Seeing a 7 on the fold of the arm, she knew it was for her. It looked as if it was an actual game day jersey made just for her. She always preferred the alternative jersey over both the home and away jerseys and Scotty knew that about her.

"Come on, get on your stuff on," said Scotty as he was prodding her. She didn't realize that she was frozen in place for a moment. She was a bit stunned but she did as she was told and started to suit up for hockey.

They both started to get ready. Alice put on her stuff quickly since it seemed like Scotty was in a slight rush. Yet he was putting on his stuff more slowly with a deliberate grace. Right as Alice was about ready to put on her new sweater, Scotty stopped her by saying, "Let me." With one swift move he pulled it over her head. She never had a chance to see the back of the sweater and she figured that was on purpose. Whatever it said, it was probably part of his surprise.

"Go on, I'll be out in a second," said Scotty as he urged her onwards.

"Are you sure?" asked Alice. She didn't want to move too soon without him.

"Yeah. Besides, I know you. You will want to skate a little then retie your skates. This might allow you to be fully ready by the time that I get out there."

Alice shrugged her shoulders since she knew he was right. He sometimes liked to tease her about wanting to retighten her skates, that it was more of a superstition rather than a real need. He never believed her that it was truly to get the boots to feel right on her ankles but she couldn't get the feel of it until she started pushing on the blades. "What can I say, it's something I've always done, besides it was always worse with my figure skates especially if I was jumping. Then I'm retying then at least four times."

Scotty stole a kiss from her and said, "I have those if you'd rather."

"Nah, I'm good," said Alice. Scotty just had on a wide smile with hearing that she wanted to keep the hockey stuff on. He continued to put on his shoulder pads. If she wasn't all padded up, she might have switched to the figure skates. But at this point, it was easier to be ready to play hockey.

She grabbed her favorite stick and headed towards the ice. To her surprise, the ice was empty. After seeing so many cars in the parking lot, she thought there would be another OTA practice with The Sound. She pushed the idea out of her mind and just decided to go with it despite knowing that she would be so completely outclassed if they were going to play with his friends from the Sound. Of course, after a few strides her left boot felt weak, so she went to the bench to tighten up the skates.

She jumped off the bench and things felt much better. Almost immediately, she heard a cascade of pucks hit the ice. She knew that Scotty was on the ice. She smiled and turned to face him.

"Al!" Alice immediately saw something come her way. She smiled when he called her Al, it was a nickname that only he called her. She easily caught the puck and passed it right back at him almost immediately. That's when she realized it wasn't a puck at all but instead a small ring box. Scotty just started to laugh as he caught the box on the end of his stick. He flicked the box up into his hand. He then knelt down and opened up the box.

Oh hell. This is it and I just threw his ring back to him assuming it was a puck, thought Alice. She was more than a little upset with herself for doing that. The only thing that kept her from full on the cursing was the fact that Scotty was smiling so wide. He wasn't even remotely upset.

"Alice, I'm glad that some things never change. I told you the day that we met that you were afraid of the puck. What I didn't tell you was that I was completely taken by you and I wanted you to be in my life forever. That day, you showed your passion, your honesty and were just yourself. Then your birthday happened, we got closer and it was probably quicker than anyone expected but.......man it's been amazing to be with you each and every day. Will you make me the happiest man in the world and marry me?"

Alice was smiling. At some point she started to bite her lip to keep her from saying anything stupid. She noticed that Scotty caught himself from swearing in the middle of the proposal. He normally never stopped himself from swearing unless there were kids around. "Of course I will."

Scotty took off her left glove and slid the ring onto her finger. He then kissed her and hugged her passionately. Alice was glad he was hugging her so tightly or else she might not have been able to stay upright. He literally and metaphorically swept her off her feet. When he pulled back from the kiss, she heard stick taps and claps. Then she heard Lager's voice saying, "Get a room."

Scotty threw a glove at Lager and Alice instinctually said, "Hey" when she realized it was her glove that he'd thrown at Lager. Scotty turned her around so she could see their friends and family at the rink's edge.

It was that moment, she realized how perfect the proposal was. Okay, she probably shouldn't have given him back the ring box but everything was so sweet and so perfect. To do it in front of their friends and family was like a dream.

Scotty whispered to her, "I figured this was the perfect spot for this since you wouldn't want to do it in the exact spot where we met. Thanks for sending the ring back to me, I don't know what I would have done if you kept it on your stick. Je t'aime." He kissed her one more time. "You okay if I let you go?" That's when Alice realized he knew damn well that he was holding her up.

Alice nodded. She was pretty sure she was okay on her feet. But she was still staring up to his eyes and just so happy. She noticed that the Sound guys were setting up a net for a game on one side of the rink. Lager threw her glove back at them and Scotty caught it. Scotty then handed it to her and she tucked it under her arm. It seemed like the other half of the ice was being prepared for some free skating.

Scotty asked her, “So do you want to skate some or play hockey?”

“I don’t know,” said Alice. She was tempted to do both. But seeing all the Sound guys playing hockey, she was worried about being seriously outgunned and way too slow no matter how hard she tried.

“Well, I know what we can do until you decide,” Scott raised his hand to her face and pulled her into a kiss. She started to really enjoy it and she forgot about everyone around her. Scotty pulled back from the kiss with a wide smile. “I think you should play a little hockey with me.”

“Okay,” said Alice. She knew she could stop when things got too difficult. Before she could go anywhere her little niece skated up gingerly to the two of them. Closely behind the almost five year old was her mom and Jenna.

“Wait, Aunt Alice. Can I see what My Scotty got you?” Alice smiled widely at the little one’s question. Even though she knew that Scotty wasn’t a fan of being called My Scotty by her niece, Alice thought it was adorable. She knelt down and showed off the ring to her niece. The little one immediately exclaimed, “Wow, pretty.”

Alice was about to agree with the little one but Scotty leaned down and said, “We need to talk.” Before the little one could say anything, he handed Alice his stick, scooped Noelle off her feet and held her as they headed to do some circles on half the ice sheet that was being used for open skating.

Alice stayed still with Jenna and Allison at center ice. She was showing off the ring. They both agreed that the ring was perfect for Alice. Alice was glad to see Jenna. Seeing Jenna at the rink explained why she wasn’t available to talk earlier.

She had to be travelling and Alice assumed she was coming the next day for game seven.

Allison noted, "He's good with her. What do you think they are talking about?"

"Probably asking her not to call him 'My Scotty' anymore. He kinda hates it. That's a term only me and his mom get to use. The other option is to invite her to be in the wedding. Hell, I wouldn't be surprised if it was both."

They did a couple laps around the rink. Alice couldn't help but to keep an eye on Scotty. It was clear that Noelle was having fun. They rested for a moment by the boards. Almost immediately, Scotty came back to the boards and set down Noelle next to her mom. The little one was giggling hard and was having a hard time saying, "Mommy, Aunt Alice. He skates really fast."

Alice laughed and said, "He sure does." But her niece had no idea how fast Scotty could go. The pace he had with Noelle was only about 30% of his power, but he was taking long, sure strides throughout. He wasn't even close to being out of breath. He looked like he belonged out there skating.

Scotty took her hand and said, "Ready to play?" He had pleading eyes and Alice couldn't deny them. It was worse than looking at puppy dog eyes and she had to give in even if she didn't want to play hockey. Fortunately for them, they both knew that she wanted to play even if she was afraid of being a liability on the ice.

"I guess but I suck."

He immediately kissed her and whispered, "Don't you worry," as the two of them started to skate towards the hockey area.

Alice was surprised to see Crestie in net. She asked, "Wait

didn't you say Crestie tweaked a hip in the last game? Wouldn't coach kill everyone if he can't play tomorrow?"

Scotty laughed. "Berman would totally kill us if anything happened to him tonight. Fortunately, Crestie is over there." Alice turned to where Scotty was pointing. She saw Cresite with a woman about his age laughing. Alice was confused since it was definitely his gear in net and you don't normally just hand your gear over to anyone. Scotty filled in the blanks by saying, "His son came in for the game and I convinced him to play tonight since we needed a goalie to play. But he had to use his dad's stuff since his stuff was sent to their home in Canada."

"He's doing juniors in Western Canada, right?" asked Alice. He nodded and Alice continued to marvel at the likeness between father and son. "Damn, he's huge. He's what 16? He's going to end up bigger than Crestie."

"Yeah. They are talking about having him on the Canada U-18 team for Worlds."

"I can see why. Especially if he can play anything like his dad."

"We are going to get a taste of it soon." Scotty was clearly excited about the idea of playing against the kid. Alice wasn't sure about her chances. She just shook her head in disbelief.

Scott

Scotty was on cloud nine. Alice had the largest smile on her face since the moment he actually put the engagement ring on her finger. He knew that she was getting more concerned by the day. Between the playoffs and the court stuff, it was a lot of stress for her and hiding the plans for the proposal was just adding to the stress levels. He knew that and felt bad he was stressing her out. But the look on her face made everything completely worth it.

As soon as Scotty and Alice skated towards the pick-up area, Lager immediately said, “We should split up the Wheiland brain trust.”

The look in Alice’s eyes was sheer panic. He knew he couldn’t play against her. She needed him for support especially when she was playing against his friends. She wouldn’t trust her own skills to play if her life depended on it. Tonight more so than others, he wasn’t going to let anyone split them up. “Not a chance in hell. Maybe some other night but not tonight.”

Lager said with a smile, “Fine. I have Dykstman then.”

Scotty knew that was going to happen. He looked towards his fiancée. Damn, he loved that she was officially his fiancée. He wasn’t sure if Alice had even noticed that the jersey she was wearing had his last name on it. Her last name once they got married. But she looked good wearing that jersey with her gear on.

“Okay. So we are doing this then.” Scotty said as he cocked his head to the side knowing that even with Alice’s lack of skill, they would easily beat his best friend. The two of them could easily put together a 1000% better team than Lager. Lager would make picks just to fuck with them and was too impulsive while the two of them would have have some strategy to their team.

He looked towards Alice and she whispered, “We will need solid defense. Get Petey.”

That surprised him. Not so much the need for defense; that was a given. It was more he would have thought with her Philly roots, she would favor Wheels with his ability to do the forecheck. He liked the idea of getting Petey's speed and ability to move on the ice as an asset. He easily said, "Petey."

Lager's pick was unsurprising, Wheels. He was hoping to rattle Alice most likely. He knew that Scotty wouldn't care. Alice didn't care, she seemed to expect that as well. Scotty turned to Alice and whispered, "I want a two-way guy next." Alice nodded in agreement but didn't supply a name but they both knew who she was thinking of. He said, "Corey."

They continued to pick players. Scotty was surprised at how easy it was for them to pick a team together. They both were picking out fast defensive-minded guys who were known for producing some offense. There were a couple of wild cards with some of the kids that he didn't know all that well. Lager's team didn't have nearly as much cohesion as they did.

When they went for the opening faceoff, Alice tried to get off the playing surface. Scotty wouldn't let her hide. He wanted her to play with him. He grabbed her wrist to keep her at his right side. He gave her a look of reassurance, "Come on. I got you, Al. At least, for a few plays together." She stayed, she didn't look real sure of herself but he knew that she could keep up. Besides, she had solid passing almost to the point of threading a needle. "I just need you to pass it up to me and you got that."

He wanted to say that was why he knew that she would send the ring box back to him but she wouldn't listen to him. At least, she seemed like she was going to play with him and that's all he wanted. So she lined up to his left and Corey was on his right. Petey was out on defense for the first play.

Lager immediately said, "Really, starting with Al? You think she can keep up with us?" with a laugh. Scotty wanted to punch him for trying to intimidate Alice. Alice shot daggers into Lager. It was good to see her just settling in to play and letting her Philly side come out in spades.

"Shut the fuck up and drop the puck already," said Alice. Lager did drop the puck. Scotty easily won the puck and gave it to Corey as Scotty bypassed Dykstman. Scotty noticed Alice was struggling to get by Lager. He kept boxing her out with his speed. It wasn't until she threw an elbow that perfectly hit one of his bruised patches and she could get open. Corey passed the puck towards Alice. Scotty knew he had to be ready for the puck sooner rather than later. Unsurprisingly, the moment he was halfway open Alice passed it towards him. He shot it on net. It went to his sweet spot and the kid in the net had no chance. Crestie's kid was shaking his head over the goal.

"Don't beat yourself over it. That's probably one of my best shots" said Scotty trying to reassure the kid.

"Ugh. I tracked it but then it just tipped up. I can't believe it just tipped up."

Scotty smiled knowingly, "Yeah. It's evil. How do you think I get so many points? It's with shots like that. Oh, watch out for Lager's wrister it will shank a bit at the last minute."

"Left or right?" asked the kid.

"It depends," which was true.

Scotty saw the kid behind the mask smiling again. It was only a matter of time before the kid had an NHL contract. The kid was playing well. The only bad thing was once Scotty got to the faceoff circle, Alice slipped off the ice. That wasn't surprising but it was still disappointing for Scotty. He liked playing with her. But he knew he would only do a short shift and he could talk with Alice to make sure she was okay.

When Scotty got off the ice, he noticed that Alice was real quiet again. He just hoped he didn't overwhelm her and got her to shut down completely. He looked her way and asked, "Doing okay?"

"Yeah," she said with strained breathing. That's when he realized while it was easy going for him, she was busting her ass to keep up with them. Well sorta keeping up, she was still super slow compared to him, Lager and Dykst but she was pushing herself. Scotty couldn't ask for more. She then said, "I might only do a few more shifts."

"Kay." said a disappointed Scotty. He loved playing with her but he understood that she would be exhausted before too long. "Sit out the next shift, you don't need to kill yourself. None of us are."

Alice nodded and Scotty wrapped an arm around her waist until it was time for him to go back out on the ice. It was getting competitive. Of course, it was him against Lager's line. As soon as he got close to Lager, Lager started to whine about Alice's hitting him and asked if Scotty was going to resort to the same trick. Scotty smiled as he stripped the puck. "Yeah I don't need to do that." He skated cleanly past Lager.

He did another quick shot on net, that one was much softer but still went in. As he went to retrieve the puck, the kid said, "You're right about Lager's shot. Any other advice?"

"Don't get star struck."

That got the kid laughing. Scotty liked that and hoped it would settle the kid down when he was taking shots on net. But they both knew that he was getting away with a couple goals, especially the last one, because the kid was getting into his own head and was likely to be a bit star struck. He didn't want to bust the kid's balls too much.

Out of the corner of his eye, he saw one of the Wildcards get off the ice and Alice stepped on. Scotty couldn't help but smile at that moment. He glided up towards her, "How's your backhand shot lately?" Alice's eyes went wide in fear and that was all the answer he needed. He had a Plan B ready. "Alight, be prepared for me to screen you and I'll pass it back. Do the wrister." Alice shook her head in agreement. He looked towards Petey and said, "Get behind net when I screen Alice."

Petey looked confused at first but he agreed to do as he asked. But Alice's smile meant she knew what he was hoping to do with Petey going behind the net. Petey probably didn't realize that having him behind net would give her a passing target rather than a pure shot on goal. They all got set up for the next faceoff. Lager almost immediately asked Alice, "Think you can keep up little girl?" She flipped him off. It was good to see her handling herself against Lager's chirping and didn't need help to protect himself. Lager would complain about anything Alice did, but it was all in fair game and besides he could handle himself. If anything, he was proud of Alice.

They dropped the puck. Scotty easily won it and pushed the puck around. He was screwing around with Dykstman who was trying to stay on Scotty's ass. But that gave enough time for Alice to elbow her way past Lager. Then they could set up the screen. It was deceptive since he had the perfect shot. He passed the backhand shot to her. She almost immediately flicked the puck forward. It went through the 5 hole and Crestie Jr was still trying to get up after taking the bait on Scotty's shot before he sent it back. Scotty turned to celebrate her goal by kissing his fiancée after he popped her mask up. He loved that he set Alice up for the goal and to think that she was officially his. As she pulled back from the kiss, she said, "Sorry babe, I'm going to skate some. My legs are dead trying to keep up with you."

Scotty made a face but he understood, "Okay I might join you soon."

Alice shook her head, "You don't have to. But make sure you kick Lager's ass. We'll never hear the end of it, if his team manages a comeback."

Scotty just laughed and he grabbed her stick, helmet and gloves so he could stash them on the bench. Then the two of them parted ways. He got to the bench. He couldn't help but watch her as he was resting. She looked so relaxed as she caught up with her best friend. She was also within arms distance of her niece and Klaus. It was clear that two little ones were playing a form of tag on the ice using Alice as a sort of base. It was only when he was playing on the ice that he wasn't watching Alice.

All too soon, Ed cleared them off the ice. It felt far too early but at the same time, he knew that it was easily about 9pm and they had been on the ice for their full time.

31

ALICE

Alice was exhausted but the evening was absolutely perfect. She was still trying to process everything. After they left the arena, their families, Jenna, Corey, Pete, and the Lagerfields came back to their house. While Klaus and Noelle were forced to go to bed, the adults talked and ate food from one of their favorite sushi places. They talked for a couple hours. But one of her favorite parts of the night was how Scotty kept hugging and was always close by.

When they went to bed, Alice was so comfy in the crook of his arm. Her left hand was sprawled out on his chest and you could get a perfect view of the engagement ring. The two of them were were lazily looking at the ring. She could feel Scotty playing with the ends of her hair with his free hand.

Alice looked at her man. Before she could say anything, he pulled her to his lips for a soft kiss where his beard started to tickle her lip slightly. Once he pulled back, he asked, "You good, baby?"

"You have no idea." She turned to climb on top of her

chiseled red haired man to look at him in the eyes. "Are you ready for tomorrow?"

"You have no fucking idea. It's the only thing that could compete with today."

"That's why I was so surprised you did this today and not tomorrow."

Scotty chuckled and shook his head. "I couldn't risk you becoming second fiddle to the cup. You are just as special as the Lord Stanley. Besides the planning was getting to me." He pushed his hair out of his face slightly.

That got Alice laughing and she asked, "So is that why you played like shit in game 6?"

"Hey, you said it wasn't that bad," he said with a laugh as he started to tickle her sides. Her hair fell all over her face as she was laughing so hard from being tickled.

"I might have lied about that," she leaned to kiss his neck. "I didn't want to you to get stuck in your head and suck tomorrow. There are no more chances after this."

"You have nothing to worry about. I promise to play my ass off tomorrow. Besides there are no distractions now. I have the most gorgeous fiancée ever to come home to every night and I know that you. Plus I still owe you one last thing."

"What's that?" Asked Alice with a kiss. She was hoping it would be sex but at the same time, she couldn't imagine what he owed her. They had a full house with her sister's family spending the night. So tonight, they were pretty much done for anything crazy.

"You'll see later." Scotty said as he leaned up. He wrapped his arms around her neck and kissed her softly. He pulled her down towards the bed, "Come on, let's go to sleep."

"Do we have to?" asked Alice. While she didn't want to do

anything more than cuddle and talk, she wasn't ready to end the day. It was too perfect. There was a part of her that was afraid it was a dream. She said, "I'm not saying we do anything but this. I just don't want it to end."

"You know we should sleep. You have work in what six hours and it's game 7 of the Stanley Cup Finals. Sleep is vital, babe. Hell, coach will kill me if I'm dead at practice let alone at the game. Didn't you say you wanted me to win?"

"I did. Are you sure you're okay being alone tomorrow? I will be working up to your nap and I can't help with a house full of guests."

"I'll be fine. It's just our family." Scotty propped himself onto his elbow. He started to stare at Alice with pure tenderness and finger the engagement ring with his right hand, "I wouldn't have invited to stay if it was going to be a problem. I knew you had to work from the moment I invited them. "

"I know, but I had to ask. I feel bad that I can't help out as much. Thank you for inviting everyone. I wouldn't have wanted them to miss it." Alice said with a smile. She felt dumb for thinking that there was anything wrong with their relationship. She should have known it would be something like that. "Now I know why you were always hiding your damn phone anytime I came into the room lately. It had to be for all the damn details like who to invite."

"Sorry but I figured you would have wanted them here. I didn't want you to find out too soon." He smothered her with some kisses. Probably hoping to quiet her down and get her to actually sleep rather than just babble.

"It was perfect. Literally perfect. The only thing I would have changed is the fact, I gave you the ring back when you tossed the box my way."

"That was my favorite part." Scotty said with a smile. "Hell, in many ways I assumed that was going to happen. I told you on the ice, I needed you to pass it back to me."

"I know" said Alice. Looking slightly more seriously, "but seriously who plans on someone giving back the ring?"

"Me. I know you and love you," said Scotty. He then kissed her nose. "Hell, Lager even owes me a case of beer over it."

Alice rolled her eyes and said, "Of course, he does." Then Alice looked at him and asked, "Wait only beer?"

"It's a case of anything you want from anywhere you want." Alice was processing what he was saying. Scotty had gotten more adventurous but beer was still her thing. That meant he placed the bet for her to enjoy, not him. He continued with, "Figured if you were going to win me the prize, you should get to enjoy it."

As if Scott couldn't make Alice swoon anymore. He would say something like that which would make her heart melt. "I'm so damn lucky to have you."

"I feel the same way about you too." He then grabbed her in their normal sleep position with him spooning her and holding her tight. The one major change tonight was that he was holding his hands over hers almost as if to confirm she was still wearing both rings he gave her. She felt so safe and warm in his arms. It was like the pure feeling of being loved. "Je t'aime et je suis fatigué."

"Kay. Je t'aime."

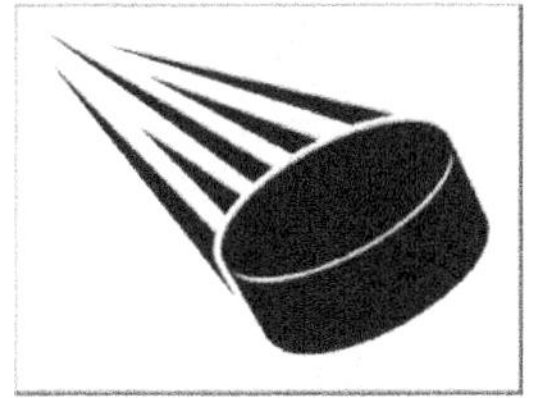

Alice came home from work. She was greeted by a very quiet house. The dogs greeted her by the door like normal but they even seemed tired. She heard the TV on but at a super quiet volume. She looked over to see her sister and brother-in-law laying comfortably with Allison's legs stretched on top of Steven's legs. She was surprised that both hers and Scotty's parents were nowhere to be seen.

Alice immediately said in a hushed voice, "Hey guys. Where's everyone?"

Allison spoke up and said, "Well, mom went home. Dad and Scott's parents went to the baseball game."

Alice nodded. It didn't take a genius to guess where the other two were, "I take it that Scotty and Noelle are napping. I know Scotty normally gets up in like an hour and a half."

"Yeah. And Noelle won't be much different."

"Please tell me that she wasn't running Scotty ragged this morning. I see the dogs are pretty wiped out from the excitement."

"She wasn't bad. She did definitely enjoy playing with the dogs the most. She's been wanting to get a pet. He was good with her too. I hope you guys have a kid soon."

"One day. We both want them but after we get married."

"Good."

Alice plopped down on the red chair to get off her feet. She was half tempted to go upstairs to either lay down with

Scotty or wake him up but with game 7, she wasn't going to mess up his gameday routine at all. She so wanted him to hoist the Stanley Cup tonight.

Alice said, "Sorry about not being around today. There wasn't a way for me to get off so last minute."

"It's okay. We all knew you had to work when Scotty invited us. But I didn't want to miss out on last night. It was really sweet and fun. It was something that seemed perfect for the two of you."

"It really was. But if he did all of that for the engagement, can you imagine what the wedding would be like? I just hope he won't tie it to the playoffs again. Cause what happens if we can't get in next year?"

"Don't worry about that baby." Alice turned to the voice that came from behind her. She turned to look at Scotty. It was clear he was having severe issues trying to fall asleep. His hair was all over the place. He wasn't in his pre-game suit or even his workout stuff, so Alice knew he wasn't trying to do anything early. She went up to give him a hug which he just enveloped her in. He laid his head on her and said, "We can get married whenever although it would be easier during the off season."

Alice nodded and wasn't all that surprised that he would let her have the day. But at the moment, her thoughts slipped away from the idea of a wedding to why he wasn't napping. She knew it was far too early for him to typically be awake. So she asked, "We weren't too loud, were we?"

"Nah, you were fine. I'm just having issues getting settled in." He just continued to hold her tight and inhale her fragrance. She just hoped there wasn't too much of a chlorine smell coming from her. Since he was holding her so tight, she couldn't smooth out his hair or at least get it going in one direction. But that was the Scotty she fell in love with. His hair used to be so shaggy and would do its own thing more often than not. It was only since returning from the IR that he had a well maintained look that made him look like he belonged in a fashion magazine. It was only in the morning and moments like this, when she got to see him when he didn't care and was just himself.

Knowing that she was always comforted when she laid down with him, she asked, "Do you want me to lie down with you or would you rather just hang out down here?"

He smiled and nibbled at her ear which caused her to giggle since his beard was tickling even more than usual. He whispered to her, "If you can be super quiet, we can do more than sleep." Alice smirked at that thought. She wasn't sure if she could pull if off and not wake up Noelle. Scotty never wanted to fool around before a game. It sounded like fun to do something a little different. So she nodded. The two of them excused themselves saying they wanted to try to nap again although Alice was sure her sister knew what they were up to.

Once the two of them got upstairs, Scotty lifted Alice up and carried her to the bedroom. He hadn't done that in months. They were both still being careful with his knee. Alice loved how flirty he was being. While it was highly unusual for him not to sleep well before a game, he was in a great mood and seemed ready to play. She couldn't wait to see how it would translate out onto the ice.

The first thing Scotty did when they got to the bedroom was to lock the door. He pushed her onto the bed. He stripped her down and soaked in her body. He just started to kiss along the contours of her body down the length of her torso. He spread her legs and started to lick her clit sending her body into a pleasured frenzy. It didn't take much time at all to climax. He almost immediately covered her mouth with his hand, fearing that she might get too loud. He said in a hushed lusty voice, "Shhhh." Alice nodded and bit her tongue.

Then she pulled off his shirt and then his bottoms. She noticed that his was huge at that moment and ready. When she knew that she got him off, she pulled back and then leaned up towards the pillows. He grabbed her and pulled her in tight.

"Nervous about tonight?" asked Alice as she laid against his chest and was looking up at his eyes and face.

He said so casually, "Nah. We have this. Honestly I was more nervous about last night."

That surprised Alice big time. She would have thought that game 7 to the Stanley Cup Finals would be more nerve racking. Everything is there for the taking. Literally it was do or die. There were no more second chances this season. But if he wasn't nervous, why wasn't he taking his pre-game nap? It really didn't seem to make much sense. Plus why would she say no to him? He was literally perfect in every way for her. So Alice called him out on it, "Really? So why aren't you napping if you aren't worried about the game?"

"Just too amped up. This is just another game that I just can't wait to win tonight. Get the big prize," he said with all the assurance and confidence in the world. There was no way to doubt his confidence levels.

"So why were you so nervous about last night then?"

Scotty closed his eyes for a second and pushed his hair

out of his face which automatically started to tame his wild mop and brought it back to being more like the GQ model look. "That you would say no or just hate it all. Sometimes, when it seems like I know you, you do something to surprise me." He then pulled her tight and said, "I'm just so glad that you are mine."

"I'm glad you're mine too. Hell a part of me still can't get over the idea that you would even want me in the first place."

"Of course, I would want you. It's even silly to think otherwise. Hell, I know the sweater is a bit early but I seriously can't wait until we have to share a last name."

"Is that why you wouldn't let me put on the new jersey? Man, I'm an idiot for not even looking at the end of the night. I mean I knew that something was up when you wouldn't let me look at the back. But then I got sidetracked with everything else and you kept kissing me as we got our gear off."

Scotty just started to laugh. He loved being able to pull a fast one on her. It was something that she should have learned much sooner. While normally she would beat herself up for not picking up on something like that, she loved hearing him laugh and seeing his enjoyment on how she forgot to follow up on her suspicion.

"Yeah. I didn't want to blow the surprise too soon. Not until you actually accepted the ring."

Alice giggled and said, "I could totally see you trying to come off as being romantic by saying you were switching your number to mine. I mean, I would think you were crazy and wouldn't fully believe it. But it wasn't out of the realms of possibility."

Scotty laughed and said, "That was the backup plan if you

saw it too early. But come on, it's time to be quiet at least for a little bit."

Alice nodded her head and knew that Scotty was right. They needed to at least try to rest a little bit. She loved being in his embrace. She didn't think that she was very tired so she intended to just lay in his arms for a while.

Somewhere along the line, she actually fell asleep since when Scotty's alarm when off, she felt the warmth of his arms lift off for a moment as he silenced his phone. Then he kissed along her neck. "Eh I'm awake" groaned Alice. He loved the kissing awake but she wanted to go back to sleep since she was comfortable.

"You don't want to be," said a joyful Scotty. It was clear that he was still in a great mood and ready for the game tonight. Plus he knew her and when she wanted to stay asleep.

Alice teased him and said, "You wake up way too damn cheerful. You know that?"

"Meh. What can I say, you make it super easy to wake up happy." Scotty said with a smile and a kiss.

"Cheesy much?" asked Alice in a teasing voice. She honestly felt the same way except when she wanted to turn back to sleep. She tossed a pillow at him which he easily caught. "Looks like you are ready for the big game tonight."

"You know it." He said with a wide smile. He then asked, "Going to work out with me or going to be social with your family?"

Alice thought for a moment and said, "I should be social." Her tone made it clear she didn't have her heart in that option but it wasn't like she wanted to work out either.

"I can't tell if you want to hide from your family or from your workout with me?"

Alice just laughed but didn't answer him on which one she was hoping to avoid at that moment. She started to climb out of bed and throw some clothes back on. He immediately put his own on and kissed her one more time.

When they were opening up their bedroom door, they heard Noelle call out. Alice smiled, "Go workout. I got her."

Alice went into the guest room where the little girl was sleeping. She saw the little blonde girl standing up in the bed. She looked confused and asked, "Where's mommy or daddy or even My Scotty?"

Alice just smiled especially and said, "There are all here. I'll take you to them. But don't forget Scotty has to get ready for work soon."

"But we will get to see him play tonight, right?"

"Yup. It will be fun!"

Scott

The arena was loud. Really loud. He never heard Cleveland fans make so much noise and it was awesome to hear them yell for him and the rest of the team. It was making the night epic and they haven't even dropped the puck yet. It was only just the warm ups.

The Sound as a whole were way looser than in game six. Then again, the team usually feed off his energy and he had been feeling super loose since Alice said yes. Now that things were perfect at home, he could fully relax. He was amped up.

He was just glad that their engagement hadn't been leaked to the media. He planned to share a couple of photos tomorrow night. The last thing he wanted was for her to get blamed if things went to shit tonight. Alice had been too awesome in his life. He was glad that Alice was at the game but it would have been impossible to keep her away. He still thought of her as a good luck charm since he had a tendency to put up big numbers when she was there. Sure his parents, Alice's sister and niece were there but the only one he wanted to impress was Alice.

He hadn't been so ready in a game in a while since coming off of IR. He didn't want to get too cocky since the game could swing quickly when that happened. The Sharks were a pesky team and desperate for a cup.

Scotty skated up for the first face off of the game. As he was getting set, he heard Lager already chirping to the Sharks. Scotty just smiled and shook his head as he got low into position. He knew if the Sound got puck possession first, it would keep the crowd in the game and just egg everyone on. But he was moving a little too much and got tossed from the circle. So he swapped with Dykstman.

Fortunately, Dykstman didn't have a problem controlling the puck. It was a footrace to the offensive zone. He tried to get some space but he wasn't able to get much room. The Sharks were swarming him. It was like they forgot that Dykst and Lager were just as much of a threat as he was. He couldn't blame the Sharks for being up his ass the entire series. He was leading the Sound in points again.

The first few shifts were going nowhere. While they were in the offensive zone, they just couldn't get set up with the Shark's pressure. They were leveling all the players into the boards.

It wasn't until the Sharks took a dumb penalty for too many men that Scotty knew he could capitalize on the power play. The Freak line was about to go out when Berman shouted, "OG PP1". That surprised Scotty but he did what he was told. Being on the point, having Lager crash the net and Dykstman on the other point wasn't super crazy. They would have Wheels QBing in the high slot and Hunt was there to push it. Scotty just wished they had practiced that formation earlier in the day, but if they talked enough on the ice and just did clean crisp passes, it wouldn't be that hard. If anything, the Sharks would be expecting that power play formation less than they did.

Going out on the power play, they were all talking about the two ways they wanted to get a goal with the old grouping off the face off. The Sharks were waiting for Lager to switch sides and weren't expecting to see Hunt at all. So they had a mismatch of players to defend against which would work in their favor as long as they kept the puck in the zone.

Scotty won the puck and sent it back to Dykstman. Dykst immediately fired it hard on the goal and it snuck by the netminder. The arena exploded in noise. This is when he loved playing at home. Everyone was into the spirit of the game and ready to see an explosion of Sound goals. The crowd helped to fire up the guys on the ice. There was nothing quite like it.

Unlike the previous games in the series, the Sharks didn't get sloppy or desperate after the first goal. Instead, they controlled themselves. If anything, they got a bit chippier and were finishing all the hits with even more gusto hoping to wear out The Sound. Scotty found himself on the end of several holds, slashes and elbows designed to slow him down. But it was part of the game and he was giving them right back to the Sharks defense. Since the refs weren't calling much for either team, it seemed fair. If anything he liked the freer reign of the play as long as both sides were given the same leeway if only to keep the pace of the game going.

Both teams had solid defense for the rest of the game. There were few real scoring opportunities for either team. With each passing moment, it seemed like the Sound was going to win the Cup. Scotty was starting to think the cup was his. He couldn't believe how magical the last few days were.

He was jumping the boards for what could have been his last shift of the year since there was less than a minute left in the game. He smiled and looked up towards where Alice would be sitting and started to think of a crazy idea.

The next thing he knew, he had a puck coming towards him. He grabbed it midair and dropped it towards his stick. He started to race towards the net, he saw that both Dykst and Lager were nearby. He heard Lager say, "Behind you."

So Scotty passed the puck towards Dykstman. But Dykstman didn't keep the puck long and sent it towards Lager. Lager took a hard shot on net but it rebounded off the leg pads of the Sharks goalie. Fortunately, it bounced onto Scotty's stick and he just ripped his wrister knowing the clock was almost out. Scotty heard the horn go off indicating it went in. That was exactly what he wanted to see happen. The arena exploded in noise and they knew that the cup was theirs.

They lined up for the next faceoff even though it was more a formality than anything. Scotty won the final faceoff and sent the puck over towards Wheels. Wheels then played away from the Sharks players for the last three seconds until the final horn went off.

From then on out, the whole team was erupting and congratulating everyone. The Stanley Cup came out and the guys all took turns hoisting it. As soon as Scotty hoisted it, he knew he had to ask Alice his crazy plan but it would be a while before he could talk to her directly. Until then he was just as happy as the rest of The Sound. He passed the Cup towards Lager and ended up getting flagged for an on-ice interview.

After what felt like hours, the party shifted to the locker room and the conference room. Scotty got switched out of the sweaty gear for some dry clothes although they didn't stay dry for long as bottles of champagne and beer were being sprayed everywhere.

Finally, he could get to the conference rooms where the families would be celebrating. He saw his Alice. He smiled and loved the fact that she was so excited to see him. He also loved the fact, her hair was down. As soon as she saw him, she rushed him for one of the biggest celebratory hugs he's ever received. He swore he heard someone say something but it was muffled by the noise in the room. He continued to hug her. He pushed back Alice's hair behind her ears as he looked deeply into her eyes. He said, "Hey Al, would it be super crazy if we got married with the cup?"

"What?" asked Alice. She was clearly caught off guard but she didn't deny him. So he knew he had a chance.

"Would it be crazy if we got married with the cup?"

She laughed and said, "Yeah, kinda."

But she didn't say no so he pitched his full idea rather quickly, "So I know you want a church wedding and I will give you that. I promise. But let's get married at city hall next month and have a small reception with our friends and family on my day with the Cup."

She laughed and said, "You're insane."

She was smiling and he knew he had her. He meant every word he said in his idea. He would give her the wedding of her dreams but he was hoping they could do both. He smiled with his cocky grin that he knew he had when he got the second goal of the night.

"But you like that about me. If you didn't, you wouldn't have said yes last night. So what do you say?"

"Okay. Why not?"

Scotty just kissed her and swung her around. He never knew everything could just fall into place. It was absolutely perfect. He literally had everything that he wanted. He was just so happy in that moment. He lowered his head on hers and relished the moment.

SNEAK PEEK: 200 FOOT GAME

This is my first look at my new novel the 200 Foot Game which is available for pre-order at Amazon. *This is unedited and is subjected to change in the editing process.*

JENNA

PROLOGUE

Jenna was rushing to meet her friend Alice. Alice was visiting from Cleveland and they had a full day planned. The plan was to pick Alice up from the train station to her place, get some pre-game drinks and go to the Flyers game that night. But Jenna got caught at work trying to reimage a machine that was taking far longer than was normal.

Jenna was crossing Samson St, not really paying attention to traffic. Most of the time, there was no traffic since the road was so narrow and would end every couple blocks. Unfortunately, today wasn't deserted. There was a car that was going down the road at a fairly high rate of speed. There was no way she could avoid the oncoming car. It also didn't stop her from trying to haul ass from crossing the street. She could really do anything other than say, "Oh shit" and try to keep her body as loose as she could since she remembered that would keep her from getting severely hurt. She only made it as far as the driver's side of the car. She felt the impact of the bumper hit her leg as she was briefly pushed up the hood before landing on her ass.

As she was starting to stand up, she saw a young, tall blonde guy get out of the car going, "Oh my god, are you alright?"

Jenna shook her head as if to knock the cobwebs free and said, "Yeah, I'm fine." To her astonishment, she really wasn't in pain. She wasn't sure if it was because her brain didn't keep with the idea that she should be feeling pain. She wasn't complaining since there was a good chance she would be feeling it soon enough.

A bleach blond model-type stepped out of the car and looked at the guy. "What are you waiting for? We're going to be late," in one of the most whiny voices ever. It was clear that she wasn't concerned about the fact they just hit someone and could have been hurt.

Fortunately, the guy didn't pay any attention to the blonde and seemed to be focused on Jenna. His full face was full of concern as he asked, "What do you need? Insurance info? Are you sure you are okay?"

"Yeah. I'm fine." Jenna said nonconchantly, trying to pretend that she wasn't just hit by the car but was pretty sure she was doing a miserable job of playing it cool. "Besides don't you need to get back to your girlfriend." Jenna realized there was a little more venom in her voice then she meant. But if she was being honest with herself, she kinda fancied the guy even if he was way too young for her. It was his girlfriend who was being a real asshole about the situation.

"She's not my girlfriend." He said it a little too quickly and a little defensively like he was repulsed by the model. That made her like him so much better. Then his voice softened as he tried to inspect Jenna over clearly looking to see if she was alright. "Are you sure you are okay?"

"Yeah. Don't worry. I'm running late and I'm just going to go." Then Jenna started walking away from the car. She didn't get his insurance information and was ready to just move on with her life. It was a steady walk, not as quick as before since she was paying more attention to her surroundings.

As she was walking away and turned the corner towards the station, she did turn around one last time to look at the guy as he was getting back into his car. She couldn't help it but she thought it was a shame the guy looked like a baby. There was something about him if he just fully filled his frame and had a little more facial hair. Then she realized she would have been her ideal guy. She regretted not getting any contact information from him but she didn't need to go to the doctor and was going to pretend that she never did just get hit. So that was a small miracle. She didn't need a way to contact the super hot guy. She just needed to forget that ever happened.

COREY

ABOUT 6 MONTHS LATER

Corey got settled into camp. He swore that this year would be different than last year. He knew in the past, he was a bit of a partier and had gotten crazy. But he was haunted from hitting that girl back in Philly. He knew he couldn't do that ever again. He still couldn't believe how lucky he was that the girl never notified anyone or wanted any money. Instead she went on with her life as if it never happened. He thought about her from time to time, wondered how she was doing and what she was up to. The biggest problem was that he had no idea who she was. She was his wake up call to clean up his act even if she would never know.

When he scanned the locker room, he saw many of the guys that he knew from either when he played with The Hamilton Crushers or The Cleveland Sound. He knew the room would be packed for the next few weeks until they whittled down which guys would make The Sound and who would get sent back down to the Crushers. He knew his own spot was technically at risk. He ended his season with The

Sound on their 4th line and played in the last 10 games of the season. Despite being tighter with the guys from The Crushers but he knew he shouldn't try to hang out with them too much and slip into old habits. He needed to play his ass off. He really wanted to make his way to the second or third line this year rather than just grind it out on the 4th line and getting minimal minutes.

Corey sat near Scotty and Lager who were already chatting as they were putting on their pads. Scott Wheiland was the captain of the team and dynamic center with great two-way skills. Andreas Lagerfield was just as (but everyone seemed to call him either Lags or Lager) who played on the same line as Scotty. There were two things that he remembered from last season about those two: they were serious about hockey with hockey IQs off the chart and they weren't known to party much. Scotty would go out more and was always in control while Lager would join for shorter periods of time while he would have more fun. Corey wanted to be on their good side and really learn from them.

Scotty turned his head and said, "Hey Cor, how was your summer?"

"Not too bad. Try to keep the training going. I worked with a few different coaches in Vermont, Quebec and Vancouver."

Scotty laughed and said, "That's what I like to hear although next year, you should train with me in Ontario."

3 months later

It was just after the All-Star break before the real practices started up. Corey was happy to show up for the practice that Scotty (The Sound's team captain) was putting together as a little OTA right before official practices started up again.

No one on the Sound seemed to care that last year that he was a bit of a wild rookie and this year he wasn't. Scotty and Lager just took him under their wing this year. They both extended their friendship and hockey knowledge even though last year he barely gave them the time of day.

It helped having Petey with him this year. Corey filled in during the injury of Hunter Kapko and secured a full time spot through strong play on the third line this year. Petey was in a similar spot this year, up from Hamilton Crushers to fill in for an injury and hoping to stay long term. Petey was his old roommate in Hamilton and Corey was pulling for him to stay. But with the trade deadline approaching, there was a strong chance that Petey could get sent back down. Petey decided to take Lager up on the offer to crash his place instead of Corey's. He didn't blame Petey, was probably afraid that there would be too many wild nights at Corey's or just wanted to soak up as much information from Lager as he could. They were still roommates on the road. Petey seemed to love the fact that Corey was much calmer and sedate in his lifestyle now. They now were both working on ways to improve his game.

Corey stepped onto the ice. He was sure of himself even if he wasn't sure what to expect with the OTA. But given Scotty's serious nature, he was sure the guy had a plan for the evening. He wasn't expecting to see a stranger step out onto the ice with a cage on their helmet rather than the clear plastic visor that all the NHL players played with. Most of the guys including both Corey and Scotty had their helmets lined up on the boards. Out of habit, he shouted out, "Who's the nerd?"

Scotty turned towards the skater so it was clear his

captain knew who it was. Then Corey started to realize who the newbie was due to the small stature and the tuft of long brown hair coming out of the helmet. It was Alice, Scotty's new girlfriend. As soon as she ditched the helmet, it was clear that it was her and he felt like a jackass for calling her a nerd.. Corey met Alice the week before when Scotty asked if they could go to the rink at his place right before Scotty left for the All-Star game since Alice was having a rough go of things at the time.

Almost immediately Scotty started to introduce everyone and laid out his plans for the evening. It was pretty standard drills initially but it was painful at times to see Alice attempt some of those drills despite her improving very quickly. She had no business playing with them even if she was some sort of coaching genius like he claimed. Only good thing about Alice being there initially was the fact she gave everyone a chance to rest up between drills and ease back into the routine since they all knew tomorrow's practice would be much tougher.

At one point, Pete skated up and said, "A little overkill to get into a girl's pants, don't you think?"

"Maybe a little. But this is Scotty...." Corey knew Scotty well enough. He wouldn't have invited his girlfriend just to get laid. He always did everything with purpose and could see the game so much farther ahead than most people. So Corey was just curious what Scotty was up to since he had a plan.

Things immediately became interesting when they broke up into teams and Alice was just to be a coach on the ice. They broke up into the normal practice grouping. Right away Alice asserted herself and switched out some of the guys. He half expected that Alice would break up the top line since the team as a whole have been relying on the scoring from Dysktman, Scotty and Lager. But he never expected that she would have Lager play on the left side or have him play with Scotty's and Lager. In some ways, it was a dream come true. Alice actually knew the game since immediately she justified the switch from an obscure hockey fact from Lager's playing AHL days.

Playing with Scotty and Lager was easy. It was a lethal grouping and the other team were having a hell of a time defending them. Corey was just having a blast. Having his own scoring pick up thanks to the passes from Lager's backhand was great for his confidence. He didn't have any problems keeping up since he's been working on his stamina since the summer. He knew according to scouts that he wouldn't be a first line guy since he didn't have the speed and stamina to maintain any pressure. As cheesy as it was, Corey was just trying to take advantage of the time playing with Lager and Scotty. The rest of practice just flew by and they easily beat Dysktman's side.

As they were getting off the ice, Lager skated up to Corey and said, "Awesome job, Cor. Glad to know you can keep up with us."

"What did you expect? For me to suck?"

"Nah. Did expect you to blow a gasket. I'm going to see if we can get this line in use more often."

"Cool." He didn't want to say too much more but he didn't want to appear to be the eager beaver but that he wanted to stay on that line. But he wanted more ice time and broke his own scoring slump.

The guys were all starting to gather in the locker room.

They were all chattering about the practice. Scotty was the last one in the locker room which wasn't unusual. Especially given that her girlfriend was out on the ice with them, Scotty would be chatting with her before coming into the locker room. As conversations started to turn towards Alice, Corey knew he wanted to get away. He just wasn't in the mood to hear about a budding love life or what was going on there. As long as the captain was happy and scoring, that's all that Corey cared about. Alice seemed to be a cool girl but he didn't want to accidentally stick his foot in his mouth. As Corey walked out, he practically steamrolled into Alice as she was exiting the locker room. "Sorry."

"No worries." Alice simply said at first. Then she said, "You did good today."

Corey smiled slyly. He knew that he played well but he didn't want to be too cocky in front of her. He had a feeling that he needed to be friends with her if he wanted to remain on good terms with Scotty and he couldn't get a good read on her. She's been so quiet until tonight and he wasn't sure how much he could say without offending her. It was bad enough, he already called her a nerd when she first got out on the ice thankfully she probably didn't realize that was him. So he just said, "That was a fun line you threw together, have you thought about that line for a while?"

"Sorta." Alice said quietly. Corey shot up an eyebrow and Alice continued on, "I knew I wanted to break up the top line some. The Sound is way too top heavy and you know that. But I also knew Scotty would have a fit if I tried to take Lager off the line. So it became more about who would work well with those two. I had no idea that Scotty would be the only true center tonight so that complicated matters some. Okay, I know Andy is a center even if he can't win a faceoff to save his life. So you made the most sense as long as we got Lager off his natural side and his backhand is actually wicked strong. You just never know it."

Corey had to laugh. She made it sound so simple and plain. He didn't want to tell her that he was impressed with her knowledge but instead just said, "Well, I'm off." He paused for a moment and said, "You know Scotty is going to be a while, right?"

"Yeah. He's a rink rat and he's going to be a while. I just can't stand to be in the sweaty stuff longer than needed. Besides, I have time to get a drink before he gets out here."

"Makes sense. I just didn't want you to be too surprised if he took forever. But I got to go."

"Hot date?"

"Nah. Been avoiding that shit lately. Just want to get home and relax."

The way Alice's eyebrow shot up, Corey knew she probably had some questions about why he was rushing off. The last thing he wanted to do was raise any suspicions. Alice knew him completely as a clean slate and not a wild child. Or at least he thought she did. But given her other hockey knowledge, she might know about his wild ways last season. By some miracle of God, she didn't actually ask any questions. "Have a great Cor."

"You too." With that Corey headed out of the back door as Alice went towards the cafeteria and vending machines near the lobby of the rink.

Jenna

Jenna was relaxing at home. Netflix was on in the background and she scrolled through Instagram when she noticed a video where her good friend was tagged by the NHL player Scott Wheiland. It was a cute video where you saw just two dogs trying to get a puck away from a hockey stick. Even if Alice wasn't tagged, Jenna would have recognized the book socks that Alice was wearing at the time.

"No fucking way!"

Jenna immediately texted Alice and said: *Girl you got some explaining to do.*

Alice didn't respond right away and that would happen but there was no way she was going to let things lie. So she sent another text: *Dude, I know Scotty plays for the Sound and you have been crushing on since he came to Cle. Why didn't you tell me?*

Jenna was hurt that one of her closest friends hid that detail from her. Sure, Alice had told her some relationship details. She knew Alice was dating a Scotty and he took her to The Sound games and got her to root for The Sound in addition to the Flyers. Alice felt safe with him and went to his place the night she was burglarized. Alice stayed at his place for a few nights but returned to her apartment for a few sleepless nights since Scotty was on a business trip. A business trip that coincided with the All-Star game. But she couldn't imagine that Alice would omit so many key details since they were super close. It's not like she would tell the world about Alice's relationship. Hell, half the time, Jenna would do internet research on any guy that Alice was interested in. Now she was kicking herself for not seeking out more details and looking up things on her own.

After what felt like ages, Alice texted back.

A: *Don't hate me. I just didn't tell you his last name. I'm sorry but I wasn't sure who I could tell.*

Jenna was about ready to send out a snarky response about how Scotty himself had no problem telling the world about Alice. But Alice beat her with a text.

A: *You will think this is insane, but I'm going to move in with Scotty.*

J: *Wait, what? Really? When?*

A: *Well, he asked earlier today and gave me a puppy when he came home from the All-Star game. I couldn't say no. It was so good before the All-Star game.*

J: *Staying at his place and living with him is a little different.*

A: *I know. It's why I'm going to keep the lease to my old place in case things go south. But I want to do it. I think I love him.*

J: *I can understand that. So when do you move in?*

A: *I guess last night? Tonight? Most of my stuff won't come over until later. But I am sleeping over again, just like last night.*

J: *Alright. Have a good night. But I want all the details, especially how you guys met.*

A: *I ran into him playing pick up. Like I always said.*

J: *Seriously? He was playing pick up with a bunch of wannabes?*

A: *No. Women will use the team locker room if they aren't using it. Everyone was supposed to be gone. He wasn't. I ran into him literally. I guess he hung around and watched pick up. I don't know. But afterwards he wanted my number so he could help improve my game. I wasn't an idiot. I gave him my info.*

A: *Seriously, I need to go. Scotty is waiting.*

Jenna had to laugh. That was Alice. But it still seemed so unreal that her friend was moving in with a famous hockey player who she had a severe crush on. So much so that Jenna was known to send photos of him when Alice was having a bad day although she would send Alice way more photos of their favorite gingers from the Flyers. They both had things for the gingers.

Jenna couldn't blame Alice for wanting to move in with him. A couple years ago, a crazy lady set their porch on fire and she moved out immediately. But she moved in with a close friend until she could get a new place to live. Jenna just didn't like how quickly Alice moved in with Scotty. She would have liked to vet him some. Maybe a lot since he was a professional athlete and so many of them were playboys and she didn't want Alice to get crushed.

Jenna started to do some internet research on Scotty now. Not that she could change Alice's mind about the guy but if there were any red flags, it was her duty to warn Alice. Jenna saw that he was basically the perfect poster boy for a team. Then again, he was the face of The Sound. It was as Jenna was looking at other posts from his Instagram use, that she recognized a familiar face from what felt like a lifetime ago. He looked older than the last time she saw him but there was no denying his features or who he was.

"No fucking way!"

It was the cute asshole who hit her last year. He had a beard and filled in his frame a bit more since he ran into her. It was unreal since both made him look about five years older and even more attractive than before. She finally knew his name, Corey Corso. It was pretty clear he was a player with The Sound just by looking at Scotty's profile. She did a quick look at his stats and such. She quickly realized why he looked like such a baby when they first met, he was nearly ten years younger than she was and was barely 21. She kicked herself yet again for not getting his information after the accident. Jenna texted Alice one last time but she knew this text, Alice wouldn't respond until the morning but she had to know since Alice had unique access to find out more.

J: *What do you know about Corey Corso?*

She knew she should go to bed, but she needed to busy herself if only to exhaust her mind. So she continued to explore the internet to learn more about Corey. It seemed like there was a huge change in his habits from last season to this season. Last season, he was a typical hot shot playboy. Tons of women, drinking and high octane style of playing. This season, he was mostly on the third line and seemed a little more consistent of a player. It was clear he was hanging out with Scotty and his friends more this year than the previous. She liked that new look but she wasn't sure what version he was presenting was his true personality.

Jenna realized that the girl that was in the car with Corey was his sister. No wonder he didn't like her being called his girlfriend. She appeared to be a model who was out of control. There were photos of her doing drugs, which was one thing that Corey had seemed not to have ever done. It was clear that Corey was spending a lot less time with his sister this year and seemed to have dialed in on hockey. There wasn't a single picture linking the two of them since shortly after the accident. Jenna was wondering if there was a falling out.

Eventually Jenna went to sleep. It was a good sleep except it was short. When she was awoken by her alarm, she saw that Alice had responded to last night's text.

A: *He's one of Scotty's friends. Seems like a good guy. Been to his rink a few times. Why do you ask?*

J: *No reason.*

A: *No reason? Are you sure? I know he's your type.*

J: *Yeah. Just curious.*

Jenna just hoped that would be enough to keep Alice from sniffing her out. Alice was one of the few people who knew about how she got hit by a car. Alice was pissed that night and wasn't sure how Alice would react to finding out that he's the one who hit her. But there was no denying that Corey was easy on the eyes At least, Alice liked Corey and she couldn't stand flashy, playboy types so maybe Corey had really changed for the better.

KEEP IN TOUCH

If you see any errors or would like to sign up for the newsletter.

Email
Facebook
Instagram
kathyobuszewski.com

ACKNOWLEDGMENTS

So of course I want to thank my family. My sister has such a big heart and is raising an amazing little girl. I love my niece so much and it's been awesome to have someone to share my love of Gritty and hockey with.

I have to do a special shoutout to my close group of friends. Lisa, you have been amazing person of support and help with everything. Having you to be a person to go turn to for story ideas and editing alone was a huge help and I wouldn't have a final product without you. Add in all the personal support over the year, you are amazing. To Jill, Mykey and Mark. You guys have been amazing and helpful where I always have someone to talk to and while I may turn to you for different reasons but I do value all the support that you give me. Not to mention my Creation family.

To the hockey community. While my love of Flyers hockey has been a long standing thing, where I've loved watching games as a distraction and a mecca of my social life; being able to play hockey again is amazing especially after ten years of being away from the ice.

Last but not least, to the readers. While the book is personal and it has allowed me to process so much, I want people to read the book. To get early feedback and praise from my beta readers has been great. So thank you!

ALSO BY KATHY OBUSZEWSKI

The Cleveland Sound Series

Deking The Puck

200 Foot Game

The Sound of Christmas

Made in the USA
Monee, IL
30 June 2020